JOHN GALSWORTHY

Collected Works

JOHN GALSWORTHY
1867–1933

JOHN GALSWORTHY

The Dark Flower
◆
Fraternity

Original Illustrations by
SANDRA ARCHIBALD

Distributed by
HERON BOOKS

Published by arrangement with
William Heinemann Ltd

© 1969, *Illustrations, Heron Books, London*

CONTENTS

THE DARK FLOWER

FRATERNITY

The Dark Flower

Take the flower from my breast, I pray thee;
Take the flower, too, from out my tresses;
And then go hence, for see, the night is fair,
The stars rejoice to watch thee on thy way.

From 'The Bard of the Dimbovitza'.

Part I

SPRING

1

HE walked along Holywell that afternoon of early June with his short gown drooping down in his arms, and no cap on his thick dark hair. A youth of middle height, and built as if he had come of two very different strains, one sturdy, the other wiry and light. His face, too, was a curious blend, for, though it was strongly formed, its expression was rather soft and moody. His eyes—dark grey, with a good deal of light in them, and very black lashes—had a way of looking beyond what they saw, so that he did not seem always to be quite present; but his smile was exceedingly swift, uncovering teeth as white as a negro's, and giving his face a peculiar eagerness. People stared at him a little as he passed—since in eighteen hundred and eighty he was before his time in not wearing a cap. Women especially were interested; they perceived that he took no notice of them, seeming rather to be looking into distance, and making combinations in his soul.

Did he know of what he was thinking—did he ever know quite definitely at that time of his life, when things, especially those beyond the immediate horizon, were so curious and interesting?—the things he was going to see and do when he had got through Oxford, where everybody was 'awfully decent' to him, and 'all right', of course, but not so very interesting.

He was on his way to his tutor's to read an essay on Oliver Cromwell; and under the old wall, which had once hedged in the town, he took out of his pocket a beast. It was a small tortoise, and, with an extreme absorption he watched it move its little inquiring head, feeling it all the time with his short, broad fingers, as though to discover exactly how it was made. It was mighty hard in the back! No wonder poor old Æschylus felt a bit sick when it fell on his head! The ancients used it to stand the world on—a pagoda world, perhaps, of men and beasts and trees, like that carving on his guardian's Chinese cabinet. The Chinese made jolly beasts and trees, as if they believed in everything having a soul, and not only being just fit for people to eat or drive or make houses of. If only

3

the Art School would let him model things 'on his own', instead of copying and copying—it was just as if they imagined it would be dangerous to let you think out anything for yourself!

He held the tortoise to his waistcoat, and let it crawl, till, noticing that it was gnawing the corner of his essay, he put it back into his pocket. What would his tutor do if he were to know it was there?—cock his head a little to one side, and say: 'Ah! there are things, Lennan, not dreamed of in my philosophy!' Yes, there were a good many not dreamed of by 'old Stormer', who seemed so awfully afraid of anything that wasn't usual; who seemed always laughing at you, for fear that you should laugh at him. There were lots of people in Oxford like that. It was stupid. You couldn't do anything decent if you were afraid of being laughed at! Mrs Stormer wasn't like that; she did things because—they came into her head. But then, of course, she was Austrian, not English, and ever so much younger than old Stormer.

And having reached the door of his tutor's house, he rang the bell. . . .

II

When Anna Stormer came into the study she found her husband standing at the window with his head a little on one side—a tall, long-legged figure in clothes of a pleasant tweed, and wearing a low turn-over collar (not common in those days) and a blue silk tie, which she had knitted, strung through a ring. He was humming and gently tapping the window-pane with his well-kept finger-nails. Though celebrated for the amount of work he got through, she never caught him doing any in this house of theirs, chosen because it was more than half a mile away from the College which held the 'dear young clowns', as he called them, of whom he was tutor.

He did not turn—it was not, of course, his habit to notice what was not absolutely necessary—but she felt that he was aware of her. She came to the window seat and sat down. He looked round at that, and said. 'Ah!'

It was a murmur almost of admiration, not usual from him, since, with the exception of certain portions of the classics, it was hardly his custom to admire. But she knew that she was looking her best sitting there, her really beautiful figure poised, the sun shining on her brown hair, and brightening her deep-set, ice-green eyes under their black lashes. It was sometimes a great comfort to her that

4

she remained so good-looking. It would have been an added vexation indeed to have felt that she ruffled her husband's fastidiousness. Even so, her cheekbones were too high for his taste, symbols of that something in her character which did not go with his—the dash of desperation, of vividness, that lack of a certain English smoothness, which always annoyed him.

'Harold!'—she would never quite flatten her r's—'I want to go to the mountains this year.'

The mountains! She had not seen them since that season at San Martino di Castrozza twelve years ago, which had ended in her marrying him.

'Nostalgia!'

'I don't know what that means—I am homesick. Can we go?'

'If you like—why not? But no leading up the Cimone della Pala for *me!*'

She knew what he meant by that. No romance. How splendidly he had led that day! She had almost worshipped him. What blindness! What distortion! Was it really the same man standing there with those bright, doubting eyes, with grey already in his hair? Yes, romance was over! And she sat silent, looking out into the street—that little old street into which she looked day and night. A figure passed out there, came to the door, and rang.

She said softly: 'Here is Mark Lennan!'

She felt her husband's eyes rest on her just for a moment, knew that he had turned, heard him murmur. 'Ah, the angel clown!' And, quite still, she waited for the door to open. There was the boy, with his blessed dark head, and his shy, gentle gravity, and his essay in his hand.

'Well, Lennan, and how's old Noll? Hypocrite of genius, eh? Draw up; let's get him over!'

Motionless, from her seat at the window, she watched those two figures at the table—the boy reading in his queer, velvety bass voice; her husband leaning back with the tips of his fingers pressed together, his head a little on one side, and that faint, satiric smile which never reached his eyes. Yes, he was dozing, falling asleep; and the boy, not seeing, was going on. Then he came to the end and glanced up. What eyes he had! Other boys would have laughed; but he looked almost sorry. She heard him murmur: 'I'm awfully sorry, sir.'

'Ah, Lennan, you caught me! Fact is, term's fagged me out. We're going to the mountains. Ever been to the mountains? What —never! You should come with us, eh? What do you say, Anna?

5

Don't you think this young man ought to come with us?'
She got up, and stood staring at them both. Had she heard aright?
Then she answered—very gravely:
'Yes; I think he ought.'
'Good; we'll get *him* to lead up the Cimone della Pala!'

III

When the boy had said good-bye, and she had watched him out into the street, Anna stood for a moment in the streak of sunlight that came in through the open door, her hands pressed to cheeks which were flaming. Then she shut the door and leaned her forehead against the window-pane, seeing nothing. Her heart beat very fast; she was going over and over again the scene just passed through. This meant so much more than it had seemed to mean. . . .

Though she always had *Heimweh*, and especially at the end of the summer term, this year it had been a different feeling altogether that made her say to her husband: 'I want to go to the mountains!'

For twelve years she had longed for the mountains every summer, but had not pleaded for them; this year she had pleaded, but she did not long for them. It was because she had suddenly realised the strange fact that she did not want to leave England, and the reason for it, that she had come and begged to go. Yet why, when it was just to get away from thought of this boy, had she said: 'Yes, I think he ought to come!' Ah! but life for her was always a strange pull between the conscientious and the desperate; a queer, vivid, aching business! How long was it now since that day when he first came to lunch, silent and shy, and suddenly smiling as if he were all lighted up within—the day when she had said to her husband afterwards. 'Ah, he's an angel!' Not yet a year—the beginning of last October term, in fact. He was different from all the other boys; not that he was a prodigy with untidy hair, ill-fitting clothes, and a clever tongue; but because of something—something—— Ah! well—different; because he was—he; because she longed to take his head between her hands and kiss it. She remembered so well the day that longing first came to her. She was giving him tea, it was quite early in the Easter term; he was stroking the cat, who always went to him, and telling her that he meant to be a sculptor, but that his guardian objected, so that, of course, he could not start till he was of age. The lamp on the table had a rose-coloured shade; he had been rowing—a very cold day—and his face was glowing; generally it was rather pale. And suddenly he smiled, and said: 'It's rotten waiting for things, isn't it?' It was then she had almost stretched out her hands to draw his forehead to her lips. She had thought then that she wanted to kiss him, because it would have been so nice to be his mother—she might just have been her mother, if she had married at sixteen. But she had long known now that she wanted to kiss, not his forehead, but his lips. He was there in her life—a fire in a cold and unaired house; it had even become hard to understand that she could have gone on all these years without him. She had missed him so those six weeks of the Easter vacation, she had revelled so in his three queer little letters, half-shy, half-confidential; kissed them, and worn them in her dress! And in return had written him long, perfectly correct epistles in her still rather quaint English. She had never let him guess her feelings; the idea that he might shocked her inexpressibly. When the summer term began, life seemed to be all made up of thoughts of him. If, ten years ago, her baby had lived, if its cruel death—after her agony—had not killed for good her wish to have another; if for years now she had not been living with the knowledge that she had no warmth to expect, and that love was all over for her; if life in the most beautiful of all old cities had been able to grip her—there would have been forces to check this feeling. But there was nothing in the world to divert the current. And she was so brimful of life, so conscious of vitality running to sheer waste. Sometimes it had been terrific, that feeling within her, of wanting to live—to find outlet for her energy. So many hundreds of lonely walks she had taken during all these years, trying to lose herself in Nature—hurrying alone, running in the woods, over the fields, where people did not come, trying to get rid of that sense of waste, trying once more to feel as she had felt when a girl, with the whole world before her. It was not for nothing that her figure was superb, her hair so bright a brown, her eyes so full of light. She had tried many distractions. Work in the back streets, music, acting, hunting; given them up one after the other; taken to them passionately again. They had served in the past. But this year they had not served. . . . One Sunday, coming from confession unconfessed, she had faced herself. It was wicked. She would have to kill this feeling—must fly from this boy who moved her so! If she did not act quickly, she would be swept away. And then the thought had come: Why not? Life was to be lived—not torpidly dozed through in this queer cultured place,

where age was in the blood! Life was for love—to be enjoyed!
And she would be thirty-six next month! It seemed to her already
an enormous age. Thirty-six! Soon she would be old, actually old
—and never have known passion! The worship, which had made
a hero of the distinguished-looking Englishman, twelve years older
than herself, who could lead up the Cimone della Pala, had not
been passion. It might, perhaps, have become passion if he had so
willed. But he was all form, ice, books. Had he a heart at all, had
he blood in his veins? Was there any joy of life in this too beautiful city and these people who lived in it—this place where even
enthusiasms seemed to be formal and have no wings, where everything was settled and sophisticated as the very chapels and clois-
ters? And yet, to have this feeling for a boy—for one almost young
enough to be her son! It was so—shameless! That thought haunted
her, made her flush in the dark, lying awake at night. And desperately she would pray—for she was devout—pray to be made pure,
to be given the holy feelings of a mother, to be filled simply with
the sweet sense that she could do everything, suffer anything for
him, for his good. After these long prayers she would feel calmed,
drowsy, as though she had taken a drug. For hours, perhaps, she
would stay like that. And then it would all come over her again.
She never thought of his loving her; that would be—unnatural.
Why should he love her? She was very humble about it. Ever since
that Sunday, when she avoided the confessional, she had brooded
over how to make an end—how to get away from a longing that
was too strong for her. And she had hit on this plan—to beg for
the mountains, to go back to where her husband had come into her
life, and try if this feeling would not die. If it did not, she would
ask to be left out there with her own people, away from this
danger. And now the fool—the blind fool—the superior fool—with
his satiric smile, his everlasting patronage, had driven her to over-
turn her own plan. Well, let him take the consequences; she had
done her best! She would have this one fling of joy, even if
it meant that she must stay out there, and never see the boy
again!

Standing in her dusky hall, where a faint scent of woodrot crept
out into the air, whenever windows and doors were closed, she was
all tremulous with secret happiness. To be with him among her
mountains, to show him all those wonderful, glittering or tawny
crags, to go with him to the top of them and see the kingdoms
of the world spread out below; to wander with him in the pine
woods, on the Alps in all the scent of the trees and the flowers,

where the sun was hot! The first of July; and it was only the tenth of June! Would she ever live so long? They would not go to San Martino, this time, rather to Cortina—some new place that had no memories!

She moved from the window, and busied herself with a bowl of flowers. She had heard that humming sound which often heralded her husband's approach, as though warning the world to recover its good form before he reached it. In her happiness she felt kind and friendly to him. If he had not meant to give her joy, he had nevertheless given it! He came downstairs two at a time, with that air of not being a pedagogue, which she knew so well; and, taking his hat off the stand, half turned round to her.

'Pleasant youth, young Lennan; hope he won't bore us out there!'

His voice seemed to have an accent of compunction, to ask pardon for having issued that impulsive invitation. And there came to her an overwhelming wish to laugh. To hide it, to find excuse for it, she ran up to him, and, pulling his coat lapels till his face was within reach, she kissed the tip of his nose. And then she laughed. And he stood looking at her, with his head just a little on one side, and his eyebrows just a little raised.

IV

When young Mark heard a soft tapping at his door, though out of bed, he was getting on but dreamily—it was so jolly to watch the mountains lying out in this early light like huge beasts. That one they were going up, with his head just raised above his paws, looked very far away out there! Opening the door an inch, he whispered.

'Is it late?'

'Five o'clock; aren't you ready?'

It was awfully rude of him to keep her waiting! And he was soon down in the empty dining-room, where a sleepy maid was already bringing in their coffee. Anna was there alone. She had on a flax-blue shirt, open at the neck, a short green skirt, and a grey-green velvety hat, small, with one blackcock's feather. Why could not people always wear such nice things, and be as splendid-looking! And he said:

'You do look jolly, Mrs Stormer!'

She did not answer for so long that he wondered if it had been rude to say that. But she *did* look so strong, and swift, and happy-looking.

Down the hill, through a wood of larch-trees, to the river, and across the bridge, to mount at once by a path through hay-fields. How could old Stormer stay in bed on such a morning! The peasant girls in their blue linen skirts were already gathering into bundles what the men had scythed. One, raking at the edge of a field, paused and shyly nodded to them. She had the face of a Madonna, very calm and grave and sweet, with delicate arched brows—a face it was pure pleasure to see. The boy looked back at her. Everything to him, who had never been out of England before, seemed strange and glamorous. The châlets, with their long wide burnt-brown wooden balconies and low-hanging eaves jutting far beyond the walls; these bright dresses of the peasant women; the friendly little cream-coloured cows, with blunt, smoky-grey muzzles. Even the feel in the air was new, that delicious crisp burning warmth that lay so lightly as it were on the surface of frozen stillness; and the special sweetness of all places at the foot of mountains—scent of pine-gum, burning larch-wood, and all the meadow flowers and grasses. But newest of all was the feeling within him—a sort of pride, a sense of importance, a queer exhilaration at being alone with her, chosen companion of one so beautiful.

They passed all the other pilgrims bound the same way—stout square Germans with their coats slung through straps, who trailed behind them heavy alpenstocks, carried greenish bags, and marched stolidly at a pace that never varied, growling, as Anna and the boy went by: '*Aber eilen ist nichts!*'

But those two could not go fast enough to keep pace with their spirits. This was no real climb—just a training walk to the top of the Nuvolau; and they were up before noon, and soon again descending, very hungry. When they entered the little dining-room of the Cinque Torre Hütte, they found it occupied by a party of English people, eating omelettes, who looked at Anna with faint signs of recognition, but did not cease talking in voices that all had a certain half-languid precision, a slight but brisk pinching of sounds, as if determined not to tolerate a drawl, and yet to have one. Most of them had field-glasses slung round them, and cameras were dotted here and there about the room. Their faces were not really much alike, but they all had a peculiar drooping smile, and a particular lift of the eyebrows, that made them seem reproductions of a single type. Their teeth, too, for the most part were a little prominent, as though the drooping of their mouths had forced them forward. They were eating as people eat who distrust the lower senses, preferring not to be compelled to taste or smell.

'From our hotel,' whispered Anna; and, ordering red wine and *schnitzels*, she and the boy sat down. The lady who seemed in command of the English party inquired now how Mr Stormer was —he was not laid up, she hoped. No? Only lazy? Indeed! He was a great climber, she believed. It seemed to the boy that this lady somehow did not quite approve of them. The talk was all maintained between her, a gentleman with a crumpled collar and puggaree, and a short thickset grey-bearded man in a dark Norfolk jacket. If any of the younger members of the party spoke, the remark was received with an arch lifting of the brows, and drooping of the lids, as who should say: 'Ah! Very promising!'

'Nothing in my life has given me greater pain than to observe the aptitude of human nature for becoming crystallised.' It was the lady in command who spoke, and all the young people swayed their faces up and down, as if assenting. How like they were, the boy thought, to guinea-fowl, with their small heads and sloping shoulders and speckly grey coats!

'Ah! my dear lady'—it was the gentleman with the crumpled collar—'you novelists are always girding at the precious quality of conformity. The sadness of our times lies in this questioning spirit. Never was there more revolt, especially among the young. To find the individual judging for himself is a grave symptom of national degeneration. But this is not a subject——'

'Surely, the subject is of the most poignant interest to all young people.' Again all the young ones raised their faces and moved them slightly from side to side.

'My dear lady, we are too prone to let the interest that things arouse blind our judgement in regard to the advisability of discussing them. We let these speculations creep and creep until they twine themselves round our faith and paralyse it.'

One of the young men interjected suddenly: 'Madre——' and was silent.

'I shall not, I think'—it was the lady speaking—'be accused of licence when I say that I have always felt that speculation is only dangerous when indulged in by the crude intelligence. If culture has nothing to give us, then let us have no culture; but if culture be, as I think it, indispensable, then we must accept the dangers that culture brings.'

Again the young people moved their faces, and again the younger of the two young men said: 'Madre——'

11

'Dangers? Have cultured people dangers?'

Who had spoken thus? Every eyebrow was going up, every mouth was drooping, and there was silence. The boy stared at his companion. In what a strange voice she had made that little interjection! There seemed a sort of flame, too, lighted in her eyes. Then the little grey-bearded man said, and his rather whispering voice sounded hard and acid:

'We are all human, my dear madam.'

The boy felt his heart go thump at Anna's laugh. It was just as if she had said: 'Ah! but not you—surely!' And he got up to follow her towards the door.

The English party had begun already talking—of the weather.

The two walked some way from the 'hut' in silence, before Anna said:

'You didn't like me when I laughed?'

'You hurt their feelings, I think.'

'I wanted to—the English Grundys! Ah! don't be cross with me! They *were* English Grundys, weren't they—every one?'

She looked into his face so hard, that he felt the blood rush to his cheeks, and a dizzy sensation of being drawn forward.

'They have no blood, those people! Their voices, their supercilious eyes that look you up and down! Oh! I've had so much of them! That woman with her Liberalism, just as bad as any. I hate them all!'

He would have liked to hate them, too, since she did; but they had only seemed to him amusing.

'They aren't human. They don't *feel*! Some day you'll know them. They won't amuse you then!'

She went on, in a quiet, almost dreamy voice:

'Why do they come here? It's still young and warm and good out here. Why don't they keep to their Culture, where no one knows what it is to ache and feel hunger, and hearts don't beat. Feel!'

Disturbed beyond measure, the boy could not tell whether it was in her heart or in his hand that the blood was pulsing so. Was he glad or sorry when she let his hand go?

'Ah, well! They can't spoil this day. Let's rest.'

At the edge of the larch-wood where they sat, were growing numbers of little mountain pinks, with fringed edges and the sweetest scent imaginable; and she got up presently to gather them. But he stayed where he was, and odd sensations stirred in him. The blue of the sky, the feathery green of the larch-trees, the mountains, were no longer to him what they had been early that morning.

She came back with her hands full of the little pinks, spread her fingers and let them drop. They showered all over his face and neck. Never was so wonderful a scent; never such a strange feeling as they gave him. They clung to his hair, his forehead, his eyes, one even got caught on the curve of his lips; and he stared up at her through their fringed petals. There must have been something wild in his eyes then, something of the feeling that was stinging his heart, for her smile died; she walked away, and stood with her face turned from him. Confused, and unhappy, he gathered the strewn flowers, and not till he had collected every one did he get up and shyly take them to her, where she still stood, gazing into the depths of the larch-wood.

V

What did he know of women, that should make him understand? At his public school he had seen none to speak to; at Oxford, only this one. At home in the holidays, not any, save his sister Cicely. The two hobbies of their guardian, fishing, and the antiquities of his native county, rendered him averse to society; so that his little Devonshire manor-house, with its black oak panels and its wild stone-walled park along the riverside was, from year's end to year's end, innocent of all petticoats, save those of Cicely and old Miss Tring, the governess. Then, too, the boy was shy. No, there was nothing in his past, of not yet quite nineteen years, to go by. He was not of those youths who are always thinking of conquests. The very idea of conquest seemed to him vulgar, mean, horrid. There must be many signs indeed before it would come into his head that a woman was in love with him, especially the one to whom he looked up, and thought so beautiful. For before all beauty he was humble, inclined to think himself a clod. It was the part of life which was always unconsciously sacred, and to be approached trembling. The more he admired, the more tremulous and diffident he became. And so, after his one wild moment, when she plucked those sweet-scented blossoms and dropped them over him, he felt abashed; and walking home beside her he was quieter than ever, awkward to the depths of his soul.

If there were confusion in his heart which had been innocent of trouble, what must there have been in hers, that for so long had secretly desired the dawning of that confusion? And she, too, was very silent.

Passing a church with open door in the outskirts of the village, she said.

'Don't wait for me—I want to go in here a little.'

In the empty twilight within, one figure, a country-woman in her black shawl, was kneeling—marvellously still. He would have liked to stay. That kneeling figure, the smile of the sunlight filtering through into the half darkness! He lingered long enough to see Anna, too, go down on her knees in the stillness. Was she praying? Again he had the turbulent feeling with which he had watched her pluck those flowers. She looked so splendid kneeling there! It was caddish to feel like that, when she was praying, and he turned quickly away into the road. But that sharp, sweet stinging sensation did not leave him. He shut his eyes to get rid of her image—and instantly she became ten times more visible, his feeling ten times stronger. He mounted to the hotel; there on the terrace was his tutor. And oddly enough, the sight of him at that moment was no more embarrassing than if it had been the hotel concierge. Stormer did not somehow seem to count; did not seem to want you to count him. Besides, he was old—nearly fifty!

The man who was so old was posed in a characteristic attitude —hands in the pockets of his Norfolk jacket, one shoulder slightly raised, head just a little on one side, as if preparing to quiz something. He spoke as Lennan came up, smiling—but not with his eyes.

'Well, young man, and what have you done with my wife?'

'Left her in a church, sir.'

'Ah! She will do that! Has she run you off your legs? No? Then let's walk and talk a little.'

To be thus pacing up and down and talking with her husband seemed quite natural, did not even interfere with those new sensations, did not in the least increase his shame for having them. He only wondered a little how she could have married him—but so little! Quite far and academic was his wonder—like his wonder in old days how his sister could care to play with dolls. If he had any other feeling, it was just a longing to get away and go down the hill again to the church. It seemed cold and lonely after all that long day with her—as if he had left himself up there, walking along hour after hour, or lying out in the sun beside her. What was old Stormer talking about? The difference between the Greek

14

and Roman views of honour. Always in the past—seemed to think the present was bad form. And he said:

'We met some English Grundys, sir, on the mountain.'

'Ah, yes! Any particular brand?'

'Some advanced, and some not; but all the same, I think, really.'

'I see. Grundys, I think you said?'

'Yes, sir, from this hotel. It was Mrs Stormer's name for them. They were so very superior.'

'Quite.'

There was something unusual in the tone of that little word. And the boy stared—for the first time there seemed a real man standing there. Then the blood rushed up into his cheeks, for there she was! Would she come up to them? How splendid she was looking, burnt by the sun, and walking as if just starting! But she passed into the hotel without turning her head their way. Had he offended, hurt her? He made an excuse, and got away to his room.

In the window from which that same morning he had watched the mountains lying out like lions in the dim light, he stood again, and gazed at the sun dropping over the high horizon. What had happened to him? He felt so different, so utterly different. It was another world. And the most strange feeling came on him, as of the flowers falling again all over his face and neck and hands, the tickling of their soft-fringed edges, the stinging sweetness of their scent. And he seemed to hear her voice saying: 'Feel!' and to feel her heart once more beating under his hand.

VI

Alone with that black-shawled figure in the silent church, Anna did not pray. Resting there on her knees, she experienced only the sore sensation of revolt. Why had Fate flung this feeling into her heart, lighted up her life suddenly, if God refused her its enjoyment? Some of the mountain pinks remained clinging to her belt, and the scent of them, crushed against her, warred with the faint odour of age and incense. While they were there, with their enticement and their memories, prayer would never come. But did she want to pray? Did she desire the mood of that poor soul in her black shawl, who had not moved by one hair's breadth since she had been watching her, who seemed resting her humble self so utterly, letting life lift from her, feeling the relief of nothingness? Ah, yes! what would it be to have a life so toilsome, so little

exciting from day to day and hour to hour, that just to kneel there
in wistful stupor was the greatest pleasure one could know? It
was beautiful to see her, but it was sad. And there came over Anna
a longing to go up to her neighbour and say: 'Tell me your troubles;
we are both women.' She had lost a son, perhaps, some love—or
perhaps not really love, only some illusion. Ah! Love. . . . Why
should any spirit yearn, why should any body, full of strength and
joy, wither slowly away for want of love? Was there not enough
in this great world for her, Anna, to have a little? She would not
harm him, for she would know when he had had enough of her;
she would surely have the pride and grace then to let him go. For,
of course, he would get tired of her. At her age she could never
hope to hold a boy more than a few years—months, perhaps. But
would she ever hold him at all? Youth was so hard—it had no
heart! And then the memory of his eyes came back—gazing up,
troubled, almost wild—when she had dropped on him those flowers.
That memory filled her with a sort of delirium. One look from her
then, one touch, and he would have clasped her to him. She was
sure of it, yet scarcely dared to believe what meant so much. And
suddenly the torment that she must go through, whatever happened, seemed to her too brutal and undeserved! She rose. Just
one gleam of sunlight was still slanting through the doorway; it
failed by a yard or so to reach the kneeling countrywoman, and
Anna watched. Would it steal on and touch her, or would the sun
pass down behind the mountains, and fade away? Unconscious
of that issue, the black-shawled figure knelt, never moving. And
the beam crept on. 'If it touches her, then he will love me, if only
for an hour; if it fades out too soon——' And the beam crept on.
That shadowy path of light, with its dancing dust-motes, was it
indeed charged with Fate—indeed the augury of Love or Darkness?
And, slowly moving, it mounted, the sun sinking; it rose above
that bent head, hovered in a golden mist, passed—and suddenly
was gone.

Unsteadily, seeing nothing plain, Anna walked out of the church.
Why she passed her husband and the boy on the terrace without a
look she could not quite have said—perhaps because the tortured
does not salute her torturers. When she reached her room she felt
deadly tired, and lying down on her bed, almost at once fell asleep.

She was awakened by a sound, and, recognising the delicate 'rat-
tat' of her husband's knock, did not answer, indifferent whether
he came in or no. He entered noiselessly. If she did not let him
know she was awake, he would not wake her. She lay still and

watched him sit down astride of a chair, cross his arms on its back, rest his chin on them, and fix his eyes on her. Through her veil of eyelashes she had unconsciously contrived that his face should be the one object plainly seen—the more intensely visualised, because of this queer isolation. She did not feel at all ashamed of this mutual fixed scrutiny, in which she had such advantage. He had never shown her what was in him, never revealed what lay behind those bright satiric eyes. Now, perhaps, she would see! And she lay, regarding him with the intense excited absorption with which one looks at a tiny wildflower through a magnifying-lens, and watches its insignificance expanded to the size and importance of a hothouse bloom. In her mind was this thought: He is looking at me with his real self, since he has no reason for armour against me now. At first his eyes seemed masked with their customary brightness, his whole face with its usual decorous formality; then gradually he became so changed that she hardly knew him. That decorousness, that brightness, melted off what lay behind, as frosty dew melts off grass. And her very soul contracted within her, as if she had become identified with what he was seeing —a something to be passed over, a very nothing. Yes, his was the face of one looking at what was unintelligible, and therefore negligible; at that which had no soul; at something of a different and inferior species and of no great interest to a man. His face was like a soundless avowal of some conclusion, so fixed and intimate that it must surely emanate from the very core of him—be instinctive, unchangeable. This was the real he! A man despising women! Her first thought was: And he's married—what a fate! Her second: If he feels that, perhaps thousands of men do! Am I and all women really what they think us? The conviction in his stare—its through-and-through conviction—had infected her; and she gave in to it for the moment, crushed. Then her spirit revolted with such turbulence, and the blood so throbbed in her, that she could hardly lie still. How dare he think her like that—a nothing, a bundle of soulless inexplicable whims and moods and sensuality? A thousand times, No! It was *he* who was the soulless one, the dry, the godless one; who, in his sickening superiority, could thus deny her, and with her all women! That stare was as if he saw her—a doll tricked out in garments labelled soul, spirit, rights, responsibilities, dignity, freedom—all so many words. It was vile, it was horrible, that he should see her thus! And a really terrific struggle began in her between the desire to get up and cry this out, and the knowledge that it would be stupid, undignified, even mad, to show her

17

comprehension of what he would never admit or even understand that he had revealed to her. And then a sort of cynicism came to her rescue. What a funny thing was married life—to have lived all these years with him, and never known what was at the bottom of his heart! She had the feeling now that, if she went up to him and said: 'I am in love with that boy!' it would only make him droop the corners of his mouth and say in his most satiric voice: 'Really! That is very interesting!'—would not change in one iota his real thoughts of her; only confirm him in the conviction that she was negligible, inexplicable, an inferior strange form of animal, of no real interest to him.

And then, just when she felt that she could not hold herself in any longer, he got up, passed on tiptoe to the door, opened it noiselessly, and went out.

The moment he had gone, she jumped up. So, then, she was linked to one for whom she, for whom women, did not, as it were, exist! It seemed to her that she had stumbled on knowledge of almost sacred importance, on the key of everything that had been puzzling and hopeless in their married life. If he really, secretly, whole-heartedly despised her, the only feeling she need have for one so dry, so narrow, so basically stupid, was just contempt. But she knew well enough that contempt would not shake what she had seen in his face; he was impregnably walled within his clever, dull conviction of superiority. He was for ever intrenched, and she would always be only the assailant. Though—what did it matter, now?

Usually swift, almost careless, she was a long time that evening over her toilette. Her neck was very sunburnt, and she lingered, doubtful whether to hide it with powder, or accept her gipsy colouring. She did accept it, for she saw that it gave her eyes, so like glacier ice, under their black lashes, and her hair, with its surprising glints of flame colour, a peculiar value.

When the dinner-bell rang she passed her husband's door without, as usual, knocking, and went down alone.

In the hall she noticed some of the English party of the mountain hut. They did not greet her, conceiving an immediate interest in the barometer; but she could feel them staring at her very hard. She sat down to wait, and at once became conscious of the boy coming over from the other side of the room, rather like a person walking in his sleep. He said not a word. But how he looked! And her heart began to beat. Was this the moment she had longed for? If it, indeed, had come, dared she take it? Then she saw her husband descending the stairs, saw him greet the English party, heard the intoning of their drawl. She looked up at the boy, and said quickly: 'Was it a happy day?' It gave her such delight to keep that look on his face, that look as if he had forgotten everything except just the sight of her. His eyes seemed to have in them something holy at that moment, something of the wonder-yearning of Nature and of innocence. It was dreadful to know that in a moment that look must be gone; perhaps never to come back on his face—that look so precious! Her husband was approaching now! Let him see, if he would! Let him see that someone could adore—that she was not to everyone a kind of lower animal. Yes, he must have seen the boy's face; and yet his expression never changed. He noticed nothing! Or was it that he disdained to notice?

VII

Then followed for young Lennan a strange time, when he never knew from minute to minute whether he was happy—always trying to be with her, restless if he could not be, sore if she talked with and smiled at others; yet, when he was with her, restless too, unsatisfied, suffering from his own timidity.

One wet morning, when she was playing the hotel piano, and he listening, thinking to have her to himself, there came a young German violinist—pale, and with a brown, thin-waisted coat, long-ish hair, and little whiskers—rather a beast, in fact. Soon, of course, this young beast was asking her to accompany him—as if anyone wanted to hear him play his disgusting violin! Every word and smile that she gave him hurt so, seeing how much more interesting than himself this foreigner was! And his heart grew heavier and heavier, and he thought: If she likes him I ought not to mind—only, I *do* mind! How can I help minding? It was hateful to see her smiling, and the young beast bending down to her. And they were talking German, so that he could not tell what they were saying, which made it more unbearable. He had not known there could be such torture.

And then he began to want to hurt her, too. But that was mean—besides, how could he hurt her? She did not care for him. He was nothing to her—only a boy. If she really thought him only a boy, who felt so old—it would be horrible. It flashed across him that she might be playing that young violinist against him! No, she never would do that! But the young beast looked just the sort that

19

might take advantage of her smiles. If only he *would* do something that was not respectful, how splendid it would be to ask him to come for a walk in the woods, and, having told him why, give him a thrashing. Afterwards, he would not tell her, he would not try to gain credit by it. He would keep away till she wanted him back. But suddenly the thought of what he would feel if she really meant to take this young man as her friend in place of him became so actual, so poignant, so horribly painful, that he got up abruptly and went towards the door. Would she not say a word to him before he got out of the room, would she not try and keep him? If she did not, surely it would be all over; it would mean that anybody was more to her than he. That little journey to the door, indeed, seemed like a march to execution. Would she not call after him? He looked back. She was smiling. But *he* could not smile; she had hurt him too much! Turning his head away, he went out, and dashed into the rain bareheaded. The feeling of it on his face gave him a sort of dismal satisfaction. Soon he would be wet through. Perhaps he would get ill. Out here, far away from his people, she would have to offer to nurse him; and perhaps—perhaps in his illness he would seem to her again more interesting than that young beast, and then—— Ah! if only he could be ill!

He mounted rapidly through the dripping leaves towards the foot of the low mountain that rose behind the hotel. A trail went up there to the top, and he struck into it, going at a great pace. His sense of injury began dying away; he no longer wanted to be ill. The rain had stopped, the sun came out; he went on, up and up. He would get to the top quicker than anyone ever had! It was something he could do better than that young beast. The pine-trees gave way to stunted larches, and these to pine scrub and bare scree, up which he scrambled, clutching at the tough bushes, terribly out of breath, his heart pumping, the sweat streaming into his eyes. He had no feeling now but wonder whether he would get to the top before he dropped, exhausted. He thought he would die of the beating of his heart; but it was better to die than to stop and be beaten by a few yards. He stumbled up at last on to the little plateau at the top. For full ten minutes he lay there on his face without moving, then rolled over. His heart had given up that terrific thumping; he breathed luxuriously, stretched out his arms along the steaming grass—felt happy. It was wonderful up here, with the sun burning hot in a sky clear-blue already. How tiny everything looked below—hotel, trees, village, châlets—little toy things! He had never before felt the sheer joy of being high up.

The rain-clouds, torn and driven in huge white shapes along the mountains to the South, were like an army of giants with chariots and white horses hurrying away. He thought suddenly: 'Suppose I had died when my heart pumped so! Would it have mattered the least bit? Everything would be going on just the same, the sun shining, the blue up there the same; and those toy things down in the valley.' That jealousy of his an hour ago, why—it was nothing —he himself nothing! What did it matter if she were nice to that fellow in the brown coat? What did anything matter when the whole thing was so big—and he such a tiny scrap of it?

On the edge of the plateau, to mark the highest point, someone had erected a rude cross, which jutted out stark against the blue sky. It looked cruel somehow, sagged all crooked, and out of place up here; a piece of bad manners, as if people with only one idea had dragged it in, without caring whether or no it suited what was around it. One might just as well introduce one of these rocks into that jolly dark church where he had left her the other day, as put a cross up here.

A sound of bells, and of sniffing and scuffling, roused him; a large grey goat had come up and was smelling at his hair—the leader of a flock, that were soon all round him, solemnly curious, with their queer yellow oblong-pupilled eyes, and their quaint little beards and tails. Awfully decent beasts—and friendly! What jolly things to model! He lay still (having learnt from the fisherman, his guardian, that necessary habit in the presence of all beasts), while the leader sampled the flavour of his neck. The passage of that long rough tongue athwart his skin gave him an agreeable sensation, awakened a strange deep sense of comradeship. He restrained his desire to stroke the creature's nose. It appeared that they now all wished to taste his neck; but some were timid, and the touch of their tongues simply a tickle, so that he was compelled to laugh, and at that peculiar sound they withdrew and gazed at him. There seemed to be no one with them; then, at a little distance, quite motionless in the shade of a rock, he spied the goatherd, a boy about his own age. How lonely he must be up here all day! Perhaps he talked to his goats. He looked as if he might. One would get to have queer thoughts up here, get to know the rocks, and clouds, and beasts, and what they all meant. The goatherd uttered a peculiar whistle, and something, Lennan could not tell exactly what, happened among the goats—a sort of 'Here, sir!' seemed to come from them. And then the goatherd moved out from the shade and went over to the edge of the plateau, and two of the goats

21

that were feeding there thrust their noses into his hand, and rubbed themselves against his legs. The three looked beautiful standing there together on the edge against the sky. . . .

That night, after dinner, the dining-room was cleared for dancing, so that the guests might feel freedom and gaiety in the air. And, indeed, presently, a couple began sawing up and down over the polished boards, in the apologetic manner peculiar to hotel guests. Then three pairs of Italians suddenly launched themselves into space—twirling and twirling, and glaring into each other's eyes; and some Americans, stimulated by their precept, began airily backing and filling. Two of the 'English Grundys' with carefully amused faces next moved out. To Lennan it seemed that they all danced very well, better than he could. Did he dare ask *her*? Then he saw the young violinist go up, saw her rise and take his arm and vanish into the dancing-room; and leaning his forehead against a window-pane, with a sick, beaten feeling, he stayed, looking out into the moonlight, seeing nothing. He heard his name spoken; his tutor was standing beside him.

'You and I, Lennan, must console each other. Dancing's for the young, eh?'

Fortunately it was the boy's instinct and his training not to show his feelings; to be pleasant, though suffering.

'Yes, sir. Jolly moonlight, isn't it, out there?'

'Ah! very jolly; yes. When I was your age I twirled the light fantastic with the best. But gradually, Lennan, one came to see it could not be done without a partner—there was the rub! Tell me —do you regard women as responsible beings? I should like to have your opinion on that.'

It was, of course, ironical—yet there was something in those words—something.

'I think it's you, sir, who ought to give me yours.'

'My dear Lennan—my experience is a mere nothing!'

That was meant for unkindness to her! He would not answer. If only Stormer would go away! The music had stopped. They would be sitting out somewhere, talking! He made an effort, and said:

'I was up the hill at the back this morning, where the cross is. There were some jolly goats.'

And suddenly he saw her coming. She was alone—flushed, smiling; it struck him that her frock was the same colour as the moonlight.

'Harold, will you dance?'

He would say 'Yes,' and she would be gone again! But his tutor only made her a little bow, and said with that smile of his:

'Lennan and I have agreed that dancing is for the young.'

'Sometimes the old must sacrifice themselves. Mark, will you dance?'

Behind him he heard his tutor murmur:

'Ah! Lennan—you betray me!'

That little silent journey with her to the dancing-room was the happiest moment perhaps that he had ever known. And he need not have been so much afraid about his dancing. Truly, it was not polished, but it could not spoil hers, so light, firm, buoyant! It was wonderful to dance with her. Only when the music stopped and they sat down did he know how his head was going round. He felt strange, very strange indeed. He heard her say:

'What is it, dear boy? You look so white!'

Without quite knowing what he did, he bent his face towards the hand that she had laid on his sleeve, then knew no more, having fainted.

VIII

Growing boy—over-exertion in the morning! That was all! He was himself very quickly, and walked up to bed without assistance. Rotten of him! Never was anyone more ashamed of his little weakness than this boy. Now that he was really a trifle indisposed, he simply could not bear the idea of being nursed at all or tended. Almost rudely he had got away. Only when he was in bed did he remember the look on her face as he left her. How wistful and unhappy, seeming to implore him to forgive her! As if there were anything to forgive! As if she had not made him perfectly happy when she danced with him! He longed to say to her: 'If I might be close to you like that one minute every day, then I don't mind all the rest!' Perhaps he would dare say that to-morrow. Lying there he still felt a little funny. He had forgotten to close the ribs of the blinds, and moonlight was filtering in; but he was too idle, too drowsy to get up now and do it. They had given him brandy, rather a lot—that perhaps was the reason he felt so queer; not ill, but mazy, as if dreaming, as if he had lost the desire ever to move again. Just to lie there, and watch the powdery moonlight, and hear far-away music throbbing down below, and still feel the touch of her, as in the dance she swayed against him, and all the time to

23

have the scent about him of flowers! His thoughts were dreams, his dreams thoughts—all precious unreality. And then it seemed to him that the moonlight was gathered into a single slip of pallor—there was a thrumming, a throbbing, and that shape of moonlight moved towards him. It came so close that he felt its warmth against his brow; it sighed, hovered, drew back soundless, and was gone. He must have fallen then into dreamless sleep. . . .

What time was it when he was awakened by that delicate 'rat-tat' to see his tutor standing in the doorway with a cup of tea?

Was young Lennan all right? Yes, he was perfectly all right—would be down directly! It was most frightfully good of Mr Stormer to come! He really didn't want anything.

Yes, yes; but the maimed and the halt must be attended to!

His face seemed to the boy very kind just then—only to laugh at him a very little—just enough. And it was awfully decent of him to have come, and to stand there while he drank the tea. He was really all right, but for a little headache. Many times while he was dressing he stood still, trying to remember. That white slip of moonlight? Was it moonlight? Was it part of a dream; or was it, could it have been she, in her moonlight-coloured frock? Why had he not stayed awake? He would not dare to ask her, and now would never know whether the vague memory of warmth on his brow had been a kiss.

He breakfasted alone in the room where they had danced. There were two letters for him. One from his guardian enclosing money, and complaining of the shyness of the trout; the other from his sister. The man she was engaged to—he was a budding diplomat, attached to the Embassy at Rome—was afraid that his leave was going to be curtailed. They would have to be married at once. They might even have to get a special licence. It was lucky Mark was coming back so soon. They simply *must* have him for best man. The only bridesmaid now would be Sylvia. . . . Sylvia Doone? Why, she was only a kid! And the memory of a little girl in a very short holland frock, with flaxen hair, pretty blue eyes, and a face so fair that you could almost see through it, came up before him. But that, of course, was six years ago; she would not still be in a frock that showed her knees, or wear beads, or be afraid of bulls that were never there. It was stupid being best man—they might have got some decent chap! And then he forgot all—for there was *she*, out on the terrace. In his rush to join her he passed several of the 'English Grundys', who stared at him askance. Indeed, his conduct of the night before might well have upset them. An

24

Oxford man, fainting in an hotel! Something wrong there! . . .

And then, when he reached her, he did find courage.

'Was it really moonlight?'

'All moonlight.'

'But it was warm!'

And, when she did not answer that, he had within him just the same light, intoxicated feeling as after he had won a race at school.

But now came a dreadful blow. His tutor's old guide had suddenly turned up, after a climb with a party of Germans. The warhorse had been aroused in Stormer. He wished to start that afternoon for a certain hut, and go up a certain peak at dawn next day. But Lennan was not to go. Why not? Because of last night's faint; and because, forsooth, he was not some stupid thing they called 'an expert'. As if——! Where she could go he could! This was to treat him like a child. Of course he could go up this rotten mountain. It was because she did not care enough to take him! She did not think him man enough! Did she think that he could not climb what—her husband—could? And if it were dangerous *she* ought not to be going, leaving him behind—that was simply cruel! But she only smiled, and he flung away from her, not having seen that all this grief of his only made her happy.

And that afternoon they went off without him. What deep, dark thoughts he had then! What passionate hatred of his own youth! What schemes he wove, by which she might come back, and find him gone—up some mountain far more dangerous and fatiguing! If people did not think him fit to climb with, he would climb by himself. That, anyway, everyone admitted, was dangerous. And it would be her fault. She would be sorry then. He would get up, and be off before dawn; he put his things out ready, and filled his flask. The moonlight that evening was more wonderful than ever, the mountains like great ghosts of themselves. And she was up there at the hut, among them! It was very long before he went to sleep, brooding over his injuries—intending not to sleep at all, so as to be ready to be off at three o'clock. At *nine* o'clock he woke. His wrath was gone; he only felt restless and ashamed. If, instead of flying out, he had made the best of it, he could have gone with them as far as the hut, could have stayed the night there. And now he cursed himself for being such a fool and idiot. Some little of that idiocy he could, perhaps, retrieve. If he started for the hut at once, he might still be in time to meet them coming down, and accompany them home. He swallowed his coffee, and set off. He knew the way at first, then in woods lost it, recovered the right track again at last, but did not reach the hut till nearly two o'clock. Yes, the party had made the ascent that morning—they had been seen, been heard jödelling on the top. *Gewiss! Gewiss!* But they would not come down the same way. Oh no! They would be going home down to the west and over the other pass. They would be back in the house before the young *Herr* himself.

He heard this, oddly, almost with relief. Was it the long walk alone, or being up there so high? Or simply that he was very hungry? Or just these nice friendly folk in the hut, and their young daughter with her fresh face, queer little black cloth sailor hat with long ribbons, velvet bodice, and perfect simple manners; or the sight of the little silvery-dun cows, thrusting their broad black noses against her hand? What was it that had taken away from him all his restless feeling, made him happy and content? . . . He did not know that the newest thing always fascinates the puppy in its gambols! . . . He sat a long while after lunch, trying to draw the little cows, watching the sun on the cheek of that pretty maiden, trying to talk to her in German. And when at last he said: 'Adieu!' and she murmured *'Küss die Hand. Adieu!'* there was quite a little pang in his heart. . . . Wonderful and queer is the heart of a man! . . . For all that, as he neared home he hastened, till he was actually running. Why had he stayed so long up there? She would be back—she would expect to see him; and that young beast of a violinist would be with her, perhaps, instead! He reached the hotel just in time to rush up and dress, and rush down to dinner. Ah! They were tired, no doubt—were resting in their rooms. He sat through dinner as best he could; got away before dessert, and flew upstairs. For a minute he stood there doubtful; on which door should he knock? Then timidly he tapped on hers. No answer! He knocked loud on his tutor's door. No answer! They were not back, then. Not back? What could that mean? Or could it be that they were both asleep. Once more he knocked on her door; then desperately turned the handle, and took a flying glance. Empty, tidy, untouched! Not back! He turned and ran downstairs again. All the guests were streaming out from dinner, and he became entangled with a group of 'English Grundys' discussing a climbing accident which had occurred in Switzerland. He listened, feeling suddenly quite sick. One of them, the short grey-bearded Grundy with the rather whispering voice, said to him; 'All alone again to-night? The Stormers not back?' Lennan did his best to answer, but something had closed his throat; he could only shake his head.

'They had a guide, I think?' said the 'English Grundy'.

This time Lennan managed to get out: 'Yes, sir.'

'Stormer, I fancy, is quite an expert!' and turning to the lady whom the young 'Grundys' addressed as 'Madre' he added:

'To me the great charm of mountain-climbing was always the freedom from people—the remoteness.'

The mother of the young 'Grundys', looking at Lennan with her half-closed eyes, answered:

'That, to me, would be the disadvantage; I always like to be mixing with my own kind.'

The grey-bearded 'Grundy' murmured in a muffled voice:

'Dangerous thing, that, to say—in an hotel!'

And they went on talking, but of what Lennan no longer knew, lost in this sudden feeling of sick fear. In the presence of these 'English Grundys', so superior to all vulgar sensations, he could not give vent to his alarm; already they viewed him as unsound for having fainted. Then he grasped that there had begun all round him a sort of luxurious speculation on what might have happened to the Stormers. The descent was very nasty; there was a particularly bad traverse. The 'Grundy', whose collar was not now crumpled, said he did not believe in women climbing. It was one of the signs of the times that he most deplored. The mother of the young 'Grundys' countered him at once: In practice she agreed that they were out of place, but theoretically she could not see why they should not climb. An American standing near threw all into confusion by saying he guessed that it might be liable to develop their understandings. Lennan made for the front door. The moon had just come up over in the south, and exactly under it he could see their mountain. What visions he had then! He saw her lying dead, saw himself climbing down in the moonlight and raising her still-living, but half-frozen, form from some perilous ledge. Even that was almost better than this actuality of not knowing where she was, or what had happened. People passed out in to the moonlight, looking curiously at his set face staring so fixedly. One or two asked him if he were anxious, and he answered: 'Oh no, thanks!' Soon there would have to be a search party. How soon? He would, he must be, of it! They should not stop him this time. And suddenly he thought: Ah, it is all because I stayed up there this afternoon talking to that girl, all because I forgot *her*!

And then he heard a stir behind him. There they were, coming down the passage from a side door—she in front with her alpenstock and rücksack—smiling. Instinctively he recoiled behind some plants. They passed. Her sunburned face, with its high cheek-bones and its deep-set eyes, looked so happy; smiling, tired, triumphant. Somehow he could not bear it, and when they were gone by he stole out into the wood and threw himself down in shadow, burying his face, and choking back a horrible dry sobbing that would keep rising in his throat.

IX

Next day he was happy; for all the afternoon he lay out in the shade of that same wood at her feet, gazing up through larch-boughs. It was so wonderful, with nobody but Nature near. Nature so alive, and busy, and so big!

Coming down from the hut the day before, he had seen a peak that looked exactly like the figure of a woman with a garment over her head, the biggest statue in the world; from further down it had become the figure of a bearded man, with his arm bent over ·his eyes. Had she seen it? Had she noticed how all the mountains in moonlight or very early morning took the shape of beasts? What he wanted most in life was to be able to make images of beasts and creatures of all sorts, that were like—that had—that gave out the spirit of—Nature; so that by just looking at them one could have all those jolly feelings one had when one was watching trees, and beasts, and rocks, and even some sorts of men —but not 'English Grundys'.

So he was quite determined to study Art?

Oh yes, of course!

He would want to leave—Oxford, then!

No, oh no! Only some day he would have to.

She answered : 'Some never get away!'

And he said quickly : 'Of course, I shall never want to leave Oxford while you are there.'

He heard her draw her breath in sharply.

'Oh yes, you will! Now help me up!' And she led the way back to the hotel.

He stayed out on the terrace when she had gone in, restless and unhappy the moment he was away from her. A voice close by said :

'Well, friend Lennan—brown study, or blue devils, which?'

There, in one of those high wicker chairs that insulate their occupants from the world, he saw his tutor leaning back, head a little to one side, and tips of fingers pressed together. He looked like

28

an idol sitting there inert, and yet—yesterday he had gone up that mountain!

'Cheer up! You will break your neck yet! When I was your age, I remember feeling it deeply that I was not allowed to risk the lives of others.'

Lennan stammered out:

'I didn't think of that; but I thought where Mrs Stormer could go, I could.'

'Ah For all our admiration we cannot quite admit—can we, when it comes to the point?'

The boy's loyalty broke into flame:

'It's not that. I think Mrs Stormer as good as any man—only—only——'

'Not quite so good as you, eh?'

'A hundred times better, sir.'

Stormer smiled. Ironic beast!

'Lennan,' he said, 'distrust hyperbole.'

'Of course, I know I'm no good at climbing,' the boy broke out again; 'but—but—I thought where she was allowed to risk her life, I ought to be!'

'Good! I like that.' It was said so entirely without irony for once, that the boy was disconcerted.

'You are young, Brother Lennan,' his tutor went on. 'Now, at what age do you consider men develop discretion? Because, there is just one thing always worth remembering—women have none of that better part of valour.'

'I think women are the best things in the world,' the boy blurted out.

'May you long have that opinion!' His tutor had risen, and was ironically surveying his knees. 'A bit stiff!' he said. 'Let me know when you change your views!'

'I never shall, sir.'

'Ah, ah! Never is a long word, Lennan. I am going to have some tea;' and gingerly he walked away, quizzing, as it were, with a smile, his own stiffness.

Lennan remained where he was, with burning cheeks. His tutor's words again had seemed directed against her. How could a man say such things about women! If they were true, he did not want to know; if they were not true, it was wicked to say them. It must be awful never to have generous feelings; always to have to be satirical. Dreadful to be like the 'English Grundys'; only different, of course, because, after all, old Stormer was much more interesting and intelligent—ever so much more; only, just as 'superior'. 'Some never get away!' Had she meant—from that superiority? Just down below were a family of peasants scything and gathering in the grass. One could imagine her doing that, and looking beautiful, with a coloured handkerchief over her head; one could imagine her doing anything simple—one could not imagine old Stormer doing anything but what he did do. And suddenly the boy felt miserable, oppressed by these dim glimmerings of lives misplaced. And he resolved that he would not be like Stormer when he was old! No, he would rather be a regular beast than be like that! . . .

When he went to his room to change for dinner he saw in a glass of water a large clove carnation. Who had put it there? Who could have put it there—but she? It had the same scent as the mountain pinks she had dropped over him, but deeper, richer—a scent moving, dark, and sweet. He put his lips to it before he pinned it into his coat.

There was dancing again that night—more couples this time, and a violin beside the piano; and she had on a black frock. He had never seen her in black. Her face and neck were powdered over their sunburn. The first sight of that powder gave him a faint shock. He had not somehow thought that ladies ever put on powder. But if *she* did—then it must be right! And his eyes never left her. He saw the young German violinist hovering round her, even dancing with her twice; watched her dancing with others, but all without jealousy, without troubling; all in a sort of dream. What was it? Had he been bewitched into that queer state, bewitched by the gift of that flower in his coat? What was it, when he danced with her, that kept him happy in her silence and his own? There was no expectation in him of anything that she would say, or do—no expectation, no desire. Even when he wandered out with her on to the terrace, even when they went down the bank and sat on a bench above the fields where the peasants had been scything, he had still no feeling but that quiet, dreamy adoration. The night was black and dreamy too, for the moon was still well down behind the mountains. The little band was playing the next waltz; but he sat, not moving, not thinking, as if all power of action and thought had been stolen out of him. And the scent of the flower in his coat rose, for there was no wind. Suddenly his heart stopped beating. She had leaned against him, he felt her shoulder press his arm, her hair touch his cheek. He closed his eyes then, and turned to face her. He felt her lips press his mouth with a swift, burning kiss. He sighed, stretched out his arms. There was nothing there but air.

The rustle of her dress against the grass was all! The flower—it, too, was gone.

X

Not one minute all that night did Anna sleep. Was it remorse that kept her awake, or the intoxication of memory? If she felt that her kiss had been a crime, it was not against her husband, or herself, but against the boy—the murder of illusion, of something sacred. But she could not help feeling a delirious happiness too, and the thought of trying to annul what she had done did not even occur to her.

He was ready, then, to give her a little love! Ever so little, compared to hers, but still a little! There could be no other meaning to that movement of his face with the closed eyes, as if he would nestle it down on her breast.

Was she ashamed of her little manoeuvres of these last few days —ashamed of having smiled at the young violinist, of that late return from the mountain climb, of the flower she had given him, of all the conscious siege she had laid since the evening her husband came in and sat watching her, without knowing that she saw him? No; not really ashamed! Her remorse rose only from the kiss. It hurt to think of that, because it was death, the final extinction of the mother-feeling in her; the awakening of—who knew what—in the boy! For if she was mysterious to him, what was he not to her, with his eagerness, and his dreaminess, his youthful warmth, his innocence! What if it had killed in him trust, brushed off the dew, tumbled a star down? Could she forgive herself for that? Could she bear it if she were to make him like so many other boys, like that young violinist; just a cynical youth, looking on women as what they called 'fair game'? But *could* she make him into such—would he ever grow like that? Oh! surely not; or she would not have loved him from the moment she first set eyes on him and spoke of him as 'an angel'.

After that kiss—that crime, if it were one—in the dark she had not known what he had done, where gone—perhaps wandering, perhaps straight up to his room. Why had she refrained, left him there, vanished out of his arms? This she herself hardly understood. Not shame, not fear; reverence perhaps—for what? For love—for the illusion, the mystery, all that made love beautiful; for youth, and the poetry of it; just for the sake of the black still night itself,

31

and the scent of that flower—dark flower of passion that had won him to her, and that she had stolen back, and now wore all night long close to her neck, and in the morning placed withered within her dress. She had been starved so long, and so long waited for that moment—it was little wonder if she did not clearly know why she had done just this, and not that!

And now how should she meet him, how first look into his eyes? Would they have changed? Would they no longer have the straight look she so loved? It would be for her to lead, to make the future. And she kept saying to herself: I am not going to be afraid. It is done. I will take what life offers! Of her husband she did not think at all.

But the first moment she saw the boy, she knew that something from outside, and untoward, had happened since that kiss. He came up to her, indeed, but he said nothing, stood trembling all over, and handed her a telegram that contained these words: 'Come back at once Wedding immediate Expect you day after to-morrow. Cicely.' The words grew indistinct even as she read them, and the boy's face all blurred. Then, making an effort, she said quietly:

'Of course, you must go. You cannot miss your only sister's wedding.'

Without protest he looked at her; and she could hardly bear that look—it seemed to know so little, and ask so much. She said: 'It is nothing—only a few days. You will come back, or we will come to you.'

His face brightened at once.

'Will you really come to us soon, at once—if they ask you? Then I don't mind—I—I——' And then he stopped, choking.

She said again:

'Ask us. We will come.'

He seized her hand; pressed and pressed it in both his own, then stroked it gently, and said:

'Oh! I'm hurting it!'

She laughed, not wishing to cry.

In a few minutes he would have to start to catch the only train that would get him home in time. She went and helped him to pack. Her heart felt like lead, but, not able to bear that look on his face again, she kept cheerfully talking of their return, asking about his home, how to get to it, speaking of Oxford and next term. When his things were ready she put her arms round his neck, and for a moment pressed him to her. Then she escaped. Looking back from his door, she saw him standing exactly as when she had withdrawn her arms. Her cheeks were wet; she dried them as she went downstairs. When she felt herself safe, she went out on the terrace. Her husband was there, and she said to him:

'Will you come with me into the town? I want to buy some things.'

He raised his eyebrows, smiled dimly, and followed her. They walked slowly down the hill into the long street of the little town. All the time she talked of she knew not what, and all the time she thought: His carriage will pass—his carriage will pass!

Several carriages went jingling by. At last he came. Sitting there, and staring straight before him, he did not see them. She heard her husband say:

'Hullo! Where is our young friend Lennan off to, v ith his luggage—looking like a lion cub in trouble?'

She answered in a voice that she tried to make clear and steady:

'There must be something wrong; or else it is his sister's wedding.'

She felt that her husband was gazing at her, and wondered what her face was like; but at that moment the word 'Madre!' sounded close in her ear, and they were surrounded by a small drove of 'English Grundys'.

XI

That twenty mile drive was perhaps the worst part of the journey for the boy. It is always hard to sit still and suffer.

When Anna left him the night before, he had wandered about in the dark, not knowing quite where he went. Then the moon came up, and he found himself sitting under the eave of a barn close to a châlet where all was dark and quiet; and down below him the moon-whitened valley village—its roofs and spires and little glamorous unreal lights.

In his evening suit, his dark ruffled hair uncovered, he would have made a quaint spectacle for the owners of that châlet, if they had chanced to see him seated on the hay-strewn boards against their barn, staring before him with such wistful rapture. But they were folk to whom sleep was precious. . . .

And now it was all snatched away from him, relegated to some immensely far-off future. Would it indeed be possible to get his guardian to ask them down to Hayle? And would they really come? His tutor would surely never care to visit a place right away

33

in the country—far from books and everything! He frowned, thinking of his tutor, but it was with perplexity—no other feeling. And yet, if he could not have them down there, how could he wait the two whole months till next term began! So went his thoughts, round and round, while the horses jogged, dragging him further and further from her.

It was better in the train; the distraction of all the strange crowd of foreigners, the interest of new faces and new country; and then sleep—a long night of it, snoozed up in his corner, thoroughly fagged out. And next day more new country, more new faces; and slowly, his mood changing from ache and bewilderment to a sense of something promised, delightful to look forward to. Then Calais at last, and a night-crossing in a wet little steamer, a summer gale blowing spray in his face, waves leaping white in a black sea, and the wild sound of the wind. On again to London, the early drive across the town, still sleepy in August haze; an English breakfast—porridge, chops, marmalade. And, at last, the train for home. At all events he could write to her, and tearing a page out of his little sketch-book, he began:

'I am writing in the train, so please forgive this joggly writing——'

Then he did not know how to go on, for all that he wanted to say was such as he had never even dreamed of writing—things about his feelings which would look horrible in words; besides, he must not put anything that might not be read by anyone, so what was there to say?

'It has been such a long journey,' he wrote at last, 'away from the Tyrol;' (he did not dare even to put 'from you,') 'I thought it would never end. But at last it has—very nearly. I have thought a great deal about the Tyrol. It was a lovely time—the loveliest time I have ever had. And now it's over, I try to console myself by thinking of the future, but not the immediate future—*that* is not very enjoyable. I wonder how the mountains are looking to-day. Please give my love to them, especially the lion ones that come and lie out in the moonlight—you will not recognize them from this'—then followed a sketch. 'And this is the church we went to, with someone kneeling. And this is meant for the "English Grundys", looking at someone who is coming in very late with an alpenstock—only, I am better at the "English Grundys" than at the person

34

with the alpenstock. I wish I were the "English Grundys" now, still in the Tyrol. I hope I shall get a letter from you soon; and that it will say you are getting ready to come back. My guardian will be awfully keen for you to come and stay with us. He is not half bad when you know him, and there will be his sister, Mrs Doone, and her daughter left there after the wedding. It will be simply disgusting if you and Mr Stormer don't come. I wish I could write all I feel about my lovely time in the Tyrol, but you must please imagine it.'

And just as he had not known how to address her, so he could not tell how to subscribe himself, and only put 'Mark Lennan'.

He posted the letter at Exeter, where he had some time to wait; and his mind moved still more from past to future. Now that he was nearing home he began to think of his sister. In two days she would be gone to Italy; he would not see her again for a long time, and a whole crowd of memories began to stretch out hands to him. How she and he used to walk together in the walled garden, and on the sunk croquet ground; she telling him stories, her arm round his neck, because she was two years older, and taller than he in those days. Their first talk each holidays, when he came back to her; the first tea—with unlimited jam—in the old mullion-windowed, flower-chintzed schoolroom, just himself and her and old Tingle (Miss Tring, the ancient governess, whose chaperonage would now be gone), and sometimes that kid Sylvia, when she chanced to be staying there with her mother. Cicely had always understood him when he explained to her how inferior school was, because nobody took any interest in beasts or birds except to kill them; or in drawing, or making things, or anything decent. They would go off together, rambling along the river, or up the park, where everything looked so jolly and wild—the ragged oak-trees, and huge boulders, of whose presence old Godden, the coachman, had said: 'I can't think but what these ha' been washed here by the Flood, Mast' Mark!' These and a thousand other memories beset his conscience now. And as the train drew closer to their station, he eagerly made ready to jump out and greet her. There was the honeysuckle full out along the paling of the platform over the waiting-room; wonderful, this year—and there was she, standing alone on the platform. No, it was not Cicely! He got out with a blank sensation, as if those memories had played him false. It was a girl, indeed, but she only looked about sixteen, and wore a sun-bonnet that hid her hair and half her face. She had on a blue frock, and some honeysuckle in her waist-belt. She seemed to be smiling at him, and expecting him to smile at her; and so he did smile. She came up to him, then, and said:

'I'm Sylvia.'

He answered: 'Oh! thanks awfully—it was awfully good of you to come and meet me.'

'Cicely's so busy. It's only the T-cart. Have you got much luggage?'

She took up his hold-all, and he took it from her; she took his bag, and he took it from her; then they went out to the T-cart. A small groom stood there, holding a silver-roan cob with a black mane and black swish tail.

She said: 'D'you mind if I drive, because I'm learning.'

And he answered: 'Oh, no! rather not.'

She got up; he noticed that her eyes looked quite excited. Then his portmanteau came out and was deposited with the other things behind; and he got up beside her.

She said: 'Let go, Billy.'

The roan rushed past the little groom, whose top boots seemed to twinkle as he jumped up behind. They whizzed round the corner from the station yard, and observing that her mouth was just a little open as though this had disconcerted her, he said:

'He pulls a bit.'

'Yes—but isn't he perfectly sweet?'

'He *is* rather decent.'

Ah! when *she* came, he would drive her; they would go off alone in the T-cart, and he would show her all the country round.

He was re-awakened by the words:

'Oh! I know he's going to shy!' At once there was a swerve. The roan was cantering.

They had passed a pig.

'Doesn't he look lovely now? Ought I to have whipped him when he shied?'

'Rather not.'

'Why?'

'Because horses are horses, and pigs are pigs; it's natural for horses to shy at them.'

'Oh!'

He looked up at her then, sidelong. The curve of her cheek and chin looked very soft, and rather jolly.

'I didn't know you, you know!' he said. 'You've grown up so awfully.'

36

'I knew you at once. Your voice is still furry.'

There was another silence, till she said:

'He does pull, rather—doesn't he, going home?'

'Shall I drive?'

'Yes, please.'

He stood up and took the reins, and she slipped past under them in front of him; her hair smelt exactly like hay, as she was softly bumped against him.

She kept regarding him steadily with very blue eyes, now that she was relieved of driving.

'Cicely was afraid you weren't coming,' she said suddenly. 'What sort of people are those old Stormers?'

He felt himself grow very red, choked something down, and answered:

'It's only he that's old. She's not more than about thirty-five.'

'That *is* old.'

He restrained the words: 'Of course it's old to a kid like you!' And, instead, he looked at her. Was she exactly a kid? She seemed quite tall (for a girl) and not very thin, and there was something frank and soft about her face, and as if she wanted you to be nice to her.

'Is she very pretty?'

This time he did not go red, such was the disturbance that question made in him. If he said: 'Yes,' it was like letting the world know his adoration; but to say anything else would be horrible, disloyal. So he did say: 'Yes,' listening hard to the tone of his own voice.

'I thought she was. Do you like her very much?'

Again he struggled with that thing in his throat, and again said: 'Yes.'

He wanted to hate this girl, yet somehow could not—she looked so soft and confiding. She was staring before her now, her lips still just parted, so evidently *that* had not been because of Bolero's pulling; they were pretty all the same, and so was her short, straight little nose, and her chin, and she was awfully fair. His thoughts flew back to that other face—so splendid, so full of life. Suddenly he found himself unable to picture it—for the first time since he had started on his journey it would not come before him.

'Oh! Look!'

Her hand was pulling at his arm. There in the field over the hedge a buzzard hawk was dropping like a stone.

'Oh, Mark! Oh! Oh! It's got it!'

She was covering her face with both her hands, and the hawk, with a young rabbit in its claws, was sailing up again. It looked so beautiful that he did not somehow feel sorry for the rabbit; but he wanted to stroke and comfort her, and said:

'It's all right, Sylvia; it really is. The rabbit's dead already, you know. And it's quite natural.'

She took her hands away from a face that looked just as if she were going to cry.

'Poor little rabbit! It was such a little one!'

XII

On the afternoon of the day following he sat in the smoking-room with a prayer-book in his hand, and a frown on his forehead, reading the Marriage Service. The book had been effectively designed for not spoiling the figure when carried in a pocket. But this did not matter, for even if he could have read the words, he would not have known what they meant, seeing that he was thinking how he could make a certain petition to a certain person sitting just behind at a large bureau with a sliding top, examining artificial flies.

He fixed at last upon this form:

'Gordy!' (Why Gordy no one quite knew now—whether because his name was George, or by way of corruption from Guardian.) 'When Cis is gone it'll be rather awful, won't it?'

'Not a bit.'

Mr Heatherley was a man of perhaps sixty-four, if indeed guardians have ages, and like a doctor rather than a squire; his face square and puffy, his eyes always half-closed, and his curly mouth using bluntly a voice of that refined coarseness peculiar to people of old family.

'But it will, you know!'

'Well, supposin' it is?'

'I only wondered if you'd mind asking Mr and Mrs Stormer to come here for a little—they were awfully kind to me out there.'

'Strange man and woman! My dear fellow!'

'Mr Stormer likes fishing.'

'Does he? And what does she like?'

Very grateful that his back was turned, the boy said:

'I don't know—anything—she's awfully nice.'

'Ah! Pretty?'

He answered faintly:

'I don't know what *you* call pretty, Gordy.'

He felt, rather than saw, his guardian scrutinising him with those half-closed eyes under their gouty lids.

'All right; do as you like. Have 'em here and have done with it, by all means.'

Did his heart jump? Not quite; but it felt warm and happy, and he said:

'Thanks awfully, Gordy. It's most frightfully decent of you,' and turned again to the Marriage Service. He could make out some of it. In places is seemed to him fine, and in other places queer. About obeying, for instance. If you loved anybody, it seemed rotten to expect them to obey you. If you loved them and they loved you, there couldn't ever be any question of obeying, because you would both do the things always of your own accord. And if they didn't love you, or you them, then—oh! then it would be simply too disgusting for anything, to go on living with a person you didn't love or who didn't love you. But of course *she* didn't love his tutor. Had she once? Those bright doubting eyes, that studiously satiric mouth came very clearly up before him. You could not love them; and yet—he was really very decent. A feeling as of pity, almost of affection, rose in him for his remote tutor. It was queer to feel so, since the last time they had talked together out there, on the terrace, he had not felt at all like that.

The noise of the bureau top sliding down aroused him; Mr Heatherley was closing in the remains of the artificial flies. That meant he would be going out to fish. And the moment he heard the door shut, Mark sprang up, slid back the bureau top, and began to write his letter. It was hard work.

'DEAR MRS STORMER,

'My guardian wishes me to beg you and Mr Stormer to pay us a visit as soon as you come back from the Tyrol. Please tell Mr Stormer that only the very best fishermen—like him—can catch our trout; the rest catch our trees. This is me catching our trees (here followed a sketch). My sister is going to be married to-morrow, and it will be disgusting afterwards unless you come. So do come, please. And with my very best greetings,

'I am,

'Your humble servant,

'M. LENNAN.'

When he had stamped this production and dropped it in the letter-box, he had the oddest feeling, as if he had been let out of school; a desire to rush about, to frolic. What should he do? Cis, of course, would be busy—they were all busy about the wedding. He would go and saddle Bolero, and jump him in the park; or should he go down along the river and watch the jays. Both seemed lonely occupations. And he stood in the window—dejected. At the age of five, walking with his nurse, he had been overheard remarking: 'Nurse, I want to eat a biscuit—*all the way* I want to eat a biscuit!' and it was still rather so with him perhaps—all the way he wanted to eat a biscuit. He bethought him then of his modelling, and went out to the little empty greenhouse where he kept his masterpieces. They seemed to him now quite horrible—and two of them, the sheep and the turkey, he marked out for summary destruction. The idea occurred to him that he might try and model that hawk escaping with the little rabbit; but when he tried, no nice feeling came, and flinging the things down he went out. He ran along the unweeded path to the tennis ground—lawn tennis was then just coming in. The grass looked very rough. But then, everything about that little manor-house was left rather wild and anyhow; why, nobody quite knew, and nobody seemed to mind. He stood there scrutinizing the condition of the ground. A sound of humming came to his ears. He got up on the wall. There was Sylvia sitting in the field, making a wreath of honeysuckle. He stood very quiet and listened. She looked pretty—lost in her tune. Then he slid down off the wall, and said gently:

'Hallo!'

She looked round at him, her eyes very wide open.

'Your voice is jolly, Sylvia!'

'Oh, no!'

'It is. Come and climb a tree!'

'Where?'

'In the park, of course.'

They were some time selecting the tree, many being too easy for him, and many too hard for her; but one was found at last, an oak of great age, and frequented by rooks. Then, insisting that she must be roped to him, he departed to the house for some blind-cord. The climb began at four o'clock—named by him the ascent of the Cimone della Pala. He led the momentous expedition, taking a hitch of the blind-cord round a branch before he permitted her to move. Two or three times he was obliged to make the cord fast and return to help her, for she was not an 'expert'; her arms seemed soft, and she was inclined to straddle instead of trusting to one foot. But at last they were settled, streaked indeed with moss, on the top branch but two. They rested there, silent, listening to the rooks soothing an outraged dignity. Save for this slowly subsiding demonstration it was marvellously peaceful and remote up there, half-way to a blue sky thinly veiled from them by the crinkled brown-green leaves. The peculiar dry mossy smell of an oak-tree was disturbed into the air by the least motion of their feet or hands against the bark. They could hardly see the ground, and all around, other gnarled trees barred off any view.

He said:

'If we stay up here till it's dark we might see owls.'

'Oh, no! Owls are horrible!'

'What! They're *lovely*—especially the white ones.'

'I can't stand their eyes, and they squeak so when they're hunting.'

'Oh! but that's so jolly, and their eyes are beautiful.'

'They're always catching mice and little chickens; all sorts of little things.'

'But they don't mean to; they only want them to eat. Don't you think things are jolliest at night?'

She slipped her arm in his.

'No; I don't like the dark.'

'Why not? It's splendid—when things get mysterious.' He dwelt lovingly on that word.

'I don't like mysterious things. They frighten you.'

'Oh, Sylvia!'

'No, I like early morning—especially in spring, when it's beginning to get leafy.'

'Well, of course.'

She was leaning against him, for safety, just a little; and stretching out his arm, he took good hold of the branch to make a back for her. There was a silence. Then he said:

'If you could only have one tree, which would you have?'

'Not oaks. Limes—no—birches. Which would you?'

He pondered. There were so many trees that were perfect. Birches and limes, of course; but beeches and cypresses, and yews, and cedars, and holm-oaks—almost, and plane-trees; then he said suddenly:

'Pines; I mean the big ones with reddish stems and branches pretty high up.'

'Why?'

Again he pondered. It was very important to explain exactly

why; his feelings about everything were concerned in this. And while he mused she gazed at him, as if surprised to see anyone think so deeply. At last he said:

'Because they're independent and dignified and never quite cold, and their branches seem to brood, but chiefly because the ones I mean are generally out of the common where you find them. You know—just one or two, strong and dark, standing out against the sky.'

'They're *too* dark.'

It occurred to him suddenly that he had forgotten larches. They, of course, could be heavenly, when you lay under them and looked up at the sky, as he had that afternoon out there. Then he heard her say:

'If I could only have one flower, I should have lilies of the valley, the small ones that grow wild and smell so jolly.'

He had a swift vision of another flower, dark—very different, and was silent.

'What would you have, Mark?' Her voice sounded a little hurt. 'You *are* thinking of one, aren't you?'

He said honestly:

'Yes, I am.'

'Which?'

'It's dark, too; you wouldn't care for it a bit.'

'How d'you know?'

'A clove carnation.'

'But I do like it—only—not very much.'

He nodded solemnly.

'I knew you wouldn't.'

Then a silence fell between them. She had ceased to lean against him, and he missed the cosy friendliness of it. Now that their voices and the cawing of the rooks had ceased, there was nothing heard but the dry rustle of the leaves, and the plaintive cry of a buzzard hawk hunting over the little tor across the river. There were nearly always two up there, quartering the sky. To the boy it was lovely, that silence—like Nature talking to you—Nature always talked in silences. The beasts, the birds, the insects, only really showed themselves when you were still; you had to be awfully quiet, too, for flowers and plants, otherwise you couldn't see the real jolly separate life there was in them. Even the boulders down there, that old Godden thought had been washed up by the Flood, never showed you what queer shapes they had, and let you feel close to them, unless you were thinking of nothing else. Sylvia, after all, was better in that way than he had expected. She could keep quiet (he had thought girls hopeless); she was gentle, and it was rather jolly to watch her. Through the leaves there came the faint far tinkle of the tea-bell.

She said: 'We must get down.'

It was much too jolly to go in, really. But if she wanted her tea —girls always wanted tea! And, twisting the cord carefully round the branch, he began to superintend her descent. About to follow, he heard her cry:

'Oh, Mark! I'm stuck—I'm stuck! I can't reach it with my foot! I'm swinging!' And he saw that she *was* swinging by her hands and the cord.

'Let go; drop on to the branch below—the cord'll hold you straight till you grab the trunk.'

Her voice mounted piteously:

'I can't—I really can't—I should slip!'

He tied the cord, and slithered hastily to the branch below her; then, bracing himself against the trunk, he clutched her round the waist and knees; but the taut cord held her up, and she would not come to anchor. He could not hold her and untie the cord, which was fast round her waist. If he let her go with one hand, and got out his knife, he would never be able to cut and hold her at the same time. For a moment he thought he had better climb up again and slack off the cord, but he could see by her face that she was getting frightened; he could feel it by the quivering of her body.

'If I heave you up,' he said, 'can you get hold again above?' And, without waiting for an answer, he heaved. She caught hold frantically.

'Hold on just for a second.'

She did not answer, but he saw that her face had gone very white. He snatched out his knife and cut the cord. She clung just for that moment, then came loose into his arms, and he hauled her to him against the trunk. Safe there, she buried her face on his shoulder. He began to murmur to her and smooth her softly, with quite a feeling of its being his business to comfort her like this, to protect her. He knew she was crying, but she let no sound escape, and he was very careful not to show that he knew, for fear she should feel ashamed. He wondered if he ought to kiss her. At last he did, on the top of her head, very gently. Then she put up her face and said she was a beast. And he kissed her again on an eyebrow.

After that she seemed all right, and very gingerly they descended

43

to the ground, where shadows were beginning to lengthen over the fern and the sun to slant into their eyes.

XIII

The night after Cicely's wedding the boy stood at the window of his pleasant attic bedroom, with one wall sloping, and its faint smell of mice. He was tired and excited, and his brain full of pictures. This was his first wedding, and he was haunted by a vision of his sister's little white form, and her face with its starry eyes. She was gone—his no more! How fearful the Wedding March had sounded on that organ—that awful old wheezer; and the sermon! One didn't want to hear that sort of thing when one felt inclined to cry. Even Gordy had looked rather boiled when he was giving her away. With perfect distinctness he could still see the group before the altar rails, just as if he had not been a part of it himself. Cis in her white, Sylvia in fluffy grey; his impassive brother-in-law's tall figure; Gordy looking queer in a black coat, with a very yellow face, and eyes still half-closed. The rotten part of it all had been that you wanted to be just *feeling*, and you had to be thinking of the ring, and your gloves, and whether the lowest button on your white waistcoat was properly undone. Girls could do both, it seemed—Cis seemed to be seeing something wonderful all the time, and Sylvia had looked quite holy. He himself had been too conscious of the rector's voice, and the sort of professional manner with which he did it all, as if he were making up a prescription, with directions how to take it. And yet it was all rather beautiful in a kind of fashion, every face turned one way, and a tremendous hush—except for poor old Godden's blowing of his nose with his enormous red handkerchief; and the soft darkness up in the roof, and down in the pews; and the sunlight brightening the south windows. All the same, it would have been much jollier just taking hands by themselves somewhere, and saying out before God what they really felt—because, after all, God was everything, everywhere, not only in stuffy churches. That was how *he* would like to be married, out of doors on a starry night like this, when everything felt wonderful all round you. Surely God wasn't half as small as people seemed always making Him—a sort of superior man a little bigger than themselves! Even the very most beautiful and wonderful and awful things one could imagine or make, could only be just nothing to a God who had a temple like the night out there.

But then you couldn't be married alone, and no girl would ever like to be married without rings and flowers and dresses, and words that made it all feel small and cosy! Cis might have, perhaps, only she wouldn't because of not hurting other people's feelings; but Sylvia—never—she would be afraid. Only, of course, she was young! And the thread of his thoughts broke—and scattered like beads from a string.

Leaning out, and resting his chin on his hands, he drew the night air into his lungs. Honeysuckle, or was it the scent of lilies still? The stars all out, and lots of owls to-night—four at least. What would night be like without owls and stars? But that was it—you never could think what things would be like if they weren't just what and where they were. You never knew what was coming, either; and yet, when it came, it seemed as if nothing else ever could have come. That was queer—you could do anything you liked until you'd done it, but when you *had* done it, then you knew, of course, that you must always have had to. . . . What was that light, below and to the left? Whose room? Old Tingle's—no, the little spare room—Sylvia's! She must be awake, then! He leaned far out, and whispered in the voice she had said was still furry :

'Sylvia !'

The light flickered, he could just see her head appear, with hair all loose, and her face turning up to him. He could only half see, half imagine it, mysterious, blurry; and he whispered :

'Isn't this jolly?'

The whisper travelled back :

'Awfully.'

'Aren't you sleepy?'

'No; are you?'

'Not a bit. D'you hear the owls?'

'Rather.'

'Doesn't it smell good?'

'Perfect. Can you see me?'

'Only just, not too much. Can you?'

'I can't see your nose. Shall I get the candle?'

'No—that'd spoil it. What are you sitting on?'

'The window sill.'

'It doesn't twist your neck, does it?'

'No—o—only a little bit.'

'Are you hungry?'

'Yes.'

45

'Wait half a shake. I'll let down some chocolate in my big bath towel : it'll swing along to you—reach out.'

A dim white arm reached out.

'Catch! I say, you won't get cold?'

'Rather not.'

'It's too jolly to sleep, isn't it?'

'Mark!'

'Yes.'

'Which star is yours? Mine is the white one over the top branch of the big sycamore, from here.'

'Mine is that twinkling red one over the summer house. Sylvia!'

'Yes.'

'Catch!'

'Oh! I couldn't—what was it?'

'Nothing.'

'No, but what *was* it?'

'Only my star. It's caught in your hair.'

'Oh!'

'Listen!'

Silence, then, until her awed whisper:

'What?'

And his floating down, dying away:

'*Cave!*'

What had stirred—some window opened? Cautiously he spied along the face of the dim house. There was no light anywhere, nor any shifting blurr of white at her window below. All was dark, remote—still sweet with the scent of something jolly. And then he saw what that something was. All over the wall below his window white jessamine was in flower—stars, not only in the sky. Perhaps the sky was really a field of white flowers; and God walked there, and plucked the stars. . . .

The next morning there was a letter on his plate when he came down to breakfast. He couldn't open it with Sylvia on one side of him, and old Tingle on the other. Then with a sort of anger he did open it. He need not have been afraid. It was written so that anyone might have read; it told of a climb, of bad weather, said they were coming home. Was he relieved, disturbed, pleased at their coming back, or only uneasily ashamed? She had not got his second letter yet. He could feel old Tingle looking round at him with those queer sharp twinkling eyes of hers, and Sylvia regarding him quite frankly. And conscious that he was growing red, he said to himself: 'I won't!' And did not. In three days they would be at Oxford.

Would they come on here at once? Old Tingle was speaking. He heard Sylvia answer: 'No, I don't like "bopsies". They're so hard!' It was their old name for high cheekbones. Sylvia certainly had none, her cheeks went softly up to her eyes.

'Do you. Mark?'

He said slowly:

'On some people.'

'People who have them are strong-willed, aren't they?'

Was *she*—Anna—strong-willed? It came to him that he did not know at all what she was.

When breakfast was over and he had got away to his old greenhouse, he had a strange, unhappy time. He was a beast, he had not been thinking of her half enough! He took the letter out and frowned at it horribly. Why could he not feel more? What was the matter with him? Why was he such a brute—not to be thinking of her day and night? For long he stood, disconsolate, in the little dark greenhouse among the images of his beasts, the letter in his hand.

He stole out presently, and got down to the river unobserved. Comforting—that crisp, gentle sound of water; ever so comforting to sit on a stone, very still, and wait for things to happen round you. You lost yourself that way, just became branches, and stones, and water, and birds, and sky. You did not feel such a beast. Gordy would never understand why he did not care for fishing—one thing trying to catch another—instead of watching and understanding what things were. You never got to the end of looking into water, or grass or fern; always something queer and new. It was like that, too, with yourself, if you sat down and looked properly—most awfully interesting to see things working in your mind.

A soft rain had begun to fall, hissing gently on the leaves, but he had still a boy's love of getting wet, and stayed where he was, on the stone. Some people saw fairies in woods and down in water, or said they did; that did not seem to him much fun. What was really interesting was noticing that each thing was different from every other thing, and what made it so; you must see that before you could draw or model decently. It was fascinating to see your creatures coming out with shapes of their very own; they did that without your understanding how. But this vacation he was no good— couldn't draw or model a bit!

A jay had settled about forty yards away, and remained in full view, attending to his many-coloured feathers. Of all things, birds were the most fascinating! He watched it a long time, and when it flew on, followed it over the high wall up into the park. He heard the lunch-bell ring in the far distance, but did not go in. So long as he was out there in the soft rain with the birds and trees and other creatures, he was free from that unhappy feeling of the morning. He did not go back till nearly seven; properly wet through and very hungry.

All through dinner he noticed that Sylvia seemed to be watching him, as if wanting to ask him something. She looked very soft in her white frock, open at the neck; and her hair almost the colour of special moonlight, so goldy-pale, and he wanted her to understand that it wasn't a bit because of her that he had been out alone all day. After dinner, when they were getting the table ready to play 'red nines', he did murmur:

'Did you sleep last night—after?'

She nodded fervently to that.

It was raining really hard now, swishing and dripping out in the darkness, and he whispered:

'Our stars would be drowned to-night.'

'Do you really think we have stars?'

'We might. But mine's safe, of course; your hair *is* jolly, Sylvia.'

She gazed at him, very sweet and surprised.

XIV

Anna did not receive the boy's letter in the Tyrol. It followed her to Oxford. She was just going out when it came, and she took it up with the mingled beatitude and almost sickening tremor that a lover feels touching the loved one's letter. She would not open it in the street, but carried it all the way to the garden of a certain College, and sat down to read it under the cedar-tree. That little letter, so short, boyish, and dry, transported her halfway to heaven. She was to see him again at once, not to wait weeks, with the fear that he would quite forget her! Her husband had said at breakfast that Oxford without 'the dear young clowns' assuredly was charming, but Oxford 'full of tourists and other strange bodies' as certainly was not. Where should they go? Thank heaven, the letter could be shown him! For all that, a little stab of pain went through her that there was not one word which made it unsuitable to show. Still, she was happy. Never had her favourite College garden seemed so beautiful, with each tree and flower so cared for, and the very wind excluded; never had the birds seemed so tame and friendly. The sun shone softly, even the clouds were luminous and joyful. She sat a long time, musing, and went back forgetting all she had come out to do. Having both courage and decision she did not leave the letter to burn a hole in her corsets, but gave it to her husband at lunch, looking him in the face, and saying carelessly :

'Providence, you see, answers your question.'

He read it, raised his eyebrows, smiled, and, without looking up, murmured :

'You wish to prosecute this romantic episode?'

Did he mean anything—or was it simply his way of putting things?

'I naturally want to be anywhere but here.'

'Perhaps you would like to go alone?'

He said that of course, knowing she could not say : Yes. And she answered simply : 'No.'

'Then let us both go—on Monday. I will catch the young man's trout; thou shalt catch—h'm!—he shall catch—— What is it he catches—trees. Good! That's settled.'

And, three days later, without another word exchanged on the subject, they started.

Was she grateful to him; No. Afraid of him? No. Scornful of him? Not quite. But she was afraid of *herself*, horribly. How would she ever be able to keep herself in hand, how disguise from these people that she loved their boy? It was her desperate mood that she feared. But since she so much wanted all the best for him that life could give, surely she would have the strength to do nothing that might harm him. Yet she was afraid.

He was there at the station to meet them, in riding things and a nice rough Norfolk jacket that she did not recognise, though she thought she knew his clothes by heart; and as the train came slowly to a standstill the memory of her last moment with him, up in his room amid the luggage that she had helped to pack, very nearly overcame her. It seemed so hard to have to meet him coldly, formally, to have to wait—who knew how long—for a minute with him alone! And he was so polite, so beautifully considerate, with all the manners of a host; hoping she wasn't tired, hoping Mr Stormer had brought his fishing-rod, though they had lots, of course, they could lend him; hoping the weather would be fine; hoping that they wouldn't mind having to drive three miles, and busying himself about their luggage. All this when she just wanted to take him in her arms and push his hair back from his forehead, and look at him!

He did not drive with them—he had thought they would be too crowded—but followed, keeping quite close in the dust to point out the scenery, mounted on a 'palfrey', as her husband called the roan with the black swish tail.

This countryside, so rich and yet a little wild, the independent-looking cottages, the old dark cosy manor-house, all was very new to one used to Oxford, and to London, and to little else of England. And all was delightful. Even Mark's guardian seemed to her delightful. For Gordy, when absolutely forced to face an unknown woman, could bring to the encounter a certain bluff ingratiation. His sister, too, Mrs Doone, with her faded gentleness, seemed soothing.

When Anna was alone in her room, reached by an unexpected little stairway, she stood looking at its carved four-poster bed and the wide lattice window with chintz curtains, and the flowers in a blue bowl. Yes, all was delightful. And yet! What was it? What had she missed? Ah, she was a fool to fret! It was only his anxiety that they should be comfortable, his fear that he might betray himself. Out there those last few days—his eyes! And now! She brooded earnestly over what dress she should put on. She, who tanned so quickly, had almost lost her sunburn in the week of travelling and Oxford. To-day her eyes looked tired, and she was pale. She was not going to disdain anything that might help. She had reached thirty-six last month, and he would be nineteen to-morrow! She decided on black. In black she knew that her neck looked whiter, and the colour of her eyes and hair stranger. She put on no jewellery, did not even pin a rose to her breast, took white gloves. Since her husband did not come to her room, she went up the little stairway to his. She surprised him ready dressed, standing by the fireplace, smiling faintly. What was he thinking of, standing there with that smile? Was there blood in him at all?

He inclined his head slightly and said:

'Good! Chaste as the night! Black suits you. Shall we find our way down to these savage halls?'

And they went down.

Everyone was already there, waiting. A single neighbouring squire and magistrate, by name Trusham, had been bidden, to make numbers equal.

Dinner was announced; they went in. At the round table in a dining-room, all black oak, with many candles, and terrible por-

traits of departed ancestors, Anna sat between the magistrate and Gordy. Mark was opposite, between a quaint-looking old lady and a young girl who had not been introduced, a girl in white, with very fair hair and very white skin, blue eyes, and lips a little parted; a daughter evidently of the faded Mrs Doone. A girl like a silvery moth, like a forget-me-not! Anna found it hard to take her eyes away from this girl's face; not that she admired her exactly; pretty she was—yes; but weak, with those parted lips and soft chin, and almost wistful look, as if her deep-blue half-eager eyes were in spite of her. But she was young—so young! That was why not to watch her seemed impossible. 'Sylvia Doone?' Indeed! Yes. A soft name, a pretty name—and very like her! Every time her eyes could travel away from her duty to Squire Trusham, and to Gordy (on both of whom she was clearly making an impression), she gazed at this girl, sitting there by the boy, and whenever those two young things smiled and spoke together she felt her heart contract and hurt her. Was *this* why that something had gone out of his eyes? Ah, she was foolish! If every girl or woman the boy knew was to cause such a feeling in her, what would life be like? And her will hardened against her fears. She was looking brilliant herself; and she saw that the girl in her turn could not help gazing at her eagerly, wistfully, a little bewildered —hatefully young. And the boy? Slowly, surely, as a magnet draws, Anna could feel that she was drawing him, could see him stealing chances to look at her. Once she surprised him full. What troubled eyes! It was not the old adoring face; yet she knew from its expression that she could make him want her—make him jealous—easily fire him with her kisses, if she would.

And the dinner wore to an end. Then came the moment when the girl and she must meet under the eyes of the mother, and that sharp, quaint-looking old governess. It would be a hard moment, that! And it came—a hard moment and a long one, for Gordy sat full span over his wine. But Anna had not served her time beneath the gaze of upper Oxford for nothing; she managed to be charming, full of interest and questions in her still rather foreign accent. Miss Doone—soon she became Sylvia—must show her all the treasures and antiquities. Was it too dark to go out just to look at the old house by night? Oh, no. Not a bit. There were goloshes in the hall. And they went, the girl leading, and talking of Anna knew not what, so absorbed was she in thinking how for a moment, just a moment, she could contrive to be with the boy alone.

It was not remarkable, this old house, but it was his home—

might some day perhaps be his. And houses at night were strangely alive with their window eyes.

'That is my room,' the girl said, 'where the jessamine is—you can just see it. Mark's is above—look, under where the eave hangs out, away to the left. The other night——'

'Yes; the other night?'

'Oh, I don't——! Listen. That's an owl. We have heaps of owls. Mark likes them. I don't, much.'

Always Mark!

'He's awfully keen, you see, about all beasts and birds—he models them. Shall I show you his workshop?—it's an old greenhouse. Here, you can see in.'

There through the glass Anna indeed could just see the boy's quaint creations huddling in the dark on a bare floor, a grotesque company of small monsters. She murmured.

'Yes, I see them, but I won't really look unless he brings me himself.'

'Oh, he's sure to. They interest him more than anything in the world.'

For all her cautious resolutions Anna could not for the life of her help saying.

'What, more than you?'

The girl gave her a wistful stare before she answered.

'Oh! I don't count much.'

Anna laughed, and took her arm. How soft and young it felt! A pang went through her heart, half jealous, half remorseful.

'Do you know,' she said, 'that you are very sweet?'

The girl did not answer.

'Are you his cousin?'

'No. Gordy is only Mark's uncle by marriage; my mother is Gordy's sister—so I'm nothing.'

Nothing!

'I see—just what you English call "a connection".'

They were silent, seeming to examine the night; then the girl said:

'I wanted to see you awfully. You're not like what I thought.'

'Oh! And what *did* you think?'

'I thought you would have dark eyes, and Venetian red hair, and not be quite so tall. Of course, I haven't any imagination.'

They were at the door again when the girl said that, and the hall light was falling on her; her slip of a white figure showed clear. Young—how young she looked! Everything she said—so young!

And Anna murmured : 'And you are—more than I thought, too.'

Just then the men came out from the dining-room; her husband with the look on his face that denoted he had been well listened to; Squire Trusham laughing as a man does who has no sense of humour; Gordy having a curly, slightly asphyxiated air; and the boy his pale, brooding look, as though he had lost touch with his surroundings. He wavered towards her, seemed to lose himself, went and sat down by the old governess. Was it because he did not dare to come up to her, or only because he saw the old lady alone? It might well be that.

And the evening, so different from what she had dreamed of, closed in. Squire Trusham was gone in his high dog-cart, with his famous mare whose exploits had entertained her all through dinner. Her candle had been given her; she had said good night to all but Mark. What should she do when she had his hand in hers? She would be alone with him in that grasp, whose strength no one could see. And she did not know whether to clasp it passionately, or let it go coolly back to its owner; whether to claim him or to wait. But she was unable to help pressing it feverishly. At once in his face she saw again that troubled look; and her heart smote her. She let it go, and that she might not see him say good night to the girl, turned and mounted to her room.

Fully dressed, she flung herself on the bed, and there lay, her handkerchief across her mouth, gnawing at its edges.

XV

Mark's nineteenth birthday rose in grey mist, slowly dropped its veil to the grass and shone clear and glistening. He woke early. From his window he could see nothing in the steep park but the soft blue-grey balloon-shaped oaks suspended one above the other among the round-topped boulders. It was in early morning that he always got his strongest feeling of wanting to model things; then and after dark when for want of light it was no use. This morning he had the craving badly, and the sense of not knowing how weighed down his spirit. His drawings, his models—they were all so bad, so fumbly. If only this had been his twenty-first birthday, and he had his money, and could do what he liked. He would not stay in England. He would be off to Athens, or Rome, or even to Paris, and work till he *could* do something. And in his holidays he would study animals and birds in wild countries where there were plenty of them, and you could watch them in their haunts. It was stupid having to stay in a place like Oxford; but at the thought of what Oxford meant, his roaming fancy, like a bird hypnotised by a hawk, fluttered, stayed suspended, and dived back to earth. And that feeling of wanting to make things suddenly left him. It was as though he had woken up, his real self; then— lost that self again. Very quietly he made his way downstairs. The garden door was not shuttered, not even locked—it must have been forgotten overnight. Last night! He had never thought he would feel like this when she came—so bewildered, and confused; drawn towards her, but by something held back. And he felt impatient, angry with himself, almost with her. Why could he not be just simply happy, as this morning was happy? He got his field-glasses and searched the meadow that led down to the river. Yes, there were several rabbits out. With the white marguerites and the dew cobwebs, it was all moon-flowery and white; and the rabbits being there made it perfect. He wanted one badly to model from, and for a moment was tempted to get his rook rifle—but what was the good of a dead rabbit—besides, they looked so happy! He put the glasses down and went towards his greenhouse to get a drawing block, thinking to sit on the wall and make a sort of Midsummer Night's Dream sketch of flowers and rabbits. Someone was there, bending down and doing something to his creatures. Who had the cheek! Why, it was Sylvia—in her dressing-gown! He grew hot, then cold, with anger. He could not bear anyone in that holy place! It was hateful to have his things even looked at; and she —she seemed to be fingering them. He pulled the door open with a jerk, and said: 'What are you doing?' He was indeed so stirred by righteous wrath that he hardly noticed the gasp she gave, and the collapse of her figure against the wall. She ran past him, and vanished without a word. He went up to his creatures and saw that she had placed on the head of each one of them a little sprig of jessamine flower. Why! It was idiotic! He could see nothing at first but the ludicrousness of flowers on the heads of his beasts! Then the desperation of this attempt to imagine something grace- ful, something that would give him pleasure touched him; for he saw now that this was a birthday decoration. From that it was only a second before he was horrified with himself. Poor little Sylvia! What a brute he was! She had plucked all that jessamine, hung out of her window and risked falling to get hold of it; and she had woken up early and come down in her dressing-gown just to do something that she thought he would like! Horrible—what he had done! Now, when it was too late, he saw, only too clearly, her startled white face and quivering lips, and the way she had shrunk against the wall. How pretty she had looked in her dressing-gown with her hair all about her, frightened like that! He would do anything now to make up to her for having been such a perfect beast! The feeling, always a little with him, that he must look after her—dating, no doubt, from days when he had protected her from the bulls that were not there; and the feeling of her being so sweet and decent to him always; and some other feeling too—all these suddenly reached poignant climax. He simply must make it up to her! He ran back into the house and stole upstairs. Outside her room he listened with all his might, but could hear nothing; then tapped softly with one nail, and, putting his mouth to the keyhole, whispered: 'Sylvia!' Again and again he whispered her name. He even tried the handle, meaning to open the door an inch, but it was bolted. Once he thought he heard a noise like sob-bing, and this made him still more wretched. At last he gave it up; she would not come, would not be consoled. He deserved it, he knew, but it was very hard. And dreadfully dispirited he went up to his room, took a bit of paper, and tried to write:

'DEAREST SYLVIA,
'It was most awfully sweet of you to put your stars on my beasts. It was just about the most sweet thing you could have done. I am an awful brute, but, of course, if I had only known what you were doing, I should have loved it. Do forgive me; I deserve it, I know—only it *is* my birthday.
'Your sorrowful
'MARK.'

He took this down, slipped it under her door, tapped so that she might notice it, and stole away. It relieved his mind a little, and he went downstairs again.

Back in the greenhouse, sitting on a stool, he ruefully contem-plated those chapletted beasts. They consisted of a crow, a sheep, a turkey, two doves, a pony, and sundry fragments. She had fas-tened the jessamine sprigs to the tops of their heads by a tiny daub of wet clay, and had evidently been surprised trying to put a sprig into the mouth of one of the doves, for it hung by a little thread of clay from the beak. He detached it and put it in his buttonhole. Poor little Sylvia! she took things awfully to heart. He would be as nice as ever he could to her all day. And, balancing on his stool, he stared fixedly at the wall against which she had fallen back; the line of her soft chin and throat seemed now to be his only memory. It was very queer how he could see nothing but that, the way the throat moved, swallowed—so white, so soft. And *he* had made it go like that! It seemed an unconscionable time till breakfast.

As the hour approached he haunted the hall, hoping she might be first down. At last he heard footsteps, and waited, hidden behind the door of the empty dining-room, lest at sight of him she should turn back. He had rehearsed what he was going to do— bend down and kiss her hand and say: 'Dulcinea del Toboso is the most beautiful lady in the world, and I the most unfortunate knight upon the earth,' from his favourite passage out of his favourite book, 'Don Quixote'. She would surely forgive him then, and his heart would no longer hurt him. Certainly she could never go on making him so miserable if she knew his feelings! She was too soft and gentle for that. Alas! it was not Sylvia who came; but Anna, fresh from sleep, with her ice-green eyes and bright hair; and in sudden strange antipathy to her, that strong, vivid figure, he stood dumb. And this first lonely moment, which he had so many times in fancy spent locked in her arms, passed without even a kiss; for quickly one by one the others came. But of Sylvia only news through Mrs Doone that she had a headache, and was staying in bed. Her present was on the sideboard, a book called 'Sartor Resartus'. 'Mark—from Sylvia, August 1st, 1880,' together with Gordy's cheque, Mrs Doone's pearl pin, old Tingle's 'Stones of Venice', and one other little parcel wrapped in tissue-paper—four ties of varying shades of green, red, and blue, hand-knitted in silk —a present of how many hours made short by the thought that he would wear the produce of that clicking. He did not fail in outer gratitude, but did he realise what had been knitted into those ties? Not then.

Birthdays, like Christmas days, were made for disenchantment. Always the false gaiety of gaiety arranged—always that pistol to the head: 'Confound you! enjoy yourself!' How could he enjoy himself with the thought of Sylvia in her room, made ill by his brutality! The vision of her throat working, swallowing her grief, haunted him like a little white, soft spectre all through the long drive out on to the moor, and the picnic in the heather, and the long drive home—haunted him so that when Anna touched or looked at him he had no spirit to answer, no spirit even to try and be with her alone, but almost a dread of it instead.

And when at last they were at home again, and she whispered.
'What is it? What have I done?' he could only mutter:
'Nothing! Oh, nothing! It's only that I've been a brute!'
At that enigmatic answer she might well search his face.
'Is it my husband?'
He could answer that, at all events.
'Oh, no!'
'What is it, then? Tell me.'
They were standing in the inner porch, pretending to examine
the ancestral chart—dotted and starred with dolphins and little
full-rigged galleons sailing into harbours—which always hung just
there.
'Tell me, Mark; I don't like to suffer!'
What could he say, since he did not know himself? He stam-
mered, tried to speak, could not get anything out.
'Is it that girl?'
Startled, he looked away, and said:
'Of course not.'
She shivered, and went into the house.
But he stayed, staring at the chart with a dreadful stirred-up
feeling—of shame and irritation, pity, impatience, fear, all mixed.
What had he done, said, lost? It was that horrid feeling of when
one has not been kind and not quite true, yet might have
been kinder if one had been still less true. Ah! but it was all so
mixed up. It felt all bleak, too, and wintry in him, as if he had
suddenly lost everybody's love. Then he was conscious of his
tutor.
'Ah! friend Lennan—looking deeply into the past from the less
romantic present? Nice things, those old charts. The dolphins are
extremely jolly.'
It was difficult to remember not to be ill-mannered then. Why
did Stormer jeer like that? He just managed to answer:
'Yes, sir; I wish we had some now.'
'There are so many moons we wish for, Lennan, and they none
of them come tumbling down.'
The voice was almost earnest, and the boy's resentment fled. He
felt sorry, but why he did not know.
'In the meantime,' he heard his tutor say, 'let us dress for dinner.'
When he came down to the drawing-room, Anna in her moonlight-coloured frock was sitting on the sofa talking to—Sylvia. He
kept away from them; they could neither of them want him. But
it did seem odd to him, who knew not too much concerning

57

women, that she could be talking so gaily, when only half an hour ago she had said: 'Is it that girl?'

He sat next her at dinner. Again it was puzzling that she should be laughing so serenely at Gordy's stories. Did the whispering in the porch, then, mean nothing? And Sylvia would not look at him; he felt sure that she turned her eyes away simply because she knew he was going to look in her direction. And this roused in him a sore feeling—everything that night seemed to rouse that feeling —of injustice; he was cast out, and he could not tell why. He had not meant to hurt either of them! Why should they both want to hurt him so? And presently there came to him a feeling that he did not care: Let them treat him as they liked! There were other things besides love! If they did not want him—he did not want them! And he hugged this reckless, unhappy, don't-care feeling to him with all the abandonment of youth.

But even birthdays come to an end. And moods and feelings that seem so desperately real die in the unreality of sleep.

XVI

If to the boy that birthday was all bewildered disillusionment, to Anna it was verily slow torture; *she* found no relief in thinking that there were things in life other than love. But next morning brought readjustment, a sense of yesterday's extravagance, a renewal of hope. Impossible surely that in one short fortnight she had lost what she had made so sure of! She had only to be resolute. Only to grasp firmly what was hers. After all these empty years was she not to have her hour? To sit still meekly and see it snatched from her by a slip of a soft girl? A thousand times, no! And she watched her chance. She saw him about noon sally forth towards the river, with his rod. She had to wait a little, for Gordy and his bailiff were down there by the tennis lawn, but they soon moved on. She ran out then to the park gate. Once through that she felt safe; her husband, she knew, was working in his room; the girl somewhere invisible; the old governess still at her housekeeping; Mrs Doone writing letters. She felt full of hope and courage. This old wild tangle of a park, that she had not yet seen, was beautiful —a true trysting-place for fauns and nymphs, with its mossy trees and boulders and the high bracken. She kept along under the wall in the direction of the river, but came to no gate, and began to be afraid that she was going wrong. She could hear the river on the other side, and looked for some place where she could climb and see exactly where she was. An old ash-tree tempted her. Scrambling up into its fork, she could just see over. There was the little river within twenty yards, its clear dark water running between thick foliage. On its bank lay a huge stone balanced on another stone still more huge. And with his back to this stone stood the boy, his rod leaning beside him. And there, on the ground, her arms resting on her knees, her chin on her hands, that girl sat looking up. How eager his eyes now—how different from the brooding eyes of yesterday!

'So, you see, that was all. You might forgive me, Sylvia!'

And to Anna it seemed verily as if those two young faces formed suddenly but one—the face of youth.

If she had stayed there looking for all time, she could not have had graven on her heart a vision more indelible. Vision of Spring, of all that was gone from her for ever! She shrank back out of the fork of the old ash-tree, and, like a stricken beast, went hurrying, stumbling away, amongst the stones and bracken. She ran thus perhaps a quarter of a mile, then threw up her arms, fell down amongst the fern, and lay there on her face. At first her heart hurt her so that she felt nothing but that physical pain. If she could have died! But she knew it was nothing but breathlessness. It left her, and that which took its place she tried to drive away by pressing her breast against the ground, by clutching the stalks of the bracken—an ache, an emptiness too dreadful! Youth to youth! He was gone from her—and she was alone again! She did not cry. What good in crying? But gusts of shame kept sweeping through her; shame and rage. So this was all she was worth! The sun struck hot on her back in that lair of tangled fern, where she had fallen; she felt faint and sick. She had not known till now quite what this passion for the boy had meant to her; how much of her very belief in herself was bound up with it; how much clinging to her own youth. What bitterness! One soft slip of a white girl—one *young* thing—and she had become as nothing! But was that true? Could she not even now wrench him back to her with the passion that this child knew nothing of! Surely! Oh, surely! Let him but once taste the rapture she could give him! And at that thought she ceased clutching at the bracken stalks, lying as still as the very stones around her. Could she not? Might she not, even now? And all feeling, except just a sort of quivering, deserted her—as if she had fallen into a trance. Why spare this girl? Why falter? She was first! He had been hers out there. And she still had the power to draw him. At dinner the first evening she had dragged his gaze to her, away from that girl—away from youth, as a magnet draws steel. She could still bind him with chains that for a little while at all events he would not want to break! Bind him? Hateful word! Take him, hankering after what she could not give him—youth, white innocence, Spring? It would be infamous, infamous! She sprang up from the fern, and ran along the hillside, not looking where she went, stumbling among the tangled growth, in and out of the boulders, till she once more sank breathless on to a stone. It was bare of trees just here, and she could see, across the river valley, the high larch-crowned tor on the far side. The sky was clear—the sun bright. A hawk was wheeling over that hill; far up, very near the blue! Infamous! She could not do that! Could not drug him, drag him to her by his senses, by all that was least high in him, when she wished for him all the finest things that life could give, as if she had been his mother. She could not. It would be wicked! In that moment of intense spiritual agony, those two down there in the sun, by the grey stone and the dark water, seemed guarded from her, protected. The girl's white flower-face trembling up, the boy's gaze leaping down! Strange that a heart which felt that, could hate at the same moment that flower-face, and burn to kill with kisses that eagerness in the boy's eyes. The storm in her slowly passed. And she prayed just to feel nothing. It was natural that she should lose her hour! Natural that her thirst should go unslaked, and her passion never bloom; natural that youth should go to youth, this boy to his own kind, by the law of—love. The breeze blowing down the valley fanned her cheeks, and brought her a faint sensation of relief. Nobility! Was it just a word? Or did those that gave up happiness feel noble?

She wandered for a long time in the park. Not till late afternoon did she again pass out by the gate, through which she had entered, full of hope. She met no one before she reached her room; and there, to be safe, took refuge in her bed. She dreaded only lest the feeling of utter weariness should leave her. She wanted no vigour of mind or body till she was away from here. She meant neither to eat nor drink; only to sleep, if she could. To-morrow, if there were any early train, she could be gone before she need see any-one; her husband must arrange. As to what he would think, and she could say—time enough to decide that. And what did it matter? The one vital thing now was not to see the boy, for she could not again go through hours of struggle like those. She rang the bell, and sent the startled maid with a message to her husband. And while she waited for him to come, her pride began revolting. She must not let him see. That would be horrible. And slipping out of bed she got a handkerchief and the eau-de-Cologne flask, and bandaged her forehead. He came almost instantly, entering in his quick, noiseless way, and stood looking at her. He did not ask what was the matter, but simply waited. And never before had she realised so completely how he began, as it were, where she left off; began on a plane from which instinct and feeling were so carefully ruled out as though they had been blasphemous. She summoned all her courage, and said: 'I went into the park; the sun must have been too hot. I should like to go home to-morrow, if you don't mind. I can't bear not feeling well in other people's houses.'

She was conscious of a smile flickering over his face; then it grew grave.

'Ah!' he said; 'yes. The sun, a touch of that will last some days. Will you be fit to travel, though?'

She had a sudden conviction that he knew all about it, but that—since to know all about it was to feel himself ridiculous—he had the power of making himself believe that he knew nothing. Was this fine of him, or was it hateful?

She closed her eyes and said:

'My head is bad, but I *shall* be able. Only I don't want a fuss made. Could we go by a train before they are down?'

She heard him say:

'Yes. That will have its advantages.'

There was not the faintest sound now, but of course he was still there. In that dumb, motionless presence was all her future. Yes, that would be her future—a thing without feeling, and without motion. A fearful curiosity came on her to look at it. She opened her eyes. He was still standing just as he had been, his gaze fixed on her. But one hand, on the edge of his coat pocket—out of the picture, as it were—was nervously closing and unclosing. And suddenly she felt pity. Not for her future—which must be like that; but for him. How dreadful to have grown so that all emotion was exiled—how dreadful! And she said, gently:

'I am sorry, Harold.'

As if he had heard something strange and startling, his eyes dilated in a curious way, he buried that nervous hand in his pocket, turned, and went out.

XVII

When young Mark came on Sylvia by the logan-stone it was less surprising to him than if he had not known she was there—having watched her go. She was sitting, all humped together, brooding over the water, her sunbonnet thrown back; and that hair, in which his star had caught, shining faint-gold under the sun. He came on her softly through the grass, and, when he was a little way off, thought it best to halt. If he startled her she might run away, and he would not have the heart to follow. How still she was, lost in her brooding! He wished he could see her face. He spoke at last, gently:

'Sylvia! . . . Would you mind?'

And, seeing that she did not move, he went up to her. Surely she could not still be angry with him!

'Thanks most awfully for that book you gave me—it looks splendid!'

She made no answer. And leaning his rod against the stone, he sighed. That silence of hers seemed to him unjust; what was it she wanted him to say or do? Life was not worth living, if it was to be bottled up like this.

'I never meant to hurt you. I hate hurting people. It's only that my beasts are so bad—I can't bear people to see them—especially you—I want to please you—I do really. So, you see, that was all. You *might* forgive me, Sylvia!'

Something over the wall, a rustling, a scattering in the fern—deer, no doubt! And again he said eagerly, softly:

'You might be nice to me, Sylvia; you really might.'

Very quickly, turning her head away, she said:

'It isn't that any more. It's—it's something else.'

'What else?'

'Nothing—only, that I don't count—now——'

He knelt down beside her. What did she mean? But he knew well enough.

'Of course, you count! Most awfully! Oh, don't be unhappy! I hate people being unhappy. Don't be unhappy, Sylvia!' And he began gently to stroke her arm. It was all strange and troubled within him; one thing only plain—he must not admit anything! As if reading that thought, her blue eyes seemed suddenly to search right into him. Then she pulled some blades of grass, and began plaiting them.

'*She* counts.'

Ah! He was not going to say: She doesn't! It would be caddish to say that. Even if she didn't count——Did she still?—it would be mean and low. And in his eyes just then there was the look that had made his tutor compare him to a lion cub in trouble.

Sylvia was touching his arm.

'Mark!'

'Yes.'

'Don't!'

He got up and took his rod. What was the use? He could not stay there with her, since he could not—must not speak.

'Are you going?'

'Yes.'

'Are you angry? *Please* don't be angry with me.'

He felt a choke in his throat, bent down to her hand, and kissed it; then shouldered his rod, and marched away. Looking back once, he saw her still sitting there, gazing after him, forlorn, by that great stone. It seemed to him, then, there was nowhere he could go; nowhere except among the birds and beasts and trees, who did not mind even if you were all mixed up and horrible inside. He lay down in the grass on the bank. He could see the tiny trout moving round and round the stones; swallows came all about him, flying very low; a hornet, too, bore him company for a little. But he could take interest in nothing; it was as if his spirit were in prison. It would have been nice, indeed, to be that water, never staying, passing, passing; or wind, touching everything, never caught. To be able to do nothing without hurting someone—that was what was so ghastly. If only one were like a flower, that just sprang up and lived its life all to itself, and died. But whatever he did, or said now, would be like telling lies, or else being cruel. The only thing was to keep away from people. And yet how keep away from his own guests?

He went back to the house for lunch, but both those guests were out, no one seemed quite to know where. Restless, unhappy, puzzled, he wandered round and about all the afternoon. Just before dinner he was told of Mrs Stormer's not being well, and that they would be leaving to-morrow. Going—after three days! That plunged him deeper into his strange and sorrowful confusion. He was reduced now to a complete brooding silence. He knew he was attracting attention, but could not help it. Several times during dinner he caught Gordy's eyes fixed on him, from under those puffy half-closed lids, with asphyxiated speculation. But he simply *could* not talk—everything that came into his mind to say seemed false. Ah! it was a sad evening—with its glimmering vision into another's sore heart, its confused gnawing sense of things broken, faith betrayed; and yet always the perplexed wonder—'How could I have helped it?' And always Sylvia's wistful face that he tried not to look at.

He stole out, leaving Gordy and his tutor still over their wine, and roamed about the garden a long time, listening sadly to the owls. It was a blessing to get upstairs, though of course he would not sleep.

But he did sleep, all through a night of many dreams, in the last of which he was lying on a mountain side, Anna looking down into his eyes, and bending her face to his. He woke just as her lips touched him. Still under the spell of that troubling dream, he became conscious of the sound of wheels and horses' hoofs on the gravel, and sprang out of bed. There was the waggonette moving from the door, old Godden driving, luggage piled up beside him, and the Stormers sitting opposite each other in the carriage. Going away like that—having never even said good-bye! For a moment he felt as people must when they have unwittingly killed someone —utterly stunned and miserable. Then he dashed into his clothes. He would not let her go thus! He would—he must—see her again! What had he done that she should go like this. He rushed downstairs. The hall was empty; nineteen minutes to eight! The train left at eight o'clock. Had he time to saddle Bolero? He rushed round to the stables; but the cob was out, being shoed. He would —he must get there in time. It would show her anyway that he was not quite a cad. He walked till the drive curved, then began running hard. A quarter of a mile, and already he felt better, not so miserable and guilty; it was something to feel you had a tough job in hand, all your work cut out—something to have to think of economising strength, picking out the best going, keeping out of the sun, saving your wind uphill, flying down any slope. It was cool still, and the dew had laid the dust; there was no traffic and scarcely anyone to look back and gape as he ran by. What he would do, if he got there in time—how explain this mad three-mile run—he did not think. He passed a farm that he knew was just half-way. He had left his watch. Indeed, he had put on only his trousers, shirt, and Norfolk jacket; no tie, no hat, not even socks under his tennis shoes, and he was as hot as fire, with his hair flying back—a strange young creature indeed for anyone to meet. But he had lost now all feeling, save the will to get there. A flock of sheep came out of a field into the lane. He pushed through them some-how, but they lost him several seconds. More than a mile still; and he was blown, and his legs beginning to give! Downhill indeed they went of their own accord, but there was the long run-in, quite level; and he could hear the train, now slowly puffing its way along the valley. Then, in spite of exhaustion, his spirit rose. He would not go in looking like a scarecrow, utterly done, and make a scene. He must pull himself together at the end, and stroll in—as if he had come for fun. But how—seeing that at any moment he felt he might fall flat in the dust, and stay there for ever! And, as he ran, he made little desperate efforts to mop his face, and brush his clothes. There were the gates, at last—two hundred yards away. The train, he could hear no longer. It must be stand-ing in the station. And a sob came from his overdriven lungs. He heard the guard's whistle as he reached the gates. Instead of making for the booking-office, he ran along the paling, where an entrance to the goods'-shed was open, and dashing through he fell back against the honeysuckle. The engine was just abreast of him; he snatched at his sleeve and passed it over his face, to wipe the sweat away. Everything was blurred. He must see—surely he had not come in time just not to see! He pushed his hands over his fore-head and hair, and spied up dizzily at the slowly passing train. She was there, at a window! Standing, looking out! He dared not step forward, for fear of falling, but he put out his hand. She saw him. Yes, she saw him! Wasn't she going to make a sign? Not one? And suddenly he saw her tear at her dress, pluck something out, and throw it. It fell close to his feet. He did not pick it up—he wanted to see her face till she was gone. It looked wonderful—very proud, and pale. She put her hand up to her lips. Then every-thing went blurred again, and when he could see once more, the train had vanished. But at his feet was what she had thrown. He picked it up! All dry and dark, it was the flower she had given him in the Tyrol, and stolen back from his buttonhole.

Creeping out, past the goods'-shed, he made his way to a field, and lay down with his face pressed to that withered thing which still had its scent. . . .

The asphyxiated speculation in his guardian's eyes had not been without significance. Mark did not go back to Oxford. He went instead to Rome—to live in his sister's house, and attend a school of sculpture. That was the beginning of a time when nothing counted except his work.

To Anna he wrote twice, but received no answer. From his tutor he had one little note:

'MY DEAR LENNAN,

'So! You abandon us for Art? Ah! well—it was your moon, if I remember—one of them. A worthy moon—a little dusty in these days—a little in her decline—but to you no doubt a virgin goddess, whose hem, etc.

'We shall retain the friendliest memories of you in spite of your defection.

'Once your tutor and still your friend,
'HAROLD STORMER.'

After that vacation it was long—very long before he saw Sylvia again.

Part II

SUMMER

I

GLEAM of a thousand lights; clack and mutter of innumerable voices, laughter, footsteps; hiss and rumble of passing trains taking gamblers back to Nice or Mentone; fevered wailing from the violins of four fiddlers with dark-white skins outside the café; and above, around, beyond, the dark sky, and the dark mountains, and the dark sea, like some great dark flower to whose heart is clinging a jewelled beetle. So was Monte Carlo on that May night of 1887.

But Mark Lennan, at one of the little marble-topped tables, was in too great maze and exaltation of spirit and of senses to be conscious of its glare and babel, even of its beauty. He sat so very still that his neighbours, with the instinctive aversion of the human creature to what is too remote from its own mood, after one good stare, turned their eyes away, as from something ludicrous, almost offensive.

He was lost, indeed, in memory of the minutes just gone by. For it had come at last, after all these weeks of ferment, after all this strange time of perturbation.

Very stealthily it had been creeping on him, ever since that chance introduction nearly a year ago, soon after he settled down in London, following those six years of Rome and Paris. First the merest friendliness, because she was so nice about his work; then respectful admiration, because she was so beautiful; then pity, because she was so unhappy in her marriage. If she had been happy, he would have fled. The knowledge that she had been unhappy long before he knew her had kept his conscience still. And at last one afternoon she said: 'Ah! if you come out there too!' Marvellously subtle, the way that one little outslipped saying had worked in him, as though it had a life of its own—like a strange bird that had flown into the garden of his heart, and established itself with its new song and flutterings, its new flight, its wistful and ever clearer call. That and one moment, a few days later in her London drawing-room, when he had told her that he *was* coming, and she did not, could not, he felt, look at him. Queer, that nothing

67

momentous said, done—or even left undone—had altered all the future!

And so she had gone with her uncle and aunt, under whose wing one might be sure she would meet with no wayward or exotic happenings. And he had received from her this little letter:

'Hôtel Coeur d'Or,
'Monte Carlo.

'My dear Mark,

'We've arrived. It is so good to be in the sun. The flowers are wonderful. I am keeping Gorbio and Roquebrune till you come.

'Your friend,
'Olive Cramier.'

That letter was the single clear memory he had of the time between her going and his following. He received it one afternoon, sitting on an old low garden wall with the spring sun shining on him through apple-trees in blossom, and a feeling as if all the desire of the world lay before him, and he had but to stretch out his arms to take it.

Then confused unrest, all things vague; till at the end of his journey he stepped out of the train at Beaulieu with a furiously beating heart. But why? Surely he had not expected her to come out from Monte Carlo to meet him!

A week had gone by since then in one long effort to be with her and appear to others as though he did not greatly wish to be; two concerts, two walks with her alone, when all that he had said seemed as nothing said, and all her sayings but ghosts of what he wished to hear; a week of confusion, day and night, until, a few minutes ago, her handkerchief had fallen from her glove on to the dusty road, and he had picked it up and put it to his lips. Nothing could take away the look she had given him then. Nothing could ever again separate her from him utterly. She had confessed in it to the same sweet, fearful trouble that he himself was feeling. She had not spoken, but he had seen her lips part, her breast rise and fall. And *he* had not spoken. What was the use of words?

He felt in the pocket of his coat. There, against his fingers, was that wisp of lawn and lace, soft, yet somehow alive; and stealthily he took it out. The whole of her, with her fragrance, seemed pressed to his face in the touch of that lawn border, roughened by little white stars. More secretly than ever he put it back; and for the first time looked round. These people! They belonged to a world that he had left. They gave him the same feeling that her uncle and aunt had given him just now, when they said good-night, following her into their hotel. That good Colonel, that good Mrs Ercott! The very concretion of the world he had been brought up in, of the English point of view; symbolic figures of health, reason, and the straight path, on which at that moment, seemingly, he had turned his back. The Colonel's profile, ruddy through its tan, with grey moustache guiltless of any wax, his cheery, high-pitched: 'Good-night, young Lennan!' His wife's curly smile, her flat, cosy, confidential voice—how strange and remote they had suddenly become! And all these people here, chattering, drinking—how queer and far away! Or was it just that he was queer and remote to them?

And getting up from his table, he passed the fiddlers with the dark-white skins out into the *Place*.

II

He went up the side streets to the back of her hotel, and stood by the railings of the garden—one of those hotel gardens which exist but to figure in advertisements, with its few arid palms, its paths staring white between them, and a fringe of dusty lilacs and mimosas.

And there came to him the oddest feeling—that he had been there before, peering through blossoms at those staring paths and shuttered windows. A scent of wood-smoke was abroad, and some dry plant rustled ever so faintly in what little wind was stirring. What was there of memory in this night, this garden? Some dark sweet thing, invisible, to feel whose presence was at once ecstasy, and the irritation of a thirst that will not be quenched.

And he walked on. Houses, houses! At last he was away from them, alone on the high road, beyond the limits of Monaco. And walking thus through the night he had thoughts that he imagined no one had ever had before him. The knowledge that she loved him had made everything seem very sacred and responsible. Whatever he did, he must not harm her. Women were so helpless!

For in spite of six years of art in Rome and Paris, he still had a fastidious reverence for women. If she had loved her husband she would have been safe enough from him; but to be bound to a companionship that she gave unwillingly—this had seemed to him atrocious, even before he loved her. How could any husband ask that? Have so little pride—so little pity? The unpardonable thing!

69

What was there to respect in such a marriage? Only, he must not do her harm! But now that her eyes had said, I love you!—What then? It was simply miraculous to know *that*, under the stars of this warm Southern night, burning its incense of trees and flowers!

Climbing up above the road, he lay down. If only she were there beside him! The fragrance of the earth, not yet chilled, crept to his face; and for just a moment it seemed to him that she did come. If he could keep her there for ever in that embrace that was no embrace—in that ghostly rapture, on this wild fragrant bed that no lovers before had ever pressed, save the creeping things, and the flowers; save sunlight and moonlight with their shadows; and the wind kissing the earth! . . .

Then she was gone; his hands touched nothing but the crumbled pine dust, and the flowers of the wild thyme fallen into sleep.

He stood on the edge of the little cliff, above the road between the dark mountains and the sea black with depth. Too late for any passer-by; as far from what men thought and said and did as the very night itself with its whispering warmth. And he conjured up her face, making certain of it—the eyes, clear and brown, and wide apart; the close, sweet mouth; the dark hair; the whole flying loveliness.

Then he leaped down into the road, and ran—one could not walk, feeling this miracle, that no one had ever felt before, the miracle of love.

III

In their most reputable hotel 'Le Coeur d'Or', long since remodelled and renamed, Mrs Ercott lay in her brass-bound bed looking by starlight at the Colonel in his brass-bound bed. Her ears were carefully freed from the pressure of her pillow, for she thought she heard a mosquito. Companion for thirty years to one whose life had been feverishly punctuated by the attentions of those little beasts, she had no love for them. It was the one subject on which perhaps her imagination was stronger than her common sense. For in fact there was not, and could not be, a mosquito, since the first thing the Colonel did, on arriving at any place farther South than Parallel 46 of latitude, was to open the windows very wide, and nail with many tiny tacks a piece of mosquito netting across that refreshing space, while she held him firmly by the coat-tails. The fact that other people did not so secure their windows did not at all trouble the Colonel, a true Englishman, who loved to act in his own way, and to think in the ways of other people. After that they would wait till night came, then burn a peculiar little lamp with a peculiar little smell, and, in the full glare of the gaslight, stand about on chairs, with slippers, and their eyes fixed on true or imaginary beasts. Then would fall little slaps, making little messes, and little joyous or doleful cries would arise: 'I've got that one!' 'Oh, John, I missed him!' And in the middle of the room, the Colonel, in pyjamas, and spectacles (only worn in very solemn moments, low down on his nose), would revolve slowly, turning his eyes, with that look in them of outfacing death which he had so long acquired, on every inch of wall and ceiling, till at last he would say: 'Well, Dolly, that's the lot!' At which she would say: 'Give me a kiss, dear!' and he would kiss her, and get into his bed.

There was, then, no mosquito, save that general ghost of him which lingered in the mind of one devoted to her husband. Spying out his profile, for he was lying on his back, she refrained from saying: 'John, are you awake?' A whiffling sound was coming from a nose, to which—originally straight—attention to military duties had given a slight crook, half an inch below the level of grizzled eyebrows raised a little, as though surprised at the sounds beneath. She could hardly see him, but she thought: 'How good he looks!' And, in fact, he did. It was the face of a man incapable of evil, having in its sleep the candour of one at heart a child— that simple candour of those who have never known how to seek adventures of the mind, and have always sought adventures of the body. Then somehow she did say:

'John! Are you asleep?'

The Colonel, instantly alive, as at some old-time attack, answered:

'Yes.'

'That poor young man!'

'Which?'

'Mark Lennan. Haven't you seen?'

'What?'

'My dear, it was under your nose. But you never do see these things!'

The Colonel slowly turned his head. His wife was an imaginative woman! She had always been so. Dimly he perceived that something romantic was about to come from her. But with that almost professional gentleness of a man who has cut the heads and arms off people in his time, he answered:

'What things?'

'He picked up her handkerchief.'

'Whose?'

'Olive's. He put it in his pocket. I distinctly saw him.'

There was silence; then Mrs Ercott's voice rose again, impersonal, far away.

'What always astonishes me about young people is the way they think they're not seen—poor dears!'

Still there was silence.

'John! Are you thinking?'

For a considerable sound of breathing, not mere whiffling now, was coming from the Colonel—to his wife a sure sign.

And indeed he *was* thinking. Dolly was an imaginative woman, but something told him that in this case she might not be riding past the hounds.

Mrs Ercott raised herself. He looked more good than ever; a little perplexed frown had climbed up with his eyebrows and got caught in the wrinkles across his forehead.

'I'm very fond of Olive,' he said.

Mrs Ercott fell back on her pillows. In her heart there was just that little soreness natural to a woman over fifty, whose husband has a niece.

'No doubt,' she murmured.

Something vague moved deep down in the Colonel; he stretched out his hand. In that strip of gloom between the beds it encountered another hand, which squeezed it rather hard.

He said: 'Look here, old girl!' and there was silence.

Mrs Ercott in her turn was thinking. Her thoughts were flat and rapid like her voice, but had that sort of sentiment which accompanies the mental exercise of women with good hearts. Poor young man! And poor Olive! But was a woman ever to be pitied, when she was so pretty as that! Besides, when all was said and done, she had a fine-looking man for husband; in Parliament, with a career, and fond of her—decidedly. And their little house in London, so close to Westminster, was a distinct dear; and nothing could be more charming than their cottage by the river. Was Olive, then, to be pitied? And yet—she was not happy. It was no good pretending that she was happy. All very well to say that such things were within one's control, but if you read novels at all, you knew they weren't. There was such a thing as incompatibility. Oh yes! And there was the matter of difference in their ages! Olive was twenty-six, Robert Cramier forty-two. And now this young Mark Lennan

72

was in love with her. What if she were in love with him! John
would realise then, perhaps, that the young flew to the young. For
men—even the best, like John, were funny! She would never dream
of feeling for any of her nephews as John clearly felt for Olive.

The Colonel's voice broke in on her thoughts.

'Nice young fellow—Lennan! Great pity! Better sheer off—if
he's getting——'

And, rather suddenly, she answered:

'Suppose he can't!'

'Can't?'

'Did you never hear of a *"grande passion"*?'

The Colonel rose on his elbow. This was another of those occasions that showed him how, during the later years of his service in
Madras and Upper Burmah, when Dolly's health had not been equal
to the heat, she had picked up in London a queer way of looking
at things—as if they were not—not so right or wrong as—as he
felt them to be. And he repeated those two French words in his
own way, adding:

'Isn't that just what I'm saying? The sooner he stands clear, the
better.'

But Mrs Ercott, too, sat up.

'Be human,' she said.

The Colonel experienced the same sensation as when one suddenly knows that one is not digesting food. Because young Lennan
was in danger of getting into a dishonourable fix, he was told to be
human! Really, Dolly was——! The white blur of her new boudoir
cap suddenly impinged on his consciousness. Surely she was not
getting—un-English! At her time of life!

'I'm thinking of Olive,' he said; 'I don't want her worried with
that sort of thing.'

'Perhaps Olive can manage for herself. In these days it doesn't do
to interfere with love.'

'Love!' muttered the Colonel. 'What? Phew!'

If one's own wife called this—this sort of—thing, love—then,
why had he been faithful to her—in very hot climates—all these
years? A sense of waste, and of injustice, tried to rear its head
against all the side of him that attached certain meanings to certain
words, and acted up to them. And this revolt gave him a feeling,
strange and so unpleasant. Love! It was not a word to use thus
loosely! Love led to marriage; this could not lead to marriage,
except through—the Divorce Court. And suddenly the Colonel had
a vision of his dead brother Lindsay, Olive's father, standing there

73

in the dark, with his grave, clear-cut, ivory-pale face, under the
black hair supposed to be derived from a French ancestress who
had escaped from the massacre of St Bartholomew. Upright fellow
always, Lindsay—even before he was made bishop! Queer somehow that Olive should be his daughter. Not that she was not upright; not at all! But she was soft! Lindsay was not! Imagine him
seeing that young fellow putting her handkerchief in his pocket.
But had young Lennan really done such a thing? Dolly was imaginative! He had mistaken it probably for his own; if he had chanced
to blow his nose, he would have realised. For, coupled with the
almost child-like candour of his mind, the Colonel had real admin-
istrative vigour, a true sense of practical values; an ounce of illus-
tration was always worth to him a pound of theory! Dolly was
given to riding off on theories. Thank God! she never acted on 'em!

He said gently:

'My dear! Young Lennan may be an artist and all that, but he's
a gentleman! I know old Heatherley, his guardian. Why I introduced him to Olive myself!'

'What has that to do with it? He's in love with her.'

One of the countless legion that hold a creed taken at face value,
into whose roots and reasons they have never dreamed of going,
the Colonel was staggered. Like some native on an island surrounded by troubled seas, which he has stared at with a certain contemptuous awe all his life, but never entered, he was disconcerted
by thus being asked to leave the shore. And by his own wife!

Indeed, Mrs Ercott had not intended to go so far; but there was
in her, as in all women whose minds are more active than their
husband's, a something worrying her always to go a little farther
than she meant. With real compunction she heard the Colonel
say:

'I must get up and drink some water.'

She was out of bed in a moment. 'Not without boiling!'

She had seriously troubled him, then! Now he would not sleep
—the blood went to his head so quickly. He would just lie awake,
trying not to disturb her. She could not bear him not to disturb
her. It seemed so selfish of her! She ought to have known that the
whole subject was too dangerous to discuss at night.

She became conscious that he was standing just behind her; his
figure in its thin covering looked very lean, his face strangely worn.

'I'm sorry you put that idea into my head!' he said. 'I'm fond of
Olive.'

Again Mrs Ercott felt that jealous twinge, soon lost this time in

74

the motherliness of a childless woman for her husband. He must not be troubled! He should not be troubled. And she said:

'The water's boiling! Now sip a good glass slowly, and get into bed, or I'll take your temperature!'

Obediently the Colonel took from her the glass, and as he sipped, she put her hand up and stroked his head.

IV

In the room below them the subject of their discussion was lying very wide awake. She knew that she had betrayed herself, made plain to Mark Lennan what she had never until now admitted to herself. But the love-look, which for the life of her she could not keep back, had been followed by a feeling of having 'lost caste'. For, hitherto, the world of women had been strictly divided by her into those who did and those who did not do such things; and to be no longer quite sure to which half she belonged was frightening. But what was the good of thinking, of being frightened?—it could not lead to anything. Yesterday she had not known this would come; and now she could not guess at tomorrow! To-night was enough! To-night with its swimming loveliness! Just to feel! To love, and to be loved!

A new sensation for her—as different from those excited by the courtships of her girlhood, or by her marriage, as light from darkness. For she had never been in love, not even with her husband. She knew it now. The sun was shining in a world where she had thought there was none. Nothing could come of it. But the sun was shining; and in that sunshine she must warm herself a little.

Quite simply she began to plan what he and she would do. There were six days left. They had not yet been to Gorbio, nor to Castellar —none of those long walks or rides they had designed to do for the beauty of them. Would he come early to-morrow? What could they do together? No one should know what these six days would be to her—not even he. To be with him, watch his face, hear his voice, and now and then just touch him! She could trust herself to show no one. And then, it would be—over! Though, of course, she would see him again in London.

And, lying there in the dark, she thought of their first meeting, one Sunday morning, in Hyde Park. The Colonel religiously observed Church Parade, and would even come all the way down to Westminster, from his flat near Knightsbridge, in order to fetch his niece up to it. She remembered how, during their stroll, he had stopped suddenly in front of an old gentleman with a puffy yellow face and eyes half open.

'Ah! Mr Heatherley—you up from Devonshire? How's your nephew—the—er—sculptor?'

And the old gentleman, glaring a little, as it seemed to her, from under his eyelids and his grey top hat, had answered: 'Colonel Ercott, I think? Here's the fellow himself—Mark!' And a young man had taken off his hat. She had only noticed at first that his dark hair grew—not long—but very thick; and that his eyes were very deep-set. Then she saw him smile; it made his face all eager, yet it left it shy; and she decided that he was nice. Soon after, she had gone with the Ercotts to see his 'things'; for it was, of course, and especially in those days, quite an event to know a sculptor— rather like having a zebra in your park. The Colonel had been delighted and a little relieved to find that the 'things' were nearly all of beasts and birds. 'Very interestin'' to one full of curious lore about such, having in his time killed many of them, and finding himself at the end of it with a curious aversion to killing any more —which he never put into words.

Acquaintanceship had ripened fast after that first visit to his studio, and now it was her turn to be relieved that Mark Lennan devoted himself almost entirely to beasts and birds instead of to the human form, so-called divine. Ah! yes—she would have suffered; now that she loved him, she saw that. At all events she could watch his work and help it with sympathy. That could not be wrong. . . .

She fell asleep at last, and dreamed that she was in a boat alone on the river near her country cottage, drifting along among spiky flowers like asphodels, with birds singing and flying round her. She could move neither face nor limbs, but that helpless feeling was not unpleasant, till she became conscious that she was drawing nearer and nearer to what was neither water nor land, light nor darkness, but simply some unutterable feeling. And then she saw, gazing at her out of the rushes on the banks, a great bull head. It moved as she moved—it was on both sides of her, yet all the time only one head. She tried to raise her hands and cover her eyes, but could not—and woke with a sob. . . . It was light.

Nearly six o'clock already! Her dreams made her disinclined to trust again to sleep. Sleep was a robber now—of each minute of these few days! She got up, and looked out. The morning was fine, the air warm already, sweet with dew, and heliotrope nailed to the wall outside her window. She had but to open her shutters and walk into the sun. She dressed, took her sunshade, stealthily slipped the shutters back, and stole forth. Shunning the hotel garden, where the eccentricity of her early wandering might betray the condition of her spirit, she passed through into the road towards the Casino. Without perhaps knowing it, she was making for where she had sat with him yesterday afternoon, listening to the band. Hatless, but defended by her sunshade, she excited the admiration of the few connoisseurs as yet abroad, strolling in blue blouses to their labours; and this simple admiration gave her pleasure. For once she was really conscious of the grace in her own limbs, actually felt the gentle vividness of her own face, with its nearly black hair and eyes, and creamy skin—strange sensation, and very comforting!

In the Casino gardens she walked more slowly, savouring the aromatic trees, and stopping to bend and look at almost every flower; then, on the seat, where she had sat with him yesterday, she rested. A few paces away were the steps that led to the railway-station, trodden upwards eagerly by so many, day after day, night after night, and lightly or sorrowfully descended. Above her, two pines, a pepper-tree, and a palm mingled their shade—so fantastic the jumbling of trees and souls in this strange place! She furled her sunshade and leaned back. Her gaze, free and friendly, passed from bough to bough. Against the bright sky, unbesieged as yet by heat or dust, they had a spiritual look, lying sharp and flat along the air. She plucked a cluster of pinkish berries from the pepper-tree, crushing and rubbing them between her hands to get their fragrance. All these beautiful and sweet things seemed to be a part of her joy at being loved, part of this sudden summer in her heart. The sky, the flowers, that jewel of green-blue sea, the bright acacias, were nothing in the world but love.

And those few who passed, and saw her sitting there under the pepper-tree, wondered no doubt at the stillness of this *dame bien mise*, who had risen so early.

V

In the small hours, which so many wish were smaller, the Colonel had awakened, with the affair of the handkerchief swelling visibly. His niece's husband was not a man that he had much liking for—a taciturn fellow, with possibly a bit of the brute in him, a man who rather rode people down; but, since Dolly and he were in charge of Olive, the notion that young Lennan was falling in love with her under their very noses was alarming to one naturally punctilious. It was not until he fell asleep again, and woke in full morning light, that the remedy occurred to him. She must be taken out of herself! Dolly and he had been slack; too interested in this queer place, this queer lot of people! They had neglected her, left her to . . . Boys and girls!—One ought always to remember. But it was not too late. She was old Lindsay's daughter; would not forget herself. Poor old Lindsay—fine fellow; bit too much, perhaps, of the—Huguenot in him! Queer, those throw-backs! Had noticed it in horses, time and again—white hairs about the tail, carriage of the head—skip generations and then pop out. And Olive had something of his look—the same ivory skin, same colour of eyes and hair! Only she was not severe, like her father, not exactly! And once more there shot through the Colonel a vague dread, as of a trusteeship neglected. It disappeared, however, in his bath.

He was out before eight o'clock, a thin upright figure in hard straw hat and grey flannel clothes, walking with the indescribable loose poise of the soldier Englishman, with that air, different from the French, German, what not, because of shoulders ever asserting, through their drill, the right to put on mufti; with that perfectly quiet and modest air of knowing that, whatever might be said, there was only one way of wearing clothes and moving legs. And, as he walked, he smoothed his drooping grey moustache, considering how best to take his niece out of herself. He passed along by the Terrace, and stood for a moment looking down at the sea beyond the pigeon-shooting ground. Then he moved on round under the Casino into the gardens at the back. A beautiful spot! Wonderful care they had taken with the plants! It made him think a little of Tushawore, where his old friend the Rajah—precious old rascal! —had gardens to his palace rather like these. He paced again to the front. It was nice and quiet in the early mornings, with the sea down there, and nobody trying to get the better of anybody else. There were fellows never happy unless they were doing someone in the eye. He had known men who would ride at the devil himself, make it a point of honour to swindle a friend out of a few pounds! Odd place this 'Monte'—sort of a Garden of Eden gone wrong. And all the real, but quite inarticulate love of Nature, which had supported the Colonel through deserts and jungles, on transports at sea, and in mountain camps, awoke in the sweetness of

these gardens. His dear mother! He had never forgotten the words with which she had shown him the sunset through the coppice down at old Withes Norton, when he was nine years old: 'That is beauty, Jack! Do you feel it, darling?' He had not felt it at the time—not he; a thick-headed, scampering youngster. Even when he first went to India he had had no eye for a sunset. The rising generation were different. That young couple, for instance, under the pepper-tree, sitting there without a word, just looking at the trees. How long, he wondered, had they been sitting like that? And suddenly something in the Colonel leaped; his steel-coloured eyes took on their look of out-facing death. Choking down a cough, he faced about, back to where he had stood above the pigeon-shooting ground. . . . Olive and that young fellow! An assignation! At this time in the morning! The earth reeled. His brother's child—his favourite niece! The woman whom he most admired—the woman for whom his heart was softest. Leaning over the stone parapet, no longer seeing either the smooth green of the pigeon-shooting ground, or the smooth blue of the sea beyond, he was moved, distressed, bewildered beyond words. Before breakfast! That was the devil of it!· Confession, as it were, of everything. Moreover, he had seen their hands touching on the seat. The blood rushed up to his face; he had seen, spied out, what was not intended for his eyes. Nice position—that! Dolly, too, last night, had seen. But that was different. Women might see things—it was expected of them. But for a man—a—gentleman! The fullness of his embarrassment gradually disclosed itself. His hands were tied. Could he even consult Dolly? He had a feeling of isolation, of utter solitude. Nobody—not anybody in the world—could understand his secret and intense discomfort. To take up a position—the position he was bound to take up, as Olive's nearest relative and protector, and—what was it—chaperon, by the aid of knowledge come at in such a way, however unintentionally! Never in all his days in the regiment—and many delicate matters affecting honour had come his way—had he had a thing like this to deal with. Poor child! But he had no business to think of her like that. No, indeed! She had not behaved—as—— And there he paused, curiously unable to condemn her. Suppose they got up and came that way!

He took his hands off the stone parapet, and made for his hotel. His palms were white from the force of his grip. He said to himself as he went along: 'I must consider the whole question calmly; I must think it out.' This gave him relief. With young Lennan, at all events, he could be angry. But even there he found, to his dismay, no finality of judgement. And this absence of finality, so unwonted, distressed him horribly. There was something in the way the young man had been sitting there beside her—so quiet, so almost timid—that had touched him. This was bad, by Jove—very bad! The two of them, they made, somehow, a nice couple! Confound it! This would not do! The chaplain of the little English church passing at this moment, called out, 'Fine morning, Colonel Ercott.' The Colonel saluted, and did not answer. The greeting at the moment seemed to him paltry. No morning could be fine that contained such a discovery. He entered the hotel, passed into the dining-room, and sat down. Nobody was there. They all had their breakfast upstairs, even Dolly. Olive alone was in the habit of supporting him while he ate an English breakfast. And suddenly he perceived that he was face to face already with this dreadful situation. To have breakfast without, as usual, waiting for her, seemed too pointed. She might be coming in at any minute now. To wait for her, and have it, without showing anything—how could he do that?

He was conscious of a faint rustling behind him. There she was, and nothing decided. In this moment of hopeless confusion the Colonel acted by pure instinct, rose, patted her cheek, and placed a chair.

'Well, my dear,' he said; 'hungry?'

She was looking very dainty, very soft. That creamy dress showed off her dark hair and eyes, which seemed somehow to be—flying off somewhere; yes—it was queer, but that was the only way to put it. He got no reassurance, no comfort, from the sight of her. And slowly he stripped the skin from the banana with which he always commenced breakfast. One might just as well be asked to shoot a tame dove or tear a pretty flower to pieces as be expected to take her to task, even if he could, in honour. And he sought refuge in the words:

'Been out?' Then could have bitten his tongue off. Suppose she answered: 'No.'

But she did not so answer. The colour came into her cheeks, indeed, but she nodded: 'It's so lovely!'

How pretty she looked saying that! He had put himself out of court now—could never tell her what he had seen, after setting, as it were, that trap for her; and presently he asked:

'Got any plans to-day?'

She answered, without flinching in the least:

'Mark Lennan and I were going to take mules from Mentone up to Gorbio.'

He was amazed at her steadiness—never, to his knowledge, having encountered a woman armoured at every point to preserve a love that flies against the world. How tell what was under her smile! And in confusion of feeling that amounted almost to pain he heard her say:

'Will you and Aunt Dolly come?'

Between sense of trusteeship and hatred of spoiling sport; between knowledge of the danger she was in and half-pitying admiration at the sight of her; between real disapproval of an illicit and underhand business (what else was it, after all?) and some dim perception that here was something he did not begin to be able to fathom—something that perhaps no one but those two themselves could deal with—between these various extremes he was lost indeed. And he stammered out:

'I must ask your aunt; she's—she's not very good on a mule.'

Then, in an impulse of sheer affection, he said with startling suddenness: 'My dear, I've often meant to ask, are you happy at home?'

'At home?'

There was something sinister about the way she repeated that, as if the word home were strange to her.

She drank her coffee and got up; and the Colonel felt afraid of her, standing there—afraid of what she was going to tell him. He grew very red. But, worse than all, she said absolutely nothing; only shrugged her shoulders with a little smile that went to his heart.

VI

On the wild thyme, under the olives below the rock village of Gorbio, with their mules cropping at a little distance, those two sat after their lunch, listening to the cuckoos. Since their uncanny chance meeting that morning in the gardens, when they sat with their hands just touching, amazed and elated by their own good fortune, there was not much need to say what they felt, to break with words this rapture of belonging to each other—so shyly, so wildly, so, as it were, without reality. They were like epicures with old wine in their glasses, not yet tired of its fragrance and the spell of anticipation.

81

And so their talk was not of love, but, in that pathetic way of star-crossed lovers, of the things they loved; leaving out—each other.

It was the telling of her dream that brought the words from him at last; but she drew away, and answered:

'It can't—it mustn't be!'

Then he just clung to her hand; and presently, seeing that her eyes were wet, took courage enough to kiss her cheek.

Trembling and fugitive indeed that first passage of their love. Not much of the conquering male in him, nor in her of the ordinary enchantress.

And then they went, outwardly sober enough, riding their mules down the stony slopes back to Mentone.

But in the grey, dusty railway-carriage, when she had left him, he was like a man drugged, staring at where she had sat opposite.

Two hours later, at dinner in her hotel, between her and Mrs Ercott, with the Colonel opposite, he knew for the first time what he was faced with. To watch every thought that passed within him, lest it should by the slightest sign betray him; to regulate and veil every look and every word he spoke to her; never for a second to forget that these other persons were actual and dangerous, not merely the insignficant and grotesque shadows that they seemed. It would be perhaps for ever a part of his love for her to seem not to love her. He did not dare dream of fulfilment. He was to be her friend, and try to bring her happiness—burn and long for her, and not think about reward. This was his first real overwhelming passion—so different to the loves of spring—and he brought to it all that naïveté, that touching quality of young Englishmen, whose secret instinct is to back away from the full nature of love, even from admitting that it has that nature. They two were to love, and —not to love! For the first time he understood a little of what that meant. A few stolen adoring minutes now and then, and, for the rest, the presence of a world that must be deceived. Already he had almost a hatred of that orderly, brown-faced Colonel, with his eyes that looked so steady and saw nothing; of that flat, kindly lady, who talked so pleasantly throughout dinner, saying things that he had to answer without knowing what they signified. He realized, with a sense of shock, that he was deprived of all interests in life but one; not even his work had any meaning apart from *her*. It lit no fire within him to hear Mrs Ercott praise certain execrable pictures in the Royal Academy, which she had religiously visited the day before leaving home. And as the interminable meal wore on, he began even to feel grief and wonder that Olive could be so smiling, so gay, and calm; so, as it seemed to him, indifferent to this intolerable impossibility of exchanging even one look of love. Did she really love him—could she love him, and show not one little sign of it? And suddenly he felt her foot touch his own. It was the faintest sidelong, supplicating pressure, withdrawn at once, but it said: 'I know what you are suffering; I, too, but I love you!' Characteristically, he felt that it cost her dear to make use of that little primitive device of common loves; the touch awoke within him only chivalry. He would burn for ever sooner than cause her the pain of thinking that he was not happy.

After dinner, they sat out on a balcony. The stars glowed above the palms; a frog was croaking. He managed to draw his chair so that he could look at her unseen. How deep, and softly dark her eyes, when for a second they rested on his! A moth settled on her knee—a cunning little creature, with its hooded, horned owl's face, and tiny black slits of eyes! Would it have come so confidingly to anyone but her? The Colonel knew its name—he had collected it. Very common, he said. The interest in it passed; but Lennan stayed, bent forward, gazing at that silk-covered knee.

The voice of Mrs Ercott, sharper than its wont, said: 'What day does Robert say he wants you back, my dear?'

He managed to remain gazing at the moth, even to take it gently from her knee, while he listened to her calm answer.

'Tuesday, I believe.'

Then he got up, and let the moth fly into the darkness; his hands and lips were trembling, and he was afraid of their being seen. He had never known, had not dreamed, of such a violent, sick feeling. That this man could thus hale her home at will! It was grotesque, fantastic, awful, but—it was true! Next Tuesday she would journey back away from him to be again at the mercy of her Fate! The pain of this thought made him grip the railing, and grit his teeth, to keep himself from crying out. And another thought came to him: I shall have to go about with this feeling, day and night, and keep it secret.

They were saying good-night; and he had to smirk and smile, and pretend—to her above all—that he was happy, and he could see that she knew it was pretence.

Then he was alone, with the feeling that he had failed her at the first shot; torn, too, between horror of what he suddenly saw before him, and longing to be back in her presence at any cost. . . . And all this on the day of that first kiss which had seemed to him to make her so utterly his own.

He sat down on a bench facing the Casino. Neither the lights, nor the people passing in and out, not even the gipsy bandsmen's music, distracted his thoughts for a second. Could it be less than twenty-four hours since he had picked up her handkerchief, not thirty yards away? In that twenty-four hours he seemed to have known every emotion that man could feel. And in all the world there was now not one soul to whom he could speak his real thoughts—not even to her, because from her, beyond all, he must keep at any cost all knowledge of his unhappiness. So this was illicit love—as it was called! Loneliness, and torture! Not jealousy —for her heart was his; but amazement, outrage, fear. Endless lonely suffering! And nobody, if they knew, would care, or pity him one jot!

Was there really, then, as the ancients thought, a Daemon that liked to play with men, as men liked to stir an earwig and turn it over and put a foot on it in the end?

He got up and made his way towards the railway-station. There was the bench where she had been sitting when he came on her that very morning. The stars in their courses had seemed to fight for them then; but whether for joy he no longer knew. And there on the seat were still the pepper berries she had crushed and strewn. He broke off another bunch and bruised them. That scent was the ghost of sacred minutes when her hand lay against his own. The stars in their courses—for joy or sorrow!

VII

There was no peace now for Colonel and Mrs Ercott. They felt themselves conspirators, and of conspiracy they had never had the habit. Yet how could they openly deal with anxieties which had arisen solely from what they had chanced secretly to see? What was not intended for one's eyes and ears did not exist; no canon of conduct could be quite so sacred. As well defend the opening of another person's letters as admit the possibility of making use of adventitious knowledge. So far tradition, and indeed character, made them feel at one, and conspire freely. But they diverged on a deeper plane. Mrs Ercott had *said*, indeed, that here was something which could not be controlled; the Colonel had felt it—a very different thing! Less tolerant in theory, he was touched at heart; Mrs Ercott, in theory almost approving—she read that dangerous authoress, George Eliot—at heart felt cold towards her husband's niece. For these reasons they could not in fact conspire without, in the end, saying suddenly: 'Well, it's no good talking about it!' and almost at once beginning to talk about it again.

In proposing to her that mule, the Colonel had not had time, or, rather, not quite conviction enough as to his line of action, to explain so immediately the new need for her to sit upon it. It was only when, to his somewhat strange relief, she had refused the expedition, and Olive had started without them, that he told her of the meeting in the Gardens, of which he had been witness. She then said at once that if she had known, she would, of course, have put up with anything in order to go; not because she approved of interfering, but because they must think of Robert! And the Colonel had said: 'D——n the fellow!' And there the matter had rested for the moment, for both of them were wondering a little which fellow it was that he had damned. That indeed was the trouble. If the Colonel had not cared so much about his niece, and had liked, instead of rather disliking Cramier; if Mrs Ercott had not found Mark Lennan a 'nice boy', and had not secretly felt her husband's niece rather dangerous to her peace of mind; if, in few words, those three had been puppets made of wood and worked by law, it would have been so much simpler for all concerned. It was the discovery that there was a personal equation in such matters, instead of just a simple rule of three, which disorganised the Colonel and made him almost angry; which depressed Mrs Ercott and made her almost silent. . . . These two good souls had stumbled on a problem which has divided the world from birth. Shall cases be decided on their individual merits, or according to formal codes?

Beneath an appearance of a vocabulary more orthodox than ever, the Colonel's allegiance to Authority and the laws of Form was really shaken; he simply could not get out of his head the sight of those two young people sitting side by side, nor the tone of Olive's voice, when she had repeated his regrettable words about happiness at home.

If only the thing had not been so human! If only she had been someone else's niece, it would clearly have been her duty to remain unhappy. As it was, the more he thought, the less he knew what to think. A man who had never had any balance to speak of at his bank, and from the nomadic condition of his life had no exaggerated feeling for a settled social status—deeming Society in fact rather a bore—he did not unduly exaggerate the worldly dangers of this affair; neither did he honestly believe that she would burn in everlasting torment if she did not succeed in remaining true to 'that great black chap', as he secretly called Cramier. His feeling was simply that it was an awful pity; a sort of unhappy conviction that it was not like the women of his family to fall upon such ways; that his dead brother would turn in his grave; in two words that it was 'not done'. Yet he was by no means of those who, giving latitude to women in general, fall with whips on those of their own family who take it. On the contrary, believing that Woman in general should be stainless to the world's eye, he was inclined to make allowance for any individual woman that he knew and loved. A suspicion he had always entertained, that Cramier was not by breeding 'quite the clean potato' may insensibly have influenced him just a little. He had heard indeed that he was not even entitled to the name of Cramier, but had been adopted by a childless man, who had brought him up and left him a lot of money. There was something in this that went against the grain of the childless Colonel. He had never adopted, nor been adopted by, anyone himself. There was a certain lack about a man who had been adopted, of reasonable guarantee—he was like a non-vintage wine, or a horse without a pedigree; you could not quite rely on what he might do, having no tradition in his blood. His appearance, too, and manner somehow lent colour to this distrust. A touch of the tar-brush somewhere, and a stubborn, silent, pushing fellow. Why on earth had Olive ever married him! But then women were such kittle cattle, poor things! and old Lindsay, with his vestments and his views on obedience, must have been a Tartar as a father, poor old chap! Besides, Cramier, no doubt, was what most women would call good-looking; more taking to the eye than such a quiet fellow as young Lennan, whose features were rather anyhow, though pleasant enough, and with a nice smile—the sort of young man one could not help liking, and who certainly would never hurt a fly! And suddenly there came the thought: Why should he not go to young Lennan and put it to him straight? That he was in love with Olive? Not quite—but the way to do it would come to him. He brooded long over this idea, and spoke of it to Mrs Ercott, while shaving, the next morning. Her answer: 'My dear John, bosh!' removed his last doubt.

Without saying where he was going, he strolled out the moment after breakfast—and took a train to Beaulieu. At the young man's hotel he sent in his card, and was told that this Monsieur had already gone out for the day. His mood of marching straight up to the guns thus checked, he was left pensive and distraught. Not having seen Beaulieu (they spoke of it then as a coming place), he made his way up an incline. That whole hillside was covered with rose-trees. Thousands of these flowers were starring the lower air, and the strewn petals of blown and fallen roses covered the light soil. The Colonel put his nose to blossoms here and there, but they had little scent, as if they knew that the season was already over. A few blue-bloused peasants were still busy among them. And suddenly he came on young Lennan himself, sitting on a stone and dabbing away with his fingers at a lump of putty stuff. The Colonel hesitated. Apart from obvious reasons for discomfiture, he had that feeling towards Art common to so many of his caste. It was not work, of course, but it was very clever—a mystery to him how anyone could do it! On seeing him, Lennan had risen, dropping his handkerchief over what he was modelling—but not before the Colonel had received a dim impression of something familiar. The young man was very red—the Colonel, too, was conscious suddenly of the heat. He held out his hand.

'Nice quiet place this,' he stammered; 'never seen it before. I called at your hotel.'

Now that he had his chance, he was completely at a loss. The sight of the face emerging from that lump of 'putty stuff' had quite unnerved him. The notion of this young man working at it up here all by himself, just because he was away an hour or two from the original, touched him. How on earth to say what he had come to say? It was altogether different from what he had thought. And it suddenly flashed through him—Dolly was right! She's always right —hang it!

'You're busy,' he said; 'I mustn't interrupt you.'

'Not at all, sir. It was awfully good of you to look me up.'

The Colonel stared. There was something about young Lennan that he had not noticed before; a 'Don't take liberties with me!' look that made things difficult. But still he lingered, staring wistfully at the young man, who stood waiting with such politeness. Then a safe question shot into his mind:

'Ah! And when do you go back to England? We're off on Tuesday.'

While he spoke, a puff of wind lifted the handkerchief from the modelled face. Would the young fellow put it back? He did not. And the Colonel thought:

'It would have been bad form. He knew I wouldn't take advantage. Yes! He's a gentleman!'

Lifting his hand to the salute, he said: 'Well, I must be getting back. See you at dinner perhaps?' And turning on his heel he marched away.

The remembrance of that face in the 'putty stuff' up there by the side of the road accompanied him home. It was bad—it was serious! And the sense that he counted for nothing in all of it grew and grew in him. He told no one of where he had been. . . .

When the Colonel turned with ceremony and left him, Lennan sat down again on the flat stone, took up his 'putty stuff', and presently effaced that image. He sat still a long time, to all appearance watching the little blue butterflies playing round the red and tawny roses. Then his fingers began to work, feverishly shaping a head; not of a man, not of a beast, but a sort of horned, heavy mingling of the two. There was something frenetic in the movement of those rather short, blunt-ended fingers, as though they were strangling the thing they were creating.

VIII

In those days, such as had served their country travelled, as befitted Spartans, in ordinary first-class carriages, and woke in the morning at La Roche or some strange-sounding place, for paler coffee and the pale brioche. So it was with Colonel and Mrs Ercott and their niece, accompanied by books they did not read, viands they did not eat, and one somnolent Irishman returning from the East. In the disposition of legs there was the usual difficulty, no one quite liking to put them up, and all ultimately doing so, save Olive. More than once during that night the Colonel, lying on the seat opposite, awoke and saw her sitting, withdrawn into her corner, with eyes still open. Staring at that little head which he admired so much, upright and unmoving, in its dark toque against the cushion, he would become suddenly alert. Kicking the Irishman slightly in the effort, he would slip his legs down, bend across to her in the darkness, and, conscious of a faint fragrance as of violets, whisper huskily: 'Anything I can do for you, my dear?' When she had smiled and shaken her head, he would retreat, and after holding his breath to see if Dolly were asleep, would restore his feet, slightly kicking the Irishman. After one such expedition, for full ten minutes he remained awake, wondering at her tireless immobility. For indeed she was spending this night entranced, with the feeling that Lennan was beside her, holding her hand in his. She seemed actually to feel the touch of his finger against the tiny patch of her bare palm where the glove opened. It was wonderful, this uncanny communion in the dark rushing night—she would not have slept for worlds! Never before had she felt so close to him, not even when he had kissed her that once under the olives; nor even when at the concert yesterday his arm pressed hers; and his voice whispered words she heard so thirstily. And that golden fortnight passed and passed through her on an endless band of reminiscence. Its memories were like flowers, such scent and warmth and colour in them; and of all, none perhaps quite so poignant as the memory of the moment, at the door of their carriage, when he said, so low that she just heard: 'Good-bye, my darling!' He had never before called her that. Not even his touch on her cheek under the olives equalled the simple treasure of that word. And above the roar and clatter of the train, and the snoring of the Irishman, it kept sounding in her ears, hour after dark hour. It was perhaps not wonderful, that through all that night she never once looked the future in the face—made no plans, took no stock of her position; just yielded to memory, and to the half-dreamed sensation of his presence close beside her. Whatever might come afterwards, she was his this night. Such was the trance that gave to her the strange, soft, tireless immobility which so moved her Uncle whenever he woke up.

In Paris they drove from station to station in a vehicle unfit for three—'to stretch their legs'—as the Colonel said. Since he saw in his niece no signs of flagging, no regret, his spirits were rising, and he confided to Mrs Ercott in the buffet at the Gare du Nord, when Olive had gone to wash, that he did not think there was much in it, after all, looking at the way she'd travelled.

But Mrs Ercott answered:

'Haven't you ever noticed that Olive never shows what she does not want to? She has not got those eyes for nothing.'

'What eyes?'

'Eyes that see everything, and seem to see nothing.'

Conscious that something was hurting her, the Colonel tried to take her hand.

But Mrs Ercott rose quickly, and went where he could not follow.

Thus suddenly deserted, the Colonel brooded, drumming on the little table. What now! Dolly was unjust! Poor Dolly! He was as fond of her as ever! Of course! How could he help Olive's being young—and pretty; how could he help looking after her, and wanting to save her from this mess! Thus he sat wondering, dismayed by the unreasonableness of women. It did not enter his head that Mrs Ercott had been almost as sleepless as his niece, watching through closed eyes every one of those little expeditions of his, and saying to herself: 'Ah! He doesn't care how *I* travel!'

She returned serene enough, concealing her 'grief', and soon they were once more whirling towards England.

But the future had begun to lay its hand on Olive; the spell of the past was already losing power; the sense that it had all been a dream grew stronger every minute. In a few hours she would re-enter the little house close under the shadow of that old Wren church, which reminded her somehow of childhood, and her austere father with his chiselled face. The meeting with her husband! How go through that! And to-night! But she did not care to contemplate to-night. And all those to-morrows wherein there was nothing she had to do of which it was reasonable to complain, yet nothing she could do without feeling that all the friendliness and zest and colour was out of life, and she a prisoner. Into those to-morrows she felt she would slip back, out of her dream; lost, with hardly perhaps an effort. To get away to the house on the river, where her husband came only at week-ends, had hitherto been a refuge; only she would not see Mark there—unless——! Then, with the thought that she would, must still see him some-times, all again grew faintly glamorous. If only she did see him, what would the rest matter? Never again as it had before!

The Colonel was reaching down her handbag; his cheery: 'Looks as if it would be rough!' aroused her. Glad to be alone, and tired enough now, she sought the ladies' cabin, and slept through the crossing, till the voice of the old stewardess awakened her: 'You've had a nice sleep. We're alongside, miss.' Ah! if she were but *that* now! She had been dreaming that she was sitting in a flowery field, and Lennan had drawn her up by the hands, with the words: 'We're here, my darling!'

On deck, the Colonel, laden with bags, was looking back for her, and trying to keep a space between him and his wife. He signalled with his chin. Threading her way towards him, she happened to look up. By the rails of the pier above she saw her husband. He was leaning there, looking intently down; his tall broad figure made the people on each side of him seem insignificant. The clean-shaved, square-cut face, with those almost epileptic, forceful eyes, had a stillness and intensity beside which the neighbouring faces seemed to disappear. She saw him very clearly, even noting the touch of silver in his dark hair, on each side under his straw hat; noting that he seemed too massive for his neat blue suit. His face relaxed; he made a little movement of one hand. Suddenly it shot through her: Suppose Mark had travelled with them, as he had wished to do? For ever and ever now, that dark massive creature, smiling down at her, was her enemy; from whom she must guard and keep herself if she could; keep, at all events, each one of her real thoughts and hopes! She could have writhed, and cried out; instead, she tightened her grip on the handle of her bag, and smiled. Though so skilled in knowledge of his moods, she felt, in his greeting, his fierce grip of her shoulders, the smouldering of some feeling the nature of which she could not quite fathom. His voice had a grim sincerity: 'Glad you're back—thought you were never coming!' Resigned to his charge, a feeling of sheer physical faintness so beset her that she could hardly reach the compartment he had reserved. It seemed to her that, for all her foreboding, she had not till this moment had the smallest inkling of what was now before her; and at his muttered: 'Must we have the old fossils in?' she looked back to assure herself that her Uncle and Aunt were following. To avoid having to talk, she feigned to have travelled badly, leaning back with closed eyes, in her corner. If only she could open them and see, not this square-jawed face with its intent gaze of possession, but that other with its eager eyes humbly adoring her. The interminable journey ended all too soon. She clung quite desperately to the Colonel's hand on the platform at Charing Cross. When his kind face vanished she would be lost indeed! Then, in the closed cab, she heard her husband's: 'Aren't you going to kiss me?' and submitted to his embrace.

She tried so hard to think: What does it matter? It's not I, not my soul, my spirit—only my miserable lips!

She heard him say: 'You don't seem too glad to see me!' And then: 'I hear you had young Lennan out there. What was *he* doing?'

She felt the turmoil of sudden fear, wondered whether she was showing it, lost it in unnatural alertness—all in the second before she answered: 'Oh! just a holiday.'

Some seconds passed, and then he said:

'You didn't mention him in your letters.'

She answered coolly: 'Didn't I? We saw a good deal of him.'

She knew that he was looking at her—an inquisitive, half-menacing regard. Why—oh, why!—could she not then and there cry out: 'And I love him—do you hear?—I love him!' So awful did it seem to be denying her love with these half lies! But it was all so much more grim and hopeless than even she had thought. How inconceivable, now, that she had ever given herself up to this man for life! If only she could get away from him to her room, and scheme and think! For his eyes never left her, travelling over her with their pathetic greed, their menacing inquiry, till he said: 'Well, it's not done you any harm. You look very fit.' But his touch was too much even for her self-command, and she recoiled as if he had struck her.

'What's the matter? Did I hurt you?'

It seemed to her that he was jeering—then realised as vividly that he was not. And the full danger to her, perhaps to Mark himself, of shrinking from this man, striking her with all its pitiable force, she made a painful effort, slipped her hand under his arm, and said: 'I'm very tired. You startled me.'

But he put her hand away, and turning his face, stared out of the window. And so they reached their home.

When he had left her alone, she remained where she was standing, by her wardrobe, without sound or movement, thinking: What am I going to do? How am I going to live?

IX

When Mark Lennan, travelling through from Beaulieu, reached his rooms in Chelsea, he went at once to the little pile of his letters, twice hunted through them, then stood very still, with a stunned, sick feeling. Why had she not sent him that promised note? And now he realised—though not yet to the full—what it meant to be in love with a married woman. He must wait in this suspense for eighteen hours at least, till he could call, and find out what had happened to prevent her, till he could hear from her lips that she still loved him. The chilliest of legal lovers had access to his love, but he must possess a soul that was on fire, in this deadly patience, for fear of doing something that might jeopardise her. Telegraph? He dared not. Write? She would get it by the first post; but what could he say that was not dangerous, if Cramier chanced to see? Call? Still more impossible till three o'clock, at very earliest, to-morrow. His gaze wandered round the studio. Were these household gods, and all these works of his, indeed the same he had left twenty days ago? They seemed to exist now only in so far as she might come to see them—come and sit in such a chair, and drink out of such a cup, and let him put this cushion

for her back, and that footstool for her feet. And so vividly could
he see her lying back in that chair looking across at him, that
he could hardly believe she had never yet sat there. It was odd how
—without any resolution taken, without admission that their love
could not remain platonic, without any change in their relations,
save one humble kiss and a few whispered words—everything was
changed. A month or so ago, if he had wanted, he would have
gone at once calmly to her house. It would have seemed harmless,
and quite natural. Now it was impossible to do openly the least
thing that strict convention did not find desirable. Sooner or later
they would find him stepping over convention, and take him for
what he was not—a real lover! A real lover! He knelt down before
the empty chair and stretched out his arms. No substance—no
warmth—no fragrance—nothing! Longing that passed through air,
as the wind through grass.

He went to the little round window, which overlooked the river.
The last evening of May; gloaming above the water, dusk resting
in the trees, and the air warm! Better to be out, and moving in the
night, out in the ebb and flow of things, among others whose hearts
were beating, than stay in this place that without her was so cold
and meaningless.

Lamps—the passion-fruit of towns—were turning from pallor
to full orange, and the stars were coming out. Half-past nine! At
ten o'clock, and not before, he would walk past her house. To
have this something to look forward to, however furtive and barren, helped. But on a Saturday night there would be no sitting at
the House. Cramier would be at home; or they would both be out;
or perhaps have gone down to their river cottage. Cramier! What
cruel demon had presided over that marring of her life! Why had
he never met her till after she had bound herself to this man! From
a negative contempt for one who was either not sensitive enough
to recognise that his marriage was a failure, or not chivalrous
enough to make that failure bear as little hardly as possible on his
wife, he had come already to jealous hatred as of a monster. To
be face to face with Cramier in a mortal conflict could alone have
satisfied his feeling. . . . Yet he was a young man by nature
gentle!

His heart beat desperately as he approached that street—one of
those little old streets, so beautiful, that belong to a vanished London. It was very narrow, there was no shelter; and he thought con-
fusedly of what he could say, if met in this remote backwater that
led nowhere. He would tell some lie, no doubt. Lies would now be

93

his daily business. Lies and hatred, those violent things of life, would come to seem quite natural, in the violence of his love.

He stood a moment, hesitating, by the rails of the old church. Black, white-veined, with shadowy summits, in that half darkness, it was like some gigantic vision. Mystery itself seemed modelled there. He turned and walked quickly down the street close to the houses on the further side. The windows of her house were lighted! So, she was not away! Dim light in the dining-room, lights in the room above—her bedroom, doubtless. Was there no way to bring her to the window, no way his spirit could climb up there and beckon hers out to him? Perhaps she was not there, perhaps it was but a servant taking up hot water. He was at the end of the street by now, but to leave without once more passing was impossible. And this time he went slowly, his head down, feigning abstraction, grudging every inch of pavement, and all the time furtively searching that window with the light behind the curtains. Nothing! Once more he was close to the railings of the church, and once more could not bring himself to go away. In the little, close, deserted street, not a soul was moving, not even a cat or dog; nothing alive but many discreet, lighted windows. Like veiled faces, showing no emotion, they seemed to watch his indecision. And he thought: 'Ah, well! I dare say there are lots like me. Lots as near, and yet as far away! Lots who have to suffer!' But what would he not have given for the throwing open of those curtains. Then, suddenly scared by an approaching figure, he turned and walked away.

X

At three o'clock next day he called.

In the middle of her white drawing-room, whose latticed window ran the whole length of one wall, stood a little table on which was a silver jar full of early larkspurs, evidently from her garden by the river. And Lennan waited, his eyes fixed on those blossoms so like to little blue butterflies and strange-hued crickets, tethered to the pale green stems. In this room she passed her days, guarded from him. Once a week, at most, he would be able to come there —once a week for an hour or two out of the hundred and. sixty-eight hours that he longed to be with her.

And suddenly he was conscious of her. She had come in without sound, and was standing by the piano, so pale, in her cream-white dress, that her eyes looked jet black. He hardly knew that face, like a flower closed against cold.

What had he done? What had happened in these five days to make her like this to him? He took her hands and tried to kiss them; but she said quickly:

'He's in!'

At that he stood silent, looking into that face, frozen to a dreadful composure, on the breaking up of which his very life seemed to depend. At last he said:

'What is it? Am I nothing to you, after all?'

But as soon as he had spoken he saw that he need not have asked, and flung his arms round her. She clung to him with desperation; then freed herself, and said:

'No, no; let's sit down quietly!'

He obeyed, half-divining, half-refusing to admit all that lay behind that strange coldness, and this desperate embrace; all the self-pity, and self-loathing, shame, rage, and longing of a married woman for the first time face to face with her lover in her husband's house.

She seemed now to be trying to make him forget her strange behaviour; to be what she had been during that fortnight in the sunshine. But, suddenly, just moving her lips, she said:

'Quick! When can we see each other? I will come to you to tea—to-morrow,' and, following her eyes, he saw the door opening, and Cramier coming in. Unsmiling, very big in the low room, he crossed over to them, and offered his hand to Lennan; then drawing a low chair forward between their two chairs, sat down.

'So you're back,' he said. 'Have a good time?'

'Thanks, yes; very.'

'Luck for Olive you were there; those places are dull holes.'

'It was luck for me.'

'No doubt.' And with those words he turned to his wife. His elbows rested along the arms of his chair, so that his clenched palms were upwards; it was as if he knew that he was holding those two, gripped one in each hand.

'I wonder,' he said slowly, 'that fellows like you, with nothing in the world to tie them, ever sit down in a place like London. I should have thought Rome or Paris were your happy hunting-grounds.'

In his voice, in those eyes of his, a little bloodshot, with their look of power, in his whole attitude, there was a sort of muffled menace, and contempt, as though he were thinking: 'Step into my path, and I will crush you!'

And Lennan thought:

'How long must I sit here?' Then, past that figure planted solidly between them, he caught a look from her, swift, sure, marvellously timed—again and again—as if she were being urged by the very presence of this danger. One of those glances would surely—surely be seen by Cramier. Is there need for fear that a swallow should dash itself against the wall over which it skims? But he got up, unable to bear it longer.

'Going?' That one suave word had an inimitable insolence.

He could hardly see his hand touching Cramier's heavy fist. Then he realised that she was standing so that their faces when they must say good-bye could not be seen. Her eyes were smiling, yet imploring; her lips shaped the word: 'To-morrow!' And squeezing her hand desperately, he got away.

He had never dreamed that to see her in the presence of the man who owned her would be so terrible. For a moment he thought that he must give her up, give up a love that would drive him mad.

He climbed on to an omnibus travelling West. Another twenty-four hours of starvation had begun. It did not matter at all what he did with them. They were simply so much aching that had to be got through somehow—so much aching; and what relief at the end? An hour or two with her, desperately holding himself in.

Like most artists, and few Englishmen, he lived on feelings rather than on facts; so, found no refuge in decisive resolutions. But he made many—the resolution to give her up; to be true to the ideal of service for no reward; to beseech her to leave Cramier and come to him—and he made each many times.

At Hyde Park Corner he got down, and went into the Park, thinking that to walk would help him.

A great number of people were sitting there, taking mysterious anodyne, doing the right thing; to avoid them, he kept along the rails, and ran almost into the arms of Colonel and Mrs Ercott, who were coming from the direction of Knightsbridge, slightly flushed, having lunched and talked of 'Monte' at the house of a certain General.

They greeted him with the surprise of those who had said to each other many times: 'That young man will come rushing back!' It was very nice—they said—to run across him. When did he arrive? They had thought he was going on to Italy—he was looking rather tired. They did not ask if he had seen her—being too kind, and perhaps afraid that he would say 'Yes', which would be embarrassing; or that he would say 'No', which would be still more embarrassing when they found that he ought to have said 'Yes'. Would he not come and sit with them a little—they were going presently to see how Olive was? Lennan perceived that they were warning him. And, forcing himself to look at them very straight, he said: 'I have just been there.'

Mrs Ercott phrased her impressions that same evening: 'He looks quite hunted, poor young man! I'm afraid there's going to be fearful trouble there. Did you notice how quickly he ran away from us? He's thin, too; if it wasn't for his tan, he'd look really ill. The boy's eyes are so pathetic; and he used to have such a nice smile in them.'

The Colonel, who was fastening her hooks, paused in an operation that required concentration.

'It's a thousand pities,' he muttered, 'that he hasn't any work to do. That puddling about with clay or whatever he does is no good at all.' And slowly fastening one hook, he unhooked several others.

Mrs Ercott went on:

'And I saw Olive, when she thought I wasn't looking; it was just as if she'd taken off a mask. But Robert Cramier will never put up with it. He's in love with her still; I watched him. It's tragic, John.'

The Colonel let his hands fall from the hooks.

'If I thought that,' he said, 'I'd do something.'

'If you could, it would not be tragic.'

The Colonel stared. There was always *something* to be done.

'You read too many novels,' he said, but without spirit.

Mrs Ercott smiled, and made no answer to an aspersion she had heard before.

XI

When Lennan reached his rooms again after that encounter with the Ercotts, he found in his letter-box a visiting card: 'Mrs Doone' 'Miss Sylvia Doone', and on it pencilled the words: 'Do come and see us before we go down to Hayle—Sylvia.' He stared blankly at the round handwriting he knew so well.

Sylvia! Nothing perhaps could have made so plain to him how in this tornado of his passion the world was drowned. Sylvia! He had almost forgotten her existence; and yet, only last year, after he definitely settled down in London, he had once more seen a

97

good deal of her; and even had soft thoughts of her again—with her pale-gold hair, her true look, her sweetness. Then they had gone for the winter to Algiers for her mother's health.

When they came back, he had already avoided seeing her, though that was before Olive went to Monte Carlo, before he had even admitted his own feeling. And since—he had not once thought of her. Not once! The world had indeed vanished. 'Do come and see us—Sylvia.' The very notion was an irritation. No rest from aching and impatience to be had that way.

And then the idea came to him: Why not kill these hours of waiting for to-morrow's meeting by going on the river and passing by her cottage? There was still one train that he could catch.

He reached the village after dark, and spent the night at the inn; got up early next morning, took a boat, and pulled down-stream. The bluffs of the opposite bank were wooded with high trees. The sun shone softly on their leaves, and the bright stream was ruffled by a breeze that bent all the reeds and slowly swayed the water-flowers. One thin white line of wind streaked the blue sky. He shipped his sculls and drifted, listening to the wood-pigeons, watching the swallows chasing. If only she were here! To spend one long day thus, drifting with the stream! To have but one such rest from longing! Her cottage, he knew, lay on the same side as the village, and just beyond an island. She had told him of a hedge of yew-trees, and a white dove-cote almost at the water's edge. He came to the island, and let his boat slide into the backwater. It was all overgrown with willow trees and alders, dark even in this early morning radiance, and marvellously still. There was no room to row; he took the boathook and tried to punt, but the green water was too deep and entangled with great roots, so that he had to make his way by clawing with the hook at branches. Birds seemed to shun this gloom, but a single magpie crossed the one little clear patch of sky, and flew low behind the willows. The air here had a sweetish, earthy odour of too rank foliage; all brightness seemed entombed. He was glad to pass out again under a huge poplar-tree into the fluttering gold and silver of the morning. And almost at once he saw the yew-hedge at the border of some bright green turf, and a pigeon-house, high on its pole, painted cream-white. About it a number of ringdoves and snow-white pigeons were perched or flying; and beyond the lawn he could see the dark veranda of a low house, covered by wistaria just going out of flower. A drift of scent from late lilacs, and new-mown grass, was borne out to him, together with the sound of a mowing-machine, and the humming of many bees. It was beautiful here, and seemed, for all its restfulness, to have something of that flying quality he so loved about her face, about the sweep of her hair, the quick, soft turn of her eyes —or was that but the darkness of the yew-trees, the whiteness of the dove-cote, and the doves themselves, flying?

He lay there a long time quietly beneath the bank, careful not to attract the attention of the old gardener, who was methodically pushing his machine across and across the lawn. How he wanted her with him then! Wonderful that there could be in life such beauty and wild softness as made the heart ache with the delight of it, and in that same life grey rules and rigid barriers—coffins of happiness! That doors should be closed on love and joy! There was not so much of it in the world! She, who was the very spirit of this flying, nymph-like summer, was untimely wintered-up in bleak sorrow. There was a hateful unwisdom in that thought; it seemed so grim and violent, so corpse-like, gruesome, narrow and extravagant! What possible end could it serve that she should be unhappy! Even if he had not loved her, he would have hated her fate just as much—all such stories of imprisoned lives had roused his anger even as a boy.

Soft white clouds—those bright angels of the river, never very long away—had begun now to spread their wings over the woods; and the wind had dropped so that the slumbrous warmth and murmuring of summer gathered full over the water. The old gardener had finished his job of mowing, and came with a little basket of grain to feed the doves. Lennan watched them going to him, the ring-doves, very dainty, and capricious, keeping to themselves. In place of that old fellow, he was really seeing *her*, feeding from her hands those birds of Cypris. What a group he could have made of her with them perching and flying round her! If she were his, what could he not achieve—to make her immortal—like the old Italians, who, in their work, had rescued their mistresses from Time! . . .

He was back in his rooms in London two hours before he dared begin expecting her. Living alone there but for a caretaker who came every morning for an hour or two, made dust, and departed, he had no need for caution. And when he had procured flowers, and the fruits and cakes which they certainly would not eat— when he had arranged the tea-table, and made the grand tour at least twenty times, he placed himself with a book at the little round window, to watch for her approach. There, very still, he sat, not reading a word, continually moistening his dry lips and sighing, to relieve the tension of his heart. At last he saw her coming. She was walking close to the railings of the houses, looking neither to right nor left. She had on a lawn frock, and a hat of the palest coffee-coloured straw, with a narrow black velvet ribbon. She crossed the side street, stopped for a second, gave a swift look round, then came resolutely on. What was it made him love her so? What was the secret of her fascination? Certainly, no conscious enticements. Never did anyone try less to fascinate. He could not recall one single little thing that she had done to draw him to her. Was it, perhaps, her very passivity, her native pride that never offered or asked anything, a sort of soft stoicism in her fibre; that and some mysterious charm, as close and intimate as scent was to a flower?

He waited to open till he heard her footstep just outside. She came in without a word, not even looking at him. And he, too, said not a word till he had closed the door, and made sure of her. Then they turned to each other. Her breast was heaving a little, under her thin frock, but she was calmer than he, with that wonderful composure of pretty women in all the passages of love, as who should say: This is my native air!

They stood and looked at each other, as if they could never have enough, till he said at last:

'I thought I should die before this moment came. There isn't a minute that I don't long for you so terribly that I can hardly live.'

'And do you think that I don't long for you?'

'Then come to me!'

She looked at him mournfully and shook her head.

Well, he had known that she would not. He had not earned her. What right had he to ask her to fly against the world, to brave everything, to have such faith in him—as yet? He had no heart to press his words, beginning then to understand the paralysing truth that there was no longer any resolving this or that; with love like his he had ceased to be a separate being with a separate will. He was entwined with her, could act only if her will and his were one. He would never be able to say to her: 'You must!' He loved her too much. And she knew it. So there was nothing for it but to forget the ache, and make the hour happy. But how about that other truth—that in love there is no pause, no resting? . . . With any watering, however scant, the flower will grow till its time comes to be plucked. . . . This oasis in the desert—these few minutes with her alone, were swept through and through with a feverish wind. To be closer! How not try to be that? How not long for her lips when he had but her hand to kiss? And how not be poisoned with the thought that in a few minutes she would leave him and go back to the presence of that other, who, even though she loathed him, could see and touch her when he would? She was leaning back in the very chair where in fancy he had seen her, and he only dared sit at her feet and look up. And this, which a week ago would have been rapture, was now almost torture, so far did it fall short of his longing. It was torture, too, to keep his voice in tune with the sober sweetness of her voice. And bitterly he thought: How can she sit there, and not want me, as I want her? Then at a touch of her fingers on his hair, he lost control, and kissed her lips. Her surrender lasted only for a second.

'No, no—you must not!'

That mournful surprise sobered him at once.

He got up, stood away from her, begged to be forgiven.

And, when she was gone, he sat in the chair where she had sat. That clasp of her, the kiss he had begged her to forget—to forget! —nothing could take that from him. He had done wrong; had startled her, had fallen short of chivalry! And yet—a smile of utter happiness would cling about his lips. His fastidiousness, his imagination almost made him think that this was all he wanted. If he could close his eyes, now, and pass out, before he lost that moment of half-fulfilment!

And, the smile still on his lips, he lay back watching the flies wheeling and chasing round the hanging-lamp. Sixteen of them there were, wheeling and chasing—never still!

XII

When, walking from Lennan's studio, Olive re-entered her dark little hall, she approached its alcove and glanced first at the hat-stand. They were all there—the silk hat, the bowler, the straw! So he was in! And within each hat, in turn, she seemed to see her husband's head—with the face turned away from her—so distinctly as to note the leathery look of the skin of his cheek and neck. And she thought: 'I pray that he will die! It is wicked, but I pray that he will die!' Then, quietly, that he might not hear, she mounted to her bedroom. The door into his dressing-room was open, and she went to shut it. He was standing there at the window.

'Ah! You're in! Been anywhere?'

'To the National Gallery.'

It was the first direct lie she had ever told him, and she was surprised to feel neither shame nor fear, but rather a sense of pleasure at defeating him. He was the enemy, all the more the enemy because she was still fighting against herself, and, so strangely, on his behalf.

'Alone?'

'Yes.'

'Rather boring, wasn't it? I should have thought you'd have got young Lennan to take you there.'

'Why?'

By instinct she had seized on the boldest answer; and there was nothing to be told from her face. If he were her superior in strength, he was her inferior in quickness.

He lowered his eyes, and said:

'His line, isn't it?'

With a shrug she turned away and shut the door. She sat down on the edge of her bed, very still. In that little passage of wits she had won, she could win in many such; but the full hideousness of things had come to her. Lies, lies! That was to be her life! That; or to say farewell to all she now cared for, to cause despair not only in herself, but in her lover, and—for what? In order that her body might remain at the disposal of that man in the next room—her spirit having flown from him for ever. Such were the alternatives, unless those words: 'Then come to me,' were to be more than words. Were they? Could they be? They would mean such happiness if—if his love for her were more than a summer love? And hers for him? Was it—were they—more than summer loves? How know? And, without knowing, how give such pain to everyone? How break a vow she had thought herself quite above breaking? How make such a desperate departure from all the traditions and beliefs in which she had been brought up! But in the very nature of passion is that which resents the intrusion of hard and fast decisions. . . . And suddenly she thought: If our love cannot stay what it is, and if I cannot yet go to him for always, is there not still another way?

She got up and began to dress for dinner. Standing before her glass she was surprised to see that her face showed no signs of the fears and doubts that were now her comrades. Was it because, whatever happened, she loved and was beloved! She wondered how she had looked when he kissed her so passionately; had she shown her joy before she checked him?

In her garden by the river were certain flowers that, for all her care, would grow rank and of the wrong colour—wanting a different soil. Was she, then, like those flowers of hers? Ah! Let her but have her true soil, and she would grow straight and true enough!

Then in the doorway she saw her husband. She had never, till to-day, quite hated him; but now she did, with a real blind horrible feeling. What did he want of her, standing there with those eyes fixed on her—those forceful eyes, touched with blood, that seemed at once to threaten, covet, and beseech! She drew her wrapper close round her shoulders. At that he came up and said:

'Look at me, Olive!'

Against instinct and will she obeyed, and he went on:

'Be careful! I say, be careful!'

Then he took her by the shoulders, and raised her up to him. And, quite unnerved, she stood without resisting.

'I want you,' he said; 'I mean to keep you.'

Then, suddenly letting her go, he covered his eyes with his hands. That frightened her most—it was so unlike him. Not till now had she understood between what terrifying forces she was balancing. She did not speak, but her face grew white. From behind those hands he uttered a sound, not quite like a human noise, turned sharply, and went out. She dropped back into the chair before her mirror, overcome by the most singular feeling she had ever known; as if she had lost everything, even her love for Lennan, and her longing for his love. What was it all worth, what was anything worth in a world like this? All was loathsome, herself loathsome! All was a void! Hateful, hateful, hateful! It was like having no heart at all! And that same evening, when her husband had gone down to the House, she wrote to Lennan:

'Our love must never turn to earthiness as it might have this afternoon. Everything is black and hopeless. *He* suspects. For you to come here is impossible, and too dreadful for us both. And I have no right to ask you to be furtive, I can't bear to think of you like that, and I can't bear it myself. I don't know what to do or say. Don't try to see me yet. I must have time, I must think.'

XIII

Colonel Ercott was not a racing man, but he had in common with others of his countrymen a religious feeling in the matter of the Derby. His remembrances of it went back to early youth, for he had been born and brought up almost within sound of the coaching-road to Epsom. Every Derby and Oaks day he had gone out on his pony to watch the passing of the tall hats and feathers of the great, and the pot-hats and feathers of the lowly; and afterwards, in the fields at home, had ridden races with old Lindsay, finishing between a cow that judged and a clump of bullrushes representing the Grand Stand.

But for one reason or another he had never seen the great race, and the notion that it was his duty to see it had now come to him. He proposed this to Mrs Ercott with some diffidence. She read so many books—he did not quite know whether she would approve. Finding that she did, he added casually:

'And we might take Olive.'

Mrs Ercott answered dryly:

'You know the House of Commons has a holiday?'

The Colonel murmured:

'Oh! I don't want that chap!'

'Perhaps,' said Mrs Ercott, 'you would like Mark Lennan.'

The Colonel looked at her most dubiously. Dolly could talk of it as a tragedy, and a—a grand passion, and yet make a suggestion like that! Then his wrinkles began slowly to come alive, and he gave her waist a squeeze.

Mrs Ercott did not resist that treatment.

'Take Olive alone,' she said. 'I don't really care to go.'

When the Colonel went to fetch his niece he found her ready, and very half-heartedly he asked for Cramier. It appeared she had not told him.

Relieved, yet somewhat disconcerted, he murmured:

'He won't mind not going, I suppose?'

'If he went, I should not.'

At this quiet answer the Colonel was beset again by all his fears. He put his white 'topper' down, and took her hand.

'My dear,' he said, 'I don't want to intrude upon your feelings; but—but is there anything I can do? It's dreadful to see things going unhappily with you!' He felt his hand being lifted, her face pressed against it; and, suffering acutely, with his other hand, cased in a bright new glove, he smoothed her arm. 'We'll have a jolly good day, sweetheart,' he said, 'and forget all about it.'

She gave the hand a kiss and turned away. And the Colonel vowed to himself that she should not be unhappy—lovely creature that she was, so delicate, and straight, and fine in her pearly frock.

And he pulled himself together, brushing his white 'topper' vigorously with his sleeve, forgetting that this kind of hat has no nap.

And so he was tenderness itself on the journey down, satisfying all her wants before she had them, telling her stories of Indian life, and consulting her carefully as to which horse they should back. There was the Duke's, of course, but there was another animal that appealed to him greatly. His friend Tabor had given him the tip—Tabor, who had the best Arabs in all India—and at a nice price. A man who practically never gambled, the Colonel liked to feel that his fancy would bring him in something really substantial—if it won; the idea that it could lose not really troubling him. However, they would see it in the paddock, and judge for themselves. The paddock was the place, away from all the dust and racket—Olive would enjoy the paddock! Once on the course, they neglected the first race; it was more important, the Colonel thought, that they should lunch. He wanted to see more colour in her cheeks, wanted to see her laugh. He had an invitation to his old regiment's drag, where the champagne was sure to be good. And he was so proud of her—would not have missed those young fellow's admiration of her for the world; though to take a lady amongst them was, in fact, against the rules. It was not, then, till the second race was due to start that they made their way into the paddock. Here the Derby horses were being led solemnly, attended each by a little posse of persons, looking up their legs and down their ribs to see whether they were worthy of support, together with a few who liked to see a whole horse at a time. Presently they found the animal which had been recommended to the Colonel. It was a chestnut, with a starred forehead, parading in a far corner. The Colonel, who really loved a horse, was deep in admiration. He liked its head and he liked its hocks; above all, he liked its eye. A fine creature, all sense and fire—perhaps just a little straight in the shoulder for coming down the hill! And in the midst of his examination he found himself staring at his niece. What breeding the child showed, with her delicate arched brows, little ears, and fine, close nostrils; and the way she moved—so sure and springy. She was too pretty to suffer! A shame! If she hadn't been so pretty that young fellow wouldn't have fallen in love with her. If she weren't so pretty—that husband of hers wouldn't——! And the Colonel dropped his gaze, startled by the discovery he had stumbled on. If she hadn't been so pretty! Was that the meaning of it all? The cynicism of his own reflection struck him between wind and water. And yet something in himself seemed to confirm it somehow. What then? Was he to let them tear her in two between them, destroying her, because she was so pretty? And somehow this discovery of his—that passion springs from worship of beauty and warmth, of form and colour—disturbed him horribly, for he had no habit of philosophy. The thought seemed to him strangely crude, even immoral. That she should be thus between two ravening desires—a bird between two hawks, a fruit between two mouths! It was a way of looking at things that had never before occurred to him. The idea of a husband clutching at his wife, the idea of that young man who looked so gentle, swooping down on her; and the idea that if she faded, lost her looks, went off, their greed, indeed, any man's, would die away— all these horrible ideas hurt him the more for the remarkable suddenness with which they had come to him. A tragic business! Dolly had said so. Queer and quick—were women! But his resolution that the day was to be jolly soon recurred to him, and he hastily resumed inspection of his fancy. Perhaps they ought to have a ten-pound note on it, and they had better get back to the Stand! And as they went the Colonel saw, standing beneath a tree at a little distance, a young man that he could have sworn was Lennan. Not likely for an artist chap to be down here! But it *was* undoubtedly young Lennan, brushed-up, in a top-hat. Fortunately, however, his face was not turned in their direction. He said nothing to Olive, not wishing—especially after those unpleasant thoughts —to take responsibility, and he kept her moving towards the gate, congratulating himself that his eyes had been so sharp. In the crush there he was separated from her a little, but she was soon beside him again; and more than ever he congratulated himself that nothing had occurred to upset her and spoil the day. Her cheeks were warm enough now, her dark eyes glowing. She was excited no doubt by thoughts of the race, and of the 'tenner' he was going to put on for her.

He recounted the matter afterwards to Mrs Ercott. 'That chestnut Tabor put me on to finished nowhere—couldn't get down the hill —knew it wouldn't the moment I set eyes on it. But the child enjoyed herself. Wish you'd been there, my dear!' Of his deeper thoughts and of that glimpse of young Lennan he did not speak, for on the way home an ugly suspicion had attacked him. Had the young fellow, after all, seen and managed to get close to her in the crush at the paddock gateway?

XIV

That letter of hers fanned the flame in Lennan as nothing had yet fanned it. Earthiness! Was it earthiness to love as he did? If so, then not for all the world would he be otherwise than earthy. In the shock of reading it, he crossed his Rubicon, and burned his boats behind him. No more did the pale ghost, chivalrous devotion, haunt him. He knew now that he could not stop short. Since she asked him, he must not, of course, try to see her just yet. But when he did, then he would fight for his life; the thought that she might be meaning to slip away from him was too utterly unbearable. But she could not be meaning that! She would never be so cruel! Ah! she would—she must come to him in the end! The world, life itself, would be well lost for love of her!

Thus resolved, he was even able to work again; and all that Tuesday he modelled at a big version of the fantastic, bull-like figure he had conceived after the Colonel left him up on the hillside at Beaulieu. He worked at it with a sort of evil joy. Into this creature he would put the spirit of possession that held her from him. And while his fingers forced the clay, he felt as if he had Cramier's neck within his grip. Yet, now that he had resolved to take her if he could, he had not quite the same hatred. After all, this man loved her too, could not help it that she loathed him; could not help it that he had the disposition of her, body and soul!

June had come in with skies of a blue that not even London glare and dust could pale. In every square and park and patch of green the air simmered with life and with the music of birds swaying on little boughs Piano organs in the streets were no longer wistful for the South; lovers already sat in the shade of trees.

To remain indoors, when he was not working, was sheer torture; for he could not read, and had lost all interest in the little excitements, amusements, occupations that go to make up the normal life of man. Every outer thing seemed to have dropped off, shrivelled, leaving him just a condition of the spirit, a state of mind.

Lying awake he would think of things in the past, and they would mean nothing—all dissolved and dispersed by the heat of this feeling in him. Indeed, his sense of isolation was so strong that he could not even believe that he had lived through the facts which his memory apprehended. He had become one burning mood—that, and nothing more.

To be out, especially amongst trees, was the only solace.

And he sat for a long time that evening under a large lime-tree on a knoll above the Serpentine. There was very little breeze, just enough to keep alive a kind of whispering. What if men and women, when they had lived their gusty lives, became trees! What if someone who had burned and ached were now spreading over him this leafy peace—this blue-black shadow against the stars? Or were the stars, perhaps, the souls of men and women escaped for ever from love and longing? He broke off a branch of the lime and drew it across his face. It was not yet in flower, but it smelled lemony and fresh even here in London. If only for a moment he could desert his own heart, and rest with the trees and stars!

No further letter came from her next morning, and he soon lost his power to work. It was Derby Day. He determined to go down. Perhaps she would be there. Even if she were not, he might find some little distraction in the crowd and the horses. He had seen her in the paddock long before the Colonel's sharp eyes detected him; and, following in the crush, managed to touch her hand in the crowded gateway, and whisper: 'To-morrow, the National Gallery, at four o'clock—by the Bacchus and Ariadne. For God's sake!' Her gloved hand pressed his hard; and she was gone. He stayed in the paddock, too happy almost to breathe. . . .

Next day, while waiting before that picture, he looked at it with wonder. For there seemed his own passion transfigured in the darkening star-crowned sky, and the eyes of the leaping god. In spirit, was he not always rushing to her like that? Minutes passed, and she did not come. What should he do if she failed him? Surely die of disappointment and despair. . . . He had little enough experience as yet of the toughness of the human heart; how life bruises and crushes, yet leaves it beating. . . . Then, from an unlikely quarter, he saw her coming.

They walked in silence down to the quiet rooms where the Turner watercolours hung. No one, save two Frenchmen and an old official, watched them passing slowly before those little pictures, till they came to the end wall, and, unseen, unheard by any but her, he could begin!

The arguments he had so carefully rehearsed were all forgotten; nothing left but an incoherent pleading. Life without her was not life; and they had only one life for love—one summer. It was all dark where she was not—the very sun itself was dark. Better to die than to live such false, broken lives, apart from each other. Better to die at once than to live wanting each other, longing and longing, and watching each other's sorrow. And all for the sake of what? It maddened, killed him, to think of that man touching her when he knew she did but hate him. It shamed all manhood; it could not be good to help such things to be. A vow when the spirit of it was gone was only superstition; it was wicked to waste one's life for the sake of that. Society—she knew, she must know —only cared for the forms, the outsides of things. And what did it matter what Society thought? It had no soul, no feeling, nothing. And if it were said they ought to sacrifice themselves for the sake of others, to make things happier in the world, she must know that was only true when love was light and selfish; but not when people loved as they did, with all their hearts and souls, so that they would die for each other any minute, so that without each other there was no meaning in anything. It would not help a single soul, for them to murder their love and all the happiness of their lives; to go on in a sort of living death. Even if it were wrong, he would rather do that wrong, and take the consequences! But it was not, it *could* not be wrong, when they felt like that!

And all the time that he was pouring forth those supplications, his eyes searched and searched her face. But there only came from her: 'I don't know—I can't tell—if only I knew!' And then he was silent, stricken to the heart; till, at a look or a touch from her, he would break out again: 'You do love me—you do; then what does anything else matter?'

And so it went on and on that summer afternoon, in the deserted room meant for such other things, where the two Frenchmen were too sympathetic, and the old official too drowsy, to come. Then it all narrowed to one fierce, insistent question:

'What is it—*what* is it you're afraid of?'

But to that, too, he got only the one mournful answer, paralysing in its fateful monotony.

'I don't know—I can't tell!'

It was awful to go on thus beating against this uncanny, dark, shadowy resistance; these unreal doubts and dreads, that by their very dumbness were becoming real to him, too. If only she could tell him what she feared! It could not be poverty—that was not like her—besides, he had enough for both. It could not be loss of a social position, which was but irksome to her! Surely it was not fear that he would cease to love her! What was it? In God's name —what?

To-morrow—she had told him—she was to go down alone, to the river-house; would she not come now, this very minute, to him

109

instead? And they would start off—that night, back to the South where their love had flowered. But again it was: 'I can't! I don't know—I must have time!' And yet her eyes had that brooding love-light. How *could* she hold back and waver? But, utterly exhausted, he did not plead again; did not even resist when she said: 'You must go, now; and leave me to get back! I will write. Perhaps—soon—I shall know.' He begged for, and took one kiss; then, passing the old official, went quickly up and out.

XV

He reached his rooms overcome by a lassitude that was not, however, quite despair. He had made his effort, failed—but was still within him the unconquerable hope of the passionate lover. . . . As well try to extinguish in full June the beating of the heart of summer; deny to the flowers their deepening hues, or to winged life its slumbrous buzzing, as stifle in such a lover his conviction of fulfilment. . . .

He lay down on a couch, and there stayed a long time quite still, his forehead pressed against the wall. His will was already beginning to recover for a fresh attempt. It was merciful that she was going away from Cramier, going to where he had in fancy watched her feed her doves. No laws, no fears, not even her commands could stop his fancy from conjuring her up by day and night. He had but to close his eyes, and she was there.

A ring at the bell, repeated several times, roused him at last to go to the door. His caller was Robert Cramier. And at sight of him, all Lennan's lethargy gave place to a steely feeling. What had brought him here? Had he been spying on his wife? The old longing for physical combat came over him. Cramier was perhaps fifteen years his senior, but taller, heavier, thicker. Chances, then, were pretty equal!

'Won't you come in?' he said.

'Thanks.'

The voice had in it the same mockery as on Sunday; and it shot through him that Cramier had thought to find his wife here. If so, he did not betray it by any crude look round. He came in with his deliberate step, light and well-poised for so big a man.

'So this,' he said, 'is where you produce your masterpieces! Anything great since you came back?'

Lennan lifted the cloths from the half-modelled figure of his bull-man. He felt malicious pleasure in doing that. Would Cramier recognise himself in this creature with the horn-like ears, and great bossed forehead? If this man who had her happiness beneath his heel had come here to mock, he should at all events get what he had come to give. And he waited.

'I see. You are giving the poor brute horns!'

If Cramier had seen, he had dared to add a touch of cynical humour, which the sculptor himself had never thought of. And this even evoked in the young man a kind of admiring compunction.

'Those are not horns,' he said gently; 'only ears.'

Cramier lifted a hand and touched the edge of his own ear.

'Not quite like that, are they—human ears? But I suppose you would call this symbolic. What, if I may ask, does it represent?'

All the softness in Lennan vanished.

'If you can't gather that from looking, it must be a failure.'

'Not at all. If I am right, you want something for it to tread on, don't you, to get your full effect?'

Lennan touched the base of the clay.

'The broken curve here'—then, with sudden disgust at this fencing, was silent. What had the man come for? He must want something. And, as if answering, Cramier said:

'To pass to another subject—you see a good deal of my wife. I just wanted to tell you that I don't very much care that you should. It is as well to be quite frank, I think.'

Lennan bowed.

'Is that not,' he said, 'perhaps rather a matter for *her* decision?'

That heavy figure—those threatening eyes! The whole thing was like a dream come true!

'I do not feel it so. I am not one of those who let things drift. Please understand me. You come between us at your peril.'

Lennan kept silence for a moment, then he said quietly:

'Can one come between two people who have ceased to have anything in common?'

The veins in Cramier's forehead were swollen, his face and neck had grown crimson. And Lennan thought with strange elation: Now he's going to hit me! He could hardly keep his hands from shooting out and seizing in advance that great strong neck. If he could strangle, and have done with him!

But, quite suddenly, Cramier turned on his heel. 'I have warned you,' he said, and went.

Lennan took a long breath. So! That was over, and he knew

111

where he was. If Cramier had struck out, he would surely have seized his neck and held on till life was gone. Nothing should have shaken him off. In fancy he could see himself swaying, writhing, reeling, battered about by those heavy fists, but always with his hands on the thick neck, squeezing out its life. He could feel, absolutely feel, the last reel and stagger of that great bulk crashing down, dragging him with it, till it lay upturned, still. He covered his eyes with his hands. . . . Thank God! The fellow had not hit out!

He went to the door, opened it, and stood leaning against the door-post. All was still and drowsy out there in that quiet backwater of a street. Not a soul in sight! How still, for London! Only the birds. In a neighbouring studio someone was playing Chopin. Queer! He had almost forgotten there was such a thing as Chopin. A mazurka! Spinning like some top thing, round and round—weird little tune! . . . Well, and what now? Only one thing certain. Sooner give up life than give her up! Far sooner! Love her, achieve her—or give up everything, and drown to that tune going on and on, that little dancing dirge of summer!

XVI

At her cottage Olive stood often by the river.

What lay beneath all that bright water—what strange, deep, swaying life, so far below the ruffling of wind, and the shadows of the willow trees? Was love down there, too? Love between sentient things, where it was almost dark; or had all passion climbed up to rustle with the reeds, and float with the water-flowers in the sunlight? Was there colour? Or had colour been drowned? No scent and no music; but movement there would be, for all the dim groping things bending one way to the current—movement, no less than in the aspen-leaves, never quite still, and the winged droves of the clouds. And if it were dark down there, it was dark, too, above the water; and hearts ached, and eyes just as much searched for that which did not come.

To watch it always flowing by to the sea; never looking back, never swaying this way or that; drifting along, quiet as Fate—dark, or glamorous with the gold and moonlight of these beautiful days and nights, when every flower in her garden, in the fields, and along the river banks, was full of sweet life; when dog-roses starred the lanes, and in the wood the bracken was nearly a foot high.

She was not alone there, though she would much rather have been; two days after she left London her Uncle and Aunt had joined her. It was from Cramier they had received their invitation. He himself had not yet been down.

Every night, having parted from Mrs Ercott and gone up the wide shallow stairs to her room, she would sit down at the window to write to Lennan, one candle beside her—one pale flame for comrade, as it might be his spirit. Every evening she poured out to him her thoughts, and ended always: 'Have patience!' She was still waiting for courage to pass that dark hedge of impalpable doubts and fears and scruples, of a dread that she could not make articulate even to herself. Having finished, she would lean out into the night. The Colonel, his black figure cloaked against the dew, would be pacing up and down the lawn, with his good-night cigar, whose fiery spark she could just discern; and, beyond, her ghostly dovehouse; and, beyond, the river—flowing. Then she would clasp herself close—afraid to stretch out her arms, lest she should be seen.

Each morning she rose early, dressed, and slipped away to the village to post her letter. From the woods across the river wild pigeons would be calling—as though Love itself pleaded with her afresh each day. She was back well before breakfast, to go up to her room and come down again as if for the first time. The Colonel, meeting her on the stairs, or in the hall, would say: 'Ah, my dear! just beaten you! Slept well?' And, while her lips touched his cheek, slanted at the proper angle for uncles, he never dreamed that she had been three miles already through the dew.

Now that she was in the throes of an indecision, whose ending, one way or the other, must be so tremendous, now that she was in the very swirl, she let no sign at all escape her; the Colonel and even his wife were deceived into thinking that after all no great harm had been done. It was grateful to them to think so, because of that stewardship at Monte Carlo, of which they could not render too good account. The warm sleepy days, with a little croquet and a little paddling on the river, and much sitting out of doors, when the Colonel would read aloud from Tennyson, were very pleasant. To him—if not to Mrs Ercott—it was especially jolly to be out of Town 'this confounded crowded time of year'. And so the days of early June went by, each finer than the last.

And then Cramier came down, without warning on a Friday evening. It was hot in London . . . the session dull. . . . The Jubilee turning everything upside down. . . . They were lucky to be out of Town!

A silent dinner—that!

Mrs Ercott noticed that he drank wine like water, and for minutes at a time fixed his eyes, that looked heavy as if he had not been sleeping, not on his wife's face but on her neck. If Olive really disliked and feared him—as John would have it—she disguised her feelings very well! For so pale a woman she was looking brilliant that night. The sun had caught her cheeks, perhaps. That black low-cut frock suited her, with old Milanesepoint lace matching her skin so well, and one carnation, of darkest red, at her breast. Her eyes were really sometimes like black velvet. It suited pale women to have those eyes, that looked so black at night! She was talking, too, and laughing more than usual. One would have said: A wife delighted to welcome her husband! And yet there was something—something in the air, in the feel of things—the lowering fixity of that man's eyes, or—thunder coming, after all this heat! Surely the night was unnaturally still and dark, hardly a breath of air, and so many moths out there, passing the beam of light, like little pale spirits crossing a river! Mrs Ercott smiled, pleased at that image. Moths! Men were like moths; there were women from whom they could not keep away. Yes, there was something about Olive that drew men to her. Not meretricious—to do her justice, not that at all; but something soft, and—fatal; like one of these candle-flames to the poor moths. John's eyes were never quite as she knew them when he was looking at Olive; and Robert Cramier's —what a queer, drugged look they had! As for that other poor young fellow—she had never forgotten his face when they came on him in the Park!

And when after dinner they sat on the veranda, they were all more silent still, just watching, it seemed, the smoke of their cigarettes, rising quite straight, as though wind had been withdrawn from the world. The Colonel twice endeavoured to speak about the moon: It ought to be up by now! It was going to be full.

And then Cramier said: 'Put on that scarf thing, Olive, and come round the garden with me.'

Mrs Ercott admitted to herself now that what John said was true. Just one gleam of eyes, turned quickly this way and that, as a bird looks for escape; and then Olive had got up and quietly gone with him down the path, till their silent figures were lost to sight.

Disturbed to the heart, Mrs Ercott rose and went over to her husband's chair. He was frowning, and staring at his evening shoe balanced on a single toe. He looked up at her and put out his hand. Mrs Ercott gave it a squeeze; she wanted comfort.

The Colonel spoke:
'It's heavy to-night, Dolly. I don't like the feel of it.'

XVII

They had passed without a single word spoken, down through the laurels and guelder roses to the river bank; then he had turned to the right, and gone along it under the dove-house, to the yew-trees. There he had stopped, in the pitch darkness of that foliage. It seemed to her dreadfully still; if only there had been the faintest breeze, the faintest lisping of reeds on the water, one bird to make a sound; but nothing, nothing save his breathing, deep, irregular, with a quiver in it. What had he brought her here for? To show her how utterly she was his? Was he never going to speak, never going to say whatever it was he had in mind to say? If only he would not touch her!

Then he moved, and a stone dislodged fell with a splash into the water. She could not help a little gasp. How black the river looked! But slowly, beyond the dim shape of the giant poplar, a shiver of light stole outwards across the blackness from the far bank—the moon, whose rim she could now see rising, of a thick gold like a coin, above the woods. Her heart went out to that warm light. At all events there was one friendly inhabitant of this darkness.

Suddenly she felt his hands on her waist. She did not move, her heart beat too furiously; but a sort of prayer fluttered up from it against her lips. In the grip of those heavy hands was such quivering force!

His voice sounded very husky and strange: 'Olive, this can't go on. I suffer. My God! I suffer!'

A pang went through her, a sort of surprise. Suffer! She might wish him dead, but she did not want him to suffer—God knew! And yet, gripped by those hands, she could not say: I am sorry!

He made a sound that was almost a groan, and dropped on his knees. Feeling herself held fast, she tried to push his forehead back from her waist. It was fiery hot; and she heard him mutter: 'Have mercy! Love me a little!' But the clutch of his hands, never still on the thin silk of her dress, turned her faint. She tried to writhe away, but could not; stood still again, and at last found her voice.

'Mercy? Can I *make* myself love? No one ever could since the world began. Please, please get up! Let me go!'

But he was pulling her down to him so that she was forced on to her knees on the grass, with her face close to his. A low moaning was coming from him. It was horrible—so horrible! And he went on pleading, the words all confused, not looking in her face. It seemed to her that it would never end, that she would never get free of that grip, away from that stammering, whispering voice. She stayed by instinct utterly still, closing her eyes. Then she felt his gaze for the first time that evening on her face, and realised that he had not dared to look until her eyes were closed, for fear of reading what was in them. She said very gently:

'Please let me go. I think I'm going to faint.'

He relaxed the grip of his arms; she sank down and stayed unmoving on the grass. After such utter stillness that she hardly knew whether he were there or not, she felt his hot hand on her bare shoulder. Was it all to begin again? She shrank down lower still, and a little moan escaped her. He let her go suddenly, and when at last she looked up, was gone.

She got to her feet trembling, and moved quickly from under the yew-trees. She tried to think—tried to understand exactly what this portended for her, for him, for her lover. But she could not. There was around her thoughts the same breathless darkness that brooded over this night. Ah! but to the night had been given that pale-gold moon-ray, to herself nothing, no faintest gleam; as well try to pierce below the dark surface of that water!

She passed her hands over her face, and hair, and dress. How long had it lasted? How long had they been out here? And she began slowly moving back towards the house. Thank God! She had not yielded to fear or pity, not uttered falsities, not pretended she could love him, and betrayed her heart. That would have been the one unbearable thing to have been left remembering! She stood long looking down, as if trying to see the future in her dim flower-beds; then, bracing herself, hurried to the house. No one was on the veranda, no one in the drawing-room. She looked at the clock. Nearly eleven. Ringing for the servant to shut the windows, she stole up to her room. Had her husband gone away as he had come? Or would she presently again be face to face with that dread, the nerve of which never stopped aching now, dread of the night when he was near. She determined not to go to bed, and drawing a long chair to the window, wrapped herself in a gown, and lay back.

The flower from her dress, miraculously uncrushed in those dark minutes on the grass, she set in water beside her at the window— Mark's favourite flower, he had once told her; it was a comfort, with its scent, and hue, and memory of him.

Strange that in her life, with all the faces seen, and people known, she had not loved one till she had met Lennan! She had even been sure that love would never come to her; had not wanted it—very much; had thought to go on well enough, and pass out at the end, never having known, or much cared to know, full summer. Love had taken its revenge on her now for all slighted love offered her in the past; for the one hated love that had to-night been on its knees to her. They said it must always come once to every man and woman—this witchery, this dark sweet feeling, springing up, who knew how or why? She had not believed, but now she knew. And whatever might be coming, she would not have this different. Since all things changed, she must change and get old and be no longer pretty for him to look at, but this in her heart could not change. She felt sure of that. It was as if something said : This is for ever, beyond life, beyond death, this is for ever! He will be dust, and you dust, but your love will live! Somewhere—in the woods, among the flowers, or down in the dark water, it will haunt! For it only you have lived! . . . Then she noticed that a slender silvery-winged thing, unlike any moth she had ever seen, had settled on her gown, close to her neck. It seemed to be sleeping, so delicate and drowsy, having come in from the breathless dark, thinking, perhaps, that her whiteness was a light. What dim memory did it rouse; something of *him*, something *he* had done— in darkness, on a night like this. Ah, yes! that evening after Gorbio, the little owl-moth on her knee! He had touched her when he took that cosy wan velvet-eyed thing off her!

She leaned out for air. What a night!—whose stars were hiding in the sheer heavy warmth; whose small, round, golden moon had no transparency! A night like a black pansy with a little gold heart. And silent! For, of the trees, that whispered so much at night, not even the aspens had voice. The unstirring air had a dream-solidity against her cheeks. But in all the stillness, what sentiency, what passion—as in her heart! Could she not draw *him* to her from those woods, from that dark gleaming river, draw him from the flowers and trees and the passion-mood of the sky—draw him up to her waiting here, so that she was no more this craving creature, but one with him and the night! And she let her head droop down on her hands.

All night long she stayed there at the window. Sometimes dozing in the chair; once waking with a start, fancying that her husband was bending over her. Had he been—and stolen away? And the dawn came; dew-grey, filmy and wistful, woven round each black tree, and round the white dove-cot, and falling scarf-like along the river. And the chirrupings of birds stirred among leaves as yet invisible.

She slept then.

XVIII

When she awoke once more, in daylight, smiling, Cramier was standing beside her chair. His face, all dark and bitter, had the sodden look of a man very tired.

'So!' he said: 'Sleeping this way doesn't spoil your dreams. Don't let me disturb them. I am just going back to Town.'

Like a frightened bird, she stayed, not stirring, gazing at his back as he leaned in the window, till, turning round on her again, he said:

'But remember this: What I can't have, no one else shall! Do you understand? No one else!' And he bent down close, repeating: 'Do you understand—you bad wife!'

Four years' submission to a touch she shrank from; one long effort not to shrink! Bad wife! Not if he killed her would she answer now!

'Do you hear?' he said once more: 'Make up your mind to that. I mean it.'

He had gripped the arms of her chair, till she could feel it quiver beneath her. Would he drive his fist into her face that she managed to keep still smiling? But there only passed into his eyes an expression which she could not read.

'Well,' he said, 'you know!' and walked heavily towards the door.

The moment he had gone she sprang up: Yes, she was a bad wife! A wife who had reached the end of her tether. A wife who hated instead of loving. A wife in prison! Bad wife! Martyrdom, then, for the sake of a faith in her that was lost already, could be but folly. If she seemed bad and false to him, there was no longer reason to pretend to be otherwise. No longer would she, in the words of the old song: 'sit and sigh—pulling bracken, pulling bracken.' No more would she starve for want of love, and watch the nights throb and ache, as last night had throbbed and ached, with the passion that she might not satisfy.

And while she was dressing she wondered why she did not look tired. To get out quickly! To send her lover word at once to hasten

118

to her while it was safe—that she might tell him she was coming
to him out of prison! She would telegraph for him to come that
evening with a boat, opposite the tall poplar. She and her Aunt and
Uncle were to go to dinner at the Rectory, but she would plead
headache at the last minute. When the Ercotts had gone she would
slip out, and he and she would row over to the wood, and be together for two hours of happiness. And they must make a clear
plan, too—for to-morrow they would begin their life together. But
it would not be safe to send that message from the village; she
must go down and over the bridge to the post-office on the other
side, where they did not know her. It was too late now before
breakfast. Better after, when she could slip away, knowing for
certain that her husband had gone. It would still not be too late for
her telegram—Lennan never left his rooms till the midday post
which brought her letters.

She finished dressing, and knowing that she must show no trace
of her excitement, sat quite still for several minutes, forcing herself
into languor. Then she went down. Her husband had breakfasted
and gone. At everything she did, and every word she spoke, she
was now smiling with a sort of wonder, as if she were watching a
self, that she had abandoned like an old garment, perform for her
amusement. It even gave her no feeling of remorse to think she was
going to do what would be so painful to the good Colonel. He was
dear to her—but it did not matter. She was past all that. Nothing
mattered—nothing in the world! It amused her to believe that her
Uncle and Aunt misread her last night's walk in the dark garden,
misread her languor and serenity. And at the first moment possible
she flew out, and slipped away under cover of the yew-trees towards the river. Passing the spot where her husband had dragged
her down to him on her knees in the grass, she felt a sort of surprise that she could ever have been so terrified. What was he? The
past—nothing! And she flew on. She noted carefully the river bank
opposite the tall poplar. It would be quite easy to get down from
there into a boat. But they would not stay in that dark backwater.
They would go over to the far side into those woods from which
last night the moon had risen, those woods from which the pigeons
mocked her every morning, those woods so full of summer. Coming
back, no one would see her landing; for it would be pitch dark in
the backwater. And, while she hurried, she looked back across her
shoulder, marking where the water, entering, ceased to be bright.
A dragon-fly brushed her cheek; she saw it vanish where the sunlight failed. How suddenly its happy flight was ·quenched in that

dark shade, as a candle flame blown out. The tree growth there was too thick—the queer stumps and snags had uncanny shapes, as of monstrous creatures, whose eyes seemed to peer out at you. She shivered. She had seen those monsters with their peering eyes somewhere. Ah! In her dream at Monte Carlo of that bull-face staring from the banks, while she drifted by, unable to cry out. No! The backwater was not a happy place—they would not stay there a single minute. And more swiftly than ever she flew on along the path. Soon she had crossed the bridge, sent off her message, and returned. But there were ten hours to get through before eight o'clock, and she did not hurry now. She wanted this day of summer to herself alone, a day of dreaming till he came; this day for which all her life till now had been shaping her—the day of love. Fate was very wonderful! If she had ever loved before; if she had known joy in her marriage—she could never have been feeling what she was feeling now, what she well knew she would never feel again. She crossed a new-mown hayfield, and finding a bank, threw herself down on her back among its uncut grasses. Far away at the other end men were scything. It was all very beautiful—the soft clouds floating, the clover-stalks pushing themselves against her palms, and stems of the tall couch grass cool to her cheeks; little blue butterflies; a lark, invisible; the scent of the ripe hay; and the gold-fairy arrows of the sun on her face and limbs. To grow and reach the hour of summer; all must do that! That was the meaning of Life! She had no more doubts and fears. She had no more dreads, no bitterness, and no remorse for what she was going to do. She was doing it because she must. . . . As well might grass stay its ripening because it shall be cut down! She had, instead, a sense of something blessed and uplifting. Whatever Power had made her heart, had placed within it this love. Whatever it was, whoever it was, could not be angry with her!

A wild bee settled on her arm, and she held it up between her and the sun, so that she might enjoy its dusky glamour. It would not sting her—not to-day! The little blue butterflies, too, kept alighting on her, who lay there so still. And the love-songs of the wood-pigeons never ceased, nor the faint swish of scything.

At last she rose to make her way home. A telegram had come saying simply: 'Yes.' She read it with an unmoved face, having resorted again to her mask of languor. Towards tea-time she confessed to headache, and said she would lie down. Up there in her room she spent those three hours writing—writing as best she could all she had passed through in thought and feeling, before making her decision. It seemed to her that she owed it to herself to tell her lover how she had come to what she had never thought to come to. She put what she had written in an envelope and sealed it. She would give it to him, that he might read and understand, when she had shown him with all of her how she loved him. It would pass the time for him, until to-morrow—until they set out on their new life together. For to-night they would make their plans, and to-morrow start.

At half-past seven she sent word that her headache was too bad to allow her to go out. This brought a visit from Mrs Ercott: The Colonel and she were so distressed; but perhaps Olive was wise not to exert herself! And presently the Colonel himself spoke, lugubriously through the door: Not well enough to come? No fun without her! But she mustn't on any account strain herself! No, no!

Her heart smote her at that. He was always so good to her.

At last, watching from the corridor, she saw them sally forth down the drive—the Colonel a little in advance, carrying his wife's evening shoes. How nice he looked—with his brown face, and his grey moustache; so upright, and concerned with what he had in hand!

There was no languor in her now. She had dressed in white, and now she took a blue silk cloak with a hood, and caught up the flower that had so miraculously survived last night's wearing and pinned it at her breast. Then making sure no servant was about, she slipped downstairs and out. It was just eight, and the sun still glistened on the dove-cot. She kept away from that lest the birds should come fluttering about her, and betray her by cooing. When she had nearly reached the tow-path, she stopped affrighted. Surely something had moved, something heavy, with a sound of broken branches. Was it the memory of last night come on her again; or, indeed, someone there? She walked back a few steps. Foolish alarm! In the meadow beyond a cow was brushing against the hedge. And, stealing along the grass, out on to the tow-path, she went swiftly towards the poplar.

XIX

A hundred times in these days of her absence Lennan had been on the point of going down, against her orders, just to pass the house, just to feel himself within reach, to catch a glimpse of her, perhaps, from afar. If his body haunted London, his spirit had passed down on to that river where he had drifted once already, reconnoitring. A hundred times—by day in fancy, and by night in dreams—pulling himself along by the boughs, he stole down that dim backwater, till the dark yews and the white dove-cot came into view.

For he thought now only of fulfilment. She was wasting cruelly away! Why should he leave her where she was? Leave her to profane herself and all womanhood in the arms of a man she hated?

And on that day of mid-June, when he received her telegram, it was as if he had been handed the key of Paradise.

Would she—could she mean to come away with him that very night? He would prepare for that at all events. He had so often in mind faced this crisis in his affairs, that now it only meant translating into action what had been carefully thought out. He packed, supplied himself liberally with money, and wrote a long letter to his guardian. It would hurt the old man—Gordy was over seventy now—but that could not be helped. He would not post it till he knew for certain.

After telling how it had all come about, he went on thus: 'I know that to many people, and perhaps to you, Gordy, it will seem very wrong, but it does not to me, and that is the simple truth. Everybody has his own views on such things, I suppose; and as I would not—on my honour, Gordy—ever have held or wished to hold, or ever will hold in marriage or out of marriage, any woman who does not love me, so I do not think it is acting as I would resent others acting towards me, to take away from such unhappiness this lady for whom I would die at any minute. I do not mean to say that pity has anything to do with it—I thought so at first, but I know now that it is all swallowed up in the most mighty feeling I have ever had or ever shall have. I am not a bit afraid of conscience. If God is Universal Truth, He cannot look hardly upon us for being true to ourselves. And as to people, we shall just hold up our heads; I think that they generally take you at your own valuation. But, anyway, Society does not much matter. We shan't want those who don't want us—you may be sure. I hope he will divorce her quickly—there is nobody much to be hurt by that except you and Cis; but if he doesn't—it can't be helped. I don't think she has anything; but with my six hundred, and what I can make, even if we have to live abroad, we shall be all right for money. You have been awfully good to me always,

Gordy, and I am very grieved to hurt you, and still more sorry if you think I am being ungrateful; but when one feels as I do—body and soul and spirit—there isn't any question; there wouldn't be if death itself stood in the way. If you receive this, we shall be gone together; I will write to you from wherever we pitch our tent, and, of course, I shall write to Cicely. But will you please tell Mrs Doone and Sylvia, and give them my love if they still care to have it. Good-bye, dear Gordy. I believe you would have done the same, if you had been I. Always your affectionate—MARK.'

In all those preparations he forgot nothing, employing every minute of the few hours in a sort of methodic exaltation. The last thing before setting out he took the damp cloths off his 'bull-man'. Into the face of the monster there had come of late a hungry, yearning look. The artist in him had done his work that unconscious justice; against his will had set down the truth. And, wondering whether he would ever work at it again, he re-damped the cloths and wrapped it carefully.

He did not go to her village, but to one five or six miles down the river—it was safer, and the row would steady him. Hiring a skiff, he pulled up stream. He travelled very slowly to kill time, keeping under the far bank. And as he pulled, his very heart seemed parched with nervousness. Was it real that he was going to her, or only some fantastic trick of Fate, a dream from which he would wake to find himself alone again? He passed the dove-cot at last, and kept on till he could round into the backwater and steal up under cover to the poplar. He arrived a few minutes before eight o'clock, turned the boat round, and waited close beneath the bank, holding to a branch, and standing so that he could see the path. If a man could die from longing and anxiety, surely Lennan must have died then!

All wind had failed, and the day was fallen into a wonderful still evening. Gnats were dancing in the sparse strips of sunlight that slanted across the dark water, now that the sun was low. From the fields, bereft of workers, came the scent of hay and the heavy scent of meadow-sweet; the musky odour of the backwater was confused with them into one brooding perfume. No one passed. And sounds were few and far to that wistful listener, for birds did not sing just there. How still and warm was the air, yet seemed to vibrate against his cheeks as though about to break into flame. That fancy came to him vividly while he stood waiting—a vision of heat simmering in little pale red flames. On the thick reeds some large, slow, dusky flies were still feeding, and now and then a moor-

123

hen a few yards away splashed a little, or uttered a sharp, shrill note. When she came—if she did come!—they would not stay here, in this dark earthy backwater; he would take her over to the other side, away to the woods! But the minutes passed, and his heart sank. Then it leaped up. Someone was coming—in white, with bare head, and something blue or black flung across her arm. It was she! No one else walked like that! She came very quickly. And he noticed that her hair looked like little wings on either side of her brow, as if her face were a white bird with dark wings, flying to love! Now she was close, so close that he could see her lips parted, and her eyes love-lighted—like nothing in the world but darkness wild with dew and starlight. He reached up and lifted her down into the boat, and the scent of some flower pressed against his face seemed to pierce into h m and reach his very heart, awakening the memory of something past, forgotten. Then, seizing the branches, snapping them in his haste, he dragged the skiff along through the sluggish water, the gnats dancing in his face. She seemed to know where he was taking her, and neither of them spoke a single word, while he pulled out into the open, and over to the far bank.

There was but one field between them and the wood—a field of young wheat, with a hedge of thorn and alder. And close to that hedge they set out, their hands clasped. They had nothing to say yet—like children saving up. She had put on her cloak to hide her dress, and its silk swished against the silvery blades of the wheat. What had moved her to put on this blue cloak? Blue of the sky, and flowers, of birds' wings, and the black-burning blue of the night! The hue of all holy things! And how still it was in the late gleam of the sun! Not one little sound of beast or bird or tree; not one bee humming! And not much colour—only the starry white hemlocks and globe-campion flowers, and the low-flying glamour of the last warm light on the wheat.

XX

. . . Now over wood and river the evening drew in fast. And first the swallows, that had looked as if they would never stay their hunting, ceased; and the light, that had seemed fastened above the world, for all its last brightenings, slowly fell wingless and dusky.

The moon would not rise till ten! And all things waited. The creatures of night were slow to come forth after that long bright summer's day, watching for the shades of the trees to sink deeper into the now chalk-white water; watching for the chalk-white face of the sky to be masked with velvet. The very black-plumed trees themselves seemed to wait in suspense for the grape-bloom of night. All things stared, wan in that hour of passing day—all things had eyes wistful and unblessed. In those moments glamour was so dead that it was as if meaning had abandoned the earth. But not for long. Winged with darkness, it stole back; not the soul of meaning that had gone, but a witch-like and brooding spirit harbouring in the black trees, in the high dark spears of the rushes, and on the grim-snouted snags that lurked along the river bank. Then the owls came out, and night-flying things. And in the wood there began a cruel bird-tragedy—some dark pursuit in the twilight above the bracken; the piercing shrieks of a creature into whom talons have again and again gone home; and mingled with them, hoarse raging cries of triumph. Many minutes they lasted, those noises of the night, sound-emblems of all the cruelty in the heart of Nature; till at last death appeased that savagery. And any soul abroad, that pitied fugitives, might once more listen, and not weep . . .

Then a nightingale began to give forth its long liquid gurgling; and a corn-crake churred in the young wheat. Again the night brooded, in the silent tops of the trees, in the more silent depths of the water. It sent out at long intervals a sigh or murmur, a tiny scuttling splash, an owl's hunting cry. And its breath was still hot and charged with heavy odour, for no dew was falling. . . .

XXI

It was past ten when they came out from the wood. She had wanted to wait for the moon to rise; not a gold coin of a moon as last night, but ivory pale, and with a gleaming radiance level over the fern, and covering the lower boughs, as it were, with a drift of white blossom.

Through the wicket gate they passed once more beside the moon-coloured wheat, which seemed of a different world from that world in which they had walked but an hour and a half ago.

And in Lennan's heart was a feeling such as a man's heart can only know once in all his life—such humble gratitude, and praise, and adoration of her who had given him her all. There should be nothing for her now but joy—like the joy of this last hour. She should never know less happiness! And kneeling down before her at the water's edge he kissed her dress, and hands, and feet, which to-morrow would be his for ever.

Then they got into the boat.

The smile of the moonlight glided over each ripple, and reed, and closing water-lily; over her face, where the hood had fallen back from her loosened hair; over one hand trailing the water, and the other touching the flower at her breast; and, just above her breath, she said:

'Row, my dear love; it's late!'

Dipping his sculls, he shot the skiff into the darkness of the backwater. . . .

What happened then he never knew, never clearly—in all those after years. A vision of her white form risen to its feet, bending forward like a creature caught, that cannot tell which way to spring; a crashing shock, his head striking something hard! Nothingness! And then—an awful, awful struggle with roots and weeds and slime, a desperate agony of groping in that pitchy blackness, among tree-stumps, in dead water that seemed to have no bottom —he and that other, who had leaped at them in the dark with his boat, like a murdering beast; a nightmare search more horrible than words could tell, till in a patch of moonlight on the bank they laid her, who for all their efforts never stirred. . . . There she lay all white, and they two crouched at her head and feet—like dark creatures of the woods and waters over that which with their hunting they had slain.

How long they stayed there, not once looking at each other, not once speaking, not once ceasing to touch with their hands that dead thing—he never knew. How long in the summer night, with its moonlight and its shadows quivering round them, and the night wind talking in the reeds!

And then the most enduring of all sentient things had moved in him again; so that he once more felt. . . . Never again to see those eyes that had loved him with their light! Never again to kiss her lips! Frozen—like moonlight to the earth, with the flower still clinging at her breast. Thrown out on the bank like a plucked water-lily! Dead? No, no! Not dead! Alive in the night—alive to him—somewhere! Not on this dim bank, in this hideous back-water, with that dark dumb creature who had destroyed her! Out there on the river—in the wood of their happiness—somewhere alive! . . . And, staggering up past Cramier, who never moved,

he got into his boat, and like one demented pulled out into the stream.

But once there in the tide, he fell huddled forward, motionless above his oars. . . .

And the moonlight flooded his dark skiff drifting down. And the moonlight effaced the ripples on the water that had stolen away her spirit. Her spirit mingled now with the white beauty and the shadows, for ever part of the stillness and the passion of a summer night; hovering, floating, listening to the rustle of the reeds, and the whispering of the woods; one with the endless dream —that spirit passing out, as all might wish to pass, in the hour of happiness.

Part III

AUTUMN

I

WHEN on that November night Lennan stole to the open door of his dressing-room, and stood watching his wife asleep, Fate still waited for an answer.

A low fire was burning—one of those fires that throw faint shadows everywhere, and once and again glow so that some object shines for a moment, some shape is clearly seen. The curtains were not quite drawn, and a plane-tree branch with leaves still hanging, which had kept them company all the fifteen years they had lived there, was moving darkly in the wind, now touching the glass with a frail tap, as though asking of him, who had been roaming in that wind so many hours, to let it in. Unfailing comrades—London plane-trees!

He had not dared hope that Sylvia would be asleep. It was merciful that she was, whichever way the issue went—that issue so cruel! Her face was turned towards the fire, and one hand rested beneath her cheek. So she often slept. Even when life seemed all at sea, its landmarks lost, one still did what was customary. Poor tender-hearted thing—she had not slept since he told her, forty-eight hours, that seemed such years, ago! With her flaxen hair, and her touching candour, even in sleep, she looked like a girl lying there, not so greatly changed from what she had been that summer of Cicely's marriage down at Hayle. Her face had not grown old in all those twenty-eight years. There had been till now no special reason why it should. Thought, strong feeling, suffering, those were what changed faces; Sylvia had never thought very deeply, never suffered much, till now. And was it for him, who had been careful of her—very careful on the whole, despite man's selfishness, despite her never having understood the depths of him —was it for him of all people to hurt her so, to stamp her face with sorrow, perhaps destroy her utterly?

He crept a little farther in and sat down in the armchair beyond the fire. What memories a fire gathered into it, with its flaky ashes, its little leaf-like flames, and that quiet glow and flicker!

What tale of passions! How like to a fire was a man's heart! The first young fitful leapings, the sudden, fierce, mastering heat, the long, steady sober burning, and then—that last flaming-up, that clutch back at its own vanished youth, the final eager flight of flame, before the ashes wintered it to nothing! Visions and memories he saw down in the fire, as only can be seen when a man's heart, by the agony of long struggle, has been stripped of skin, and quivers at every touch. Love! A strange haphazard thing was love —so spun between ecstasy and torture! A thing insidious, irresponsible, desperate. A flying sweetness, more poignant than anything on earth, more dark in origin and destiny. A thing without reason or coherence. A man's love-life—what say had he in the ebb and flow of it? No more than in the flights of autumn birds, swooping down, alighting here and there, passing on. The loves one left behind—even in a life by no means vagabond in love, as men's lives went! The love that thought the Tyrol skies would fall if he were not first with a certain lady. The love whose star had caught in the hair of Sylvia, now lying there asleep. A so-called love—that half-glamorous, yet sordid little meal of pleasure, which youth, however sensitive, must eat, it seems, some time or other with some young light of love—a glimpse of life that beforehand had seemed much and had meant little, save to leave him disillusioned with himself and sorry for his partner. And then the love that he could not, even after twenty years, bear to remember; that all-devouring summer passion, which in one night had gained all and lost all terribly, leaving on his soul a scar that could never be quite healed, leaving his spirit always a little lonely, haunted by the sense of what might have been. Of his share in that night of tragedy —that 'terrible accident on the river'—no one had ever dreamed. And then the long despair which had seemed the last death of love had slowly passed, and yet another love had been born—or rather born again, pale, sober, but quite real; the fresh springing-up of a feeling long forgotten, of that protective devotion of his boyhood. He still remembered the expression on Sylvia's face when he passed her by chance in Oxford Street, soon after he came back from his four years of exile in the East and Rome—that look, eager, yet reproachful, then stoically ironic, as if saying: 'Oh, no! after forgetting me four years and more—you can't remember me now!' And when he spoke, the still more touching pleasure in her face. Then uncertain months, with a feeling of what the end would be; and then their marriage. Happy enough—gentle, not very vivid, nor spiritually very intimate—his work always secretly as remote from her as when she had thought to please him by putting jessamine stars on the heads of his beasts. A quiet successful union, not meaning, he had thought, so very much to him nor so very much to her—until forty-eight hours ago he told her; and she had shrunk, and wilted, and gone all to pieces. And what was it he had told her?

A long story—that!

Sitting there by the fire, with nothing yet decided, he could see it all from the start, with its devilish, delicate intricacy, its subtle slow enchantment spinning itself out of him, out of his own state of mind and body, rather than out of the spell cast over him, as though a sort of fatal force, long dormant, were working up again to burst into dark flower. . . .

II

Yes, it had begun within him over a year ago, with a queer unhappy restlessness, a feeling that life was slipping, ebbing away within reach of him, and his arms never stretched out to arrest it. It had begun with a sort of long craving, stilled only when he was working hard—a craving for he knew not what, an ache which was worst whenever the wind was soft.

They said that about forty-five was a perilous age for a man—especially for an artist. All the autumn of last year he had felt this vague misery rather badly. It had left him alone most of December and January, while he was working so hard at his group of lions; but the moment that was finished it had gripped him hard again. In those last days of January he well remembered wandering about in the parks day after day, trying to get away from it. Mild weather, with a scent in the wind! With what avidity he had watched children playing, the premature buds on the bushes, anything, everything young—with what an ache, too, he had been conscious of innumerable lives being lived round him, and loves loved, and he outside, unable to know, to grasp, to gather them; and all the time the sands of his hourglass running out! A most absurd and unreasonable feeling for a man with everything he wanted, with work that he loved, quite enough money, and a wife so good as Sylvia—a feeling that no Englishman of forty-six, in excellent health, ought for a moment to have been troubled with. A feeling such as, indeed, no Englishman ever admitted having—so that there was not even, as yet, a Society for its suppression.

For what was this disquiet feeling, but the sense that he had had his day, would never again know the stir and fearful joy of falling in love, but only just hanker after what was past and gone! Could anything be more reprehensible in a married man?

It was—yes—the last day of January, when, returning from one of those restless rambles in Hyde Park, he met Dromore. Queer to recognise a man hardly seen since school-days. Yet unmistakably, Johnny Dromore, sauntering along the rails of Piccadilly on the Green Park side, with that slightly rolling gait of his thin, horse-man's legs, his dandified hat a little to one side, those strange, chaffing, goggling eyes, that look, as if making a perpetual bet. Yes —the very same teasing, now moody, now reckless, always astute Johnny Dromore, with a good heart beneath an outside that seemed ashamed of it. Truly to have shared a room at school—to have been at College together, were links mysteriously indestructible.

'Mark Lennan! By gum! haven't seen you for ages. Not since you turned out a full-blown—what d'you call it? Awfully glad to meet you, old chap!'

Here was the past indeed, long vanished in feeling and thought and all; and Lennan's head buzzed, trying to find some common interest with this hunting, racing man-about-town.

Johnny Dromore come to life again—he whom the Machine had stamped with astute simplicity by the time he was twenty-two, and for ever after left untouched in thought and feeling—Johnny Dromore, who would never pass beyond the philosophy that all was queer and freakish which had not to do with horses, women, wine, cigars, jokes, good-heartedness, and that perpetual bet; Johnny Dromore, who, somewhere in him, had a pocket of depth, a streak of hunger, that was not just Johnny Dromore.

How queer was the sound of that jerky talk!

'You ever see old Fookes now? Been racin' at all? You live in Town? Remember good old Blenker?' And then silence, and then another spurt: 'Ever go down to "Bambury's"? Ever go racin'? . . . Come on up to my "digs". You've got nothin' to do.' No per-suading Johnny Dromore that a "what d'you call it" could have anything to do. 'Come on, old chap. I've got the hump. It's this damned east wind.'

Well he remembered it, when they shared a room at 'Bambury's' —that hump of Johnny Dromore's, after some reckless spree or bout of teasing.

And down that narrow bye-street of Piccadilly he had gone, and up into those 'digs' on the first floor, with their little dark hall, their Van Beers' drawing and *Vanity Fair* cartoons, and prints of racehorses, and of the old Nightgown Steeplechase; with the big chairs, and all the paraphernalia of Race Guides and race-glasses, fox-masks and stags'-horns, and hunting-whips. And yet, something that from the first moment struck him as not quite in keeping, foreign to the picture—a little jumble of books, a vase of flowers, a grey kitten.

'Sit down, old chap. What'll you drink?'

Sunk into the recesses of a marvellous chair, with huge arms of tawny leather, he listened and spoke drowsily. 'Bambury's', Oxford, Gordy's clubs—dear old Gordy, gone now!—things long passed by; they seemed all round him once again. And yet, always that vague sense, threading this resurrection, threading the smoke of their cigars, and Johnny Dromore's clipped talk—of something that did not quite belong. Might it be, perhaps, that sepia drawing—above the 'Tantalus' on the oak sideboard at the far end—of a woman's face gazing out into the room? Mysteriously unlike every-thing else, except the flowers, and this kitten that was pushing its furry little head against his hand. Odd how a single thing some-times took possession of a room, however remote in spirit! It seemed to reach like a shadow over Dromore's outstretched limbs, and weathered, long-nosed face, behind his huge cigar; over the queer, solemn, chaffing eyes, with something brooding in the depths of them.

'Ever get the hump? Bally awful, isn't it? It's getting old. We're bally old, you know, Lenny!' Ah! No one had called him 'Lenny' for twenty years. And it was true; they were unmentionably old.

'When a fellow begins to feel old, you know, it's time he went broke—or something; doesn't bear sittin' down and lookin' at. Come out to "Monte" with me!'

'Monte!' That old wound, never quite healed, started throbbing at the word, so that he could hardly speak his: 'No, I don't care for "Monte".'

And, at once, he saw Dromore's eyes probing, questioning:

'You married?'

'Yes.'

'Never thought of you as married!'

So Dromore did think of him. Queer! He never thought of Johnny Dromore.

'Winter's bally awful, when you're not huntin'. You've changed a lot; should hardly have known you. Last time I saw you, you'd just come back from Rome or somewhere. What's it like bein' a

—a sculptor? Saw something of yours once. Ever do things of horses?'

Yes; he had done a 'relief' of ponies only last year.

'You do women, too, I s'pose?'

'Not often.'

The eyes goggled slightly. Quaint, that unholy interest! Just like boys, the Johnny Dromores—would never grow up, no matter how life treated them. If Dromore spoke out his soul, as he used to speak it out at 'Bambury's' he would say: 'You get a pull there; you have a bally good time, I expect.' That was the way it took them; just a converse manifestation of the very same feeling towards Art that the pious Philistines had, with their deploring eyebrows and their 'peril to the soul'. Babes all! Not a glimmering of what Art meant—of its effort, and its yearnings!

'You make money at it?'

'Oh, yes.'

Again that appreciative goggle, as who should say: 'Ho! there's more in this than I thought!'

A long silence, then, in the dusk with the violet glimmer from outside the windows, the fire flickering in front of them, the grey kitten purring against his neck, the smoke of their cigars going up, and such a strange, dozing sense of rest, as he had not known for many days. And then—something, someone at the door, over by the sideboard! And Dromore speaking in a queer voice:

'Come in, Nell! D'you know my daughter?'

A hand took Lennan's, a hand that seemed to waver between the aplomb of a woman of the world, and a child's impulsive warmth. And a voice, young, clipped, clear, said:

'How d'you do? She's rather sweet, isn't she—my kitten?'

Then Dromore turned the light up. A figure fairly tall, in a grey riding-habit, stupendously well cut; a face not quite so round as a child's nor so shaped as a woman's, blushing slightly, very calm; crinkly light-brown hair tied back with a black ribbon under a neat hat; and eyes like those eyes of Gainsborough's 'Perdita'—slow, grey, mesmeric, with long lashes curling up, eyes that draw things to them, still innocent.

And just on the point of saying: 'I thought you'd stepped out of that picture'—he saw Dromore's face, and mumbled instead:

'So it's *your* kitten?'

'Yes; she goes to everbody. Do you like Persians? She's all fur really. Feel!'

Entering with his fingers the recesses of the kitten, he said:

'Cats without fur are queer.'

'Have you seen one without fur?'

'Oh, yes! In my profession we have to go below fur—I'm a sculptor.'

'That must be awfully interesting.'

What a woman of the world! But what a child, too! And now he could see that the face in the sepia drawing was older altogether —lips not so full, look not so innocent, cheeks not so round, and something sad and desperate about it—a face that life had rudely touched. But the same eyes it had—and what charm, for all its disillusionment, its air of a history! Then he noticed, fastened to the frame, on a thin rod, a dust-coloured curtain, drawn to one side. The self-possessed young voice was saying:

'Would you mind if I showed you my drawings? It would be awfully good of you. You could tell me about them.' And with dismay he saw her open a portfolio. While he scrutinised those school-girl drawings, he could feel her looking at him, as animals do when they are making up their minds whether or no to like you; then she came and stood so close that her arm pressed his. He redoubled his efforts to find something good about the drawings. But in truth there was nothing good. And if, in other matters, he could lie well enough to save people's feelings, where Art was concerned he never could; so he merely said:

'You haven't been taught, you see.'

'Will you teach me?'

But before he could answer, she was already effacing that naïve question in her most grown-up manner.

'Of course I oughtn't to ask. It would bore you awfully.'

After that he vaguely remembered Dromore's asking if he ever rode in the Row; and those eyes of hers following him about; and her hand giving his another childish squeeze. Then he was on his way again down the dimly-lighted stairs, past an interminable array of *Vanity Fair* cartoons, out into the east wind.

III

Crossing the Green Park on his way home, was he more, or less, restless? Difficult to say. A little flattered, certainly, a little warmed; yet irritated, as always when he came into contact with people to whom the world of Art was such an amusing unreality. The notion of trying to show that child how to draw—that feather-pate, with her riding and her kitten; and her 'Perdita' eyes! Quaint, how she had at once made friends with him! He was a little different, perhaps, from what she was accustomed to. And how daintily she spoke! A strange, attractive, almost lovely child! Certainly not more than seventeen—and—Johnny Dromore's daughter!

The wind was bitter, the lamps bright among the naked trees. Beautiful always—London at night, even in January, even in an east wind, with a beauty he never tired of. Its great dark, chiselled shapes, its gleaming lights, like droves of flying stars come to earth; and all warmed by the beat and stir of innumerable lives—those lives that he ached so to know and to be part of.

He told Sylvia of his encounter. Dromore! The name struck her. She had an old Irish song, 'The Castle of Dromore', with a queer, haunting refrain.

It froze hard all the week, and he began a life-size group of their two sheep-dogs. Then a thaw set in with that first south-west wind, which brings each February a feeling of Spring such as is never again recaptured, and men's senses, like sleepy bees in the sun, go roving. It awakened in him more violently than ever the thirst to be living, knowing, loving—the craving for something new. Not this, of course, took him back to Dromore's rooms; oh, no! just friendliness, since he had not even told his old room-mate where he lived, or said that his wife would be glad to make his acquaintance, if he cared to come round. For Johnny Dromore had assuredly not seemed too happy, under all his hard-bitten air. Yes! it was but friendly to go again.

Dromore was seated in his long arm-chair, a cigar between his lips, a pencil in his hand, a Ruff's Guide on his knee; beside him was a large green book. There was a festive air about him, very different from his spasmodic gloom of the other day; and he murmured without rising:

'Hallo, old man!—glad to see you. Take a pew! Look here! Agapemone—which d'you think I ought to put her to—San Diavolo or Ponte Canet?—not more than four crosses of St Paul. Goin' to get a real good one from her this time!'

He, who had never heard these sainted names, answered:

'Oh! Ponte Canet, without doubt. But if you're working I'll come in another time.'

'Lord! no! Have a smoke. I'll just finish lookin' out their blood—and take a pull.'

And so Lennan sat down to watch those researches, wreathed in cigar smoke and punctuated by muttered expletives. They were as sacred and absorbing, no doubt, as his own efforts to create in clay; for before Dromore's inner vision was the perfect racehorse—he, too, was creating. Here was no mere dodge for making money, but a process hallowed by the peculiar sensation felt when one rubbed the palms of the hands together, the sensation that accompanied all creative achievement. Once only Dromore paused to turn his head and say:

'Bally hard, gettin' a taproot right!'

Real Art! How well an artist knew that desperate search after the point of balance, the central rivet that must be found before a form would come to life. . . . And he noted that to-day there was no kitten, no flowers, no sense at all of an extraneous presence—even the picture was curtained. Had the girl been just a dream—a fancy conjured up by his craving after youth?

Then he saw that Dromore had dropped the large green book, and was standing before the fire.

'Nell took to you the other day. But you always were a lady's man. Remember the girl at Coaster's?'

Coaster's tea-shop, where he would go every afternoon that he had money, just for the pleasure of looking shyly at a face. Something beautiful to look at—nothing more! Johnny Dromore would no better understand that now than when they were at 'Bambury's'. Not the smallest good even trying to explain! He looked up at the goggling eyes; he heard the bantering voice:

'I say—you *are* goin' grey. We're bally old, Lenny! A fellow gets old when he marries.'

And he answered:

'By the way, I never knew that *you* had been.'

From Dromore's face the chaffing look went, like a candle-flame blown out; and a coppery flush spread over it. For some seconds he did not speak, then, jerking his head towards the picture, he muttered gruffly:

'Never had the chance of marrying, there; Nell's "outside".'

A sort of anger leaped in Lennan; why should Dromore speak that word as if he were ashamed of his own daughter? Just like his sort—none so hidebound as men-about-town! Flotsam on the tide of other men's opinions; poor devils adrift, without the one true anchorage of their own real feelings! And doubtful whether Dromore would be pleased, or think him gushing, or even distrustful of his morality, he said:

'As for that, it would only make any decent man or woman nicer to her. When is she going to let me teach her drawing?'

Dromore crossed the room, drew back the curtain of the picture, and in a muffled voice, said:

'My God, Lenny! Life's unfair. Nell's coming killed her mother. I'd rather it had been me—bar chaff! Women have no luck.'

Lennan got up from his comfortable chair. For, startled out of the past, the memory of that summer night, when yet another woman had no luck, was flooding his heart with its black, inextinguishable grief. He said quietly:

'The past *is* past, old man.'

Dromore drew the curtain again across the picture, and came back to the fire. And for a full minute he stared into it.

'What am I to do with Nell? She's growing up.'

'What have you done with her so far?'

'She's been at school. In the summer she goes to Ireland—I've got a bit of an old place there. She'll be eighteen in July. I shall have to introduce her to women, and all that. It's the devil! How? Who?'

Lennan could only murmur: 'My wife, for one.'

He took his leave soon after. Johnny Dromore! Bizarre guardian for that child! Queer life she must have of it, in that bachelor's den, surrounded by Ruff's Guides! What would become of her? Caught up by some young spark about town; married to him, no doubt—her father would see to the thoroughness of that, his standard of respectability was evidently high! And after—go the way, maybe, of her mother—that poor thing in the picture with the alluring, desperate face. Well! It was no business of his!

IV

No business of his! The merest sense of comradeship, then, took him once more to Dromore's after that disclosure, to prove that the word 'outside' had no significance save in his friend's own fancy; to assure him again that Sylvia would be very glad to welcome the child at any time she liked to come.

When he had told her of that little matter of Nell's birth, she had been silent a long minute, looking in his face, and then had said: 'Poor child! I wonder if she knows! People are so unkind, even nowadays!' He could not himself think of anyone who would pay attention to such a thing, except to be kinder to the girl; but in such matters Sylvia was the better judge, in closer touch with general thought. She met people that he did not—and of a more normal species.

It was rather late when he got to Dromore's diggings on that third visit.

'Mr Dromore, sir,' the man said—he had one of those strictly confidential faces bestowed by an all-wise Providence on servants in the neighbourhood of Piccadilly—'Mr Dromore, sir, is not in. But he will be almost sure to be in to dress. Miss Nell is in, sir.'

And there she was, sitting at the table, pasting photographs into an album—lonely young creature in that abode of male middle-age! Lennan stood, unheard, gazing at the back of her head, with its thick crinkly-brown hair tied back on her dark red frock. And, to the confidential man's soft:

'Mr Lennan, miss,' he added a softer: 'May I come in?'

She put her hand into his with intense composure.

'Oh, yes, do! if you don't mind the mess I'm making;' and, with a little squeeze of the tips of his fingers, added: 'Would it bore you to see my photographs?'

And down they sat together before the photographs—snapshots of people with guns or fishing-rods, little groups of schoolgirls, kittens, Dromore and herself on horseback, and several of a young man with a broad, daring, rather good-looking face. 'That's Oliver —Oliver Dromore—Dad's first cousin once removed. Rather nice, isn't he? Do you like his expression?'

Lennan did not know. Not her second cousin; her father's first cousin once removed! And again there leaped in him that un-reasoning flame of indignant pity.

'And how about drawing? You haven't come to be taught yet.'

She went almost as red as her frock.

'I thought you were only being polite. I oughtn't to have asked. Of course, I want to awfully—only I know it'll bore you.'

'It won't at all.'

She looked up at that. What peculiar languorous eyes they were! 'Shall I come to-morrow, then?'

'Any day you like, between half-past twelve and one.'

'Where?'

He took out a card.

'Mark Lennan—yes—I like your name. I liked it the other day. It's awfully nice!'

What was in a name that she should like him because of it? His fame as a sculptor—such as it was—could have nothing to do with that, for she would certainly not know of it. Ah! but there was a lot in a name—for children. In his childhood what fascination there had been in the words macaroon, and Spaniard, and Carniola, and Aldebaran, and Mr McCrae. For quite a week the whole world had been Mr McCrae—a most ordinary friend of Gordy's.

By whatever fascination moved, she talked freely enough now —of her school; of riding and motoring—she seemed to love going very fast; about Newmarket—which was 'perfect'; and theatres— plays of the type that Johnny Dromore might be expected to approve; these together with 'Hamlet' and 'King Lear' were all she had seen. Never was a girl so untouched by thought, or Art— yet not stupid, having, seemingly, a certain natural good taste; only, nothing, evidently, had come her way. How could it— 'Johnny Dromore *duce, et auspice* Johnny Dromore!' She had been taken, indeed, to the National Gallery while at school. And Lennan had a vision of eight or ten young maidens trailing round at the skirts of one old maiden, admiring Landseer's dogs, giggling faintly at Botticelli's angels, gaping, rustling, chattering like young birds in a shrubbery.

But with all her surroundings, this child of Johnny Dromoredom was as yet more innocent than cultured girls of the same age. If those grey, mesmeric eyes of hers followed him about, they did so frankly, unconsciously. There was no minx in her, so far.

An hour went by, and Dromore did not come. And the loneliness of this young creature in her incongruous abode began telling on Lennan's equanimity.

What did she do in the evenings?

'Sometimes I go to the theatre with Dad, generally I stay at home.'

'And then?'

'Oh! I just read, or talk French.'

'What? To yourself?'

'Yes, or to Oliver sometimes, when he comes in.'

So Oliver came in!

'How long have you known Oliver?'

'Oh! ever since I was a child.'

He wanted to say: And how long is that? But managed to refrain, and got up to go instead. She caught his sleeve and said:

'You're not to go!' Saying that, she looked as a dog will, going to bite in fun, her upper lip shortened above her small white teeth set fast on her lower lip, and her chin thrust a little forward. A glimpse of a wilful spirit! But as soon as he had smiled, and murmured:

'Ah! but I must, you see!' she at once regained her manners, only saying rather mournfully: 'You don't call me by my name. Don't you like it?'

'Nell?'

'Yes. It's really Eleanor, of course. *Don't* you like it?'

If he had detested the name, he could only have answered: 'Very much.'

'I'm awfully glad! Good-bye.'

When he got out into the street, he felt terribly like a man who, instead of having had his sleeve touched, has had his heart plucked at. And that warm, bewildered feeling lasted him all the way home.

Changing for dinner, he looked at himself with unwonted attention. Yes, his dark hair was still thick, but going distinctly grey; there were very many lines about his eyes, too, and those eyes, still eager when they smiled, were particularly deepset, as if life had forced them back. His cheekbones were almost 'bopsies' now, and his cheeks very thin and dark, and his jaw looked too set and bony below the almost black moustache. Altogether a face that life had worn a good deal, with nothing for a child to take a fancy to and make friends with, that he could see.

Sylvia came in while he was thus taking stock of himself, bringing a freshly-opened flask of eau-de-Cologne. She was always bringing him something—never was anyone so sweet in those ways. In that grey, low-cut frock, her white, still prettiness and pale-gold hair, so little touched by Time, only just fell short of real beauty for lack of a spice of depth and of incisiveness, just as her spirit lacked he knew not what of poignancy. He would not for the world have let her know that he ever felt that lack. If a man could not hide little rifts in the lute from one so good and humble and affectionate, he was not fit to live.

She sang 'The Castle of Dromore' again that night with its queer haunting lilt. And when she had gone up, and he was smoking over the fire, the girl in her dark-red frock seemed to come, and sit opposite with her eyes fixed on his, just as she had been sitting while they talked. Dark red had suited her! Suited the look on her face when she said: 'You're not to go!' Odd, indeed, if she had not some devil in her, with that parentage!

V

Next day they had summoned him from the studio to see a peculiar phenomenon—Johnny Dromore, very well groomed, talking to Sylvia with unnatural suavity, and carefully masking the goggle in his eyes! Mrs Lennan ride? Ah! Too busy, of course. Helped Mark with his—er—— No! Really! Read a lot, no doubt? Never had any time for readin' himself—awful bore not havin' time to read! And Sylvia listening and smiling, very still and soft.

What had Dromore come for? To spy out the land, discover why Lennan and his wife thought nothing of the word 'outside'—whether, in fact, their household was respectable. . . . A man must always look twice at 'what-d'you-call-ems', even if they have shared his room at school! . . . To his credit, of course, to be so careful of his daughter, at the expense of time owed to the creation of the perfect racehorse! On the whole he seemed to be coming to the conclusion that they might be useful to Nell in the uncomfortable time at hand when she would have to go about; seemed even to be falling under the spell of Sylvia's transparent goodness —abandoning his habitual vigilance against being scored off in life's perpetual bet; parting with his armour of chaff. Almost a relief, indeed, once out of Sylvia's presence, to see that familiar, unholy curiosity creeping back into his eyes, as though they were hoping against parental hope to find something—er—amusing somewhere about that mysterious Mecca of good times—a 'what-d'you-call-it's' studio. Delicious to watch the conflict between relief and disappointment. Alas! no model—not even a statue without clothes; nothing but portrait heads, casts of animals, and such-like sobrieties—absolutely nothing that could bring a blush to the cheek of the young person, or a glow to the eyes of a Johnny Dromore.

With what curious silence he walked round and round the group of sheep-dogs, inquiring into them with that long crinkled nose of his! With what curious suddenness, he said: 'Damned good! You wouldn't do me one of Nell on horseback?' With what dubious watchfulness he listened to the answer:

'I might, perhaps, do a statuette of her; if I did, you should have a cast.'

Did he think that in some way he was being outmanoeuvred?

For he remained some seconds in a sort of trance before muttering, as though clinching a bet:

'Done! And if you want to ride with her to get the hang of it, I can always mount you.'

When he had gone, Lennan remained staring at his unfinished sheep-dogs in the gathering dusk. Again that sense of irritation at contact with something strange, hostile, uncomprehending! Why let these Dromores into his life like this? He shut the studio, and went back to the drawing-room. Sylvia was sitting on the fender, gazing at the fire, and she edged along so as to rest against his knees. The light from a candle on her writing-table was shining on her hair, her cheek, and chin, that years had so little altered. A pretty picture she made, with just that candle flame, swaying there, burning slowly, surely down the pale wax—candle flame, of all lifeless things most living, most like a spirit, so bland and vague, one would hardly have known it was fire at all. A drift of wind blew it this way and that: he got up to shut the window, and as he came back, Sylvia said:

'I like Mr Dromore. I think he's nicer than he looks.'

'He's asked me to make a statuette of his daughter on horseback.'

'And will you?'

'I don't know.'

'If she's really so pretty, you'd better.'

'Pretty's hardly the word—but she's not ordinary.'

She turned round, and looked up at him, and instinctively he felt that something difficult to answer was coming next.

'Mark.'

'Yes.'

'I wanted to ask you: Are you really happy nowadays?'

'Of course. Why not?'

What else to be said? To speak of those feelings of the last few months—those feelings so ridiculous to anyone who had them not—would only disturb her horribly.

And having received her answer, Sylvia turned back to the fire, resting silently against his knees. . . .

Three days later the sheep-dogs suddenly abandoned the pose into which he had lured them with such difficulty, and made for the studio door. There in the street was Nell Dromore, mounted on a narrow little black horse with a white star, a white hoof, and devilish little goat's ears, pricked, and very close together at the tips.

'Dad said I had better ride round and show you Magpie. He's not very good at standing still. Are those your dogs? What darlings!'

She had slipped her knee already from the pummel, and slid down; the sheep-dogs were instantly on their hind-feet, propping themselves against her waist. Lennan held the black horse—a bizarre little beast, all fire and whipcord, with a skin like satin, liquid eyes, very straight hocks, and a thin bang-tail reaching down to them. The little creature had none of those commonplace good looks so discouraging to artists.

He had forgotten its rider till she looked up from the dogs, and said: 'Do you like him? It *is* nice of you to be going to do us.'

When she had ridden away, looking back until she turned the corner, he tried to lure the two dogs once more to their pose. But they would sit no more, going continually to the door, listening and sniffing; and everything felt disturbed and out of gear.

That same afternoon at Sylvia's suggestion he went with her to call on the Dromore's.

While they were being ushered in he heard a man's voice rather high-pitched speaking in some language not his own; then the girl:

'No, no, Oliver. "*Dans l'amour il y a toujours un qui aime, et l'autre qui se laisse aimer."* '

She was sitting in her father's chair, and on the window-sill they saw a young man lolling, who rose and stood stock-still, with an almost insolent expression on his broad, good-looking face. Lennan scrutinised him with interest—about twenty-four he might be, rather dandified, clean-shaved, with crisp dark hair and wide-set hazel eyes, and, as in his photograph, a curious look of daring. His voice, when he vouchsafed a greeting, was rather high and not unpleasant, with a touch of lazy drawl.

They stayed but a few minutes, and going down those dimly lighted stairs again, Sylvia remarked:

'How prettily she said good-bye—as if she were putting up her face to be kissed! I think she's lovely. So does that young man. They go well together.'

Rather abruptly Lennan answered:

'Ah! I suppose they do.'

VI

She came to them often after that, sometimes alone, twice with Johnny Dromore, sometimes with young Oliver, who, under Sylvia's spell, soon lost his stand-off air. And the statuette was begun. Then came Spring in earnest, and that real business of life—the racing of horses 'on the flat', when Johnny Dromore's genius was no longer hampered by the illegitimate risks of 'jumpin''. He came to dine with them the day before the first Newmarket meeting.. He had a soft spot for Sylvia, always saying to Lennan as he went away: 'Charmin' woman—your wife!' She, too, had a soft spot for him, having fathomed the utter helplessness of this worldling's wisdom, and thinking him pathetic.

After he was gone that evening, she said:

'Ought we to have Nell to stay with us while you're finishing her? She must be very lonely now her father's so much away.'

It was like Sylvia to think of that; but would it be pleasure or vexation to have in the house this child with her quaint grown-upness, her confiding ways, and those 'Perdita' eyes? In truth he did not know.

She came to them with touching alacrity—very like a dog, who, left at home when the family goes for a holiday, takes at once to those who make much of it.

And she was no trouble, too well accustomed to amuse herself; and always quaint to watch, with her continual changes from child to woman of the world. A new sensation, this—of a young creature in the house. Both he and Sylvia had wanted children, without luck. Twice illness had stood in the way. Was it, perhaps, just that little lack in her—that lack of poignancy, which had prevented her from becoming a mother? An only child herself, she had no nieces or nephews; Cicely's boys had always been at school, and now were out in the world. Yes, a new sensation, and one in which Lennan's restless feelings seemed to merge and vanish.

Outside the hours when Nell sat to him, he purposely saw but little of her, leaving her to nestle under Sylvia's wing; and this she did, as if she never wanted to come out. Thus he preserved his amusement at her quaint warmths, and quainter calmness, his aesthetic pleasure in watching her, whose strange, half-hypnotised, half-hypnotic gaze, had a sort of dreamy and pathetic lovingness, as if she were brimful of affections that had no outlet.

Every morning after 'sitting' she would stay an hour bent over her own drawing, which made practically no progress; and he would often catch her following his movements with those great eyes of hers, while the sheep-dogs would lie perfectly still at her feet, blinking horribly—such was her attraction. His birds also, a jackdaw and an owl, who had the run of the studio, tolerated her as they tolerated no other female, save the housekeeper. The jack-daw would perch on her and peck her dress; but the owl merely engaged her in combats of mesmeric gazing, which never ended in victory for either.

Now that she was with them, Oliver Dromore began to haunt the house, coming at all hours, on very transparent excuses. She behaved to him with extreme capriciousness, sometimes hardly speaking, sometimes treating him like a brother; and in spite of all his nonchalance, the poor youth would just sit glowering, or gazing out his adoration, according to her mood.

One of these July evenings Lennan remembered beyond all others. He had come, after a hard day's work, out from his studio into the courtyard garden to smoke a cigarette and feel the sun on his cheek before it sank behind the wall. A piano-organ far away was grinding out a waltz; and on an hydrangea tub, under the drawing-room window, he sat down to listen. Nothing was visible from there, save just the square patch of a quite blue sky, and one soft plume of smoke from his own kitchen chimney; nothing audible save that tune, and the never-ending street murmur. Twice birds flew across—starlings. It was very peaceful, and his thoughts went floating like the smoke of his cigarette, to meet who-knew-what other thoughts—for thoughts, no doubt, had little swift lives of their own; desired, found their mates, and, lightly blending, sent forth offspring. Why not? All things were possible in this wonder-house of a world. Even that waltz tune, floating away, would find some melody to wed, and twine with, and produce a fresh chord that might float in turn to catch the hum of a gnat or fly, and breed again. Queer—how everything sought to entwine with something else! On one of the pinkish blooms of the hydrangea he noted a bee—of all things, in this hidden-away garden of tiles and gravel and plants in tubs! The little furry, lonely thing was drowsily clinging there, as if it had forgotten what it had come for—seduced, maybe, like himself, from labour by these last rays of the sun. Its wings, close-furled, were glistening; its eyes seemed closed. And the piano-organ played on, a tune of yearning, waiting, yearning. . . .

Then, through the window above his head, he heard Oliver Dromore—a voice one could always tell, pitched high, with its slight drawl—pleading, very softly at first, then insistent, imperious; and suddenly Nell's answering voice:

'I won't, Oliver! I won't! I won't!'

He rose to go out of earshot. Then a door slammed, and he saw her at the window above him, her waist on a level with his head; flushed, with her grey eyes ominously bright, her full lips parted. And he said:

'What is it, Nell?'

She leaned down and caught his hand; her touch was fiery hot. 'He kissed me! I won't let him—I won't kiss him!'

Through his head went a medley of sayings to soothe children that are hurt; but he felt unsteady, unlike himself. And suddenly she knelt, and put her hot forehead against his lips.

It was as if she had really been a little child, wanting the place kissed to make it well.

VII

After that strange outburst, Lennan considered long whether he should speak to Oliver. But what could he say, from what standpoint say it, and—with that feeling? Or should he speak to Dromore? Not very easy to speak on such a subject to one off whose turf all spiritual matters were so permanently warned. Nor somehow could he bring himself to tell Sylvia; it would be like violating a confidence to speak of the child's outburst and that quivering moment, when she had kneeled and put her hot forehead to his lips for comfort. Such a disclosure was for Nell herself to make, if she so wished.

And then young Oliver solved the difficulty by coming to the studio himself next day. He entered with 'Dromore' composure, very well groomed, in a silk hat, a cut-away black coat and charming lemon-coloured gloves; what, indeed, the youth did, besides belonging to the Yeomanry and hunting all the winter, seemed known only to himself. He made no excuse for interrupting Lennan, and for some time sat silently smoking his cigarette, and

pulling the ears of the dogs. And Lennan worked on, waiting. There was always something attractive to him in this young man's broad, good-looking face, with its crisp dark hair, and half-insolent good humour, now so clouded.

At last Oliver got up, and went over to the unfinished 'Girl on the Magpie Horse'. Turning to it so that his face could not be seen, he said:

'You and Mrs Lennan have been awfully kind to me; I behaved rather like a cad yesterday. I thought I'd better tell you. I want to marry Nell, you know.'

Lennan was glad that the young man's face was so religiously averted. He let his hands come to anchor on what he was working at before he answered: 'She's only a child, Oliver;' and then, watching his fingers making an inept movement with the clay, was astonished at himself.

'She'll be eighteen this month,' he heard Oliver say. 'If she once gets out—amongst people—I don't know what I shall do. Old Johnny's no good to look after her.'

The young man's face was very red; he was forgetting to hide it now. Then it went white, and he said through clenched teeth: 'She sends me mad! I don't know how not to—— If I don't get her, I shall shoot myself. I shall, you know—I'm that sort. It's her eyes. They draw you right out of yourself—and leave you——' And from his gloved hand the smoked-out cigarette-end fell to the floor. 'They say her mother was like that. Poor old Johnny! D'you think I've got a chance, Mr Lennan? I don't mean now, this minute; I know she's too young!'

Lennan forced himself to answer.

'I dare say, my dear fellow, I dare say. Have you talked with my wife?'

Oliver shook his head.

'She's so good—I don't think she'd quite understand my sort of feeling.'

A queer little smile came up on Lennan's lips.

'Ah, well!' he said, 'you must give the child time. Perhaps when she comes back from Ireland, after the summer.'

The young man answered moodily:

'Yes. I've got the run of that, you know. And I shan't be able to keep away.' He took up his hat. 'I suppose I oughtn't to have come and bored you about this, but Nell thinks such a lot of you; and, you being different to most people—I thought you wouldn't mind.' He turned again at the door. 'It wasn't gas what I said just now—about not getting her. Fellows say that sort of thing, but I mean it.'

He put on that shining hat and went.

And Lennan stood, staring at the statuette. So! Passion broke down even the defences of Dromoredom. Passion! Strange hearts it chose to bloom in!

'Being different to most people—I thought you wouldn't mind!' How had this youth known that Sylvia would not understand passion so out of hand as this? And what had made it clear that he (Lennan) would? Was there, then, something in his face? There must be! Even Johnny Dromore—most reticent of creatures—had confided to him that one hour of his astute existence, when the wind had swept him out to sea!

Yes! And that statuette would never be any good, try as he might. Oliver was right—it was her eyes! How they had smoked —in their childish anger—if eyes could be said to smoke, and how they had drawn and pleaded when she put her face to his in her still more childish entreaty! If they were like this now, what would they be when the woman in her woke? Just as well not to think of her too much! Just as well to work, and take heed that he would soon be forty-seven! Just as well that next week she would be gone to Ireland!

And the last evening before she went they took her to see 'Carmen' at the Opera. He remembered that she wore a nearly high white frock, and a dark carnation in the ribbon tying her crinkly hair, that still hung loose. How wonderfully entranced she sat, drunk on that opera that he had seen a score of times; now touching his arm, now Sylvia's, whispering questions: 'Who's that?' 'What's coming now?' The Carmen roused her to adoration, but Don José was 'too fat in his funny little coat,' till, in the maddened jealousy of the last act, he rose superior. Then, quite lost in excitement, she clutched Lennan's arm; and her gasp, when Carmen at last fell dead, made all their neighbours jump. Her emotion was far more moving than that on the stage; he wanted badly to stroke, and comfort her and say: 'There, there, my dear, it's only make-believe!' And, when it was over, and the excellent murdered lady and her poor fat little lover appeared before the curtain, finally forgetting that she was a woman of the world, she started forward in her seat and clapped, and clapped. Fortunate that Johnny Dromore was not there to see! But all things coming to an end, they had to get up and go. And, as they made their way out to the hall, Lennan felt a hot little finger crooked into his own, as if she simply

148

must have something to squeeze. He really did not know what to do with it. She seemed to feel this half-heartedness, soon letting it go. All the way home in the cab she was silent. With that same abstraction she ate her sandwiches and drank her lemonade; took Sylvia's kiss, and, quite a woman of the world once more, begged that they would not get up to see her off—for she was to go at seven in the morning, to catch the Irish mail. Then, holding out her hand to Lennan, she very gravely said:

'Thanks most awfully for taking me to-night. Good-bye!'

He stayed full half an hour at the window, smoking. No street lamp shone just there, and the night was velvety black above the plane-trees. At last, with a sigh, he shut up, and went tiptoe-ing upstairs in darkness. Suddenly in the corridor the white wall seemed to move at him. A warmth, a fragrance, a sound like a tiny sigh, and something soft was squeezed into his hand. Then the wall moved back, and he stood listening—no sound, no anything! But in his dressing-room he looked at the soft thing in his hand. It was the carnation from her hair. What had possessed the child to give him that? Carmen! Ah! Carmen! And gazing at the flower, he held it away from him with a sort of terror; but its scent arose. And suddenly he thrust it, all fresh as it was, into a candle-flame, and held it, burning, writhing, till it blackened to velvet. Then his heart smote him for so cruel a deed. It was still beautiful, but its scent was gone. And turning to the window he flung it far out into the darkness.

VIII

Now that she was gone, it was curious how little they spoke of her, considering how long she had been with them. And they had from her but one letter written to Sylvia, very soon after she left, ending: 'Dad sends his best respects, please; and with my love to you and Mr Lennan, and all the beasts.—NELL.

'Oliver is coming here next week. We are going to some races.'

It was difficult, of course, to speak of her, with that episode of the flower, too bizarre to be told—the sort of thing Sylvia would see out of all proportion—as, indeed, any woman might. Yet—what had it really been, but the uncontrolled impulse of an emotional child longing to express feelings kindled by the excitement of that opera? What but a child's feathery warmth, one of those flying peeps at the mystery of passion that young things take? He could not give away that pretty foolishness. And because he would not give it away, he was more than usually affectionate to Sylvia.

They had made no holiday plans, and he eagerly fell in with her suggestion that they should go down to Hayle. There, if anywhere, this curious restlessness would leave him. They had not been down to the old place for many years; indeed, since Gordy's death it was generally let.

They left London late in August. The day was closing in when they arrived. Honeysuckle had long been improved away from that station paling, against which he had stood twenty-nine years ago, watching the train carrying Anna Stormer away. In the hired fly Sylvia pressed close to him, and held his hand beneath the ancient dust-rug. Both felt the same excitement at seeing again this old home. Not a single soul of the past days would be there now— only the house and the trees, the owls and the stars; the river, park, and logan stone! It was dark when they arrived; just their bedroom and two sitting-rooms had been made ready, with fires burning, though it was still high summer. The same old execrable Heatherleys looked down from the black oak panellings. The same scent of apples and old mice clung here and there about the dark corridors with their unexpected stairways. It was all curiously unchanged, as old houses are when they are let furnished.

Once in the night he woke. Through the wide-open, uncurtained windows the night was simply alive with stars, such swarms of them swinging and trembling up there; and, far away, rose the melancholy, velvet-soft hooting of an owl.

Sylvia's voice, close to him, said:

'Mark, that night when your star caught in my hair? Do you remember?'

Yes, he remembered. And in his drowsy mind just roused from dreams, there turned and turned the queer nonsensical refrain: 'I never—never—will desert Mr Micawber. . . .'

A pleasant month that—of reading, and walking with the dogs the country round, of lying out long hours amongst the boulders or along the river banks, watching beasts and birds.

The little old greenhouse temple of his early masterpieces was still extant, used now to protect watering pots. But no vestige of impulse towards work came to him down there. He was marking time; not restless, not bored, just waiting—but for what, he had no notion. And Sylvia, at any rate, was happy, blooming in these old haunts, losing her fairness in the sun; even taking again to a sunbonnet, which made her look extraordinarily young. The trout that poor old Gordy had so harried were left undisturbed. No gun was fired; rabbits, pigeons, even the few partridges enjoyed those first days of autumn unmolested. The bracken and leaves turned very early, so that the park in the hazy September sunlight had an almost golden hue. A gentle mellowness reigned over all that holiday. And from Ireland came no further news, save one picture postcard with the words: 'This is our house.—NELL.'

In the last week of September they went back to London. And at once there began in him again that restless, unreasonable aching —that sense of being drawn away out of himself; so that he once more took to walking the Park for hours, over grass already strewn with leaves, always looking—craving—and for what?

At Dromore's the confidential man did not know when his master would be back; he had gone to Scotland with Miss Nell after the St Leger. Was Lennan disappointed? Not so—relieved, rather. But his ache was there all the time, feeding on its secrecy and loneliness, unmentionable feeling that it was. Why had he not realised long ago that youth was over, passion done with, autumn upon him? How never grasped the fact that 'Time steals away'? And, as before, the only refuge was in work. The sheep-dogs and 'The Girl on the Magpie Horse' were finished. He began a fantastic 'relief'— a nymph peering from behind a rock, and a wild-eyed man creeping, through reeds, towards her. If he could put into the nymph's face something of this lure of Youth and Life and Love that was dragging at him, into the man's face the state of his own heart, it might lay that feeling to rest. Anything to get it out of himself! And he worked furiously, laboriously, all October, making no great progress. . . . What could he expect when Life was all the time knocking with that muffled tapping at his door?

It was on the Tuesday, after the close of the last Newmarket meeting, and just getting dusk, when Life opened the door and walked in. She wore a dark-red dress, a new one, and surely her face—her figure—were very different from what he had remembered! They had quickened and become poignant. She was no longer a child—that was at once plain. Cheeks, mouth, neck, waist —all seemed fined, shaped; the crinkly, light-brown hair was coiled up now under a velvet cap; only the great grey eyes seemed quite the same. And at sight of her his heart gave a sort of dive and flight, as if all its vague and wistful sensations had found their goal.

Then, in sudden agitation, he realised that his last moment with this girl—now a child no longer—had been a secret moment of warmth and of emotion; a moment which to her might have meant, in her might have bred, feelings that he had no inkling of. He tried to ignore that flighting and diving of his heart, held out his hand, and murmured:

'Ah, Nell! Back at last! You've grown.'

Then, with a sensation of every limb gone weak, he felt her arms round his neck, and herself pressed against him. There was time for the thought to flash through him: This is terrible! He gave her a little convulsive squeeze—could a man do less?—then just managed to push her gently away, trying with all his might to think: She's a child! It's nothing more than after Carmen! She doesn't know what I'm feeling! But he was conscious of a mad desire to clutch her to him. The touch of her had demolished all his vagueness, made things only too plain, set him on fire.

He said uncertainly:

'Come to the fire, my child, and tell me all about it.'

If he did not keep to the notion that she was just a child, his head would go. Perdita—'the lost one'! A good name for her, indeed, as she stood there, her eyes shining in the firelight—more mesmeric than ever they had been! And, to get away from the lure of those eyes, he bent down and raked the grate, saying:

'Have you seen Sylvia?' But he knew that she had not, even before she gave that impatient shrug. Then he pulled himself together, and said:

'What has happened to you, child?'

'I'm not a child.'

'No, we've both grown older. I was forty-seven the other day.'

She caught his hand—Heavens! how supple she was!—and murmured:

'You're not old a bit; you're quite young.'

At his wits' end, with his heart thumping, but still keeping his eyes away from her, he said:

'Where is Oliver?'

She dropped his hand at that.

'Oliver? I hate him!'

Afraid to trust himself near her, he had begun walking up and down. And she stood, following him with her gaze—the firelight playing on her red frock. What extraordinary stillness! What power she had developed in these few months! Had he let her see that he felt that power? And had all this come of one little moment in a dark corridor, of one flower pressed into his hand? Why had he not spoken to her roughly then—told her she was a romantic little fool? God knew what thoughts she had been feeding on!

But who could have supposed—who dreamed—? And again he
fixed his mind resolutely on that thought: She's a child—only a
child!

'Come!' he said: 'tell me all about your time in Ireland?'

'Oh! it was just dull—it's all been dull away from you.'

It came out without hesitancy or shame, and he could only
murmur:

'Ah! you've missed your drawing!'

'Yes. Can I come to-morrow?'

That was the moment to have said: No! You are a foolish child,
and I an elderly idiot! But he had neither courage nor clearness of
mind enough; nor—the desire. And, without answering, he went
towards the door to turn up the light.

'Oh, no! please don't! It's so nice like this!'

The shadowy room, the bluish dusk painted on all the windows,
the fitful shining of the fire, the pallor and darkness of the dim
casts and bronzes, and that one glowing figure there before the
hearth! And her voice, a little piteous, went on:

'Aren't you glad I'm back? I can't see you properly out there.'

He went back into the glow, and she gave a little sigh of satisfaction. Then her calm young voice said, ever so distinctly:

'Oliver wants me to marry him, and I won't, of course.'

He dared not say: Why not? He dared not say anything. It was
too dangerous. And then followed those amazing words: 'You
know why, don't you? Of course you do.'

It was ridiculous, almost shameful to understand their meaning.
And he stood, staring in front of him, without a word; humility,
dismay, pride, and a sort of mad exultation, all mixed and seething
within him in the queerest pudding of emotion. But all he said was:

'Come, my child; we're neither of us quite ourselves to-night.
Let's go to the drawing-room.'

IX

Back in the darkness and solitude of the studio, when she was
gone, he sat down before the fire, his senses in a whirl. Why was
he not just an ordinary animal of a man that could enjoy what
the gods had sent? It was as if on a November day someone had
pulled aside the sober curtains of the sky and there in a chink
had been April standing—thick white blossom, a purple cloud, a
rainbow, grass vivid green, light flaring from one knew not where,

153

and such a tingling passion of life on it all as made the heart stand still! This, then, was the marvellous, enchanting, maddening end of all that year of restlessness and wanting! This bit of Spring suddenly given to him in the midst of Autumn. Her lips, her eyes, her hair; her touching confidence; above all—quite unbelievable—her love. Not really love perhaps, just childish fancy. But on the wings of fancy this child would fly far, too far—all wistfulness and warmth beneath that light veneer of absurd composure.

To live again—to plunge back into youth and beauty—to feel Spring once more—to lose the sense of all being over, save just the sober jogtrot of domestic bliss; to know, actually to know, ecstasy again, in the love of a girl; to rediscover all that youth yearns for, and feels, and hopes, and dreads, and loves. It was a prospect to turn the head even of a decent man. . . .

By just closing his eyes he could see her standing there with the firelight glow on her red frock; could feel again that marvellous thrill when she pressed herself against him in the half-innocent, seducing moment when she first came in; could feel again her eyes drawing—drawing him! She was a witch, a grey-eyed, brown-haired witch—even unto her love of red. She had the witch's power of lighting fever in the veins. And he simply wondered at himself, that he had not, as she stood there in the firelight, knelt, and put his arms round her and pressed his face against her waist. Why had he not? But he did not want to think; the moment thought began he knew he must be torn this way and that, tossed here and there between reason and desire, pity and passion. Every sense struggled to keep him wrapped in the warmth and intoxication of this discovery that he, in the full of Autumn, had awakened love in Spring. It was amazing that she could have this feeling; yet there was no mistake. Her manner to Sylvia just now had been almost dangerously changed; there had been a queer cold impatience in her look, frightening from one who but three months ago had been so affectionate. And, going away, she had whispered, with that old trembling-up at him, as if offering to be kissed: 'I may come, mayn't I? And don't be angry with me, please; I can't help it.' A monstrous thing at his age to let a young girl love him—compromise her future! A monstrous thing by all the canons of virtue and gentility! And yet—what future?—with that nature—those eyes—that origin—with that father, and that home? But he would not—simply must not think!

Nevertheless, he showed the signs of thought, and badly; for after dinner Sylvia, putting her hand on his forehead, said:

'You're working too hard, Mark. You don't go out enough.'

He held those fingers fast. Sylvia! No, indeed, he must not think! But he took advantage of her words, and said that he would go out and get some air.

He walked at a great pace—to keep thought away—till he reached the river close to Westminster, and, moved by sudden impulse, seeking perhaps an antidote, turned down into that little street under the big Wren church, where he had never been since the summer night when he lost what was then more to him than life. There *she* had lived; there was the house—those windows which he had stolen past and gazed at with such distress and longing. Who lived there now? Once more he seemed to see that face out of the past, the dark hair, and dark soft eyes, and sweet gravity; and it did not reproach him. For this new feeling was not a love like that had been. Only once could a man feel the love that passed all things, the love before which the world was but a spark in a draught of wind; the love that, whatever dishonour, grief, and unrest it might come through, alone had in it the heart of peace and joy and honour. Fate had torn that love from him, nipped it off as a sharp wind nips off a perfect flower. This new feeling was but a fever, a passionate fancy, a grasping once more at Youth and Warmth. Ah, well! but it was real enough! And, in one of those moments when a man stands outside himself, seems to be lifted away and see his own life twirling, Lennan had a vision of a shadow driven here and there; a straw going round and round; a midge in the grip of a mad wind. Where was the home of this mighty secret feeling that sprang so suddenly out of the dark, and caught you by the throat? Why did it come now and not then, for this one and not that other? What did man know of it, save that it made him spin and hover—like a moth intoxicated by a light, of a bee by some dark sweet flower; save that it made of him a distraught, humble, eager puppet of its fancy? Had it not once already driven him even to the edge of death; and must it now come on him again with its sweet madness, its drugging scent? What was it? Why was it? Why these passionate obsessions that could not decently be satisfied? Had civilisation so outstripped man that his nature was cramped into shoes too small—like the feet of a Chinese woman? What was it? Why was it?

And faster than ever he walked away.

Pall Mall brought him back to that counterfeit presentment of the real—reality. There, in St James's Street, was Johnny Dromore's Club; and, again moved by impulse, he pushed open its swing door.

No need to ask; for there was Dromore in the hall, on his way from dinner to the card-room. The glossy tan of hard exercise and good living lay on his cheeks as thick as clouted cream. His eyes had the peculiar shine of superabundant vigour; a certain sub-festive air in face and voice and movements suggested that he was going to make a night of it. And the sardonic thought flashed through Lennan: Shall I tell him?

'Hallo, old chap! Awfully glad to see you! What you doin' with yourself? Workin' hard? How's your wife? You been away? Been doin' anything great?' And then the question that would have given him his chance, if he had liked to be so cruel:

'Seen Nell?'

'Yes, she came round this afternoon.'

'What d'you think of her? Comin' on nicely, isn't she?'

That old query, half furtive and half proud, as much as to say: 'I know she's not in the stud-book, but, d——n it, I sired her!' And then the old sudden gloom, which lasted but a second, and gave way again to chaff.

Lennan stayed very few minutes. Never had he felt farther from his old school-chum.

No. Whatever happened, Johnny Dromore must be left out. It was a position he had earned with his goggling eyes, and his astute philosophy; from it he should not be disturbed.

He passed along the railings of the Green Park. On the cold air of this last October night a thin haze hung, and the acrid fragrance from little bonfires of fallen leaves. What was there about that scent of burned-leaf smoke that had always moved him so? Symbol of parting!—that most mournful thing in all the world. For what would even death be, but for parting? Sweet, long sleep, or new adventure. But, if a man loved others—to leave them, or be left! Ah! and it was not death only that brought partings!

He came to the opening of the street where Dromore lived. She would be there, sitting by the fire in the big chair, playing with her kitten, thinking, dreaming, and—alone! He passed on at such a pace that people stared; till, turning the last corner for home, he ran almost into the arms of Oliver Dromore.

The young man was walking with unaccustomed indecision, his fur coat open, his opera-hat pushed up on his crisp hair. Dark under the eyes, he had not the proper gloss of a Dromore at this season of the year.

'Mr Lennan! I've just been round to you.'

And Lennan answered dazedly:

156

'Will you come in, or shall I walk your way a bit?'

'I'd rather—out here, if you don't mind.'

So in silence they went back into the Square. And Oliver said:
'Let's get over by the rails.'

They crossed to the railings of the Square's dark garden, where nobody was passing. And with every step Lennan's humiliation grew. There was something false and undignified in walking with this young man who had once treated him as a father confessor to his love for Nell. And suddenly he perceived that they had made a complete circuit of the Square garden without speaking a single word.

'Yes?' he said.

Oliver turned his face away.

'You remember what I told you in the summer. Well, it's worse now. I've been going a mucker lately in all sorts of ways to try and get rid of it. But it's all no good. She's got me!'

And Lennan thought: You're not alone in that! But he kept silence. His chief dread was of saying something that he would remember afterwards as the words of Judas.

Then Oliver suddenly burst out:

'Why can't she care? I suppose I'm nothing much, but she's known me all her life, and she used to like me. There's something —I can't make out. Could you do anything for me with her?'

Lennan pointed across the street.

'In every other one of those houses, Oliver,' he said, 'there's probably some creature who can't make out why another creature doesn't care. Passion comes when it will, goes when it will; and we poor devils have no say in it.'

'What do you advise me, then?'

Lennan had an almost overwhelming impulse to turn on his heel and leave the young man standing there. But he forced himself to look at his face, which even then had its attraction—perhaps more so than ever, so pallid and desperate it was. And he said slowly, staring mentally at every word:

'I'm not up to giving you advice. The only thing I might say is: One does not press oneself where one isn't wanted; all the same —who knows? So long as she feels you're there, waiting, she might turn to you at any moment. The more chivalrous you are, Oliver, the more patiently you wait, the better chance you have.'

Oliver took those words of little comfort without flinching. 'I see,' he said. 'Thanks! But, my God! it's hard. I never could wait.'

And with that epigram on himself, holding out his hand, he turned away.

Lennan went slowly home, trying to gauge exactly how anyone who knew all would judge him. It was a little difficult in this affair to keep a shred of dignity.

Sylvia had not gone up, and he saw her looking at him anxiously. The one strange comfort in all this was that his feeling for her, at any rate, had not changed. It seemed even to have deepened—to be more real to him.

How could he help staying awake that night? How could he help thinking, then? And long time he lay, staring at the dark.

As if thinking were any good for fever in the veins!

X

Passion never plays the game. It, at all events, is free from self-consciousness, and pride; from dignity, nerves, scruples, cant, moralities; from hypocrisies, and wisdom, and fears for pocket, and position in this world and the next. Well did the old painters limn it as an arrow or a wind! If it had not been as swift and darting, Earth must long ago have drifted through space untenanted—to let. . . .

After that fevered night Lennan went to his studio at the usual hour and naturally did not do a stroke of work. He was even obliged to send away his model. The fellow had been his hair-dresser, but, getting ill, and falling on dark days, one morning had come to the studio, to ask with manifest shame if his head were any good. After having tested his capacity for standing still, and giving him some introductions, Lennan had noted him down: 'Five feet nine, good hair, lean face, something tortured and pathetic. Give him a turn, if possible.' The turn had come, and the poor man was posing in a painful attitude, talking, whenever permitted, of the way things had treated him, and the delights of cutting hair. This morning he took his departure with the simple pleasure of one fully paid for services not rendered.

And so, walking up and down, up and down, the sculptor waited for Nell's knock. What would happen now? Thinking had made nothing clear. Here was offered what every warm-blooded man whose Spring is past desires—youth and beauty, and in that youth a renewal of his own; what all men save hypocrites and English-men would even admit that they desired. And it was offered to one who had neither religious nor moral scruples, as they are commonly understood. In theory he could accept. In practice he did not as yet know what he could do. One thing only he had discovered during the night's reflections: That those who scouted belief in the principle of Liberty made no greater mistake than to suppose that Liberty was dangerous because it made a man a libertine. To those with any decency, the creed of Freedom was—of all—the most enchaining. Easy enough to break the chains imposed by others, fling his cap over the windmill, and cry for the moment at least: I am unfettered, free! Hard, indeed, to say the same to his own unfettered Self! Yes, his own Self was in the judgment-seat; by his own verdict and decision he must abide. And though he ached for the sight of her, and his will seemed paralysed—many times already he had thought: It won't do! God help me!

Then twelve o'clock had come, and she had not. Would 'The Girl on the Magpie Horse' be all he would see of her to-day—that unsatisfying work, so cold, and devoid of witchery? Better have tried to paint her—with a red flower in her hair, a pout on her lips, and her eyes fey, or languorous. Goya could have painted her!

And then, just as he had given her up, she came.

After taking one look at his face, she slipped in ever so quietly, like a very good child. . . . Marvellous the instinct and finesse of the young when they are women . . . Not a vestige in her of yesterday's seductive power; not a sign that there had been a yesterday at all—just confiding, like a daughter. Sitting there, telling him about Ireland, showing him the little batch of drawings she had done while she was away. Had she brought them because she knew they would make him feel sorry for her? What could have been less dangerous, more appealing to the protective and paternal side of him than she was that morning; as if she only wanted what her father and her home could not give her—only wanted to be a sort of daughter to him!

She went away demurely, as she had gone, refusing to stay to lunch, manifestly avoiding Sylvia. Only then he realised that she must have taken alarm from the look of strain on his face, been afraid that he would send her away; only then perceived that, with her appeal to his protection, she had been binding him closer, making it harder for him to break away and hurt her. And the revered aching began again—worse than ever—the moment he lost sight of her. And more than ever he felt in the grip of something beyond his power to fight against; something that, however he swerved, and backed, and broke away, would close in on him, find means to bind him again hand and foot.

In the afternoon Dromore's confidential man brought him a note. The fellow, with his cast down eyes, and his well-parted hair, seemed to Lennan to be saying: 'Yes, sir—it is quite natural that you should take the note out of eyeshot, sir—*but I know*; fortunately, there is no necessity for alarm—I am strictly confidential.'

And this was what the note contained:

'You promised to ride with me once—you *did* promise, and you never have. Do please ride with me to-morrow; then you will get what you want for the statuette instead of being so cross with it. You can have Dad's horse—he has gone to Newmarket again, and I'm so lonely. Please—to-morrow, at half-past two—starting from here.—NELL.'

To hesitate in view of those confidential eyes was not possible; it must be 'Yes' or 'No'; and if 'No', it would only mean that she would come in the morning instead. So he said:

'Just say "All right!"'

'Very good, sir.' Then from the door: 'Mr Dromore will be away till Saturday, sir.'

Now, why had the fellow said that? Curious how this desperate secret feeling of his own made him see sinister meaning in this servant, in Oliver's visit of last night—in everything. It was vile— this suspiciousness! He could feel, almost see, himself deteriorating already, with this furtive feeling in his soul. It would soon be written on his face! But what was the use of troubling? What would come, would—one way or the other.

And suddenly he remembered with a shock that it was the first of November—Sylvia's birthday! He had never before forgotten it. In the disturbance of that discovery he was very near to going and pouring out to her the whole story of his feelings. A charming birthday present, that would make! Taking his hat, instead, he dashed round to the nearest flower shop. A Frenchwoman kept it.

What had she?

What did Monsieur desire? '*Des oeillets rouges? J'en ai de bien beaux ce soir.*'

No—not those. White flowers!

'*Une belle azalée?*'

Yes, that would do—to be sent at once—at once!

Next door was a jeweller's. He had never really known if Sylvia cared for jewels, since one day he happened to remark that they were vulgar. And feeling that he had fallen low indeed, to be trying to atone with some miserable gewgaw for never having thought of her all day, because he had been thinking of another, he went in and bought the only ornament whose ingredients did not make his gorge rise, two small pear-shaped black pearls, one at each end of a fine platinum chain. Coming out with it, he noticed over the street, in a clear sky fast deepening to indigo, the thinnest slip of a new moon, like a bright swallow, with wings bent back, flying towards the ground. That meant—fine weather! If it could only be fine weather in his heart! And in order that the azalea might arrive first, he walked up and down the Square which he and Oliver had patrolled the night before.

When he went in, Sylvia was just placing the white azalea in the window of the drawing-room; and stealing up behind her he clasped the little necklet round her throat. She turned round and clung to him. He could feel that she was greatly moved. And remorse stirred and stirred in him that he was betraying her with his kiss.

But, even while he kissed her, he was hardening his heart.

XI

Next day, still following the lead of her words about fresh air and his tired look, he told her that he was going to ride, and did not say with whom. After applauding his resolution, she was silent for a little—then asked:

'Why don't you ride with Nell?'

He had already so lost his dignity, that he hardly felt disgraced in answering:

'It might bore her!'

'Oh, no; it wouldn't bore her.'

Had she meant anything by that? And feeling as if he were fencing with his own soul, he said:

'Very well, I will.'

He had perceived suddenly that he did not know his wife, having always till now believed that it was she who did not quite know him.

If she had not been out at lunch-time, he would have lunched out himself—afraid of his own face. For feverishness in sick persons mounts steadily with the approach of a certain hour. And surely his face, to anyone who could have seen him being conveyed to Piccadilly, would have suggested a fevered invalid rather than a healthy, middle-aged sculptor in a cab.

The horses were before the door—the little magpie horse, and a thoroughbred bay mare, weeded from Dromore's racing stable. Nell, too, was standing ready, her cheeks very pink, and her eyes very bright. She did not wait for him to mount her, but took the aid of the confidential man. What was it that made her look so perfect on that little horse—shape of limb, or something soft and fiery in her spirit that the little creature knew of?

They started in silence, but as soon as the sound of hoofs died on the tan of Rotten Row, she turned to him.

'It was lovely of you to come! I thought you'd be afraid—you *are* afraid of me.'

And Lennan thought: You're right!

'But please don't look like yesterday. To-day's too heavenly. Oh! I love beautiful days, and I love riding, and——' She broke off and looked at him. 'Why can't you just be nice to me'—she seemed to be saying—'and love me as you ought!' That was her power—the conviction that he did, and ought to love her; that she ought to and did love him. How simple!

But riding, too, is a simple passion; and simple passions distract each other. It was a treat to be on that bay mare. Who so to be trusted to ride the best as Johnny Dromore?

At the far end of the Row she cried out: 'Let's go on to Richmond now,' and trotted off into the road, as if she knew she could do with him what she wished. And, following meekly, he asked himself: Why? What was there in her to make up to him for all that he was losing—his power of work, his dignity, his self-respect? What was there? Just those eyes, and lips, and hair?

And as if she knew what he was thinking, she looked round and smiled.

So they jogged on over the Bridge and across Barnes Common into Richmond Park.

But the moment they touched turf, with one look back at him, she was off. Had she all the time meant to give him this breakneck chase—or had the loveliness of that autumn day gone to her head—blue sky and coppery flames of bracken in the sun, and the beech leaves and the oak leaves; pure Highland colouring come South for once.

When in the first burst he had tested the mare's wind, this chase of her, indeed, was sheer delight. Through glades, over fallen tree-trunks, in bracken up to the hocks, out across the open, past a herd of amazed and solemn deer, over rotten ground all rabbit-burrows, till just as he thought he was up to her, she slipped away by a quick turn round trees. Mischief incarnate, but something deeper than mischief, too! He came up with her at last, and leaned over to seize her rein. With a cut of her whip that missed his hand by a bare inch, and a wrench, she made him shoot past, wheeled in her tracks, and was off again like an arrow, back amongst the trees— lying right forward under the boughs, along the neck of her little horse. Then out from amongst the trees she shot downhill. Right down she went, full tilt, and after her went Lennan, lying back, and expecting the bay mare to come down at every stride. This was her idea of fun! She switched round at the bottom and went galloping along the foot of the hill; and he thought: Now I've got her! She could not break back up that hill, and there was no other cover for fully half a mile.

Then he saw, not thirty yards in front, an old sandpit; and Great God she was going straight at it! Shouting frantically, he reined his mare outwards. But she only raised her whip, cut the magpie horse over the flank, and rode right on. He saw that little demon gather its feet and spring—down, down, saw him pitch, struggle, sink— and she, flung forward, roll over and lie on her back. He felt nothing at the moment, only had that fixed vision of a yellow patch of sand, the blue sky, a rook flying, and her face upturned. But when he came on her she was on her feet, holding the bridle of her dazed horse. No sooner did he touch her, than she sank down. Her eyes were closed, but he could feel that she had not fainted; and he just held her, and kept pressing his lips to her eyes and forehead. Suddenly she let her head fall back, and her lips met his. Then opening her eyes, she said: 'I'm not hurt, only—funny. Has Magpie cut his knees?'

Not quite knowing what he did, he got up to look. The little horse was cropping at some grass, unharmed—the sand and fern had saved his knees. And the languid voice behind him said: 'It's all right—you can leave the horses. They'll come when I call.'

Now that he knew she was unhurt, he felt angry. Why had she behaved in this mad way—given him this fearful shock? But in that same languid voice she went on: 'Don't be cross with me. I thought at first I'd pull up, but then I thought: "If I jump, he can't help being nice"—so I did—— Don't leave off loving me because I'm not hurt, please.'

163

Terribly moved, he sat down beside her, took her hands in his, and said:

'Nell! Nell! it's all wrong—it's madness!'

'Why? Don't think about it! I don't want you to think—only to love me.'

'My child, you don't know what love is!'

For answer she only flung her arms round his neck; then, since he held back from kissing her, let them fall again, and jumped up.

'Very well. But I love you. You can think of *that*—you can't prevent me!' And without waiting for help, she mounted the magpie horse from the sand-heap where they had fallen.

Very sober that ride home! The horses, as if ashamed of their mad chase, were edging close to each other, so that now and then his arm would touch her shoulder. He asked her once what she had felt while she was jumping.

'Only to be sure my foot was free. It was rather horrid coming down, thinking of Magpie's knees'; and touching the little horse's goat-like ears, she added softly: 'Poor dear! He'll be stiff to-morrow.'

She was again only the confiding, rather drowsy, child. Or was it that the fierceness of those past moments had killed his power of feeling? An almost dreamy hour—with the sun going down, the lamps being lighted one by one—and a sort of sweet oblivion over everything!

At the door, where the groom was waiting, Lennan would have said good-bye, but she whispered: 'Oh, no, please! I *am* tired now —you might help me up a little.'

And so, half carrying her, he mounted past the *Vanity Fair* cartoons, and through the corridor with the red paper and the Van Beers' drawings, into the room where he had first seen her.

Once settled back in Dromore's great chair, with the purring kitten curled up on her neck, she murmured:

'Isn't it nice? You can make tea; and we'll have hot buttered toast.'

And so Lennan stayed, while the confidential man brought tea and toast; and, never once looking at them, seemed to know all that had passed, all that might be to come.

Then they were alone again, and, gazing down at her stretched out in that great chair, Lennan thought:

'Thank God that I'm tired too—body and soul!'

But suddenly she looked up at him, and pointing to the picture that to-day had no curtain drawn, said:

'Do you think I'm like her? I made Oliver tell me about—myself this summer. That's why you needn't bother. It doesn't matter what happens to me, you see. And I don't care—because you can love me, without feeling bad about it. And you will, won't you?'

Then, with her eyes still on his face, she went on quickly:

'Only we won't talk about that now, will we? It's too cosy. I *am* nice and tired. Do smoke!'

But Lennan's fingers trembled so that he could hardly light that cigarette. And, watching them, she said: 'Please give me one. Dad doesn't like my smoking.'

The virtue of Johnny Dromore! Yes! It would always be by proxy! And he muttered:

'How do you think he would like to know about this afternoon, Nell?'

'I don't care.' Then peering up through the kitten's fur she murmured: 'Oliver wants me to go to a dance on Saturday—it's for charity. Shall I?'

'Of course; why not?'

'Will *you* come?'

'I?'

'Oh, do! You must! It's my very first, you know. I've got an extra ticket.'

And against his will, his judgment—everything, Lennan answered: 'Yes.'

She clapped her hands, and the kitten crawled down to her knees.

When he got up to go, she did not move, but just looked up at him; and how he got away he did not know.

Stopping his cab a little short of home, he ran, for he felt cold and stiff, and letting himself in with his latch-key, went straight to the drawing-room. The door was ajar, and Sylvia standing at the window. He heard her sigh; and his heart smote him. Very still, and slender, and lonely she looked out there, with the light shining on her fair hair so that it seemed almost white. Then she turned and saw him. He noticed her throat working with the effort she made not to show him anything, and he said:

'Surely you haven't been anxious! Nell had a bit of a fall—jumping into a sandpit. She's quite mad sometimes. I stayed to tea with her—just to make sure she wasn't really hurt.' But as he spoke he loathed himself; his voice sounded so false.

She only answered: 'It's all right, dear,' but he saw that she kept her eyes—those blue, too true eyes—averted, even when she kissed him.

And so began another evening and night and morning of fever, subterfuge, wariness, aching. A round of half-ecstatic torment, out of which he seemed no more able to break than a man can break through the walls of a cell. . . .

Though it live but a day in the sun, though it drown in tenebrous night, the dark flower of passion will have its hour. . . .

XII

To deceive undoubtedly requires a course of training. And, unversed in this art, Lennan was fast finding it intolerable to scheme and watch himself, and mislead one who had looked up to him ever since they were children. Yet, all the time, he had a feeling that, since he alone knew all the circumstances of his case, he alone was entitled to blame or to excuse himself. The glib judgments that moralists would pass upon his conduct could be nothing but the imbecilities of smug and pharisaic fools—of those not under this drugging spell—of such as had not blood enough, perhaps, ever to fall beneath it!

The day after the ride Nell had not come, and he had no word from her. Was she, then, hurt, after all? She had lain back very inertly in that chair! And Sylvia never asked if he knew how the girl was after her fall, nor offered to send round to inquire. Did she not wish to speak of her, or had she simply—not believed? When there was so much he could not talk of it seemed hard that just what happened to be true should be distrusted. She had not yet, indeed, by a single word suggested that she felt he was deceiving her, but at heart he knew that she was not deceived. . . . Those feelers of a woman who loves—can anything check their delicate apprehension? . . .

Towards evening, the longing to see the girl—a sensation as if she were calling him to come to her—became almost insupportable; yet, whatever excuse he gave, he felt that Sylvia would know where he was going. He sat on one side of the fire, she on the other, and they both read books; the only strange thing about their reading was, that neither of them ever turned a leaf. It was 'Don Quixote' he read, the page which had these words: 'Let Altisidora weep or sing, still I am Dulcinea's and hers alone, dead or alive, dutiful and unchanged, in spite of all the necromantic powers in the world.' And so the evening passed. When she went up to bed, he was very near to stealing out, driving up to the Dromore's door, and inquiring of the confidential man; but the thought of the confounded fellow's eyes was too much for him, and he held out. He took up Sylvia's book, De Maupassant's 'Fort comme la mort'—open at the page where the poor woman finds that her lover has passed away from her to her own daughter. And as he read, the tears rolled down his cheek. Sylvia! Sylvia! Were not his old favourite words from that old favourite book still true? 'Dulcinea del Toboso is the most beautiful woman in the world, and I the most unfortunate knight upon the earth. It were unjust that such perfection should suffer through my weakness. No, pierce my body with your lance, knight, and let my life expire with my honour. . . .' Why could he not wrench this feeling from his heart, banish this girl from his eyes? Why could he not be wholly true to her who was and always had been wholly true to him? Horrible —this will-less, nerveless feeling, this paralysis, as if he were a puppet moved by a cruel hand. And, as once before, it seemed to him that the girl was sitting there in Sylvia's chair in her dark red frock, with her eyes fixed on him. Uncannily vivid—that impression! . . . A man could not go on long with his head in Chancery like this, without becoming crazed!

It was growing dusk on Saturday afternoon when he gave up that intolerable waiting and opened the studio door to go to Nell. It was now just two days since he had seen or heard of her. She had spoken of a dance for that very night—of his going to it. She *must* be ill!

But he had not taken six steps when he saw her coming. She had on a grey furry scarf, hiding her mouth, making her look much older. The moment the door was shut she threw it off, went to the hearth, drew up a little stool, and, holding her hands out to the fire, said:

'Have you thought about me? Have you thought enough now?'

And he answered: 'Yes, I've thought, but I'm no nearer.'

'Why? Nobody need ever know you love me. And if they did, I wouldn't care.'

Simple! How simple! Glorious, egoistic youth!

He could not speak of Sylvia to this child—speak of his married life, hitherto so dignified, so almost sacred. It was impossible. Then he heard her say:

'It can't be wrong to love *you*! I don't care if it is wrong,' and saw her lips quivering, and her eyes suddenly piteous and scared, as if for the first time she doubted of the issue. Here was fresh torment! To watch an unhappy child. And what was the use of even trying to make clear to her—on the very threshold of life—

the hopeless maze that he was wandering in! What chance of making her understand the marsh of mud and tangled weeds he must drag through to reach her. 'Nobody need know.' So simple! What of his heart and his wife's heart? And, pointing to his new work—the first man bewitched by the first nymph—he said:

'Look at this, Nell! That nymph is you; and this man is me.' She got up, and came to look. And while she was gazing he greedily drank her in. What a strange mixture of innocence and sorcery! What a wonderful young creature to bring to full knowledge of love within his arms! And he said: 'You had better understand what you are to me—all that I shall never know again; there it is in that nymph's face. Oh, no! not *your* face. And there am I struggling through slime to reach you—not *my* face, of course.'

She said: 'Poor face!' then covered her own. Was she going to cry, and torture him still more? But, instead, she only murmured: 'But you *have* reached me!' swayed towards him, and put her lips to his.

He gave way then. From that too stormy kiss of his she drew back for a second, then, as if afraid of her own recoil, snuggled close again. But the instinctive shrinking of innocence had been enough for Lennan—he dropped his arms and said:

'You must go, child.'

Without a word she picked up her fur, put it on, and stood waiting for him to speak. Then, as he did not, she held out something white. It was the card for the dance.

'You said you were coming?'

And he nodded. Her eyes and lips smiled at him; she opened the door, and, still with that slow, happy smile, went out. . . .

Yes, he would be coming; wherever she was, whenever she wanted him! . . .

His blood on fire, heedless of everything but to rush after happiness, Lennan spent those hours before the dance. He had told Sylvia that he would be dining at his Club—a set of rooms owned by a small coterie of artists in Chelsea. He had taken this precaution, feeling that he could not sit through dinner opposite her and then go out to that dance—and Nell! He had spoken of a guest at the Club, to account for evening dress—another lie, but what did it matter? He was lying all the time, if not in words, in action—must lie, indeed, to save her suffering!

He stopped at the Frenchwoman's flower shop.

'Que désirez-vous, monsieur? Des oeillets rouges—j'en ai de bien beaux, ce soir.'

168

Des oeillets rouges? Yes, those to-night! To this address. No green with them; no card!

How strange the feeling—with the die once cast for love—of rushing, of watching his own self being left behind!

In the Brompton Road, outside a little restaurant, a thin musician was playing on a violin. Ah! and he knew this place; he would go in there, not to the Club—and the fiddler should have all he had to spare, for playing those tunes of love. He turned in. He had not been there since the day before that night on the river, twenty years ago. Never since; and yet it was not changed. The same tarnished gilt, and smell of cooking; the same macaroni in the same tomato sauce; the same Chianti flasks; the same staring, light-blue walls wreathed with pink flowers. Only the waiter different—hollow-cheeked, patient, dark of eye. He, too, should be well tipped! And that poor, over-hatted lady, eating her frugal meal—to her, at all events, a look of kindness. For all desperate creatures he must feel, this desperate night! And suddenly he thought of Oliver. Another desperate one! What should he say to Oliver at this dance—he, aged forty-seven, coming there without his wife! Some imbecility, such as: 'Watching the human form divine in motion,' 'Catching sidelights on Nell for the statuette'—some cant; it did not matter! The wine was drawn, and he must drink!

It was still early when he left the restaurant—a dry night, very calm, not cold. When had he danced last? With Olive Cramier, before he knew he loved her. Well, *that* memory could not be broken, for he would not dance to-night! Just watch, sit with the girl a few minutes, feel her hand cling to his, see her eyes turned back to him; and—come away! And then—the future! For the wine was drawn! The leaf of a plane-tree, fluttering down, caught on his sleeve. Autumn would soon be gone, and after Autumn—only Winter! She would have done with him long before he came to Winter. Nature would see to it that Youth called for her, and carried her away. Nature in her courses! But just to cheat Nature for a little while! To cheat Nature—what greater happiness!

Here was the place, with red-striped awning, carriages driving away, loiterers watching. He turned in, with a beating heart. Was he before her? How would she come to this first dance? With Oliver alone? Or had some chaperon been found? To have come because she—this child so lovely, born 'outside'—might have need of chaperonage, would have been some comfort to dignity, so wistful, so lost as his. But, alas! he knew he was only there because he could not keep away!

169

Already they were dancing in the hall upstairs; but not she, yet; and he stood leaning against the wall where she must pass. Lonely and out of place he felt; as if everyone must know why he was there. People stared, and he heard a girl ask: 'Who's that against the wall with the hair and dark moustache?'—and her partner murmuring his answer, and her voice again: 'Yes, he looks as if he were seeing sand and lions.' For whom, then, did they take him? Thank heaven! They were all the usual sort. There would be no one that he knew. Suppose Johnny Dromore himself came with Nell! He was to be back on Saturday! What could he say, then? How meet those doubting, knowing eyes, goggling with the fixed philosophy that a man has but one use for woman? God! and it would be true! For a moment he was on the point of getting his coat and hat, and sneaking away. That would mean not seeing her till Monday; and he stood his ground. But after to-night there must be no more such risks—their meetings must be wisely planned, must sink underground. And then he saw her at the foot of the stairs in a dress of a shell-pink colour, with one of his flowers in her light-brown hair and the other tied to the handle of a tiny fan. How self-possessed she looked, as if this were indeed her native element—her neck and arms bare, her cheeks a deep soft pink, her eyes quickly turning here and there. She began mounting the stairs, and saw him. Was ever anything so lovely as she looked just then? Behind her he marked Oliver, and a tall girl with red hair, and another young man. He moved deliberately to the top of the stairs on the wall side, so that from behind they should not see her face when she greeted him. She put the little fan with the flower to her lips; and, holding out her hand, said, quickly and low:

'The fourth, it's a polka; we'll sit out, won't we?'

Then swaying a little, so that her hair and the flower in it almost touched his face, she passed, and there in her stead stood Oliver.

Lennan had expected one of his old insolent looks but the young man's face was eager and quite friendly.

'It was awfully good of you to come, Mr Lennan. Is Mrs Lennan——'

And Lennan murmured:

'She wasn't able; she's not quite——' and could have sunk into the shining floor. Youth with its touching confidence, its eager trust! This was the way he was fulfilling his duty towards Youth!

When they had passed into the ballroom he went back to his position against the wall. They were dancing Number Three; his

170

time of waiting, then, was drawing to a close. From where he stood he could not see the dancers—no use to watch her go round in someone else's arms.

Not a true waltz—some French or Spanish pavement song played in waltz time; bizarre, pathetic, whirling after its own happiness. That chase for happiness! Well, life, with all its prizes and its possibilities, had nothing that quite satisfied—save just the fleeting moments of passion! Nothing else quite poignant enough to be called pure joy! Or so it seemed to him.

The waltz was over. He could see her now, on a rout seat against the wall with the other young man, turning her eyes constantly as if to make sure that he was still standing there. What subtle fuel was always being added to the fire by that flattery of her inexplicable adoration—of those eyes that dragged him to her, yet humbly followed him, too! Five times while she sat there he saw the red-haired girl or Oliver bring men up; saw youths cast longing glances; saw girls watching her with cold appraisement, or with a touching, frank delight. From the moment that she came in, there had been, in her father's phrase, 'only one in it'. And she could pass all this by, and still want him. Incredible!

At the first notes of the polka he went to her. It was she who found their place of refuge—a little alcove behind two palm-plants. But sitting there, he realised, as never before, that there was no spiritual communion between him and this child. She could tell him her troubles or her joys; he could soothe or sympathise; but never would the gap between their natures and their ages be crossed. His happiness was only in the sight and touch of her. But that, God knew, was happiness enough—a feverish, craving joy, like an over-tired man's thirst, growing with the drink on which it tries to slake itself. Sitting there, in the scent of those flowers and of some sweet essence in her hair, with her fingers touching his, and her eyes seeking his, he tried loyally not to think of himself, to grasp her sensations at this her first dance, and just help her to enjoyment. But he could not—paralysed, made drunk by that insensate longing to take her in his arms and crush her to him as he had those few hours back. He could see her expanding like a flower, in all this light, and motion, and intoxicating admiration round her. What business had he in her life, with his dark hunger after secret hours; he—a coin worn thin already—a destroyer of the freshness and the glamour of her youth and beauty!

Then, holding up the flowers, she said:

'Did you give me these because of the one I gave you?'

'Yes.'

'What did you do with that?'

'Burned it.'

'Oh! but why?'

'Because you are a witch—and witches must be burned with all their flowers.'

'Are you going to burn me?'

He put his hand on her cool arm.

'Feel! The flames are lighted.'

'You may! I don't care!'

She took his hand and laid her cheek against it; yet, to the music, which had begun again, the tip of her shoe was already beating time. And he said:

'You ought to be dancing, child.'

'Oh, no! Only it's a pity you don't want to.'

'Yes! Do you understand that it must all be secret—underground?'

She covered his lips with the fan, and said: 'You're not to think; you're not to think—never! When can I come?'

'I must find the best way. Not to-morrow. Nobody must know, Nell—for your sake—for hers—nobody!'

She nodded, and repeated with a soft, mysterious wisdom: 'Nobody.' And then, aloud: 'Here's Oliver! It was awfully good of you to come. Good-night!'

And as, on Oliver's arm, she left their little refuge, she looked back.

He lingered—to watch her through this one dance. How they made all the other couples sink into insignificance, with that something in them both that was better than mere good looks—that something not *outré* or eccentric, but poignant, wayward. They went well together, those two Dromores—his dark head and her fair head; his clear, brown, daring eyes, and her grey, languorous, mesmeric eyes. Ah! Master Oliver was happy now, with her so close to him! It was not jealousy that Lennan felt. Not quite—one did not feel jealous of the young; something very deep—pride, sense of proportion, who knew what—prevented that. She, too, looked happy, as if her soul were dancing, vibrating with the music and the scent of the flowers. He waited for her to come round once more, to get for a last time that flying glance turned back; then found his coat and hat and went.

172

XIII

Outside, he walked a few steps, then stood looking back at the windows of the hall through some trees, the shadows of whose trunks, in the light of a street lamp, were spilled out along the ground like the splines of a fan. A church clock struck eleven. For hours yet she would be there, going round and round in the arms of Youth! Try as he might he could never recapture for himself the look that Oliver's face had worn—the look that was the symbol of so much more than he himself could give her. Why had she come into his life—to her undoing, and his own? And the bizarre thought came to him: If she were dead should I really care? Should I not be almost glad? If she were dead her witchery would be dead, and I, could stand up straight again and look people in the face! What was this power that played with men, darted into them, twisted their hearts to rags; this power that had looked through her eyes when she put her fan, with his flowers, to her lips?

The thrumming of the music ceased; he walked away:

It must have been nearly twelve when he reached home. Now, once more, would begin the gruesome process of deception—flinching of soul, and brazening of visage. It would be better when the whole thievish business was irretrievably begun and ordered in its secret courses!

There was no light in the drawing-room, save just the glow of the fire. If only Sylvia might have gone to bed! Then he saw her, sitting motionless out there by the uncurtained window.

He went over to her, and began his hateful formula:

'I'm afraid you've been lonely. I had to stay rather late. A dull evening.' And, since she did not move or answer, but just sat there very still and white, he forced himself to go close, bend down to her, touch her cheek; even to kneel beside her. She looked round then; her face was quiet enough, but her eyes were strangely eager. With a pitiful little smile she broke out:

'Oh, Mark! What is it—what is it? Anything is better than this!'

Perhaps it was the smile, perhaps her voice or eyes—but something gave way in Lennan. Secrecy, precaution went by the board. Bowing his head against her breast, he poured it all out, while they clung, clutched together in the half dark like two frightened children. Only when he had finished did he realise that if she had pushed

173

him away, refused to let him touch her, it would have been far less piteous, far easier to bear, than her wan face and her hands clutching him, and her words: 'I never thought—you and I—oh! Mark —you and I——' The trust in their life together, in himself, that those words revealed! Yet, not greater than he had had—still had! She could not understand—he had known that she could never understand; it was why he had fought so for secrecy, all through. She was taking it as if she had lost everything; and in his mind she had lost nothing. This passion, this craving for Youth and Life, this madness—call it what one would—was something quite apart, not touching his love and need of her. If she would only believe that! Over and over he repeated it; over and over again perceived that she could not take it in. The only thing she saw was that his love had gone from her to another—though that was not true! Suddenly she broke out of his arms, pushing him from her, and cried: 'That girl—hateful, horrible, false!' Never had he seen her look like this, with flaming spots in her white cheeks, soft lips and chin distorted, blue eyes flaming, breast heaving, as if each breath were drawn from lungs that received no air. And then, as quickly, the fire went out of her; she sank down on the sofa, covering her face with her arms, rocking to and fro. She did not cry, but a little moan came from her now and then. And each one of those sounds was to Lennan like the cry of something he was murdering. At last he went and sat down on the sofa by her and said:

'Sylvia! Sylvia! Don't! oh! don't!' And she was silent, ceasing to rock herself; letting him smooth and stroke her. But her face she kept hidden, and only once she spoke, so low that he could hardly hear: 'I can't—I won't keep you from her.' And with the awful feeling that no words could reach or soothe the wound in that tender heart, he could only go on stroking and kissing her hands.

It was atrocious—horrible—this that he had done! God knew that he had not sought it—the thing had come on him. Surely even in her misery she could see that! Deep down beneath his grief and self-hatred, he knew, what neither she nor anyone else could know —that he could not have prevented this feeling, which went back to days before he ever saw the girl—that no man could have stopped that feeling in himself. This craving and roving was as much part of him as his eyes and hands, as overwhelming and natural a longing as his hunger for work, or his need of the peace that Sylvia gave, and alone could give him. That was the tragedy —it was all sunk and rooted in the very nature of a man. Since the

girl had come into their lives he was no more unfaithful to his wife in thought than he had been before. If only she could look into him, see him exactly as he was, as, without part or lot in the process, he had been made—then she would understand, and even might not suffer; but she could not, and he could never make it plain. And solemnly, desperately, with a weary feeling of the futility of words, he went on trying: Could she not see? It was all a thing outside him—a craving, a chase after beauty and life, after his own youth! At that word she looked at him:

'And do you think *I* don't want my youth back?'

He stopped.

For a woman to feel that her beauty—the brightness of her hair and eyes, the grace and suppleness of her limbs—were slipping from her and from the man she loved! Was there anything more bitter? —or any more sacred duty than not to add to that bitterness, not to push her with suffering into old age, but to help keep the star of her faith in her charm intact!

Man and woman—they both wanted youth again; she, that she might give it all to him; he, because it would help him towards something—new! Just that world of difference!

He got up, and said:

'Come, dear, let's try and sleep.'

He had not once said that he could give it up. The words would not pass his lips, though he knew she must be conscious that he had not said them, must be longing to hear them. All he had been able to say was:

'So long as you want me, you shall never lose me' . . . and, 'I will never keep anything from you again.'

Up in their room she lay hour after hour in his arms, quite unresentful, but without life in her, and with eyes that, when his lips touched them, were always wet.

What a maze was a man's heart, wherein he must lose himself every minute! What involved and intricate turnings and turnings on itself; what fugitive replacement of emotion by emotion! What strife between pities and passions; what longing for peace! . . .

And in his feverish exhaustion, which was almost sleep, Lennan hardly knew whether it was the thrum of music or Sylvia's moaning that he heard; her body or Nell's within his arms. . . .

But life had to be lived, a face preserved against the world, engagements kept. And the nightmare went on for both of them, under the calm surface of an ordinary Sunday. They were like people walking at the edge of a high cliff, not knowing from step to step whether they would fall; or like swimmers struggling for issue out of a dark whirlpool.

In the afternoon they went together to a concert. It was just something to do—something that saved them for an hour or two from the possibility of speaking on the one subject left to them. The ship had gone down, and they were clutching at anything that for a moment would help to keep them above water.

In the evening some people came to supper; a writer and two painters, with their wives. A grim evening—never more so than when the conversation turned on that perennial theme—the freedom, spiritual, mental, physical, requisite for those who practise Art. All the stale arguments were brought forth, and had to be joined in with unmoved faces. And for all their talk of freedom, Lennan could see the *volte-face* his friends would be making, if they only knew. It was not 'the thing' to seduce young girls—as if, forsooth, there were freedom in doing only what people thought 'the thing'! Their cant about the free artist spirit experiencing everything, would wither the moment it came up against a canon of 'good form', so that in truth it was no freer than the bourgeois spirit, with its conventions; or the priest spirit, with its cry of 'Sin!' No, no! To resist—if resistance were possible to this dragging power—maxims of 'good form', dogmas of religion and morality, were no help—nothing was any help, but some feeling stronger than passion itself. Sylvia's face, forced to smile!—that, indeed, was a reason why they should condemn him! None of their doctrines about freedom could explain that away—the harm, the death that came to a man's soul when he made a loving, faithful creature suffer.

But they were gone at last—with their 'Thanks so much!' and their 'Delightful evening!'

And those two were face to face for another night.

He knew that it must begin all over again—inevitable, after the stab of that wretched argument plunged into their hearts and turned and turned all the evening.

'I won't, I mustn't keep you starved, and spoil your work. Don't think of me, Mark! I can bear it!'

And then a breakdown worse than the night before. What genius, what sheer genius Nature had for torturing her creatures! If anyone had told him, even so little as a week ago, that he could have caused such suffering to Sylvia—Sylvia, whom as a child with wide blue eyes and a blue bow on her flaxen head he had guarded across fields full of imaginary bulls; Sylvia, in whose hair his star had caught; Sylvia, who day and night for fifteen years, had been his devoted wife; whom he loved and still admired—he would have given him the lie direct. It would have seemed incredible, monstrous, silly. Had all married men and women such things to go through—was this but a very usual crossing of the desert? Or was it, once for all, shipwreck? death—unholy, violent death—in a storm of sand?

Another night of misery, and no answer to that question yet.

He had told her that he would not see Nell again without first letting her know. So, when morning came, he simply wrote the words: 'Don't come to-day!'—showed them to Sylvia, and sent them by a servant to Dromore's.

Hard to describe the bitterness with which he entered his studio that morning. In all this chaos, what of his work? Could he ever have peace of mind for it again? Those people last night had talked of 'inspiration of passion, of experience'. In pleading with her he had used the words himself. She—poor soul!—had but repeated them, trying to endure them, to believe them true. And were they true? Again no answer, or certainly none that he could give. To have had the waters broken up; to be plunged into emotion; to feel desperately, instead of stagnating—some day he might be gratefull—who knew? Some day there might be fair country again beyond this desert, where he could work even better than before. But just now, as well expect creative work from a condemned man. It seemed to him that he was equally destroyed whether he gave Nell up, and with her, once for all, that roving, seeking instinct, which ought, forsooth, to have been satisfied, and was not; or whether he took Nell, knowing that in doing so he was torturing a woman dear to him! That was as far as he could see to-day. What he would come to see in time God only knew! But: 'Freedom of the Spirit'! That was a phrase of bitter irony indeed! And, there, like a man tied hand and foot, with his work all round him, he was swept by such a feeling of exasperated rage as he had never known. Women! These women! Only let him be free of both, of all women, and the passions and pities they aroused, so that his brain and his hands might live and work again! They should not strangle, they should not destroy him!

Unfortunately, even in his rage, he knew that flight from them both could never help him. One way or the other the thing would have to be fought through. If it had been a straight fight even; a clear issue between passion and pity! But both he loved, and both he pitied. There was nothing straight and clear about it anywhere;

it was all too deeply rooted in full human nature. And the appalling sense of rushing ceaselessly from barrier to barrier began really to affect his brain.

True, he had now and then a lucid interval of a few minutes, when the ingenious nature of his own torments struck him as supremely interesting and queer; but this was not precisely a relief, for it only meant, as in prolonged toothache, that his power of feeling had for a moment ceased. A very pretty little hell indeed!

All day he had the premonition, amounting to certainty, that Nell would take alarm at those three words he had sent her, and come in spite of them. And yet, what else could he have written? Nothing save what must have alarmed her more, or plunged him deeper. He had the feeling that she could follow his moods, that her eyes could see him everywhere, as a cat's eyes can see in darkness. That feeling had been with him, more or less, ever since the last evening of October, the evening she came back from her summer—grown-up. How long ago? Only six days—was it possible? Ah, yes! She knew when her spell was weakening, when the current wanted, as it were, renewing. And about six o'clock—dusk already—without the least surprise, with only a sort of empty quivering, he heard her knock. And just behind the closed door, as near as he could get to her, he stood, holding his breath. He had given his word to Sylvia—of his own accord had given it. Through the thin wood of the old door he could hear the faint shuffle of her feet on the pavement, moved a few inches this way and that, as though supplicating the inexorable silence. He seemed to see her head, bent a little forward, listening. Three times she knocked and each time Lennan writhed. It was so cruel! With that seeing-sense of hers she must know he was there; his very silence would be telling her—for his silence had its voice, its pitiful breathless sound. Then, quite distinctly, he heard her sigh, and her footsteps move away; and covering his face with his hands he rushed to and fro in the studio, like a madman.

No sound of her any more! Gone! It was unbearable; and, seizing his hat, he ran out. Which way? At random he ran towards the Square. There she was, over by the railings; languidly, irresolutely moving towards home.

XIV

But now that she was within reach, he wavered; he had given his word—was he going to break it? Then she turned, and saw him; he could not go back. In the biting easterly wind her face looked small, and pinched, and cold, but her eyes only the larger, the more full of witchery, as if beseeching him not to be angry, not to send her away.

'I had to come; I got frightened. Why did you write such a tiny little note?'

He tried to make his voice sound quiet and ordinary.

'You must be brave, Nell. I have had to tell her.'

She clutched at his arm; then drew herself up, and said in her clear, clipped voice:

'Oh! I suppose she hates me, then!'

'She is terribly unhappy.'

They walked a minute, that might have been an hour, without a word; not round the Square, as he had walked with Oliver, but away from the house. At last she said in a half-choked voice: 'I only want a little bit of you.'

And he answered dully: 'In love, there are no little bits—no standing still.'

Then, suddenly, he felt her hand in his, the fingers lacing, twining restlessly amongst his own; and again the half-choked voice said:

'But you *will* let me see you sometimes! You must!'

Hardest of all to stand against was this pathetic, clinging, frightened child. And, not knowing very clearly what he said, he murmured:

'Yes—yes; it'll be all right. Be brave—you must be brave, Nell. It'll all come right.'

But she only answered:

'No, no! I'm not brave. I shall do something.'

Her face looked just as when she had ridden at that gravel pit. Loving, wild, undisciplined, without resource of any kind—what might she not do? Why could he not stir without bringing disaster upon one or other? And between these two, suffering so because of him, he felt as if he had lost his own existence. In quest of happiness, he had come to that!

Suddenly she said:

179

'Oliver asked me again at the dance on Saturday. He said you had told him to be patient. Did you?'

'Yes.'

'Why?'

'I was sorry for him.'

She let his hand go.

'Perhaps you would like me to marry him.'

Very clearly he saw those two going round and round over the shining floor.

'It would be better, Nell.'

She made a little sound—of anger or dismay.

'You don't *really* want me, then?'

That was his chance. But with her arm touching his, her face so pale and desperate, and those maddening eyes turned to him, he could not tell that lie, and answered:

'Yes—I want you, God knows!'

At that a sigh of content escaped her, as if she were saying to herself: 'If he wants me he will not let me go.' Strange little tribute to her faith in love and her own youth!

They had come somehow to Pall Mall by now. And scared to find himself so deep in the hunting-ground of the Dromores, Lennan turned hastily towards St James's Park, that they might cross it in the dark, round to Piccadilly. To be thus slinking out of the world's sight with the daughter of his old room-mate—of all men in the world the last perhaps that he should do this to! A nice treacherous business! But the thing men called honour—what was it, when her eyes were looking at him and her shoulder touching his?

Since he had spoken those words, 'Yes, I want you,' she had been silent—fearful perhaps to let other words destroy their comfort. But near the gate by Hyde Park Corner she put her hand again into his, and again her voice, so clear, said:

'I don't want to hurt anybody, but you *will* let me come some-times—you will let me see you—you won't leave me all alone, thinking that I'll never see you again?'

And once more, without knowing what he answered, Lennan murmured:

'No, no! It'll be all right, dear—it'll all come right. It must—and shall.'

Again her fingers twined amongst his, like a child's. She seemed to have a wonderful knowledge of the exact thing to say and do to keep him helpless. And she went on:

'I didn't try to love you—it isn't wrong to love—it wouldn't hurt her. I only want a little of your love.'

A little—always a little! But he was solely bent on comforting her now. To think of her going home, and sitting lonely, frightened, and unhappy, all the evening, was dreadful. And holding her fingers tight, he kept on murmuring words of would-be comfort.

Then he saw that they were out in Piccadilly. How far dared he go with her along the railings before he said good-bye? A man was coming towards them, just where he had met Dromore that first fatal afternoon nine months ago; a man with a slight lurch in his walk and a tall, shining hat a little on one side. But thank Heaven! —it was not Dromore—only one somewhat like him, who in passing stared sphinx-like at Nell. And Lennan said:

'You must go home now, child; we mustn't be seen together.'

For a moment he thought she was going to break down, refuse to leave him. Then she threw up her head, and for a second stood like that, quite motionless, looking in his face. Suddenly stripping off her glove, she thrust her warm, clinging hand into his. Her lips smiled faintly, tears stood in her eyes; then she drew her hand away and plunged into the traffic. He saw her turn the corner of her street and disappear. And with the warmth of that passionate little hand still stinging his palm, he almost ran towards Hyde Park.

Taking no heed of direction, he launched himself into its dark space, deserted in this cold, homeless wind, that had little sound and no scent, travelling its remorseless road under the grey-black sky.

The dark firmament and keen cold air suited one who had little need of aids to emotion—one who had, indeed, but the single wish to get rid, if he only could, of the terrible sensation in his head, that bruised, battered, imprisoned feeling of a man who paces his cell—never, never to get out at either end. Without thought or intention he drove his legs along; not running, because he knew that he would have to stop the sooner. Alas! what more comic spectacle for the eyes of a good citizen than this married man of middle age, striding for hours over those dry, dark, empty pastures—hunted by passion and by pity, so that he knew not even whether he had dined! But no good citizen was abroad on an autumn night in a bitter easterly wind. The trees were the sole witnesses of this grim exercise—the trees, resigning to the cold blast their crinkled leaves that fluttered past him, just a little lighter than the darkness. Here and there his feet rustled in the drifts, waiting their turn to serve the little bonfires, whose scent still clung in the air. A desperate walk, in this heart of London—round and round, up and down, hour after hour, keeping always in the dark; not a star in the sky, not a human being spoken to or even clearly seen, not a bird or beast; just the gleam of the lights far away, and the hoarse muttering of the traffic! A walk as lonely as the voyage of the human soul is lonely from birth to death with nothing to guide it but the flickering glow from its own frail spirit lighted it knows not where. . . .

And, so tired that he could hardly move his legs, but free at last of that awful feeling in his head—free for the first time for days and days—Lennan came out of the Park at the gate where he had gone in, and walked towards his home, certain that to-night, one way or the other, it would be decided. . . .

xv

This then—this long trouble of body and of spirit—was what he remembered, sitting in the armchair beyond his bedroom fire, watching the glow, and Sylvia sleeping there exhausted, while the dark plane-tree leaves tap-tapped at the window in the autumn wind; watching, with the uncanny certainty that he would not pass the limits of this night without having made at last a decision that would not alter. For even conflict wears itself out; even indecision has this measure set to its miserable powers of torture, that any issue in the end is better than the hell of indecision itself. Once or twice in those last days even death had seemed to him quite tolerable; but now that his head was clear and he had come to grips, death passed out of his mind like the shadow that it was. Nothing so simple, extravagant, and vain could serve him. Other issues had reality; death—none. To leave Sylvia, and take this young love away; there was reality in that, but it had always faded as soon as it shaped itself; and now once more it faded. To put such a public and terrible affront on a tender wife whom he loved, do her to death, as it were, before the world's eyes—and then, ever remorseful, grow old while the girl was still young? He could not. If Sylvia had not loved him, yes; or, even if he had not loved her; or if, again, though loving him she had stood upon her rights—in any of those events he might have done it. But to leave her whom he did love, and who had said to him so generously: 'I will not hamper you—go to her'—would be a black atrocity. Every memory, from their boy-and-girl lovering to the desperate clinging of her arms these last two nights—memory with its innumerable tentacles, the invincible strength of its countless threads, bound him to her too fast. What then? Must it come, after all, to giving up the girl? And sitting there, by that warm fire, he shivered. How desolate, sacrilegious, wasteful to throw love away; to turn from the most precious of all gifts; to drop and break that vase! There was not too much love in the world, nor too much warmth and beauty—not, anyway, for those whose sands were running out, whose blood would soon be cold.

Could Sylvia not let him keep both her love and the girl's? Could she not bear that? She had said she could; but her face, her eyes, her voice gave her the lie, so that every time he heard her his heart turned sick with pity. This, then, was the real issue. Could he accept from her such a sacrifice, exact a daily misery, see her droop and fade beneath it? Could he bear his own happiness at such a cost? Would it be happiness at all? He got up from the chair and crept towards her. She looked very fragile sleeping there! The darkness below her closed eyelids showed cruelly on that too fair skin; and in her flax-coloured hair he saw what he had never noticed—a few strands of white. Her softly opened lips, almost colourless, quivered with her uneven breathing; and now and again a little feverish shiver passed up as from her heart. All soft and fragile! Not much life, not much strength; youth and beauty slipping! To know that he who should be her champion against age and time would day by day be placing one more mark upon her face, one more sorrow in her heart! That he should do this—they both going down the years together!

As he stood there holding his breath, bending to look at her, that slurring swish of the plane-tree branch, flung against and against the window by the autumn wind, seemed filling the whole world. Then her lips moved in one of those little, soft hurrying whispers that unhappy dreamers utter, the words all blurred with their wistful rushing.

And he thought: I, who believe in bravery and kindness; I, who hate cruelty—if I do this cruel thing, what shall I have to live for; how shall I work; how bear myself? If I do it, I am lost—an outcast from my own faith—a renegade from all that I believe in.

And, kneeling there close to that face so sad and lonely, that heart so beaten even in its sleep, he knew that he could not do it—knew it with sudden certainty, and a curious sense of peace. Over! —the long struggle—over at last! Youth with youth, summer to summer, falling leaf with falling leaf! And behind him the fire flickered, and the plane-tree leaves tap-tapped.

He rose, and crept away stealthily downstairs into the drawing-room, and through the window at the far end out into the court-yard, where he had sat that day by the hydrangea, listening to the piano-organ. Very dark and cold and eerie it was there, and he hurried across to his studio. There, too, it was cold, and dark, and eerie, with its ghostly plaster presences, stale scent of cigarettes, and just one glowing ember of the fire he had left when he rushed out after Nell—those seven hours ago.

He went first to the bureau, turned up its lamp, and taking out some sheets of paper, marked on them directions for his various works; for the statuette of Nell, he noted that it should be taken with his compliments to Mr Dromore. He wrote a letter to his banker directing money to be sent to Rome, and to his solicitor telling him to let the house. He wrote quickly. If Sylvia woke, and found him still away, what might she not think? He took a last sheet. Did it matter what he wrote, what deliberate lie, if it helped Nell over the first shock?

'DEAR NELL,

'I write this hastily in the early hours, to say that we are called out to Italy to my only sister, who is very ill. We leave by the first morning boat, and may be away some time. I will write again. Don't fret, and God bless you.

'M.L.'

He could not see very well as he wrote. Poor, loving, desperate child! Well, she had youth and strength, and would soon have—Oliver! And he took yet another sheet.

'DEAR OLIVER,

'My wife and I are obliged to go post-haste to Italy. I watched you both at the dance the other night. Be very gentle with Nell; and—good luck to you! But don't say again that I told you to be patient; it is hardly the way to make her love you.

'M. LENNAN.'

That, then, was all—yes, all! He turned out the little lamp, and groped towards the hearth. But one thing left. To say good-bye! To her, and Youth, and Passion!—to the only salve for the aching that Spring and Beauty bring—the aching for the wild, the passionate, the new, that never quite dies in a man's heart. Ah! well, sooner or later, all men had to say good-bye to that. All men—all men!

He crouched down before the hearth. There was no warmth in that fast-blackening ember, but it still glowed like a dark-red flower. And while it lived he crouched there, as though it were that to which he was saying good-bye. And on the door he heard the girl's ghostly knocking. And beside him—a ghost among the ghostly presences—she stood. Slowly the glow blackened, till the last spark had faded out.

Then by the glimmer of the night he found his way back, softly as he had come, to his bedroom.

Sylvia was still sleeping; and, to watch for her to wake, he sat down again by the fire, in silence only stirred by the frail tap-tapping of those autumn leaves, and the little catch in her breathing now and then. It was less troubled than when he had bent over her before, as though in her sleep she knew. He must not miss the moment of her waking, must be beside her before she came to full consciousness, to say: 'There, there! It's all over; we are going away at once—at once.' To be ready to offer that quick solace, before she had time to plunge back into her sorrow, was an island in this black sea of night, a single little refuge point for his bereaved and naked being. Something to do—something fixed, real, certain. And yet another long hour before her waking, he sat forward in the chair, with that wistful eagerness, his eyes fixed on her face, staring through it at some vision, some faint, glimmering light—far out there beyond—as a traveller watches a star. . . .

Fraternity

Brother, brother, on some far shore
Hast thou a city, is there a door
That knows thy footfall, Wandering One?

Murray's *Electra of Euripides*

Chapter 1

THE SHADOW

ON the afternoon of the last day of April, 190—, a billowy sea of little broken clouds crowned the thin air above High Street, Kensington. This soft tumult of vapours, covering nearly all the firmament, was in onslaught round a patch of blue sky, shaped somewhat like a star, which still gleamed—a single gentian flower amongst innumerable grass. Each of these small clouds seemed fitted with a pair of unseen wings, and, as insects fly on their too constant journeys, they were setting forth all ways round this starry blossom which burned so clear with the colour of its far fixity. On one side they were massed in fleecy congeries, so crowding each other that no edge or outline was preserved; on the other, higher, stronger, emergent from their fellow-clouds, they seemed leading the attack on that surviving gleam of the ineffable. Infinite was the variety of those million separate vapours, infinite the unchanging unity of that fixed blue star.

Down in the street beneath this eternal warring of the various soft-winged clouds on the unmisted ether, men, women, children, and their familiars—horses, dogs, and cats—were pursuing their occupations with the sweet zest of the Spring. They streamed along, and the noise of their frequenting rose in an unbroken roar: 'I, I—I, I!'

The crowd was perhaps thickest outside the premises of Messrs Rose and Thorn. Every kind of being, from the highest to the lowest, passed in front of the hundred doors of this establishment; and before the costume window a rather tall, slight, graceful woman stood thinking: 'It really is gentian blue! But I don't know whether I ought to buy it, with all this distress about!'

Her eyes, which were greenish-grey, and often ironical lest they should reveal her soul, seemed probing a blue gown displayed in that window, to the very heart of its desirability.

'And suppose Stephen doesn't like me in it!' This doubt set her gloved fingers pleating the bosom of her frock. Into that little pleat she folded the essence of herself, the wish to have and the fear of having, the wish to be and the fear of being, and her veil, falling from the edge of her hat, three inches from her face, shrouded with its tissue her half-decided little features, her rather too high cheek-

189

bones, her cheeks that were slightly hollowed, as though Time had kissed them just a bit too much.

The old man, with a long face, eyes rimmed like a parrot's, and discoloured nose, who, so long as he did not sit down, was permitted to frequent the pavement just there and sell the *Westminster Gazette*, marked her, and took his empty pipe out of his mouth.

It was his business to know all the passers-by, and his pleasure too; his mind was thus distracted from the condition of his feet. He knew this particular lady with the delicate face, and found her puzzling; she sometimes bought the paper which Fate condemned him, against his politics, to sell. The Tory journals were undoubtedly those which her class of person ought to purchase. He knew a lady when he saw one. In fact, before Life threw him into the streets, by giving him a disease in curing which his savings had disappeared, he had been a butler, and for the gentry had a respect as incurable as was his distrust of 'all that class of people' who bought their things at 'these 'ere large establishments', and attended 'these 'ere subscription dances at the Town 'All over there'. He watched her with special interest, not, indeed, attempting to attract attention, though conscious in every fibre that he had only sold five copies of his early issues. And he was sorry and surprised when she passed from his sight through one of the hundred doors.

The thought which spurred her into Messrs Rose and Thorn's was this: 'I am thirty-eight; I have a daughter of seventeen! I cannot afford to lose my husband's admiration. The time is on me when I really must make myself look nice!'

Before a long mirror, in whose bright pool there yearly bathed hundreds of women's bodies, divested of skirts and bodices, whose unruffled surface reflected daily a dozen women's souls divested of everything, her eyes became as bright as steel; but having ascertained the need of taking two inches off the chest of the gentian frock, one off its waist, three off its hips, and of adding one to its skirt, they clouded again with doubt, as though prepared to fly from the decision she had come to. Resuming her bodice, she asked:

'When could you let me have it?'

'At the end of the week, madam.'

'Not till then?'

'We are very pressed, madam.'

'Oh, but you *must* let me have it by Thursday at the latest, please.'

The fitter sighed: 'I will do my best.'

'I shall rely on you. Mrs Stephen Dallison, 76, The Old Square.'

Going downstairs she thought: 'That poor girl looked very tired; it's a shame they give them such long hours!' and she passed into the street.

A voice said timidly behind her: '*Westminster*, marm?'

'That's the poor old creature,' thought Cecilia Dallison, 'whose nose is so unpleasant. I don't really think I——' and she felt for a penny in her little bag. Standing beside the 'poor old creature' was a woman clothed in worn but neat black clothes, and an ancient toque that had once known a better head. The wan remains of a little bit of fur lay round her throat. She had a thin face, not without refinement, mild, very clear brown eyes, and a twist of smooth black hair. Beside her was a skimpy little boy, and in her arms a baby. Mrs Dallison held out twopence for the paper, but it was at the woman that she looked.

'Oh, Mrs Hughs,' she said, 'we've been expecting you to hem the curtains!'

The woman slightly pressed the baby.

'I am very sorry, ma'am. I knew I was expected, but I've had such trouble.'

Cecilia winced. 'Oh, really?'

'Yes, m'm; it's my husband.'

'Oh, dear!' Cecilia murmured. 'But why didn't you come to us?'

'I didn't feel up to it, ma'am; I didn't really——'

A tear ran down her cheek, and was caught in a furrow near the mouth.

Mrs Dallison said hurriedly: 'Yes, yes; I'm very sorry.'

'This old gentleman, Mr Creed, lives in the same house with us, and he is going to speak to my husband.'

The old man wagged his head on its lean stalk of neck.

'He ought to know better than be'ave 'imself so disrespectable,' he said.

Cecilia looked at him, and murmured: 'I hope he won't turn on *you*!'

The old man shuffled his feet.

'I likes to live at peace with everybody. I shall have the police to 'im if he misdemeans hisself with me! . . . *Westminster*, sir?' And, screening his mouth from Mrs Dallison, he added in a loud whisper: 'Execution of the Shoreditch murderer!'

Cecilia felt suddenly as though the world were listening to her conversation with these two rather seedy persons.

'I don't really know what I can do for you, Mrs Hughs. I'll speak to Mr Dallison, and to Mr Hilary too.'

'Yes, ma'am; thank you, ma'am.'

With a smile that seemed to deprecate its own appearance, Cecilia grasped her skirts and crossed the road. 'I hope I wasn't unsympathetic,' she thought, looking back at the three figures on the edge of the pavement—the old man with his papers, and his discoloured nose thrust upwards under iron-rimmed spectacles; the seamstress in her black dress; the skimpy little boy. Neither speaking nor moving, they were looking out before them at the traffic; and something in Cecilia revolted at this sight. It was lifeless, hopeless, unaesthetic.

'What can one do,' she thought, 'for women like Mrs Hughs, who always look like that? And that poor old man! I suppose I oughtn't to have bought that dress, but Stephen *is* tired of this.'

She turned out of the main street into a road preserved from commoner forms of traffic, and stopped at a long low house half hidden behind the trees of its front garden.

It was the residence of Hilary Dallison, her husband's brother, and himself the husband of Bianca, her own sister.

The queer conceit came to Cecilia that it resembled Hilary. Its look was kindly and uncertain; its colour a palish tan; the eyebrows of its windows rather straight than arched, and those deepset eyes, the windows, twinkled hospitably; it had, as it were, a sparse moustache and beard of creepers, and dark marks here and there, like the lines and shadows on the faces of those who think too much. Beside it, and apart, though connected by a passage, a studio stood, and about that studio—of white rough-cast, with a black oak door, and peacock-blue paint—was something a little hard and fugitive, well suited to Bianca, who used it, indeed, to paint in. It seemed to stand, with its eyes on the house, shrinking defiantly from too close company, as though it could not entirely give itself to anything. Cecilia, who often worried over the relations between her sister and her brother-in-law, suddenly felt how fitting and symbolical this was.

But, mistrusting inspirations, which, experience told her, committed one too much, she walked quickly up the stone-flagged pathway to the door. Lying in the porch was a little moonlight-coloured lady bulldog, of toy breed, who gazed up with eyes like agates, delicately waving her bell-rope tail, as it was her habit to do towards everyone, for she had been handed down clearer and

192

paler with each generation, till she had at last lost all the peculiar virtues of dogs that bait the bull.

Speaking the word 'Miranda!' Mrs Stephen Dallison tried to pat this daughter of the house. The little bulldog withdrew from her caress, being also unaccustomed to commit herself. . . .

Mondays were Bianca's 'days', and Cecilia made her way towards the studio. It was a large high room, full of people.

Motionless, by himself, close to the door, stood an old man, very thin and rather bent, with silvery hair, and a thin silvery beard grasped in his transparent fingers. He was dressed in a suit of smoke-grey cottage tweed, which smelt of peat, and an Oxford shirt, whose collar, ceasing prematurely, exposed a lean brown neck; his trousers, too, ended very soon, and showed light socks. In his attitude there was something suggestive of the patience and determination of a mule. At Cecilia's approach he raised his eyes. It was at once apparent why, in so full a room, he was standing alone. Those blue eyes looked as if he were about to utter a prophetic statement.

'They have been speaking to me of an execution,' he said.

Cecilia made a nervous movement.

'Yes, Father?'

'To take life,' went on the old man in a voice which, though charged with strong emotion, seemed to be speaking to itself, 'was the chief mark of the insensate barbarism still prevailing in those days. It sprang from the most irreligious fetish, the belief in the permanence of the individual ego after death. From the worship of that fetish had come all the sorrows of the human race.'

Cecilia, with an involuntary quiver of her little bag, said:

'Father, how can you?'

'They did not stop to love each other in this life; they were so sure they had all eternity to do it in. The doctrine was an invention to enable men to act like dogs with clear consciences. Love could never come to full fruition till it was destroyed.'

Cecilia looked hastily round; no one had heard. She moved a little sideways, and became merged in another group. Her father's lips continued moving. He had resumed the patient attitude that so slightly suggested mules. A voice behind her said: 'I do think your father is such an interesting man, Mrs Dallison.'

Cecilia turned and saw a woman of middle height, with her hair done in the early Italian fashion, and very small, dark, lively eyes, which looked as though her love of living would keep her busy each minute of her day and all the minutes that she could occupy of everybody else's days.

'Mrs Tallents Smallpeace? Oh! how do you do? I've been meaning to come and see you for quite a long time, but I know you're always so busy.'

With doubting eyes, half friendly and half defensive, as though chaffing to prevent herself from being chaffed, Cecilia looked at Mrs Tallents Smallpeace, whom she had met several times at Bianca's house. The widow of a somewhat famous connoisseur, she was now secretary of the League for Educating Orphans who have Lost both Parents, vice-president of the Forlorn Hope for Maids in Peril, and treasurer to Thursday Hops for Working Girls. She seemed to know every man and woman who was worth knowing, and some besides; to see all picture-shows; to hear every new musician; and attend the opening performance of every play. With regard to literature, she would say that authors bored her; but she was always doing them good turns, inviting them to meet their critics or editors, and sometimes—though this was not generally known—pulling them out of the holes they were prone to get into, by lending them a sum of money—after which, as she would plaintively remark, she rarely saw them more.

She had a peculiar spiritual significance to Mrs Stephen Dallison, being just on the border-line between those of Bianca's friends whom Cecilia did not wish and those whom she did wish to come to her own house, for Stephen, a barrister in an official position, had a keen sense of the ridiculous. Since Hilary wrote books and was a poet, and Bianca painted, their friends would naturally be either interesting or queer; and though for Stephen's sake it was important to establish which was which, they were so very often both. Such people stimulated, taken in small doses, but neither on her husband's account nor on her daughter's did Cecilia desire that they should come to her in swarms. Her attitude of mind towards them was, in fact, similar—a sort of pleasurable dread—to that in which she purchased the *Westminster Gazette* to feel the pulse of social progress.

Mrs Tallents Smallpeace's dark little eyes twinkled.

'I hear that Mr Stone—that *is* your father's name, I think—is writing a book which will create quite a sensation when it comes out.'

Cecilia bit her lips. 'I hope it never will come out,' she was on the point of saying.

'What will it be called?' asked Mrs Tallents Smallpeace. 'I

gather that it's a book of Universal Brotherhood. That's so nice!'

Cecilia made a movement of annoyance. 'Who told you?'

'Ah!' said Mrs Tallents Smallpeace, 'I do think your sister gets such attractive people at her At Homes. They all take *such* interest in things.'

A little surprised at herself, Cecilia answered: 'Too much for me!'

Mrs Tallents Smallpeace smiled. 'I mean in art and social questions. Surely one can't be too interested in them?'

Cecilia said rather hastily:

'Oh no, of course not.' And both ladies looked around them. A buzz of conversation fell on Cecilia's ears.

'Have you seen the "Aftermath"? It's really quite wonderful!'

'Poor old chap! he's so rococo. . . .'

'There's a new man. . . .'

'She's very sympathetic. . . .'

'But the condition of the poor. . . . ?'

'Is that Mr Balladyce? Oh, really. . . .'

'It gives you such a feeling of life. . . .'

'Bourgeois! . . .'

The voice of Mrs Tallents Smallpeace broke through: 'But do please tell me who is that young girl with the young man looking at the picture over there. She's quite charming!'

Cecilia's cheeks went a very pretty pink.

'Oh, that's my little daughter.'

'Really! Have you a daughter as big as that? Why, she must be seventeen!'

'Nearly eighteen!'

'What is her name?'

'Thyme,' said Cecilia, with a little smile. She felt that Mrs Tallents Smallpeace was about to say: 'How charming!'

Mrs Tallents Smallpeace saw her smile and paused. 'Who is the young man with her?'

'My nephew, Martin Stone.'

'The son of your brother who was killed with his wife in that dreadful Alpine accident? He looks a very decided sort of young man. He's got that new look. What is he?'

'He's very nearly a doctor. I never know whether he's quite finished or not.'

'I thought perhaps he might have something to do with Art.'

'Oh no, he despises Art.'

'And does your daughter despise it, too?'

'No; she's studying it.'

'Oh, really! How interesting! I do think the rising generation amusing don't you? They're so independent.'

Cecilia looked uneasily at the rising generation. They were standing side by side before the picture, curiously observant and detached, exchanging short remarks and glances. They seemed to watch all these circling, chatting, bending, smiling people with a sort of youthful, matter-of-fact, half-hostile curiosity. The young man had a pale face, clean-shaven, with a strong jaw, a long, straight nose, a rather bumpy forehead which did not recede, and clear grey eyes. His sarcastic lips were firm and quick, and he looked at people with disconcerting straightness. The young girl wore a blue-green frock. Her face was charming, with eager, hazel-grey eyes, a bright colour, and fluffy hair the colour of ripe nuts.

'That's your sister's picture, "The Shadow", they're looking at, isn't it?' asked Mrs Tallents Smallpeace. 'I remember seeing it on Christmas Day, and the little model who was sitting for it—an attractive type! Your brother-in-law told me how interested you all were in her. Quite a romantic story, wasn't it, about her fainting from want of food when she first came to sit?'

Cecilia murmured something. Her hands were moving nervously; she looked ill at ease.

These signs passed unperceived by Mrs Tallents Smallpeace, whose eyes were busy.

'In the F.H.M.P., of course, I see a lot of young girls placed in delicate positions, just on the borders, don't you know? You should really join the F.H.M.P., Mrs Dallison. It's a first-rate thing—most absorbing work.'

The doubting deepened in Cecilia's eyes.

'Oh, it must be!' she said. 'I've so little time.'

Mrs Tallents Smallpeace went on at once.

'Don't you think that we live in the most interesting days? There are such a lot of movements going on. It's quite exciting. We all feel that we can't shut our eyes any longer to social questions. I mean the condition of the people alone is enough to give one nightmares!'

'Yes, yes,' said Cecilia; 'it is dreadful, of course.'

'Politicians and officials are so hopeless, one can't look for anything from them.'

Cecilia drew herself up. 'Oh, do you think so?' she said.

'I was just talking to Mr Balladyce. He says that Art and Literature must be put on a new basis altogether.'

'Yes,' said Cecilia; 'really? Is he that funny little man?'

'I think he's so monstrously clever.'

Cecilia answered quickly: 'I know—I know. Of course, *something* must be done.'

'Yes,' said Mrs Tallents Smallpeace absently, 'I think we all feel that. Oh, do tell me! I've been talking to such a delightful person —just the type you see when you go into the City—thousands of them, all in such good black coats. It's so unusual to really meet one nowadays; and they're so refreshing, they have such nice simple views. There he is, standing just behind your sister.'

Cecilia by a nervous gesture indicated that she recognised the personality alluded to. 'Oh yes,' she said; 'Mr Purcey. I don't know why he comes to see us.'

'I think he's so delicious!' said Mrs Tallents Smallpeace dreamily. Her little dark eyes, like bees, had flown to sip honey from the flower in question—a man of broad build and medium height, dressed with accuracy, who seemed just a little out of his proper bed. His mustachioed mouth wore a set smile; his cheerful face was rather red, with a forehead of no extravagant height or breadth, and a conspicuous jaw; his hair was thick and light in colour, and his eyes were small, grey, and shrewd. He was looking at a picture.

'He's so delightfully unconscious,' murmured Mrs Tallents Smallpeace. 'He didn't even seem to know that there was a problem of the lower classes.'

'Did he tell you that he had a picture?' asked Cecilia gloomily.

'Oh yes, by Harpignies, with the accent on the "pig". It's worth three times what he gave for it. It's nice to be made to feel that there is still all that mass of people just simply measuring everything by what they gave for it.'

'And did he tell you my grandfather Carfax's dictum in the Banstock case?' muttered Cecilia.

'Oh yes: "The man who does not know his own mind should be made an Irishman by Act of Parliament." He said it was so awfully good.'

'He would,' replied Cecilia.

'He seems to depress you, rather!'

'Oh no; I believe he's quite a nice sort of person. One can't be rude to him; he really did what he thought a very kind thing to my father. That's how we came to know him. Only it's rather trying when he will come to call regularly. He gets a little on one's nerves.'

197

'Ah, that's just what I feel is so jolly about him; no one would ever get on his nerves. I do think we've got too many nerves, don't you? Here's your brother-in-law. He's such an uncommon-looking man; I want to have a talk with him about that little model. A country girl, wasn't she?'

She had turned her head towards a tall man with a very slight stoop and a brown, thin, bearded face, who was approaching from the door. She did not see that Cecilia had flushed, and was looking at her almost angrily. The tall thin man put his hand on Cecilia's arm, saying gently: 'Hello, Cis! Stephen here yet?'

Cecilia shook her head.

'You know Mrs Tallents Smallpeace, Hilary?'

The tall man bowed. His hazel-coloured eyes were shy, gentle, and deep-set; his eyebrows, hardly ever still, gave him a look of austere whimsicality. His dark brown hair was very lightly touched with grey, and a frequent kindly smile played on his lips. His un-mannerismed manner was quiet to the point of extinction. He had long, thin, brown hands, and nothing peculiar about his dress.

'I'll leave you to talk to Mrs Tallents Smallpeace,' Cecilia said.

A knot of people round Mr Balladyce prevented her from moving far, however, and the voice of Mrs Smallpeace travelled to her ears.

'I was talking about that little model. It was so good of you to take such interest in the girl. I wondered whether we could do anything for her.'

Cecilia's hearing was too excellent to miss the tone of Hilary's reply:

'Oh, thank you; I don't think so.'

'I fancied perhaps you might feel that our Society—hers is an unsatisfactory profession for young girls!'

Cecilia saw the back of Hilary's neck turn red. She turned her head away.

'Of course, there are many very nice models indeed,' said the voice of Mrs Tallents Smallpeace. 'I don't mean that they are necessarily at all—if they're girls of strong character; and especially if they don't sit for the—the altogether.'

Hilary's dry, staccato answer came to Cecilia's ears: 'Thank you; it's very kind of you.'

'Oh, of course, if it's not necessary. Your wife's picture was so clever, Mr Dallison—such an interesting type.'

Without intention Cecilia found herself before that picture. It stood with its face a little turned towards the wall, as though somewhat in disgrace, portraying the full-length figure of a girl standing in deep shadow, with her arms half outstretched, as if asking for something. Her eyes were fixed on Cecilia, and through her parted lips breath almost seemed to come. The only colour in the picture was the pale blue of those eyes, the pallid red of those parted lips, the still paler brown of the hair; the rest was shadow. In the foreground light was falling as though from a street-lamp.

Cecilia thought: 'That girl's eyes and mouth haunt me. Whatever made Bianca choose such a subject? It is clever, of course—for her.'

Chapter 2

A FAMILY DISCUSSION

THE marriage of Sylvanus Stone, Professor of the Natural Sciences, to Anne, daughter of Mr Justice Carfax, of the well-known county family—the Carfaxes of Spring Deans, Hants—was recorded in the sixties. The baptisms of Martin, Cecilia, and Bianca, son and daughters of Sylvanus and Anne Stone, were to be discovered registered in Kensington in the three consecutive years following, as though some single-minded person had been connected with their births. After this the baptisms of no more offspring were to be found anywhere, as if that single mind had encountered opposition. But in the eighties there was noted in the register of the same church the burial of 'Anne, *née* Carfax, wife of Sylvanus Stone'. In that '*née* Carfax' there was, to those who knew, something more than met the eye. It summed up the mother of Cecilia and Bianca, and, in more subtle fashions, Cecilia and Bianca too. It summed up that fugitive, barricading look in their bright eyes, which, though spoken of in the family as 'the Carfax eyes', were in reality far from coming from old Mr Justice Carfax. They had been his wife's in turn, and had much annoyed a man of his decided character. He himself had always known his mind, and had let others know it, too; reminding his wife that she was an impracticable woman, who knew not her own mind; and devoting his lawful gains to securing the future of his progeny. It would have disturbed him if he had lived to see his grand-daughters and their times. Like so many able men of his generation, far-seeing enough in practical affairs, he had never considered the possibility that the descendants of those who, like himself, had laid up treasure for their children's children might acquire the quality of taking time, balancing pros and cons, looking ahead, and not putting one foot down before picking the other up. He had not foreseen, indeed, that to wobble might become an art, in order that, before anything was done, people might know the full necessity for doing something, and how impossible it would be to do—indeed, foolish to attempt to do—that which would fully meet the case. He, who had been a man of action all his life, had not perceived how it would grow to be matter of common instinct that to act was to commit oneself, and that, while what one had was not precisely what one wanted, what one had not (if one had it) would be as bad. He had never been self-conscious—it was not the custom of his generation—and, having but little imagination, had never suspected that he was laying up that quality for his descendants, together with a competence that secured them a comfortable leisure.

Of all the persons in his grand-daughter's studio that afternoon, that stray sheep Mr Purcey would have been, perhaps, the only one whose judgments he would have considered sound. No one had laid up a competence for Mr Purcey, who had been in business from the age of twenty.

It is is uncertain whether the mere fact that he was not in his own fold kept this visitor lingering in the studio when all other guests were gone; or whether it was simply the feeling that the longer he stayed in contact with really artistic people the more distinguished he was becoming. Probably the latter, for the possession of that Harpignies, a good specimen, which he had bought by accident, and subsequently by accident discovered to have a peculiar value, had become a factor in his life, marking him out from all his friends, who went in more for a neat type of Royal Academy landscape, together with reproductions of young ladies in eighteenth-century costumes seated on horseback, or in Scotch gardens. A junior partner in a banking-house of some importance, he lived at Wimbledon, whence he passed up and down daily in his car. To this he owed his acquaintance with the family of Dallison. For one day, after telling his chauffeur to await him at the gate of the Broad Walk, he had set out to stroll down Rotten Row, as he often did on the way home, designing to nod to anybody that he knew. It had turned out a somewhat barren expedition. No one of any consequence had met his eye; and it was with a certain, almost fretful longing for distraction that in Kensington Gardens he came on an old man feeding birds out of a paper bag. The birds having flown away on seeing him, he approached the feeder to apologise.

'I'm afraid I frightened your birds, sir,' he began.

This old man, who was dressed in smoke-grey tweeds which exhaled a poignant scent of peat, looked at him without answering.

'I'm afraid your birds saw me coming,' Mr Purcey said again.

'In those days,' said the aged stranger, 'birds were afraid of men.'

Mr Purcey's shrewd grey eyes perceived at once that he had a character to deal with.

'Ah, yes!' he said; 'I see—you allude to the present time. That's very nice. Ha, ha!'

The old man answered: 'The emotion of fear is inseparably connected with a primitive state of fratricidal rivalry.'

This sentence put Mr Purcey on his guard.

'The old chap,' he thought, 'is touched. He evidently oughtn't to be out here by himself.' He debated, therefore, whether he should hasten away towards his car, or stand by in case his assistance should be needed. Being a kind-hearted man, who believed in his capacity for putting things to rights, and noticing a certain, delicacy—a 'sort of something rather distinguished', as he phrased it afterwards—in the old fellow's face and figure, he decided to see if he could be of any service. They walked along together, Mr Purcey watching his new friend askance, and directing the march to where he had ordered his chauffeur to await him.

'You are very fond of birds, I suppose,' he said cautiously.

'The birds are our brothers.'

The answer was of a nature to determine Mr Purcey in his diagnosis of the case.

'I've got my car here,' he said. 'Let me give you a lift home.'

This new but aged acquaintance did not seem to hear; his lips moved as though he were following out some thought.

'In those days,' Mr Purcey heard him say, 'the congeries of men were known as rookeries. The expression was hardly just towards that handsome bird.'

Mr Purcey touched him hastily on the arm.

'I've got my car here, sir,' he said. 'Do let me put you down!'

Telling the story afterwards, he had spoken thus:

'The old chap knew where he lived right enough; but dash me if I believe he noticed that I was taking him there in my car—I had the A.1. Damyer out. That's how I came to make the acquaintance of these Dallisons. He's the writer, you know; and she paints—rather the new school—she admires Harpignies. Well, when I got there in the car I found Dallison in the garden. Of course I was careful not to put my foot into it. I told him: "I found this old gentleman wandering about. I've just brought him back in my car." Who should the old chap turn out to be but her father! They were awfully obliged to me. Charmin' people, but very what d'you call it—*fin de siècle*—like these professors, these artistic pigs— seem to know rather a queer set, advanced people, and all that sort of cuckoo, always talkin' about the poor, and societies, and new religions, and that kind of thing.'

Though he had since been to see them several times, the Dallisons had never robbed him of the virtuous feeling of that good action—they had never let him know that he had brought home, not, as he imagined, a lunatic, but merely a philosopher.

It had been somewhat of a quiet shock to him to find Mr Stone close to the doorway when he entered Bianca's studio that afternoon; for though he had seen him since the encounter in Kensington Gardens, and knew that he was writing a book, he still felt that he was not quite the sort of old man that one ought to meet about. He had at once begun to tell him of the hanging of the Shoreditch murderer, as recorded in the evening papers. Mr Stone's reception of that news had still further confirmed his original views. When all the guests were gone—with the exception of Mr and Mrs Stephen Dallison and Miss Dallison, 'that awfully pretty girl', and the young man 'who was always hangin' about her'— he had approached his hostess for some quiet talk. She stood listening to him, very well bred, with just that habitual spice of mockery in her smile, which to Mr Purcey's eyes made her 'a very strikin'- lookin' woman, but rather——' There he would stop, for it required a greater psychologist than he to describe a secret disharmony which a little marred her beauty. Due to some too violent cross of blood, to an environment too unsuited, to what not—it was branded on her. Those who knew Bianca Dallison better than Mr Purcey were but too well aware of this fugitive, proud spirit permeating one whose beauty would otherwise have passed unquestioned.

She was a little taller than Cecilia, her figure rather fuller and more graceful, her hair darker, her eyes, too, darker and more deeply set, her cheek-bones higher, her colouring richer. That spirit of the age, Disharmony, must have presided when a child so vivid and dark-coloured was christened Bianca.

Mr Purcey, however, was not a man who allowed the finest shades of feeling to interfere with his enjoyments. She was a 'strikin'-lookin' woman', and there was, thanks to Harpignies, a link between them.

'Your father and I, Mrs Dallison, can't quite understand each other,' he began. 'Our views of life don't seem to hit it off exactly.'

'Really,' murmured Bianca; 'I should have thought that you'd have got on so well.'

'He's a little bit too—er—scriptural for me, perhaps,' said Mr Purcey, with some delicacy.

'Did we never tell you,' Bianca answered softly, 'that my father was a rather well-known man of science before his illness?'

'Ah!' replied Mr Purcey, a little puzzled; 'that, of course. D'you know, of all your pictures, Mrs Dallison, I think that one you call "The Shadow" is the most rippin'. There's a something about it that gets hold of you. That was the original, wasn't it, at your Christmas party—attractive girl—it's an awf'ly good likeness.'

Bianca's face had changed, but Mr Purcey was not a man to notice a little thing like that.

'If ever you want to part with it,' he said, 'I hope you'll give me a chance. I mean it'd be a pleasure to me to have it. I think it'll be worth a lot of money some day.'

Bianca did not answer, and Mr Purcey, feeling suddenly a little awkward, said: 'I've got my car waiting. I must be off—really.' Shaking hands with all of them, he went away.

When the door had closed behind his back, a universal sigh went up. It was followed by a silence, which Hilary broke.

'We'll smoke, Stevie, if Cis doesn't mind.'

Stephen Dallison placed a cigarette between his moustacheless lips, always rather screwed up, and ready to nip with a smile anything that might make him feel ridiculous.

'Phew!' he said. 'Our friend Purcey becomes a little tedious. He seems to take the whole of Philistia about with him.'

'He's a very decent fellow,' murmured Hilary.

'A bit heavy, surely!' Stephen Dallison's face, though also long and narrow, was not much like his brother's. His eyes, though not unkind, were far more scrutinising, inquisitive, and practical; his hair darker, smoother.

Letting a puff of smoke escape, he added:

'Now, that's the sort of man to give you a good sound opinion. You should have asked *him*, Cis.'

Cecilia answered with a frown:

'Don't chaff, Stephen; I'm perfectly serious about Mrs Hughs.'

'Well, I don't see what I can do for the good woman, my dear.
One can't interfere in these domestic matters.'

'But it seems dreadful that we who employ her should be able
to do nothing for her. Don't you think so, B.?'

'I suppose we could do something for her if we wanted to
badly enough.'

Bianca's voice, which had the self-distrustful ring of modern
music, suited her personality.

A glance passed between Stephen and his wife.

'That's B. all over!' it seemed to say.

'Hound Street, where they live, is a horrid place.'

It was Thyme who spoke, and everybody looked round at her.

'How do you know that?' asked Cecilia.

'I went to see.'

'With whom?'

'Martin.'

The lips of the young man whose name she mentioned curled
sarcastically.

Hilary asked gently:

'Well, my dear, what *did* you see?'

'Most of the doors are open——'

Bianca murmured: 'That doesn't tell us much.'

'On the contrary,' said Martin suddenly, in a deep bass voice,
'it tells you everything. Go on.'

'The Hughs live on the top floor at No. 1. It's the best house
in the street. On the ground-floor are some people called Budgen;
he's a labourer, and she's lame. They've got one son. The Hughs
have let off the first-floor front-room to an old man named
Creed——'

'Yes, I know,' Cecilia muttered.

'He makes about one and tenpence a day by selling papers. The
back-room on that floor they let, of course, to your little model
Aunt B.'

'She is not my model now.'

There was a silence such as falls when no one knows how far
the matter mentioned is safe to touch on. Thyme proceeded with
her report.

'Her room's much the best in the house; it's airy, and it looks
out over someone's garden. I suppose she stays there because it's
so cheap. The Hugh's rooms are——' She stopped, wrinkling her
straight nose.

'So that's the household,' said Hilary. 'Two married couples, one young man, one young girl'—his eyes travelled from one to another of the two married couples, the young man, and the young girl, collected in this room—'and one old man,' he added softly.

'Not quite the sort of place for you to go poking about in, Thyme,' Stephen said ironically. 'Do you think so, Martin?'

'Why not?'

Stephen raised his brows, and glanced towards his wife. Her face was dubious, a little scared. There was a silence. Then Bianca spoke:

'Well?' That word, like nearly all her speeches, seemed rather to disconcert her hearers.

'So Hughs ill-treats her?' said Hilary.

'She says so,' replied Cecilia—'at least, that's what I understood. Of course, I don't know any details.'

'She had better get rid of him, I should think,' Bianca murmured.

Out of the silence that followed Thyme's clear voice was heard saying:

'She can't get a divorce; she could get a separation.'

Cecilia rose uneasily. These words concreted suddenly a wealth of half-acknowledged doubts about her little daughter. This came of letting her hear people talk, and go about with Martin! She might even have been listening to her grandfather—such a thought was most disturbing. And, afraid, on the one hand, of gainsaying the liberty of speech, and, on the other, of seeming to approve her daughter's knowledge of the world, she looked at her husband.

But Stephen did not speak, feeling, no doubt, that to pursue the subject would be either to court an ethical, even an abstract, disquisition, and this one did not do in anybody's presence, much less one's wife and daughter's; or to touch on sordid facts of doubtful character, which was equally distasteful in the circumstances. He, too, however, was uneasy that Thyme should know so much.

The dusk was gathering outside; the fire threw a flickering light, fitfully outlining their figures, making those faces, so familiar to each other, a little mysterious.

At last Stephen broke the silence. 'Of course, I'm very sorry for her, but you'd better let it alone—you can't tell with those sort of people; you never can make out what they want—it's safer not to meddle. At all events, it's a matter for a Society to look into first!'

Cecilia answered: 'But she's on my conscience, Stephen.'

'They're all on *my* conscience,' muttered Hilary.

Bianca looked at him for the first time; then, turning to her nephew, said: 'What do you say, Martin?'

The young man, whose face was stained by the firelight the colour of pale cheese, made no answer.

But suddenly through the stillness came a voice:

'I have thought of something.'

Everyone turned round. Mr Stone was seen emerging from behind 'The Shadow'; his frail figure, in its grey tweeds, his silvery hair and beard, were outlined sharply against the wall.

'Why, Father,' Cecilia said, 'we didn't know that you were here!'

Mr Stone looked round bewildered; it seemed as if he, too, had been ignorant of that fact.

'What is it that you've thought of?'

The firelight leaped suddenly on to Mr Stone's thin yellow hand.

'Each of us,' he said, 'has a shadow in those places—in those streets.'

There was a vague rustling, as of people not taking a remark too seriously, and the sound of a closing door.

Chapter 3

HILARY'S BROWN STUDY

'WHAT do you really think, Uncle Hilary?'

Turning at his writing-table to look at the face of his young niece, Hilary Dallison answered:

'My dear, we have had the same state of affairs since the beginning of the world. There is no chemical process, as far as my knowledge goes, that does not make waste products. What your grandfather calls our "shadows" are the waste products of the social process. That there is a submerged tenth is as certain as that there is an emerged fiftieth like ourselves; exactly who they are and how they come, whether they can ever be improved away, is, I think, as uncertain as anything can be.'

The figure of the girl seated in the big armchair did not stir. Her lips pouted contemptuously, a frown wrinkled her forehead.

'Martin says that a thing is only impossible when we think it so.'

'Faith and the mountain, I'm afraid.'

Thyme's foot shot forth; it nearly came into contact with Miranda, the little bulldog.

'Oh, duckie!'

But the little moonlight bulldog backed away.

'I hate these slums, uncle; they're so disgusting!'

Hilary leaned his face on his thin hand; it was his characteristic attitude.

'They are hateful, disgusting, and heartrending. That does not make the problem any the less difficult, does it?'

'I believe we simply make the difficulties ourselves by seeing them.'

Hilary smiled. 'Does Martin say that too?'

'Of course he does.'

'Speaking broadly,' murmured Hilary, 'I see only one difficulty —human nature.'

Thyme rose. 'I think it horrible to have a low opinion of human nature.'

'My dear,' said Hilary, 'don't you think perhaps that people who have what is called a low opinion of human nature are really more tolerant of it, more in love with it, in fact, than those who, looking to what human nature might be, are bound to hate what human nature is.'

The look which Thyme directed at her uncle's amiable, attractive face, with its pointed beard, high forehead, and peculiar little smile, seemed to alarm Hilary.

'I don't want you to have an unnecessarily low opinion of me, my dear. I'm not one of those people who tell you that everything's all right because the rich have their troubles as well as the poor. A certain modicum of decency and comfort is obviously necessary to man before we can begin to do anything but pity him; but that doesn't make it any easier to know how you're going to insure him that modicum of decency and comfort, does it?'

'We've got to do it,' said Thyme; 'it won't wait any longer.'

'My dear,' said Hilary, 'think of Mr Purcey! What proportion of the upper classes do you imagine is even conscious of that necessity? We, who have got what I call the social conscience, rise from the platform of Mr Purcey; we're just a gang of a few thousands to Mr Purcey's tens of thousands, and how many even of us are prepared, or, for the matter of that, fitted, to act on our consciousness? In spite of your grandfather's ideas, I'm afraid we're all too much divided into classes; man acts, and always has acted, in classes.'

'Oh—classes!' answered Thyme—'that's the old superstition, uncle.'

'Is it? I thought one's class, perhaps, was only oneself exaggerated—not to be shaken off. For instance, what are you and I, with our particular prejudices, going to do?'

Thyme gave him the cruel look of youth, which seemed to say: 'You are my very good uncle, and a dear; but you are more than twice my age. That, I think, is conclusive!'

'Has something been settled about Mrs Hughs?' she asked abruptly.

'What does your father say this morning?'

Thyme picked up her portfolio of drawings, and moved towards the door.

'Father's hopeless. He hasn't an idea beyond referring her to the S.P.B.'

She was gone; and Hilary, with a sigh, took his pen up, but he wrote nothing down. . . .

Hilary and Stephen Dallison were grandsons of that Canon Dallison, well known as friend, and sometime adviser, of a certain Victorian novelist. The Canon, who came of an old Oxfordshire family, which for three hundred years at least had served the Church or State, was himself the author of two volumes of 'Socratic Dialogues'. He had bequeathed to his son—a permanent official in the Foreign Office—if not his literary talent, the tradition at all events of culture. This tradition had in turn been handed on to Hilary and Stephen.

Educated at a public school and Cambridge, blessed with competent, though not large, independent incomes, and brought up never to allude to money if it could possibly be helped, the two young men had been turned out of the mint with something of the same outward stamp on them. Both were kindly, both fond of open-air pursuits, and neither of them lazy. Both, too, were very civilised, with that bone-deep decency, that dislike of violence, nowhere so prevalent as in the upper classes of a country whose settled institutions are as old as its roads, or the walls that insulate its parks. But as time went on, the one great quality which heredity and education, environment and means, had bred in both of them—self-consciousness—acted in these two brothers very differently. To Stephen it was preservative, keeping him, as it were, in ice throughout hot-weather seasons, enabling him to know exactly when he was in danger of decomposition, so that he might nip the process in the bud; it was with him a healthy, perhaps slightly chemical, ingredient, binding his component parts, causing them to work together safely, homogeneously. In Hilary the effect seemed to have been otherwise; like some slow and subtle poison, this great quality, self-consciousness, had soaked his system through and through; permeated every cranny of his spirit, so that to think a definite thought, or do a definite deed, was obviously becoming difficult to him. It took in the main the form of a sort of gentle desiccating humour.

'It's a remarkable thing,' he had one day said to Stephen, 'that by the process of assimilating little bits of chopped-up cattle one should be able to form the speculation of how remarkable a thing it is.'

Stephen had paused a second before answering—they were lunching off roast beef in the Law Courts—he had then said:

'You're surely not going to eschew the higher mammals, like our respected father-in-law?'

'On the contrary,' said Hilary, 'to chew them; but it *is* remarkable, for all that; you missed my point.'

It was clear that a man who could see anything remarkable in such a thing was far gone, and Stephen had murmured:

'My dear old chap, you're getting too introspective.'

Hilary, having given his brother the peculiar retiring smile, which seemed not only to say, 'Don't let me bore you,' but also, 'Well, perhaps you *had* better wait outside,' the conversation closed.

That smile of Hilary's, which jibbed away from things, though disconcerting and apt to put an end to intercourse, was natural enough. A sensitive man, who had passed his life amongst cultivated people in the making of books, guarded from real wants by modest, not vulgar, affluence, had not reached the age of forty-two without finding his delicacy sharpened to the point of fastidiousness. Even his dog could see the sort of man he was. She knew that he would take no liberties, either with her ears or with her tail. She knew that he would never hold her mouth ajar, and watch her teeth, as some men do; that when she was lying on her back he would gently rub her chest without giving her the feeling that she was doing wrong, as women will; and if she sat, as she was sitting now, with her eyes fixed on his study fire, he would never, she knew, even from afar, prevent her thinking of the nothing she loved to think on.

In his study, which smelt of a special mild tobacco warranted to suit the nerves of any literary man, there was a bust of Socrates, which always seemed to have a strange attraction for its owner. He had once described to a fellow-writer the impression produced on him by that plaster face, so capaciously ugly, as though comprehending the whole of human life, sharing all man's gluttony and lust, his violence and rapacity, but sharing also his strivings towards love and reason and serenity.

'He's telling us,' said Hilary, 'to drink deep, to dive down and live with mermaids, to lie out on the hills under the sun, to sweat with helots, to know all things and all men. No seat, he says, among the Wise, unless we've been through it all before we climb! That's how he strikes me—not too cheering for people of our sort!'

Under the shadow of this bust Hilary rested his forehead on his hand. In front of him were three open books and a pile of manuscript, and pushed to one side a little sheaf of pieces of green-white paper, press-cuttings of his latest book.

The exact position occupied by his work in the life of such a man is not too easy to define. He earned an income by it, but he was not dependent on that income. As poet, critic, writer of essays, he had made himself a certain name—not a great name, but enough to swear by. Whether his fastidiousness could have stood the conditions of literary existence without private means was now and then debated by his friends; it could probably have done so better than was supposed, for he sometimes startled those who set him down as a dilettante by a horny way of retiring into his shell for the finish of a piece of work.

Try as he would that morning to keep his thoughts concentrated on his literary labour, they wandered to his conversation with his niece and to the discussion on Mrs Hughs, the family seamstress, in his wife's studio the day before. Stephen had lingered behind Cecilia and Thyme when they went away after dinner, to deliver a last counsel to his brother at the garden gate.

'Never meddle between man and wife—you know what the lower classes are!'

And across the dark garden he had looked back towards the house. One room on the ground-floor alone was lighted. Through its open window the head and shoulders of Mr Stone could be seen close to a small green reading-lamp. Stephen shook his head, murmuring:

'But, I say, our old friend, eh? "In those places—in those

streets!" It's worse than simple crankiness—the poor old chap is getting almost——' And, touching his forehead lightly with two fingers, he had hurried off with the ever-springy step of one whose regularity habitually controls his imagination.

Pausing a minute amongst the bushes, Hilary too had looked at the lighted window that broke the dark front of his house, and his little moonlight bulldog, peering round his legs, had gazed up also. Mr Stone was still standing, pen in hand, presumably deep in thought. His silvered head and beard moved slightly to the efforts of his brain. He came over to the window, and, evidently not seeing his son-in-law, faced out into the night.

In that darkness were all the shapes and lights and shadows of a London night in spring: the trees in dark bloom; the wan yellow of the gas-lamps, pale emblems of the self-consciousness of towns; the clustered shades of the tiny leaves, spilled, purple, on the surface of the road, like bunches of black grapes squeezed down into the earth by the feet of the passers-by. There, too, were shapes of men and women hurrying home, and the great blocked shapes of the houses where they lived. A halo hovered above the City—a high haze of yellow light, dimming the stars. The black, slow figure of a policeman moved noiselessly along the railings opposite.

From then till eleven o'clock, when he would make himself some cocoa on a little spirit-lamp, the writer of the 'Book of Universal Brotherhood' would alternate between his bent posture above his manuscript and his blank consideration of the night. . . .

With a jerk, Hilary came back to his reflections beneath the bust of Socrates.

'Each of us has a shadow in those places—in those streets!'

There certainly was a virus in that notion. One must either take it as a jest, like Stephen; or, what must one do? How far was it one's business to identify oneself with other people, especially the helpless—how far to preserve oneself intact—*integer vitae?* Hilary was no young person, like his niece or Martin, to whom everything seemed simple; nor was he an old person like their grandfather, for whom life had lost its complications.

And, very conscious of his natural disabilities for a decision on a like, or indeed on any, subject except, perhaps, a point of literary technique, he got up from his writing-table, and, taking his little bulldog, went out. His intention was to visit Mrs Hughs in Hound Street, and see with his own eyes the state of things. But he had another reason, too, for wishing to go there. . . .

Chapter 4

THE LITTLE MODEL

WHEN in the preceding autumn Bianca began her picture called 'The Shadow', nobody was more surprised than Hilary that she asked him to find her a model for the figure. Not knowing the nature of the picture, nor having been for many years—perhaps never—admitted into the workings of his wife's spirit, he said:

'Why don't you ask Thyme to sit for you?'

Bianca answered: 'She's not the type at all—too matter-of-fact. Besides, I don't want a lady; the figure's to be half draped.'

Hilary smiled.

Bianca knew quite well that he was smiling at this distinction between ladies and other women, and understood that he was smiling, not so much at her, but at himself, for secretly agreeing with the distinction she had made.

And suddenly she smiled too.

There was the whole history of their married life in those two smiles. They meant so much: so many thousand hours of suppressed irritation, so many baffled longings and earnest efforts to bring their natures together. They were the supreme, quiet evidence of the divergence of two lives—that slow divergence which had been far from being wilful, and was the more hopeless in that it had been so gradual and so gentle. They had never really had a quarrel, having enlightened views of marriage; but they had smiled. They had smiled so often through so many years that no two people in the world could very well be further from each other. Their smiles had banned the revelation even to themselves of the tragedy of their wedded state. It is certain that neither could help those smiles, which were not intended to wound, but came on their faces as naturally as moonlight falls on water, out of their inimically constituted souls.

Hilary spent two afternoons among his artist friends, trying, by means of the indications he had gathered, to find a model for 'The Shadow'. He had found one at last. Her name, Barton, and address had been given him by a painter of still life, called French.

'She's never sat to me,' he said; 'my sister discovered her in the West Country somewhere. She's got a story of some sort. I don't know what. She came up about three months ago, I think.'

'She's not sitting to your sister now?' Hilary asked.

'No,' said the painter of still life; 'my sister's married and gone out to India. I don't know whether she'd sit for the half-draped, but I should think so. She'll have to, sooner or later; she may as well begin, especially as your wife's a woman. There's a something about her that's attractive—you might try her!' And with these words he resumed the painting of still life which he had broken off to talk to Hilary.

Hilary had written to this girl to come and see him. She had come just before dinner the same day.

He found her standing in the middle of his study, not daring, as it seemed, to go near the furniture, and as there was very little light, he could hardly see her face. She was resting a foot, very patient, very still, in an old brown skirt, an ill-shaped blouse, and a blue-green tam-o'-shanter cap. Hilary turned up the light. He saw a round little face with broad cheek-bones, flower-blue eyes, short lamp-black lashes, and slightly parted lips. It was difficult to judge of her figure in those old clothes, but she was neither short nor tall; her neck was white and well set on, her hair pale brown and abundant. Hilary noted that her chin, though not receding, was too soft and small; but what he noted chiefly was her look of patient expectancy, as though beyond the present she were seeing something, not necessarily pleasant, which had to come. If he had not known from the painter of still life that she was from the country, he would have thought her a town-bred girl, she looked so pale. Her appearance, at all events, was not 'too matter-of-fact'. Her speech, however, with its slight West-Country burr, was matter-of-fact enough, concerned entirely with how long she would have to sit, and the pay she was to get for it. In the middle of their conversation she sank down on the floor, and Hilary was driven to restore her with biscuits and liqueur, which in his haste he took for brandy. It seemed she had not eaten since her breakfast the day before, which had consisted of a cup of tea. In answer to his remonstrance, she made this matter-of-fact remark:

'If you haven't money, you can't buy things. . . . There's no one I can ask up here; I'm a stranger.'

'Then you haven't been getting work?'

'No,' the little model answered sullenly; 'I don't want to sit as most of them want me to till I'm obliged.' The blood rushed up in her face with startling vividness, then left it white again.

'Ah!' thought Hilary, 'she has had experience already.'

Both he and his wife were accessible to cases of distress, but the nature of their charity was different. Hilary was constitutionally unable to refuse his aid to anything that held out a hand for it. Bianca (whose sociology was sounder), while affirming that charity was wrong, since in a properly constituted State no one should need help, referred her cases, like Stephen, to the 'Society for the Prevention of Begging', which took much time and many pains to ascertain the worst.

But in this case what was of importance was that the poor girl should have a meal, and after that to find out if she were living in a decent house; and since she appeared not to be, to recommend her somewhere better. And as in charity it is always well to kill two birds with one expenditure of force, it was found that Mrs Hughs, the seamstress, had a single room to let unfurnished, and would be more than glad of four shillings, or even three and six, a week for it. Furniture was also found for her: a bed that creaked, a washstand, table, and chest of drawers; a carpet, two chairs, and certain things to cook with; some of those old photographs and prints that hide in cupboards, and a peculiar little clock, which frequently forgot the time of day. All these and some elementary articles of dress were sent round in a little van, with three ferns whose time had nearly come, and a piece of the plant called 'honesty'. Soon after this she came to 'sit'. She was a very quiet and passive little model, and was not required to pose half-draped, Bianca having decided that, after all, 'The Shadow' was better represented fully clothed; for, though she discussed the nude, and looked on it with freedom, when it came to painting unclothed people, she felt a sort of physical aversion.

Hilary, who was curious, as a man naturally would be, about anyone who had fainted from hunger at his feet, came every now and then to see, and would sit watching this little half-starved girl with kindly and screwed-up eyes. About his personality there was all the evidence of that saying current among those who knew him: 'Hilary would walk a mile sooner than tread on an ant.' The little model, from the moment when he poured liqueur between her teeth, seemed to feel he had a claim on her, for she reserved her small, matter-of-fact confessions for his ears. She made them in the garden, coming in or going out; or outside, and, now and then, inside his study, like a child who comes and shows you a sore finger. Thus, quite suddenly: 'I've four shillings left over this week, Mr Dallison,' or, 'Old Mr Creed's gone to the hospital today, Mr Dallison.'

Her face soon became less bloodless than on that first evening, but it was still pale, inclined to colour in wrong places on cold days, with little blue veins about the temples and shadows under the eyes. The lips were still always a trifle parted, and she still seemed to be looking out for what was coming, like a little Madonna, or Venus, in a Botticelli picture. This look of hers, coupled with the matter-of-factness of her speech, gave its flavour to her personality. . . .

On Christmas Day the picture was on view to Mr Purcey, who had chanced to 'give his car a run', and to other connoisseurs. Bianca had invited her model to be present at this function, intending to get her work. But, slipping at once into a corner, the girl had stood as far as possible behind a canvas. People, seeing her standing there and noting her likeness to the picture, looked at her with curiosity, and passed on, murmuring that she was ·an interesting type. They did not talk to her, either because they were afraid she could not talk of the things they could talk of, or that they could not talk of the things she could talk of, or because they were anxious not to seem to patronise her. She talked to no one, therefore. This occasioned Hilary some distress. He kept coming up and smiling at her, or making tentative remarks or jests, to which she would reply, 'Yes, Mr Dallison', or 'No, Mr Dallison', as the case might be.

Seeing him return from one of these little visits, an Art Critic standing before the picture had smiled, and his round, clean-shaven, sensual face had assumed a greenish tint in eyes and cheeks, as of the fat in turtle soup.

The only two other people who had noticed her particularly were those old acquaintances Mr Purcey and Mr Stone. Mr Purcey had thought, 'Rather a good-lookin' girl', and his eyes strayed somewhat continually in her direction. There was something piquant and, as it were, unlawfully enticing to him in the fact that she was a real artist's model.

Mr Stone's way of noticing her had been different. He had approached in his slightly inconvenient way, as though seeing but one thing in the whole world.

'You are living by yourself?' he had said. 'I shall come and see you.'

Made by the Art Critic or by Mr Purcey, that somewhat strange remark would have had one meaning; made by Mr Stone it obviously had another. Having finished what he had to say, the author of the book of 'Universal Brotherhood' had bowed and turned to go. Perceiving that he saw before him the door and nothing else, everybody made way for him at once. The remarks that usually arose behind his back began to be heard—'Extraordinary old man!' 'You know, he bathes in the Serpentine all the year round?' 'And he cooks his food himself, and does his own room, they say; and all the rest of his time he writes a book!' 'A perfect crank!'

Chapter 5

THE COMEDY BEGINS

THE Art Critic who had smiled was—like all men—a subject for pity rather than for blame. An Irishman of real ability, he had started life with high ideals and a belief that he could live with them. He had hoped to serve Art, to keep his service pure; but, having one day let his acid temperament out of hand to revel in an orgy of personal retaliation, he had since never known when she would slip her chain and come home smothered in mire. Moreover, he no longer chastised her when she came. His ideals had left him, one by one; he now lived alone, immune from dignity and shame, soothing himself with whisky. A man of rancour, meet for pity, and, in his cups, contented.

He had lunched freely before coming to Bianca's Christmas function, but by four o'clock the gases which had made him feel the world a pleasant place had nearly all evaporated, and he was suffering from a wish to drink again. Or it may have been that this girl, with her soft look, gave him the feeling that she ought to have belonged to him; and as she did not, he felt, perhaps, a natural irritation that she belonged, or might belong, to somebody else. Or, again, it was possibly his natural male distaste for the works of women painters that induced an awkward frame of mind.

Two days later in a daily paper, over no signature, appeared this little paragraph: 'We learn that "The Shadow", painted by Bianca Stone, who is not generally known to be the wife of the writer, Mr Hilary Dallison, will soon be exhibited at the Bencox Gallery. This very fin-de-siècle creation, with its unpleasant subject, representing a woman (presumably of the streets) standing beneath a gas-lamp, is a somewhat anaemic piece of painting. If Mr Dallison, who finds the type an interesting one, embodies her in one of his very charming poems, we trust the result will be less bloodless.'

The little piece of green-white paper containing this information was handed to Hilary by his wife at breakfast. The blood mounted slowly in his cheeks. Bianca's eyes fastened themselves on that flush. Whether or no—as philosophers say—little things are all big with the past, of whose chain they are the latest links, they frequently produce what apparently are great results.

The marital relations of Hilary and his wife, which till then had been those of, at all events, formal conjugality, changed from that moment. After ten o'clock at night their lives became as separate as though they lived in different houses. And this change came about without expostulations, reproach, or explanation, just by the turning of a key; and even this was the merest symbol, employed once only, to save the ungracefulness of words. Such a hint was quite enough for a man like Hilary, whose delicacy, sense of the ridiculous, and peculiar faculty of starting back and retiring into himself, put the need of anything further out of the question. Both must have felt, too, that there was nothing that could be explained. An anonymous *double entendre* was not precisely evidence on which to found a rupture of the marital tie. The trouble was so much deeper than that—the throbbing of a woman's wounded self-esteem, of the feeling that she was no longer loved, which had long cried out for revenge.

One morning in the middle of the week after this incident the innocent author of it presented herself in Hilary's study, and, standing in her peculiar patient attitude, made her little statements. As usual, they were very little ones; as usual, she seemed helpless, and suggested a child with a sore finger. She had no other work; she owed the week's rent; she did not know what would happen to her; Mrs Dallison did not want her any more; she could not tell what she had done! The picture was finished, she knew, but Mrs Dallison had said she was going to paint her again in another picture. . . .

Hilary did not reply.

'. . . That old gentleman, Mr—Mr Stone, had been to see her. He wanted her to come and copy out his book for two hours a day, from four to six, at a shilling an hour. Ought she to come, please? He said his book would take him years.'

Before answering her Hilary stood for a full minute staring at the fire. The little model stole a look at him. He suddenly turned and faced her. His glance was evidently disconcerting to the girl. It was, indeed, a critical and dubious look, such as he might have bent on a folio of doubtful origin.

'Don't you think,' he said at last, 'that it would be much better for you to go back into the country?'

The little model shook her head vehemently.

'Oh no!'

'Well, but why not? This is a most unsatisfactory sort of life.'

The girl stole another look at him, then said sullenly:

'I can't go back there.'

'What is it? Aren't your people nice to you?'

She grew red.

'No; and I don't want to go;' then, evidently seeing from Hilary's face that his delicacy forbade his questioning her further, she brightened up, and murmured: 'The old gentleman said it would make me independent.'

'Well,' replied Hilary, with a shrug, 'you'd better take his offer.'

She kept turning her face back as she went down the path, as though to show her gratitude. And presently, looking up from his manuscript, he saw her face still at the railings, peering through a lilac bush. Suddenly she skipped, like a child let out of school. Hilary got up, perturbed. The sight of that skipping was like the rays of a lantern turned on the dark street of another human being's life. It revealed, as in a flash, the loneliness of this child, without money and without friends, in the midst of this great town.

The months of January, February, March passed, and the little model came daily to copy the 'Book of Universal Brotherhood'.

Mr Stone's room, for which he insisted on paying rent, was never entered by a servant. It was on the ground-floor, and anyone passing the door between the hours of four and six could hear him dictating slowly, pausing now and then to spell a word. In these two hours it appeared to be his custom to read out, for fair copying, the labours of the other seven.

At five o'clock there was invariably a sound of plates and cups, and out of it the little model's voice would rise, matter-of-fact, soft, monotoned, making little statements; and in turn Mr Stone's, also making statements that clearly lacked cohesion with those of his young friend. On one occasion, the door being open, Hilary heard distinctly the following conversation:

The LITTLE MODEL: 'Mr Creed says he was a butler. He's got an ugly nose.' (A pause.)

Mr STONE: 'In those days men were absorbed in thinking of their individualities. Their occupations seemed to them important——'

The LITTLE MODEL: 'Mr Creed says his savings were all swallowed up by illness.'

Mr STONE: '——it was not so.'

The LITTLE MODEL: 'Mr Creed says he was always brought up to go to church.'

Mr STONE (suddenly): 'There has been no church worth going to since A.D. 700.'

The LITTLE MODEL: 'But he doesn't go.'

And with a flying glance through the just open door Hilary saw her holding bread-and-butter with inky fingers, her lips a little parted, expecting the next bite, and her eyes fixed curiously on Mr Stone, whose transparent hand held a teacup, and whose eyes were immovably fixed on distance.

It was one day in April that Mr Stone, heralded by the scent of Harris tweed and baked potatoes which habitually encircled him, appeared at five o'clock in Hilary's study doorway.

'She has not come,' he said.

Hilary laid down his pen. It was the first real Spring day.

'Will you come for a walk with me, sir, instead?' he asked.

'Yes,' said Mr Stone.

They walked out into Kensington Gardens, Hilary with his head rather bent towards the ground, and Mr Stone, with eyes fixed on his far thoughts, slightly poking forward his silver beard.

In their favourite firmaments the stars of crocuses and daffodils were shining. Almost every tree had its pigeon cooing, every bush its blackbird in full song. And on the paths were babies in perambulators. These were their happy hunting-grounds, and here they came each day to watch from a safe distance the little dirty girls sitting on the grass nursing little dirty boys, to listen to the ceaseless chatter of these common urchins, and learn to deal with the great problem of the lowest classes. They sat there in their perambulators, thinking and sucking indiarubber tubes. Dogs went before them, and nursemaids followed after.

The spirit of colour was flying in the distant trees, swathing them with brownish-purple haze; the sky was saffroned by dying sunlight. It was such a day as brings a longing to the heart, like that which the moon brings to the hearts of children.

Mr Stone and Hilary sat down in the Broad Walk.

'Elm-trees!' said Mr Stone. 'It is not known when they assumed their present shape. They have one universal soul. It is the same with man.' He ceased, and Hilary looked round uneasily. They were alone on the bench.

Mr Stone's voice rose again. 'Their form and balance is their single soul; they have preserved it from century to century. This is all they live for. In those days'—his voice sank; he had plainly forgotten that he was not alone—'when men had no universal conceptions, they would have done well to look at the trees. Instead of fostering a number of little souls on the pabulum of varying theories of future life, they should have been concerned to improve their present shapes, and thus to dignify man's single soul.'

'Elms were always considered dangerous trees, I believe,' said Hilary.

Mr Stone turned, and, seeing his son-in-law beside him, asked:

'You spoke to me, I think?'

'Yes, sir.'

Mr Stone said wistfully:

'Shall we walk?'

They rose from the bench and walked on. . . .

The explanation of the little model's absence was thus stated by herself to Hilary: 'I had an appointment.'

'More work?'

'A friend of Mr French.'

'Yes—who?'

'Mr Lennard. He's a sculptor; he's got a studio in Chelsea. He wants me to pose to him.'

'Ah!'

She stole a glance at Hilary, and hung her head.

Hilary turned to the window. 'You know what posing to a sculptor means, of course?'

The little model's voice sounded behind him, matter-of-fact as ever: 'He said I was just the figure he was looking for.'

Hilary continued to stare through the window. 'I thought you didn't mean to begin standing for the nude.'

'I don't want to stay poor always.'

Hilary turned round at the strange tone of these unexpected words.

The girl was in a streak of sunlight; her pale cheeks flushed; her pale, half-opened lips red; her eyes, in their setting of short black lashes, wide and mutinous; her young round bosom heaving as if she had been running.

'I don't want to go on copying books all my life.'

'Oh, very well.'

'Mr Dallison! I didn't mean that—I didn't, really! I want to do what you tell me to do—I do!'

Hilary stood contemplating her with the dubious, critical look, as though asking: 'What is there behind you? Are you really a

220

genuine edition, or what?' which had so disconcerted her before.
At last he said: 'You must do just as you like. I never advise anybody.'

'But you don't want me to—I know you don't. Of course, if *you*
don't want me to, then it'll be a pleasure not to!'

Hilary smiled.

'Don't you like copying for Mr Stone?'

The little model made a face. 'I like Mr Stone—he's such a funny
old gentleman.'

'That *is* the general opinion,' answered Hilary. 'But Mr Stone,
you know, thinks that *we* are funny.'

The little model smiled faintly, too; the streak of sunlight had
slanted past her, and, standing there behind its glamour and million floating specks of gold-dust, she looked for the moment like the
young Shade of Spring, watching with expectancy for what the
year would bring her.

With the words 'I am ready', spoken from the doorway, Mr
Stone interrupted further colloquy. . . .

But though the girl's position in the household had, to all seeming, become established, now and then some little incident—straws
blowing down the wind—showed feelings at work beneath the
family's apparent friendliness, beneath that tentative and almost
apologetic manner towards the poor or helpless, which marks out
those who own what Hilary had called the 'social conscience'.
Only three days, indeed, before he sat in his brown study, meditating beneath the bust of Socrates, Cecilia, coming to lunch, had let
fall this remark:

'Of course, I know nobody can read his handwriting; but I
can't think why father doesn't dictate to a typist, instead of to
that little girl. She could go twice the pace!'

Bianca's answer, deferred for a few seconds, was:

'Hilary perhaps knows.'

'Do you dislike her coming here?' asked Hilary.

'Not particularly. Why?'

'I thought from your tone you did.'

'I don't dislike her coming here for that purpose.'

'Does she come for any other?'

Cecilia, dropping her quick glance to her fork, said just a little
hastily: 'Father *is* extraordinary, of course.'

But the next three days Hilary was out in the afternoon when
the little model came.

This, then, was the other reason, on the morning of the first of

221

May, that made him not averse to go and visit Mrs Hughs in Hound Street, Kensington.

Chapter 6

FIRST PILGRIMAGE TO HOUND STREET

HILARY and his little bulldog entered Hound Street from its eastern end. It was a grey street of three-storied houses, all in one style of architecture. Nearly all their doors were open, and on the doorsteps babes and children were enjoying Easter holidays. They sat in apathy, varied by sudden little slaps and bursts of noise. Nearly all were dirty; some had whole boots, some half boots, and two or three had none. In the gutters more children were at play; their shrill tongues and febrile movements gave Hilary the feeling that their 'caste' exacted of them a profession of this faith: 'To-day we live; to-morrow—if there be one—will be like to-day.'

He had unconsciously chosen the very centre of the street to walk in, and Miranda, who had never in her life demeaned herself to this extent, ran at his heels, turning up her eyes, as though to say: 'One thing I make a point of—no dog must speak to me!'

Fortunately, there were no dogs; but there were many cats, and these cats were thin.

Through the upper windows of the houses Hilary had glimpses of women in poor habiliments doing various kinds of work, but stopping now and then to gaze into the street. He walked to the end, where a wall stopped him, and, still in the centre of the road, he walked the whole length back. The children stared at his tall figure with indifference; they evidently felt that he was not of those who, like themselves, had no to-morrow.

No. 1, Hound Street, abutting on the garden of a house of better class, was distinctly the show building of the street. The door, however, was not closed, and pulling the remnant of a bell, Hilary walked in.

The first thing that he noticed was a smell; it was not precisely bad, but it might have been better. It was a smell of walls and washing, varied rather vaguely by red herrings. The second thing he noticed was his moonlight bulldog, who stood on the doorstep eyeing a tiny sandy cat. This very little cat, whose back was arched with fury, he was obliged to chase away before his bulldog would come in. The third thing he noticed was a lame woman of short stature, standing in the doorway of a room. Her face, with big

222

cheek-bones, and wide-open, light grey, dark-lashed eyes, was broad and patient; she rested her lame leg by holding to the handle of the door.

'I dunno if you'll find anyone upstairs. I'd go and ask, but my leg's lame.'

'So I see,' said Hilary; 'I'm sorry.'

The woman sighed: 'Been like that for five years;' and turned back into her room.

'Is there nothing to be done for it?'

'Well, I did think so once,' replied the woman, 'but they say the bone's diseased; I neglected it at the the start.'

'Oh dear!'

'We hadn't the time to give to it,' the woman said defensively, retiring into a room so full of china cups,.photographs, coloured prints, waxwork fruits, and other ornaments, that there seemed no room for the enormous bed.

Wishing her good-morning, Hilary began to mount the stairs. On the first floor he paused. Here, in the back room, the little model lived.

He looked around him. The paper on the passage walls was of a dingy orange colour, the blind of the window torn, and still pursuing him, pervading everything, was the scent of walls and washing and red herrings. There came on him a sickness, a sort of spiritual revolt. To live here, to pass up these stairs, between these dingy, bilious walls, on this dirty carpet, with this—ugh! every day; twice, four times, six times, who knew how many times a day! And that sense, the first to be attracted or revolted, the first to become fastidious with the culture of the body, the last to be expelled from the temple of the pure spirit; that sense to whose refinement all breeding and all education is devoted; that sense which, ever an inch at least in front of man, is able to retard the development of nations, and paralyse all social schemes—this Sense of Smell awakened within him the centuries of his gentility, the ghosts of all those Dallisons who, for three hundred years and more, had served Church or State. It revived the souls of scents he was accustomed to, and with them, subtly mingled, the whole live fabric of aestheticism, woven in fresh air and laid in lavender. It roused the simple, non-extravagant demand of perfect cleanliness. And though he knew that chemists would have certified the composition of his blood to be the same as that of the dwellers in this house, and that this smell, composed of walls and washing and red herrings, was really rather healthy, he stood frowning fixedly at the girl's door, and the memory of his young niece's delicately wrinkled nose as she described the house rose before him. He went on upstairs, followed by his moonlight bulldog.

Hilary's tall thin figure appearing in the open doorway of the top-floor front, his kind and worried face, and the pale agate eyes of the little bulldog peeping through his legs, were witnessed by nothing but a baby, who was sitting in a wooden box in the centre of the room. This baby, who was very like a piece of putty to which Nature had by some accident fitted two movable black eyes, was clothed in a woman's knitted undervest, spreading beyond his feet and hands, so that nothing but his head was visible. This vest divided him from the wooden shavings on which he sat, and, since he had not yet attained the art of rising to his feet, the box divided him from contacts of all other kinds. As completely isolated from his kingdom as the Czar of all the Russias, he was doing nothing. In this realm there was a dingy bed, two chairs, and a washstand, with one lame leg, supported by an aged foot-stool. Clothes and garments were hanging on nails, pans lay about the hearth, a sewing-machine stood on a bare deal table. Over the bed was hung an oleograph, from a Christmas supplement, of the birth of Jesus, and above it a bayonet, under which was printed in an illiterate hand on a rough scroll of paper: 'Gave three of em what for at Elandslaagte. S. Hughs.' Some photographs adorned the walls, and two drooping ferns stood on the window-ledge. The room withal had a sort of desperate tidiness; in a large cupboard, slightly open, could be seen stowed all that must not see the light of day. The window of the baby's kingdom was tightly closed; the scent was the scent of walls and washing and red herrings, and— of other things.

Hilary looked at the baby, and the baby looked at him. The eyes of that tiny scrap of grey humanity seemed saying:

'You are not my mother, I believe?'

He stooped down and touched its cheek. The baby blinked its black eyes once.

'No,' it seemed to say again, 'you are *not* my mother.'

A lump rose in Hilary's throat; he turned and went downstairs. Pausing outside the little model's door, he knocked, and, receiving no answer, turned the handle. The little square room was empty; it was neat and clean enough, with a pink-flowered paper of comparatively modern date. Through its open window could be seen a pear-tree in full bloom. Hilary shut the door again with care, ashamed of having opened it.

On the half-landing, staring up at him with black eyes like the baby's, was a man of medium height and active build, whose short face, with broad cheek-bones, cropped dark hair, straight nose, and little black moustache, was burnt a dark dun colour. He was dressed in the uniform of those who sweep the streets—a loose blue blouse, and trousers tucked into boots reaching half-way up his calves; he held a peaked cap in his hand.

After some seconds of mutual admiration, Hilary said:

'Mr Hughs, I believe?'

'Yes.'

'I've been up to see your wife.'

'Have you?'

'You know me, I suppose?'

'Yes, I know you.'

'Unfortunately, there's only your baby at home.'

Hughs motioned with his cap towards the little model's room. 'I thought perhaps you'd been to see *her*,' he said. His black eyes smouldered; there was more than class resentment in the expression of his face.

Flushing slightly and giving him a keen look, Hilary passed down the stairs without replying. But Miranda had not followed. She stood, with one paw delicately held up above the topmost step.

'I don't know this man,' she seemed to say, 'and I don't like his looks.'

Hughs grinned. 'I never hurt a dumb animal,' he said; 'come on, tykie!'

Stimulated by a word she had never thought to hear, Miranda descended rapidly.

'He meant that for impudence,' thought Hilary as he walked away.

'*Westminster*, sir? Oh dear!'

A skinny trembling hand was offering him a greenish newspaper.

'Terrible cold wind for the time o' year!'

A very aged man in black-rimmed spectacles, with a distended nose and long upper lip and chin, was tentatively fumbling out change for sixpence.

'I seem to know your face,' said Hilary.

'Oh dear, yes. You deals with this 'ere shop—the tobacco department. I've often seen you when you've a-been a-goin' in. Sometimes you has the *Pell Mell* off o' this man here.' He jerked his head a trifle to the left, where a younger man was standing armed with a sheaf of whiter papers. In that gesture were years of envy,

225

heart-burning, and sense of wrong. 'That's my paper,' it seemed to say, 'by all the rights of man; and that low-class fellow sellin' it, takin' away my profits!'

'I sells this 'ere *Westminster*. I reads it on Sundays—it's a gentleman's paper, 'igh-class paper—notwithstandin' of its politics. But, Lor', sir, with this 'ere man a-sellin' the *Pell Mell*'—lowering his voice, he invited Hilary to confidence—'so many o' the gentry takes that; an' there ain't too many o' the gentry about 'ere—I mean, not o' the *real* gentry—that I can afford to 'ave 'em took away from me.'

Hilary, who had stopped to listen out of delicacy, had a flash of recollection. 'You live in Hound Street?'

The old man answered eagerly: 'Oh dear! Yes, sir—No. 1, name of Creed. You're the gentleman where the young person goes for to copy of a book!'

'It's not my book she copies.'

'Oh no; it's an old gentleman; I know 'im. He come an' see me once. He come in one Sunday morning. "Here's a pound o' tobacco for you!" 'e says. "You was a butler," 'e says. "Butlers!" 'e says, "there'll be no butlers in fifty years." An' out 'e goes. Not quite'—he put a shaky hand up to his head—'not quite—oh dear!'

'Some people called Hughs live in your house, I think?'

'I rents my room off o' them. A lady was a-speakin' to me yesterday about 'em; that's not your lady, I suppose, sir?'

His eyes seemed to apostrophise Hilary's hat, which was of soft felt: 'Yes, yes—I've seen your sort a-stayin' about in the best houses. They has you down because of your learnin'; and quite the manners of a gentleman you've got.'

'My wife's sister, I expect.'

'Oh dear! She often has a paper off o' me. A real lady—not one o' these'—again he invited Hilary to confidence—'you know what I mean, sir—that buys their things a' ready-made at these 'ere large establishments. Oh, I know her well.'

'The old gentleman that visited you is her father.'

'Is he? Oh dear!' The old butler was silent, evidently puzzled.

Hilary's eyebrows began to execute those intricate manoeuvres which always indicated that he was about to tax his delicacy.

'How—how does Hughs treat the little girl who lives in the next room to you?'

The old butler replied in a rather gloomy tone:

'She takes my advice, and don't 'ave nothin' to say to 'im.

Dreadful foreign-lookin' man 'e is. Wherever 'e was brought up I can't think!'

'A soldier, wasn't he?'

'So he says. He's one o' these that works for the Vestry; an' then 'e'll go an' get upon the drink, an' when that sets 'im off, it seems as if there wasn't no respect for nothing in 'im; he goes on against the gentry, and the Church, and every sort of institution. I never met no soldiers like *him*. Dreadful foreign—Welsh, they tell me.'

'What do you think of the street you're living in?'

'I keeps myself to myself; low class o' street it is; dreadful low class o' person there—no self-respect about 'em.'

'Ah!' said Hilary.

'These little 'ouses, they get into the hands o' little men, and *they* don't care so long as they makes their rent out o' them. They can't help themselves—low class o' man like that; 'e's got to do the best 'e can for 'imself. They say there's thousands o' these 'ouses all over London. There's some that's for pullin' of 'em down, but that's talkin' rubbish; where are you goin' to get the money for to do it? These 'ere little men, they can't afford not even to put a paper on the walls, and the big ground landlords—you can't expect *them* to know what's happenin' behind their backs. There's some ignorant fellers like this Hughs talks a lot o' wild nonsense about the duty o' ground landlords; but you can't expect the real gentry to look into these sort o' things. They've got their estates down in the country. I've lived with them, and of course I know.'

The little bulldog, incommoded by the passers-by, now took the opportunity of beating with her tail against the old butler's legs.

'Oh dear! what's this? He don't bite, do 'e? Good Sambo!'

Miranda sought her master's eye at once. 'You see what happens to her if a lady loiters in the streets,' she seemed to say.

'It must be hard standing about here all day, after the life you've led,' said Hilary.

'I mustn't complain; it's been the salvation o' me.'

'Do you get shelter?'

Again the old butler seemed to take him into confidence.

'Sometimes of a wet night they lets me stand up in the archway there; they know I'm respectable. 'Twouldn't never do for that man'—he nodded at his rival—'or any of them boys to get standin' there, obstructin' of the traffic.'

'I wanted to ask you, Mr Creed, is there anything to be done for Mrs Hughs?'

The frail old body quivered with the vindictive force of his answer.

'Accordin' to what she says, if I'm a-to believe 'er, I'd have him up before the magistrate, sure as my name's Creed, an' get a separation, an' I wouldn't never live with 'im again : that's what she ought to do. An' if he come to go for her after that, I'd have 'im in prison, if 'e killed me first! I've no patience with a low class o' man like that! He insulted of me this morning.'

'Prison's a dreadful remedy,' murmured Hilary.

The old butler answered stoutly : 'There ain't but one way o' treatin' them low fellers—ketch hold o' them until they holler!'

Hilary was about to reply when he found himself alone. At the edge of the pavement some yards away, Creed, his face upraised to heaven, was embracing with all his force the second edition of the *Westminster Gazette*, which had been thrown him from a cart.

'Well,' thought Hilary, walking on, '*you* know your own mind, anyway!'

And trotting by his side, with her jaw set very firm, his little bulldog looked above her eyes, and seemed to say : 'It was time we left that man of action!'

Chapter 7

CECILIA'S SCATTERED THOUGHTS

IN her morning room Mrs Stephen Dallison sat at an old oak bureau collecting her scattered thoughts. They lay about on pieces of stamped notepaper, beginning 'Dear Cecilia', or 'Mrs Tallents Smallpeace requests', or on bits of pasteboard headed by the names of theatres, galleries, or concert-halls; or, again, on paper of not quite so good a quality, commencing, 'Dear Friend', and ending with a single well-known name like 'Wessex', so that no suspicion should attach to the appeal contained between the two. She had before her also sheets of her own writing-paper, headed '76, The Old Square, Kensington', and two little books. One of these was bound in marbleised paper, and on it written : 'Please keep this book in safety'; across the other, cased in the skin of some small animal deceased, was inscribed the solitary word 'Engagements'.

Cecilia had on a Persian-green silk blouse with sleeves that would have hidden her slim hands, but for silver buttons made in the likeness of little roses at her wrists; on her brow was a faint frown, as though she were wondering what her thoughts were all about.

She sat there every morning catching those thoughts, and placing them in one or other of her little books. Only by thus working hard could she keep herself, her husband, and daughter, in due touch with all the different movements going on. And that the touch might be as due as possible, she had a little headache nearly every day. For the dread of letting slip one movement, or of being too much taken with another, was very real to her; there were so many people who were interesting, so many sympathies of hers and Stephen's which she desired to cultivate, that it was a matter of the utmost import not to cultivate any single one too much. Then, too, the duty of remaining feminine with all this going forward taxed her constitution. She sometimes thought enviously of the splendid isolation now enjoyed by Bianca, of which some subtle instinct, rather than definite knowledge, had informed her; but not often, for she was a loyal little person, to whom Stephen and his comforts were of the first moment. And though she worried somewhat because her thoughts *would* come by every post, she did not worry very much—hardly more than the Persian kitten on her lap, who also sat for hours trying to catch her tail, with a line between her eyes, and two small hollows in her cheeks.

When she had at last decided what concerts she would be obliged to miss, paid her subscription to the League for the Suppression of Tinned Milk, and accepted an invitation to watch a man fall from a balloon, she paused. Then, dipping her pen in ink, she wrote as follows :

'Mrs Stephen Dallison would be glad to have the blue dress ordered by her yesterday sent home at once without alteration.— Messrs Rose and Thorn, High Street, Kensington.'

Ringing the bell, she thought : 'It will be a job for Mrs Hughs, poor thing : I believe she'll do it quite as well as Rose and Thorn.— Would you please ask Mrs Hughs to come to me?—Oh, is that you, Mrs Hughs? Come in.'

The seamstress, who had advanced into the middle of the room, stood with her worn hands against her sides, and no sign of life but the liquid patience in her large brown eyes. She was an enigmatic figure. Her presence always roused a sort of irritation in Cecilia, as if she had been suddenly confronted with what might possibly have been herself if certain little accidents had omitted to occur. She was so conscious that she ought to sympathise, so anxious to show that there was no barrier between them, so eager to be all she ought to be, that her voice almost purred.

'Are you getting on with the curtains, Mrs Hughs?'

'Yes, m'm, thank you, m'm.'

'I shall have another job for you to-morrow—altering a dress. Can you come?'

'Yes, m'm, thank you, m'm.'

'Is the baby well?'

'Yes, m'm, thank you, m'm.'

There was a silence.

'It's no good talking of her domestic matters,' thought Cecilia; 'not that I don't care!' But the silence getting on her nerves, she said quickly: 'Is your husband behaving himself better?'

There was no answer; Cecilia saw a tear trickle slowly down the woman's cheek.

'Oh dear, oh dear,' she thought; 'poor thing! I'm in for it!'

Mrs Hughs' whispering voice began: 'He's behaving himself dreadful, m'm. I was going to speak to you. It's ever since that young girl'—her face hardened—'come to live down in my room there; he seem to—he seem to—just do nothing but neglect me.'

Cecilia's heart gave the little pleasurable flutter which the heart must feel at the love dramas of other people, however painful.

'You mean the little model?' she said.

The seamstress answered in an agitated voice: 'I don't want to speak against her, but she's put a spell on him, that's what she has; he don't seem able to do nothing but talk of her, and hang about her room. It was that troubling me when I saw you the other day. And ever since yesterday midday, when Mr Hilary came—he's been talking that wild—and he pushed me—and—and——' Her lips ceased to form articulate words, but, since it was not etiquette to cry before her superiors, she used them to swallow down her tears, and something in her lean throat moved up and down.

At the mention of Hilary's name the pleasurable sensation in Cecilia had undergone a change. She felt curiosity, fear, offence.

'I don't quite understand you,' she said.

The seamstress plaited at her frock. 'Of course, I can't help the way he talks, m'm. I'm sure I don't like to repeat the wicked things he says about Mr Hilary. It seems as if he were out of his mind when he gets talkin' about *that young girl*.'

The tone of those last three words was almost fierce.

Cecilia was on the point of saying: 'That will do, please; I want to hear no more.' But her curiosity and queer subtle fear forced her instead to repeat: 'I don't understand. Do you mean he insinuates that Mr Hilary has anything to do with—with this girl, or what?' And she thought: 'I'll stop that, at any rate.'

The seamstress's face was distorted by her efforts to control her voice.

'I tell him he's wicked to say such things, m'm, and Mr Hilary such a kind gentleman. And what business is it of his, I say, that's got a wife and children of his own? I've seen him in the street, I've watched him hanging about Mrs Hilary's house when I've been working there—waiting for that girl, and following her—home ——' Again her lips refused to do service, except in the swallowing of her tears.

Cecilia thought: 'I must tell Stephen at once. That man is dangerous.' A spasm gripped her heart, usually so warm and snug; vague feelings she had already entertained presented themselves now with startling force; she seemed to see the face of sordid life staring at the family of Dallison. Mrs Hughs' voice, which did not dare to break, resumed:

'I've said to him: "Whatever are you thinking of? And after Mrs Hilary's been so kind to me!" But he's like a madman when he's in liquor, and he says he'll go to Mrs Hilary——'

'Go to my sister? What about? The ruffian!'

At hearing her husband being called a ruffian by another woman the shadow of resentment passed across Mrs Hughs' face, leaving it quivering and red. The conversation had already made a strange difference in the manner of these two women to each other. It was as though each now knew exactly how much sympathy and confidence could be expected of the other, as though life had suddenly sucked up the mist, and shown them standing one on either side of a deep trench. In Mrs Hughs' eyes there was the look of those who have long discovered that they must not answer back for fear of losing what little ground they have to stand on; and Cecilia's eyes were cold and watchful. 'I sympathise,' they seemed to say, 'I sympathise; but you must please understand that you cannot expect sympathy if your affairs compromise the members of my family.' Her chief thought now was to be relieved of the company of this woman, who had been betrayed into showing what lay beneath her dumb, stubborn patience. It was not callousness, but the natural result of being fluttered. Her heart was like a bird agitated in its gilt-wire cage by the contemplation of a distant cat. She did not, however, lose her sense of what was practical, but said calmly: 'Your husband was wounded in South Africa, you told me? It looks as if he wasn't quite . . . I think you should have a doctor!'

The seamstress's answer, slow and matter-of-fact, was worse than her emotion.

'No, m'm, he isn't mad.'

Crossing to the hearth—whose Persian-blue tiling had taken her so long to find—Cecilia stood beneath a reproduction of Botticelli's 'Primavera', and looked doubtfully at Mrs Hughs. The Persian kitten, sleepy and disturbed on the bosom of her blouse, gazed up into her face. 'Consider me,' it seemed to say; 'I am worth consideration; I am of a piece with you, and everything round you. We are both elegant and rather slender; we both love warmth and kittens; we both dislike interference with our fur. You took a long time to buy me, so as to get me perfect. You see that woman over there! I sat on her lap this morning while she was sewing your curtains. She has no right in here; she's not what she seems; she can bite and scratch, I know; her lap is skinny; she drops water from her eyes. She made me wet all down my back. Be careful what you're doing, or she'll make you wet down yours!'

All that was like the little Persian kitten within Cecilia—cosiness and love of pretty things, attachment to her own abode with its high-art lining, love for her mate and her own kitten, Thyme, dread of disturbance—all made her long to push this woman from the room; this woman with the skimpy figure, and eyes that, for all their patience, had in them something virago-like; this woman who carried about with her an atmosphere of sordid grief, of squalid menaces, and scandal. She longed all the more because it could well be seen from the seamstress's helpless attitude that she too would have liked an easy life. To dwell on things like this was to feel more than thirty-eight!

Cecilia had no pocket, Providence having removed it now for some time past, but from her little bag she drew forth the two essentials of gentility. Taking her nose, which she feared was shining, gently within one, she fumbled in the other. And again she looked doubtfully at Mrs Hughs. Her heart said: 'Give the poor woman half a sovereign; it might comfort her!' But her brain said: 'I owe her four-and-six; after what she's just been saying about her husband and that girl and Hilary, it mayn't be safe to give her more.' She held out two half-crowns, and had an inspiration: 'I shall mention to my sister what you've said; you can tell your husband that!'

No sooner had she said this, however, than she saw, from a little smile devoid of merriment and quickly extinguished, that Mrs Hughs did not believe she would do anything of the kind; from which she concluded that the seamstress was convinced of Hilary's interest in the little model. She said hastily :

'You can go now, Mrs Hughs.'

Mrs Hughs went, making no noise or sign of any sort.

Cecilia returned to her scattered thoughts. They lay there still, with a gleam of sun from the low window smearing their importance; she felt somehow that it did not now matter very much whether she and Stephen, in the interests of science, saw that man fall from his balloon, or, in the interests of art, heard Herr von Kraaffe sing his Polish songs; she experienced, too, almost a revulsion in favour of tinned milk. After meditatively tearing up her note to Messrs Rose and Thorn, she lowered the bureau lid and left the room.

Mounting the stairs, whose old oak banisters on either side were a real joy, she felt she was stupid to let vague, sordid rumours, which, after all, affected her but indirectly, disturb her morning's work. And entering Stephen's dressing-room, she stood looking at his boots.

Inside each one of them was a wooden soul; none had any creases, none had any holes. The moment they wore out, their wooden souls were taken from them and their bodies given to the poor, whilst—in accordance with that theory, to hear a course of lectures on which a scattered thought was even now inviting her —the wooden souls migrated instantly to other leathern bodies.

Looking at that polished row of boots, Cecilia felt lonely and unsatisfied. Stephen worked in the Law Courts, Thyme worked at Art; both were doing something definite. She alone, it seemed, had to wait at home, and order dinner, answer letters, shop, pay calls, and do a dozen things that failed to stop her thoughts from dwelling on that woman's tale. She was not often conscious of the nature of her life, so like the lives of many hundred women in this London, which she said she could not stand, but which she stood very well. As a rule, with practical good sense, she kept her doubting eyes fixed friendlily on every little phase in turn, enjoying well enough the Chinese puzzle of her scattered thoughts, setting out on each small adventure with a certain cautious zest, and taking Stephen with her as far as he allowed. This last year or so, now that Thyme was a grown girl, she had felt at once a loss of purpose and a gain of liberty. She hardly knew whether to be glad or sorry. It freed her for the tasting of more things, more people, and more Stephen; but it left a little void in her heart, a little soreness round it. What would Thyme think if she heard this story about her uncle? The thought started a whole train of doubts that had of late beset her. Was her little daughter going to turn out like herself? If not, why not? Stephen joked about his daughter's skirts, her hockey, her friendship with young men. He joked about the way Thyme refused to let him joke about her art or about her interest in 'the people'. His joking was a source of irritation to Cecilia. For, by woman's instinct rather than by any reasoning process, she was conscious of a disconcerting change. Amongst the people she knew, young men were not now attracted by girls as they had been in her young days. There was a kind of cool and friendly matter-of-factness in the way they treated them, a sort of almost scientific playfulness. And Cecilia felt uneasy as to how far this was to go. She seemed left behind. If young people were really becoming serious, if youths no longer cared about the colour of Thyme's eyes, or dress, or hair, what would there be left to care for—that is, up to the point of definite relationship? Not that she wanted her daughter to be married. It would be time enough to think of that when she was twenty-five. But her own experiences had been so different. She had spent so many youthful hours in wondering about men, had seen so many men cast furtive looks at her; and now there did not seem in men or girls anything left worth the other's while to wonder or look furtive about. She was not of a philosophic turn of mind, and had attached no deep meaning to Stephen's jest—'If young people will reveal their ankles, they'll soon have no ankles to reveal.'

To Cecilia the extinction of the race seemed threatened; in reality her species of the race alone was vanishing, which to her, of course, was very much the same disaster. With her eyes on Stephen's boots she thought: 'How shall I prevent what I've heard from coming to Bianca's ears? I know how she would take it! How shall I prevent Thyme's hearing? I'm sure I don't know what the effect would be on her! I must speak to Stephen. He's so fond of Hilary.'

And, turning away from Stephen's boots, she mused: 'Of course it's nonsense. Hilary's much too—too nice, too fastidious, to be more than just interested; but he's so kind he might easily put himself in a false position. And—it's ugly nonsense. B. can be so disagreeable; even now she's not—on terms with him!' And suddenly the thought of Mr Purcey leaped into her mind—Mr Purcey, who, as Mrs Tallents Smallpeace had declared, was not even conscious that there was a problem of the poor. To think of him seemed somehow at that moment comforting, like rolling oneself in a blanket against a draught. Passing into her room, she opened her wardrobe door.

'Bother the woman!' she thought. 'I do want that gentian dress got ready, but now I simply *can't* give it to her to do.'

Chapter 8

THE SINGLE MIND OF MR STONE

SINCE in the flutter of her spirit caused by the words of Mrs Hughs, Cecilia felt she must do something, she decided to change her dress.

The furniture of the pretty room she shared with Stephen had not been hastily assembled. Conscious, even fifteen years ago, when they moved into this house, of the grave Philistinism of the upper classes, she and Stephen had ever kept their duty to aestheticism green; and, in the matter of their bed, had lain for two years on two little white affairs, comfortable, but purely temporary, that they might give themselves a chance. The chance had come at last —a bed in real keeping with the period they had settled on, and going for twelve pounds. They had not let it go, and now slept in it—not quite so comfortable, perhaps, but comfortable enough, and conscious of duty done.

For fifteen years Cecilia had been furnishing her house; the process approached completion. The only things remaining on her mind—apart, that is, from Thyme's development and the condition of the people—were: item, a copper lantern that would allow some light to pass its framework; item, an old oak washstand not going back to Cromwell's time. And now this tnird anxiety had come!

She was rather touching, as she stood before the wardrobe glass divested of her bodice, with dimples of exertion in her thin white arms as she hooked her skirt behind, and her greenish eyes troubled, so anxious to do their best for everyone, and save risk of any sort. Having put on a bramble-coloured frock, which laced across her breast with silver lattice-work, and a hat (without feathers, so as to encourage birds) fastened to her head with pins (bought to aid a novel school of metal-work), she went to see what sort of day it was.

The window looked out at the back over some dreary streets, where the wind was flinging light drifts of smoke athwart the sunlight. They had chosen this room, not indeed for its view over the

condition of the people, but because of the sky effects at sunset,
which were extremely fine. For the first time, perhaps, Cecilia was
conscious that a sample of the class she was so interested in was
exposed to view beneath her nose. 'The Hughs live somewhere
there,' she thought. 'After all, I think B. ought to know about that
man. She might speak to father, and get him to give up having the
girl to copy for him—the whole thing's so worrying.'

In pursuance of this thought, she lunched hastily, and went out,
making her way to Hilary's. With every step she became more
uncertain. The fear of meddling too much, of not meddling enough,
of seeming meddlesome; timidity at touching anything so awkward; distrust, even ignorance, of her sister's character, which was
like, yet so very unlike, her own; a real itch to get the matter settled, so that nothing whatever should come of it—all this she felt.
She first hurried, then dawdled, finished the adventure at a run,
then told the servant not to announce her. The vision of Bianca's
eyes, as she listened to this tale, was suddenly too much for
Cecilia. She decided to pay a visit to her father first.

Mr Stone was writing, attired in his working dress—a thick
brown woollen gown, revealing his thin neck above the line of a
blue shirt, and tightly gathered round the waist with tasselled cord;
the lower portions of grey trousers were visible above woollen-slip-
pered feet. His hair straggled over his thin long ears. The window,
wide open, admitted an east wind; there was no fire. Cecilia
shivered.

'Come in quickly,' said Mr Stone. Turning to a big high desk
of stained deal which occupied the middle of one wall, he began
methodically to place the inkstand, a heavy paper-knife, a book,
and stones of several sizes, on his fluttering sheets of manuscript.

Cecilia looked about her; she had not been inside her father's
room for several months. There was nothing in it but that desk, a
camp bed in the far corner (with blankets, but no sheets), a folding
washstand, and a narrow bookcase, the books in which Cecilia
unconsciously told off on the fingers of her memory. They never
varied. On the top shelf the Bible and the works of Plautus and
Diderot; on the second from the top the plays of Shakespeare in a
blue edition; on the third from the bottom Don Quixote, in four
volumes, covered with brown paper; a green Milton; the 'Comedies
of Aristophanes'; a leather book, partially burned, comparing the
philosophy of Epicurus with the philosophy of Spinoza; and in a
yellow binding Mark Twain's 'Huckleberry Finn'. On the second
from the bottom was lighter literature: 'The Iliad'; a 'Life of Fran-

cis of Assisi'; Speke's 'Discovery of the Sources of the Nile'; the 'Pickwick Papers'; 'Mr Midshipman Easy'; The Verses of Theocritus, in a very old translation; Renan's 'Life of Christ'; and the 'Autobiography of Benvenuto Cellini'. The bottom shelf of all was full of books on natural science.

The walls were whitewashed, and, as Cecilia knew, came off on anybody who leaned against them. The floor was stained, and had no carpet. There was a little gas cooking-stove, with cooking things ranged on it; a small bare table; and one large cupboard. No draperies, no pictures, no ornaments of any kind; but by the window an ancient golden leather chair. Cecilia could never bear to sit in that oasis; its colour in this wilderness was too precious to her spirit.

'It's an east wind, father; aren't you terribly cold without a fire?'

Mr Stone came from his writing-desk, and stood so that light might fall on a sheet of paper in his hand. Cecilia noted the scent that went about with him of peat and baked potatoes. He spoke:

'Listen to this: "In the condition of society, dignified in those days with the name of civilisation, the only source of hope was the persistence of the quality of courage. Amongst a thousand nerve-destroying habits, amongst the dram-shops, patent medicines, the undigested chaos of inventions and discoveries, while hundreds were prating in their pulpits of things believed in by a negligible fraction of the population, and thousands writing down to-day what nobody would want to read in two days' time; while men shut animals in cages, and make bears jig to please their children, and all were striving one against the other; while, in a word, like gnats above a stagnant pool on a summer's evening, man danced up and down without the faintest notion why—in this condition of affairs the quality of courage was alive. It was the only fire within that gloomy valley." ' He stopped, though evidently anxious to go on, because he had read the last word on that sheet of paper. He moved towards the writing-desk. Cecilia said hastily:

'Do you mind if I shut the window, father?'

Mr Stone made a movement of his head, and Cecilia saw that he held a second sheet of paper in his hand. She rose, and going towards him, said:

'I want to talk to you, Dad!' Taking up the cord of his dressing-gown, she pulled it by its tassel.

'Don't!' said Mr Stone; 'it secures my trousers.'

Cecilia dropped the cord. 'Father is really terrible!' she thought.

Mr Stone, lifting the second sheet of paper, began again:

' "The reason, however, was not far to seek——" '

Cecilia said desperately:

'It's about that girl who comes to copy for you.'

Mr Stone lowered the sheet of paper, and stood, slightly curved from head to foot; his ears moved as though he were about to lay them back; his blue eyes, with little white spots of light alongside the tiny black pupils, stared at his daughter.

Cecilia thought: 'He's listening now.'

She made haste. '*Must* you have her here? Can't you do without her?'

'Without whom?' said Mr Stone.

'Without the girl who comes to copy for you.'

'Why?'

'For this very good reason——'

Mr Stone dropped his eyes, and Cecilia saw that he had moved the sheet of paper up as far as his waist.

'Does she copy better than any other girl could?' she asked hastily.

'No,' said Mr Stone.

'Then, Father, I do wish, to please me, you'd get someone else. I know what I'm talking about, and I——' Cecilia stopped; her father's lips and eyes were moving; he was obviously reading to himself. 'I've no patience with him,' she thought; 'he thinks of nothing but his wretched book.'

Aware of his daughter's silence, Mr Stone let the sheet of paper sink, and waited patiently again.

'What do you want, my dear?' he said.

'Oh, Father, do listen just a minute!'

'Yes, yes.'

'It's about that girl who comes to copy for you. Is there any reason why she should come instead of any other girl?'

'Yes,' said Mr Stone.

'What reason?'

'Because she has no friends.'

So awkward a reply was not expected by Cecilia; she looked at the floor, forced to search within her soul. Silence lasted several seconds; then Mr Stone's voice rose above a whisper:

' "The reason was not far to seek. Man, differentiated from the other apes by his desire to *know*, was from the first obliged to steel himself against the penalties of knowledge. Like animals subjected to the rigors of an Arctic climate, and putting forth more fur with each reduction in the temperature, man's hide of courage thickened automatically to resist the spear-thrusts dealt him by his own insatiate curiosity. In those days of which we speak, when undigested knowledge, in a great invading horde, had swarmed all his defences, man, suffering from a foul dyspepsia, with a nervous system in the latest stages of exhaustion, and a reeling brain, survived by reason of his power to go on making courage. Little heroic as (in the then general state of petty competition) his deeds appeared to be, there never had yet been a time when man in bulk was more courageous, for there never had yet been a time when he had more need to be. Signs were not wanting that this desperate state of things had caught the eyes of the community. A little sect——" ' Mr Stone stopped; his eyes had again tumbled over the bottom edge; he moved hurriedly towards the desk. Just as his hand removed a stone and took up a third sheet, Cecilia cried out:

'Father!'

Mr Stone stopped, and turned towards her. His daughter saw that he had gone quite pink; her annoyance vanished.

'Father! About that girl——'

Mr Stone seemed to reflect. 'Yes, yes,' he said.

'I don't think Bianca likes her coming here.'

Mr Stone passed his hand across his brow.

'Forgive me for reading to you, my dear,' he said; 'it's a great relief to me at times.'

Cecilia went close to him, and refrained with difficulty from taking up the tasselled cord.

'Of course, dear,' she said; 'I quite understand that.'

Mr Stone looked full in her face, and before a gaze which seemed to go through her and see things the other side, Cecilia dropped her eyes.

'It's strange,' he said, 'how you came to be my daughter!'

To Cecilia, too, this had often seemed a problem.

'There is a great deal in atavism,' said Mr Stone, 'that we know nothing of at present.'

Cecilia cried with heat, 'I do wish you would attend a minute, Father; it's really an important matter,' and she turned towards the window, tears being very near her eyes.

The voice of Mr Stone said humbly: 'I will try, my dear.'

But Cecilia thought: 'I must give him a good lesson. He really is too self-absorbed;' and she did not move, conveying by the posture of her shoulders how gravely she was vexed.

She could see nursemaids wheeling babies towards the Gardens, and noted their faces gazing, not at the babies, but, uppishly, at other nursemaids, or, with a sort of cautious longing, at men who passed. How selfish they looked! She felt a little glow of satisfaction that she was making this thin and bent old man behind her conscious of his egoism.

'He will know better another time,' she thought. Suddenly she heard a whistling, squeaking sound—it was Mr Stone whispering the third page of his manuscript:

' "—animated by some admirable sentiments, but whose doctrines—riddled by the fact that life is but the change of form to form—were too constricted for the evils they designed to remedy; this little sect, who had as yet to learn the meaning of universal love, were making the most strenuous efforts, in advance of the community at large, to understand themselves. The necessary movement which they voiced—reaction against the high-tide of the fratricidal system then prevailing—was young, and had the freshness and honesty of youth. . . ." '

Without a word Cecilia turned round and hurried to the door. She saw her father drop the sheet of paper; she saw his face, all pink and silver, stooping after it; and remorse visited her anger.

In the corridor outside she was arrested by a noise. The uncertain light of London halls fell there; on close inspection the sufferer was seen to be Miranda, who, unable to decide whether she wanted to be in the garden or the house, was seated beneath the hat-rack snuffling to herself. On seeing Cecilia she came out.

'What do you want, you little beast?'

Peering at her over the tops of her eyes, Miranda vaguely lifted a white foot. 'Why ask me that?' she seemed to say. 'How am I to know? Are we not all like this?'

Her conduct, coming at that moment, overtried Cecilia's nerves. She threw open Hilary's study-door, saying sharply: 'Go in and find your master!'

Miranda did not move, but Hilary came out instead. He had been correcting proofs to catch the post, and wore the look of a man abstracted, faintly contemptuous of other forms of life.

Cecilia, once more saved from the necessity of approaching her sister, the mistress of the house, so fugitive, haunting, and unseen, yet so much the centre of this situation, said:

'Can I speak to you a minute, Hilary?'

They went into his study, and Miranda came creeping in behind.

To Cecilia her brother-in-law always seemed an amiable and more or less pathetic figure. In his literary preoccupations he allowed people to impose on him. He looked unsubstantial beside the bust of Socrates, which moved Cecilia strangely—it was so very massive and so very ugly! She decided not to beat about the bush.

'I've been hearing some odd things from Mrs Hughs about that little model, Hilary.'

Hilary's smile faded from his eyes, but remained clinging to his lips.

'Indeed!'

Cecilia went on nervously: 'Mrs Hughs says it's because of her that Hughs behaves so badly. I don't want to say anything against the girl, but she seems—she seems to have——'

'Yes?' said Hilary.

'To have cast a spell on Hughs, as the woman puts it.'

'On Hughs!' repeated Hilary.

Cecilia found her eyes resting on the bust of Socrates, and hastily proceeded:

'She says he follows her about, and comes down here to lie in wait for her. It's a most strange business altogether. You went to see them, didn't you?'

Hilary nodded.

'I've been speaking to Father,' Cecilia murmured; 'but he's hopeless—I couldn't get him to pay the least attention.'

Hilary seemed thinking deeply.

'I wanted him,' she went on, 'to get some other girl instead to come and copy for him.'

'Why?'

Under the seeming impossibility of ever getting any farther, without saying what she had come to say, Cecilia blurted out:

'Mrs Hughs says that Hughs has threatened *you*.'

Hilary's face became ironical.

'Really!' he said. 'That's good of him! What for?'

The frightful indelicacy of her situation at this moment, the feeling of unfairness that she should be placed in it, almost overwhelmed Cecilia. 'Goodness knows I don't want to meddle. I never meddle in anything—it's horrible!'

Hilary took her hand.

'My dear Cis,' he said, 'of course! But we'd better have this out!'

Grateful for the pressure of his hand, she gave it a convulsive squeeze.

'It's so sordid, Hilary!'

'Sordid! H'm! Let's get it over, then.'

Cecilia had grown crimson. 'Do you want me to tell you everything?'

'Certainly.'

'Well, Hughs evidently thinks you're interested in the girl. You can't keep anything from servants and people who work about your house; they always think the worst of everything—and, of course, they know that you and B. don't—aren't——'

Hilary nodded.

'Mrs Hughs actually said the man meant to go to B.!'

Again the vision of her sister seemed to float into the room, and she went on desperately: 'And, Hilary, I can see Mrs Hughs really thinks you are interested. Of course, she wants to, for if you were, it would mean that a man like her husband could have no chance.'

Astonished at this flash of cynical inspiration, and ashamed of such plain speaking, she checked herself. Hilary had turned away.

Cecilia touched his arm. 'Hilary, dear,' she said, 'isn't there any chance of you and B——?'

Hilary's lips twitched. 'I should say not.'

Cecilia looked sadly at the floor. Not since Stephen was bad with pleurisy had she felt so worried. The sight of Hilary's face brought back her doubts with all their force. It might, of course, be only anger at the man's impudence, but it might be—she hardly liked to frame her thought—a more personal feeling.

'Don't you think,' she said, 'that, anyway, she had better not come here again?'

Hilary paced the room.

'It's her only safe and certain piece of work; it keeps her independent. It's much more satisfactory than this sitting. I can't have any hand in taking it away from her.'

Cecilia had never seen him moved like this. Was it possible that he was not incorrigibly gentle, but had in him some of that animality which she, in a sense, admired? This uncertainty terribly increased the difficulties of the situation.

'But, Hilary,' she said at last, 'are you satisfied about the girl— I mean, are you satisfied that she really is worth helping?'

'I don't understand.'

'I mean,' murmured Cecilia, 'that we don't know anything about her past.' And, seeing from the movement of his eyebrows that she was touching on what had evidently been a doubt with him, she went on with great courage: 'Where are her friends and relations? I mean, she may have had a—adventures.'

Hilary withdrew into himself.

'You can hardly expect me,' he said, 'to go into that with her.'

His reply made Cecilia feel ridiculous.

'Well,' she said in a hard little voice, 'if this is what comes of helping the poor, I don't see the use of it.'

The outburst evoked no reply from Hilary; she felt more tremulous than ever. The whole thing was so confused, so unnatural. What with the dark, malignant Hughs and that haunting vision of Bianca, the matter seemed almost Italian. That a man of Hughs' class might be affected by the passion of love had somehow never come into her head. She thought of the back streets she had looked out on from her bedroom window. Could anything like passion spring up in those dismal alleys? The people who lived there, poor down-trodden things, had enough to do to keep themselves alive. She knew all about them; they were in the air; their condition was deplorable! Could a person whose condition was deplorable find time or strength for any sort of lurid exhibition such as this? It was incredible.

She became aware that Hilary was speaking.

'I daresay the man is dangerous!'

Hearing her fears confirmed, and in accordance with the secret vein of hardness which kept her living, amid all her sympathies and hesitations, Cecilia felt suddenly that she had gone as far as it was in her to go.

'I shall have no more to do with them,' she said; 'I've tried my best for Mrs Hughs. I know quite as good a needlewoman, who'll be only too glad to come instead. Any other girl will do as well to copy father's book. If you take my advice, Hilary, you'll give up trying to help them too.'

Hilary's smile puzzled and annoyed her. If she had known, this was the smile that stood between him and her sister.

'You may be right,' he said, and shrugged his shoulders.

'Very well,' said Cecilia, 'I've done all I can. I must go now. Good-bye.'

During her progress to the door she gave one look behind. Hilary was standing by the bust of Socrates. Her heart smote her to leave him thus embarrassed. But again the vision of Bianca—fugitive in her own house, and with something tragic in her mocking immobility—came to her, and she hastened away.

A voice said: 'How are you, Mrs Dallison? Your sister at home?'

Cecilia saw before her Mr Purcey, rising and falling a little

243

with the oscillation of his A.1. Damyer as he prepared to alight.

A sense as of having just left a house visited by sickness or misfortune made Cecilia murmur:

'I'm afraid she's not.'

'Bad luck!' said Mr Purcey. His face fell as far as so red and square a face could fall. 'I was hoping perhaps I might be allowed to take them for a run. She's wanting exercise.' Mr Purcey laid his hand on the flank of his palpitating car. 'Know these A.1. Damyers, Mrs Dallison? Best value you can get, simply rippin' little cars. Wish you'd try her.'

The A.1. Damyer, diffusing an aroma of the finest petrol, leaped and trembled, as though conscious of her master's praise. Cecilia looked at her.

'Yes,' she said. 'she's very sweet.'

'Now do!' said Mr Purcey. 'Let me give you a run—just to please me, I mean. I'm sure you'll like her.'

A little compunction, a little curiosity, a sudden revolt against all the discomfiture and sordid doubts she had been suffering from, made Cecilia glance softly at Mr Purcey's figure; almost before she knew it, she was seated in the A.1. Damyer. It trembled, emitted two small sounds, one large scent, and glided forward. Mr Purcey said:

'That's rippin' of you!'

A postman, dog, and baker's cart, all hurrying at top speed, seemed to stand still; Cecilia felt the wind beating her cheeks. She gave a little laugh.

'You must just take me home, please.'

Mr Purcey touched the chauffeur's elbow.

'Round the park,' he said. 'Let her have it.'

The A.1. Damyer uttered a tiny shriek. Cecilia, leaning back in her padded corner, glanced askance at Mr Purcey leaning back in his; an unholy, astonished little smile played on her lips.

'What am I doing?' it seemed to say. 'The way he got me here—really! And now I am here I'm just going to enjoy it!'

There were no Hughes, no little model—all that sordid life had vanished; there was nothing but the wind beating her cheeks and the A.1. Damyer leaping under her.

Mr Purcey said: 'It just makes all the difference to me; keeps my nerves in order.'

'Oh,' Cecilia murmured, 'have *you* got nerves?'

Mr Purcey smiled. When he smiled his cheeks formed two hard red blocks, his trim moustache stood out, and many little wrinkles ran from his light eyes.

'Chock full of them,' he said; 'least thing upsets me. Can't bear to see a hungry-lookin' child, or anything.'

A strange feeling of admiration for this man had come upon Cecilia. Why could not she, and Thyme, and Hilary, and Stephen, and all the people they knew and mixed with, be like him, so sound and healthy, so unravaged by disturbing sympathies, so innocent of 'social conscience', so content?

As though jealous of these thoughts about her master, the A.1. Damyer stopped of her own accord.

'Hallo,' said Mr Purcey, 'hallo, I say! Don't you get out; she'll be all right directly.'

'Oh,' said Cecilia, 'thanks but I must go in here, anyhow; I think I'll say good-bye. Thank you so much. I *have* enjoyed it.'

From the threshold of a shop she looked back. Mr Purcey, on foot, was leaning forward from the waist, staring at his A.1. Damyer with profound concentration.

Chapter 9

HILARY GIVES CHASE

THE ethics of a man like Hilary were not those of the million pure-bred Purceys of this life, founded on a sense of property in this world and the next; nor were they precisely the morals and religion of the aristocracy, who, though aestheticised in parts, quietly used, in bulk, their fortified position to graft on Mr Purcey's ethics the principle of 'You be damned!' In the eyes of the majority he was probably an immoral and irreligious man; but in fact his morals and religion were those of his special section of society—the cultivated classes, 'the professors, the artistic pigs, advanced people, and all that sort of cuckoo,' as Mr Purcey called them—a section of society supplemented by persons, placed beyond the realms of want, who speculated in ideas.

Had he been required to make a profession of his creed he would probably have framed it in some such way as this: 'I disbelieve in all Church dogmas, and do not go to church; I have no definite ideas about a future state, and do not want to have; but in a private way I try to identify myself as much as possible with what I see about me, feeling that if I could ever really be at one with the world I live in I should be happy. I think it foolish not to trust my senses and my reason; as for what my senses and my reason will not tell me, I assume that all is as it had to be, for if one could get to know the why of everything, one would be the Universe. I do not believe that chastity is a virtue in itself, but only so far as it ministers to the health and happiness of the community. I do not believe that marriage confers the rights of ownership, and I loathe all public wrangling on such matters; but I am temperamentally averse to the harming of my neighbours, if in reason it can be avoided. As to manners, I think that to repeat a bit of scandal, and circulate backbiting stories, are worse offences than the actions that gave rise to them. If I mentally condemn a person, I feel guilty of moral lapse. I hate self-assertion; I am ashamed of self-advertisement. I dislike loudness of any kind. Probably I have too much tendency to negation of all sorts. Small-talk bores me to extinction, but I will discuss a point of ethics or psychology half the night. To make capital out of a person's weakness is repugnant to me. I want to be a decent man, but—I really can't take myself too seriously.'

Though he had preserved his politeness towards Cecilia, he was in truth angry, and grew angrier every minute. He was angry with her, himself, and the man Hughs; and suffered from this anger as only they can who are not accustomed to the rough-and-tumble of things.

Such a retiring man as Hilary was seldom given the opportunity for an obvious display of chivalry. The tenor of his life removed him from those situations. Such chivalry as he displayed was of a negative order. And confronted suddenly with the conduct of Hughs, who, it seemed, knocked his wife about, and dogged the footsteps of the helpless girl, he took it seriously to heart.

When the little model came walking up the garden on her usual visit, he fancied her face looked scared. Quieting the growling of Miranda, who from the first had stubbornly refused to know this girl, he sat down with a book to wait for her to go away. After sitting an hour or more, turning over pages, and knowing little of their sense, he saw a man peer over his garden gate. He was there for half a minute, then lounged across the road, and stood hidden by some railings.

'So?' thought Hilary. 'Shall I go out and warn the fellow to clear off, or shall I wait to see what happens when she goes away?'

He determined on the latter course. Presently she came out, walking with her peculiar gait, youthful and pretty, but too

246

matter-of-fact, and yet, as it were, too purposeless to be a lady's. She looked back at Hilary's window, and turned uphill.

Hilary took his hat and stick and waited. In half a minute Hughs came out from under cover of the railings and followed. Then Hilary, too, set forth.

There is left in every man something of the primeval love of stalking. The delicate Hilary, in cooler blood, would have revolted at the notion of dogging people's footsteps. He now experienced the holy pleasures of the chase. Certain that Hughs was really following the girl, he had but to keep him in sight and remain unseen. This was not hard for a man given to mountain-climbing, almost the only sport left to one who thought it immoral to hurt anybody but himself.

Taking advantage of shop-windows, omnibuses, passers-by, and other bits of cover, he prosecuted the chase up the steepy heights of Campden Hill. But soon a nearly fatal check occurred; for, chancing to take his eyes off Hughs, he saw the little model returning on her tracks. Ready enough in physical emergencies, Hilary sprang into a passing omnibus. He saw her stopping before the window of a picture-shop. From the expression of her face and figure, she evidently had no idea that she was being followed, but stood with a sort of slack-lipped wonder, lost in admiration of a well-known print. Hilary had often wondered who could possibly admire that picture—he now knew. It was obvious that the girl's aesthetic sense was deeply touched.

While this was passing through his mind, he caught sight of Hughs lurking outside a public-house. The dark man's face was sullen and dejected, and looked as if he suffered. Hilary felt a sort of pity for him.

The omnibus leaped forward, and he sat down smartly almost on a lady's lap. This was the lap of Mrs Tallents Smallpeace, who greeted him with a warm, quiet smile, and made a little room.

'Your sister-in-law has just been to see me, Mr Dallison. She's such a dear—so interested in everything. I tried to get her to come on to my meeting with me.'

Raising his hat, Hilary frowned. For once his delicacy was at fault. He said:

'Ah, yes! Excuse me!' and got out.

Mrs Tallents Smallpeace looked after him, and then glanced round the omnibus. His conduct was very like the conduct of a man who had got in to keep an assignation with a lady, and found that lady sitting next his aunt. She was unable to see a soul who seemed to foster this view, and sat thinking that he was 'rather attractive'. Suddenly her dark busy eyes lighted on the figure of the little model strolling along again.

'Oh!' she thought. 'Ah! Yes, really! How very interesting!'

Hilary, to avoid meeting the girl point-blank, had turned up a by-street, and, finding a convenient corner waited. He was puzzled. If this man were persecuting her with his attentions, why had he not gone across when she was standing at the picture-shop?

She passed across the opening of the by-street, still walking in the slack way of one who takes the pleasures of the streets. She passed from view; Hilary strained his eyes to see if Hughs were following. He waited several minutes. The man did not appear. The chase was over! And suddenly it flashed across him that Hughs had merely dogged her to see that she had no assignation with anybody. They had both been playing the same game! He flushed up in that shady little street, in which he was the only person to be seen. Cecilia was right! It was a sordid business. A man more in touch with facts than Hilary would have had some mental pigeon-hole into which to put an incident like this; but, being by profession concerned mainly with ideas and thoughts, he did not quite know where he was. The habit of his mind precluded him from thinking very definitely on any subject except his literary work—precluded him especially in a matter of this sort, so inextricably entwined with that delicate, dim question, the impact of class on class.

Pondering deeply, he ascended the leafy lane that leads between high railings from Notting Hill to Kensington.

It was so far from traffic that every tree on either side was loud with the Spring songs of birds; the scent of running sap came forth shyly as the sun sank low. Strange peace, strange feeling of old Mother Earth up there above the town; wild tunes, and the quiet sight of clouds. Man in this lane might rest his troubled thoughts, and for a while trust the goodness of the Scheme that gave him birth, the beauty of each day, that laughs or broods itself into night. Some budding lilacs exhaled a scent of lemons; a sandy cat on the coping of a garden wall basking in the setting sun.

In the centre of the lane a row of elm-trees displayed their gnarled, knotted roots. Human beings were seated there, whose matted hair clung round their tired faces. Their gaunt limbs were clothed in rags; each had a stick, and some sort of dirty bundle tied to it. They were asleep. On a bench beyond, two toothless old women sat, moving their eyes from side to side, and a crimson-faced woman was snoring. Under the next tree a Cockney youth and his girl were sitting side by side—pale young things with loose mouths, and hollow cheeks, and restless eyes. Their arms were enlaced; they were silent. A little farther on two young men in working clothes were looking straight before them, with desperately tired faces. They, too, were silent.

On the last bench of all Hilary came on the little model, seated slackly by herself.

Chapter 10

THE TROUSSEAU

THIS, the first time these two had met each other at large, was clearly not a comfortable event for either of them. The girl blushed, and hastily got off her seat. Hilary, who raised his hat and frowned, sat down on it.

'Don't get up,' he said; 'I want to talk to you.'

The little model obediently resumed her seat. A silence followed. She had on the old brown skirt and knitted jersey, the old blue-green tam-o'-shanter cap, and there were marks of weariness beneath her eyes.

At last Hilary remarked: 'How are you getting on?'

The little model looked at her feet.

'Pretty well, thank you, Mr Dallison.'

'I came to see you yesterday.'

She slid a look at him which might have meant nothing or meant much, so perfect its shy stolidity.

'I was out,' she said, 'sitting to Miss Boyle.'

'So you have some work?'

'It's finished now.'

'Then you're only getting the two shillings a day from Mr Stone?'

She nodded.

'H'm!'

The unexpected fervour of this grunt seemed to animate the little model.

'Three and sixpence for my rent, and breakfast costs threepence nearly—only bread-and-butter—that's five and two; and washing's always at least tenpence—that's six; and little things last week was a shilling—even when I don't take buses—seven; that leaves five shillings for my dinners. Mr Stone always gives me tea. It's my clothes worries me.' She tucked her feet farther beneath the seat, and Hilary refrained from looking down. 'My hat is awful, and I do want some——' She looked Hilary in the face for the first time. 'I do wish I was rich.'

'I don't wonder.'

The little model gritted her teeth, and, twisting at her dirty gloves, said: 'Mr Dallison, d'you know the first thing I'd buy if I was rich?'

'No.'

'I'd buy everything new on me from top to toe, and I wouldn't ever wear any of these old things again.'

Hilary got up: 'Come with me now, and buy everything new from top to toe.'

'Oh!'

Hilary had already perceived that he had made an awkward, even dangerous, proposal; short, however, of giving her money, the idea of which offended his sense of delicacy, there was no way out of it. He said brusquely: 'Come along!'

The little model rose obediently. Hilary noticed that her boots were split, and this—as though he had seen someone strike a child —so moved his indignation that he felt no more qualms, but rather a sort of pleasant glow, such as will come to the most studious man when he levels a blow at the conventions.

He looked down at his companion—her eyes were lowered; he could not tell at all what she was thinking of.

'This is what I was going to speak to you about,' he said: 'I don't like that house you're in; I think you ought to be somewhere else. What do you say?'

'Yes, Mr Dallison.'

'You'd better make a change, I think; you could find another room, couldn't you?'

The little model answered as before: 'Yes, Mr Dallison.'

'I'm afraid that Hughs is—a dangerous sort of fellow.'

'He's a funny man.'

'Does he annoy you?'

Her expression baffled Hilary; there seemed a sort of slow enjoyment in it. She looked up knowingly.

'I don't mind him—he won't hurt me. Mr Dallison, do you think blue or green?'

Hilary answered shortly: 'Bluey-green.'

She clasped her hands, changed her feet with a hop, and went on walking as before.

'Listen to me,' said Hilary; 'has Mrs Hughs been talking to you about her husband?'

The little model smiled again.

'She goes on,' she said.

Hilary bit his lips.

'Mr Dallison, please—about my hat?'

'What about your hat?'

'Would you like me to get a large one or a small one?'

'For God's sake,' answered Hilary, 'a small one—no feathers.'

'Oh!'

'Can you attend to me a minute? Have either Hughs or Mrs Hughs spoken to you about—coming to my house, about—me?'

The little model's face remained impassive, but by the movement of her fingers Hilary saw that she was attending now.

'I don't care what they say.'

Hilary looked away; an angry flush slowly mounted in his face. With surprising suddenness the little model said:

'Of course, if I was a lady, I might mind!'

'Don't talk like that!' said Hilary; 'every woman is a lady.'

The stolidity of the girl's face, more mocking far than any smile, warned him of the cheapness of this verbiage.

'If I was a lady,' she repeated simply, 'I shouldn't be livin' there, should I?'

'No,' said Hilary; 'and you had better not go on living there, anyway.'

The little model making no answer, Hilary did not quite know what to say. It was becoming apparent to him that she viewed the situation with a very different outlook from himself, and that he did not understand that outlook.

He felt thoroughly at sea, conscious that this girl's life contained a thousand things he did not know, a thousand points of view he did not share.

Their two figures attracted some attention in the crowded street, for Hilary—tall and slight, with his thin, bearded face and soft felt hat—was what is known as 'a distinguished-looking man'; and the little model, though not 'distinguished-looking' in her old brown skirt and tam-o'-shanter cap, had the sort of face which made men and even women turn to look at her. To men she was a little bit of strangely interesting, not too usual, flesh and blood; to women, she was that which made men turn to look at her. Yet now and again there would rise in some passer-by a feeling

251

more impersonal, as though the God of Pity had shaken wings over-head, and dropped a tiny feather.

So walking, and exciting vague interest, they reached the first of the hundred doors of Messrs Rose and Thorn.

Hilary had determined on this end door, for, as the adventure grew warmer, he was more alive to its dangers. To take this child into the very shop frequented by his wife and friends seemed a little mad; but that same reason which caused them to frequent it—the fact that there was no other shop of the sort half so handy —was the reason which caused Hilary to go there now. He had acted on impulse; he knew that if he let his impulse cool he would not act at all. The bold course was the wise one; this was why he chose the end door round the corner. Standing aside for her to go in first, he noticed the girl's brightened eyes and cheeks; she had never looked so pretty. He glanced hastily round; the department was barren for their purposes, filled entirely with pyjamas. He felt a touch on his arm. The little model, rather pink, was looking up at him.

'Mr Dallison, am I to get more than one set of—underthings?'

'Three—three,' muttered Hilary; and suddenly he saw that they were on the threshold of that sanctuary. 'Buy them,' he said, 'and bring me the bill.'

He waited close beside a man with a pink face, a moustache, and an almost perfect figure, who was standing very still, dressed from head to foot in blue-and-white stripes. He seemed the apotheosis of what a man should be, his face composed in a deathless simper : 'Long, long have been the struggles of man, but civilisation has produced me at last. Further than this it cannot go. Nothing shall make me continue my line. In me the end is reached. See my back : "The Amateur. This perfect style, 8s. 11d. Great reduction." '

He would not talk to Hilary, and the latter was compelled to watch the shopmen. It was but half an hour to closing time; the youths were moving languidly, bickering a little, in the absence of their customers—like flies on a pane, that cannot get out into the sun. Two of them came and asked him what they might serve him with, they were so refined and pleasant that Hilary was on the point of buying what he did not want. The reappearance of the little model saved him.

'It's thirty shillings; five and eleven was the cheapest, and stockings, and I bought some sta——'

Hilary produced the money hastily.

'This is a very dear shop,' she said.

When she had paid the bill, and Hilary had taken from her a large brown-paper parcel, they journeyed on together. He had armoured his face now in a slightly startled quizzicality, as though, himself detached, he were watching the adventure from a distance.

On the central velvet seat of the boot and shoe department, a lady, with an egret in her hat, was stretching out a slim silk-stockinged foot, waiting for a boot. She looked with negligent amusement at this common little girl and her singular companion. This look of hers seemed to affect the woman serving, for none came near the little model. Hilary saw them eyeing her boots, and, suddenly forgetting his rôle of looker-on, he became very angry. Taking out his watch, he went up to the eldest woman.

'If somebody,' he said, 'does not attend this young lady within a minute, I shall make a personal complaint to Mr Thorn.'

The hand of the watch, however, had not completed its round before a woman was at the little model's side. Hilary saw her taking off her boot, and by a sudden impulse he placed himself between her and the lady. In doing this, he so far forgot his delicacy as to fix his eyes on the little model's foot. The sense of physical discomfort which first attacked him became a sort of aching in his heart. That brown, dingy stocking was darned till no stocking, only darning, and one toe and two little white bits of foot were seen, where the threads refused to hold together any longer.

The little model wagged the toe uneasily—she had hoped, no doubt, that it would not protrude—then concealed it with her skirt. Hilary moved hastily away; when he looked again, it was not at her, but at the lady.

Her face had changed; it was no longer amused and negligent, but stamped with an expression of offence. 'Intolerable,' it seemed to say, 'to bring a girl like that into a shop like this! I shall never come here again!' The expression was but the outward sign of that inner physical discomfort Hilary himself had felt when he first saw the little model's stocking. This naturally did not serve to lessen his anger, especially as he saw her animus mechanically reproduced on the faces of the serving women.

He went back to the little model, and sat down by her side.

'Does it fit? You'd better walk in it and see.'

The little model walked.

'It squeezes me,' she said.

'Try another, then,' said Hilary.

The lady rose, stood for a second with her eyebrows raised and her nostrils slightly distended, then went away, and left a peculiarly pleasant scent of violets behind.

The second pair of boots not 'squeezing' her, the little model was soon ready to go down. She had all her trousseau now, except the dress—selected and, indeed, paid for, but which, as she told Hilary, she was coming back to try on to-morrow, when—when—— She had obviously meant to say when she was all new underneath. She was laden with one large and two small parcels, and in her eyes there was a holy look.

Outside the shop she gazed up in his face.

'Well, you are happy now?' asked Hilary.

Between the short black lashes were seen two very bright, wet shining eyes; her parted lips began to quiver.

'Good-night, then,' he said abruptly, and walked away.

But looking round, he saw her still standing there, half buried in parcels, gazing after him. Raising his hat, he turned into the High Street towards home. . . .

The old man, known to that low class of fellow with whom he was now condemned to associate as '*Westminster*', was taking a whiff or two out of his old clay pipe, and trying to forget his feet. He saw Hilary coming, and carefully extended a copy of the last edition.

'Good-evenin', sir! Quite seasonable to-day for the time of year! Ho yes! *Westminster!*'

His eyes followed Hilary's retreat. He thought:

'Oh dear! He's a-given me an 'arf-a-crown. He does look well— I like to see 'im look as well as that—quite young! Oh dear!'

The sun—that smokey, flaring ball, which in its time had seen so many last editions of the *Westminster Gazette*—was dropping down to pass the night in Shepherd's Bush. It made the old butler's eyelids blink when he turned to see if the coin really was a half-crown, or too good to be true.

And all the spires and house-roofs, and the spaces up above and underneath them, glittered and swam, and little men and horses looked as if they had been powdered with golden dust.

Chapter 11

PEAR BLOSSOM

WEIGHED down by her three parcels, the little model pursued her way to Hound Street. At the door of No. 1 the son of the lame woman, a tall weedy youth with a white face, was resting his legs alternately, and smoking a cigarette. Closing one eye, he addressed her thus:

''Allo, miss! Kerry your parcels for you?'

The little model gave him a look. 'Mind your own business!' it said; but there was that in the flicker of her eyelashes which more than nullified this snub.

Entering her room, she deposited the parcels on her bed, and untied the strings with quick, pink fingers. When she had freed the garments from wrappings and spread them out, she knelt down, and began to touch them, putting her nose down once or twice to sniff the linen and feel its texture. There were little frills attached here and there, and to these she paid particular attention, ruffling their edges with the palms of her hands, while the holy look came back to her face. Rising at length, she locked the door, drew down the blind, undressed from head to foot, and put on the new garments. Letting her hair down, she turned herself luxuriously round and round before the too-small looking-glass. There was utter satisfaction in each gesture of that whole operation, as if her spirit, long starved, were having a good meal. In this rapt contemplation of herself, all childish vanity and expectancy, and all that wonderful quality found in simple unspiritual natures of delighting in the present moment, were perfectly displayed. So, motionless, with her hair loose on her neck, she was like one of those half-hours of Spring that have lost their restlessness and are content just to *be*.

Presently, however, as though suddenly remembering that her happiness was not utterly complete, she went to a drawer, took out a packet of pear-drops, and put one in her mouth.

The sun, near to setting, had found its way through a hole in the blind, and touched her neck. She turned as though she had received a kiss, and, raising a corner of the blind, peered out. The pear-tree, which, to the annoyance of its proprietor, was placed so close to the back court of this low-class house as almost to seem to belong to it, was bathed in slanting sunlight. No tree in all the world could have looked more fair than it did just then in its garb

255

of gilded bloom. With her hand up to her bare neck, and her cheeks indrawn from sucking the sweet, the little model fixed her eyes on the tree. Her expression did not change; she showed no signs of admiration. Her gaze passed on to the back windows of the house that really owned the pear-tree, spying out whether anyone could see her—hoping, perhaps, someone *would* see her while she was feeling so nice and new. Then, dropping the blind, she went back to the glass and began to pin her hair up. When this was done she stood for a long minute looking at her old brown skirt and blouse, hesitating to defile her new-found purity. At last she put them on and drew up the blind. The sunlight had passed off the pear-tree; its bloom was now white, and almost as still as snow. The little model put another sweet into her mouth, and producing from her pocket an ancient leather purse, counted out her money. Evidently discovering that it was no more than she expected, she sighed, and rummaged out of a top drawer an old illustrated magazine.

She sat down on the bed, and turning the leaves rapidly till she reached a certain page, rested the paper in her lap. Her eyes were fixed on a photograph in the left-hand corner—one of those effigies of writers that appear occasionally in the public press. Under it were printed the words: 'Mr Hilary Dallison'. And suddenly she heaved a sigh.

The room grew darker; the wind, getting up as the sun went down, blew a few dropped petals of the pear-tree against the window-pane.

Chapter 12

SHIPS IN SAIL

IN due accord with the old butler's comment on his looks, Hilary had felt so young that, instead of going home, he mounted an omnibus, and went down to his club—the 'Pen and Ink', so called because the man who founded it could not think at the moment of any other words. This literary person had left the club soon after its initiation, having conceived for it a sudden dislike. It had indeed a certain reputation for bad cooking, and all its members complained bitterly at times that you never could go in without meeting someone you knew. It stood in Dover Street. Unlike other clubs, it was mainly used to talk in, and had special arrangements for the safety of umbrellas and such books as had not yet vanished from the library; not, of course, owing to any peculative tendency among its members, but because, after interchanging their ideas, those members would depart, in a long row, each grasping some material object in his hand. Its maroon-coloured curtains, too, were never drawn, because, in the heat of their discussions, the members were always drawing them. On the whole, those members did not like each other much; wondering a little, one by one, why the others wrote; and when the printed reasons were detailed to them, reading them with irritation. If really compelled to hazard an opinion about each other's merits, they used to say that, no doubt 'Só-and-so' was 'very good', but they had never read him! For it had early been established as the principle underlying membership not to read the writings of another man, unless you could be certain he was dead, lest you might have to tell him to his face that you disliked his work. For they were very jealous of the purity of their literary consciences. Exception was made, however, in the case of those who lived by written criticism, the opinions of such persons being read by all, with a varying smile, and a certain cerebral excitement. Now and then, however, some member, violating every sense of decency, would take a violent liking for another member's books. This he would express in words, to the discomfort of his fellows, who, with a sudden chilly feeling in the stomach, would wonder why it was not their books that he was praising.

Almost every year, and generally in March, certain aspirations would pass into the club; members would ask each other why there was no Academy of British Letters; why there was no concerted movement to limit the production of other authors' books; why there was no prize given for the best work of the year. For a little time it almost seemed as if their individualism were in danger; but, the windows having been opened wider than usual some morning, the aspirations would pass out, and all would feel secretly as a man feels when he has swallowed the mosquito that has been worrying him all night—relieved, but just a little bit embarrassed. Socially sympathetic in their dealings with each other—they were mostly quite nice fellows—each kept a little fame-machine, on which he might be seen sitting every morning about the time the papers and his correspondence came, wondering if his fame were going up.

Hilary stayed in the club till half-past nine; then, avoiding a discussion which was just setting in, he took his own umbrella, and bent his steps towards home.

It was the moment of suspense in Piccadilly; the tide had flowed up to the theatres, and had not yet begun to ebb. The tranquil trees, still feathery, draped their branches along the farther bank of that broad river, resting from their watch over the tragi-comedies played on its surface by men, their small companions. The gentle sighs which distilled from their plume-like boughs seemed utterances of the softest wisdom. Not far beyond their trunks it was all dark velvet, into which separate shapes, adventuring, were lost, as wild birds vanishing in space, or the souls of men received into their Mother's heart.

Hilary walked, hearing no sighs of wisdom, noting no smooth darkness, wrapped in thought. The mere fact of having given pleasure was enough to produce a warm sensation in a man so naturally kind. But, as with all self-conscious, self-distrustful, natures, that sensation had not lasted. He was left with a feeling of emptiness and disillusionment, as of having given himself a good mark without reason.

While walking, he was a target for the eyes of many women, who passed him rapidly, like ships in sail. The peculiar fastidious shyness of his face attracted those accustomed to another kind of face. And though he did not precisely look at them, they in turn inspired in him the compassionate, morbid curiosity which persons who live desperate lives necessarily inspire in the leisured, speculative mind. One of them deliberately approached him from a side-street. Though taller and fuller, with heightened colour, frizzy hair, and a hat with feathers, she was the image of the little model—the same shape of face, broad cheek-bones, mouth a little open; the same flower-coloured eyes and short black lashes, all coarsened and accentuated as Art coarsens and accentuates the lines of life. Looking boldly into Hilary's startled face, she laughed. Hilary winced and walked on quickly.

He reached home at half-past ten. The lamp was burning in Mr Stone's room, and his window was, as usual, open; that which was not usual, however, was a light in Hilary's own bedroom. He went gently up. Through the door—ajar—he saw, to his surprise, the figure of his wife. She was reclining in a chair, her elbows on its arms, the tips of her fingers pressed together. Her face, with its dark hair, vivid colouring, and sharp lines, was touched with shadows; her head turned as though towards somebody beside her; her neck gleamed white. So—motionless, dimly seen—she was like a woman sitting alongside her own life, scrutinising, criticising, watching it live, taking no part in it. Hilary wondered whether to go in or slip away from his strange visitor.

'Ah! it's you,' she said.

Hilary approached her. For all her mocking of her own charms, this wife of his was strangely graceful. After nineteen years in which to learn every line of her face and body, every secret of her nature, she still eluded him; that elusiveness, which had begun by being such a charm, had got on his nerves, and extinguished the flame it had once lighted. He had so often tried to see, and never seen, the essence of her soul. Why was she made like this? Why was she for ever mocking herself, himself, and every other thing? Why was she so hard to her own life, so bitter a foe to her own happiness? Leonardo da Vinci might have painted her, less sensual and cruel than his women, more restless and disharmonic, but physically, spiritually enticing, and, by her refusals to surrender either to her spirit or her senses, baffling her own enticements.

'I don't know why I came,' she said.

Hilary found no better answer than: 'I am sorry I was out to dinner.'

'Has the wind gone round? My room is cold.'

'Yes, north-east. Stay here.'

Her hand touched his; that warm and restless clasp was agitating.

'It's good of you to ask me; but we'd better not begin what we can't keep up.'

'Stay here,' said Hilary again, kneeling down beside her chair.

And suddenly he began to kiss her face and neck. He felt her answering kisses; for a moment they were clasped together in a fierce embrace. Then, as though by mutual consent, their arms relaxed; their eyes grew furtive, like the eyes of children who have egged each other on to steal; and on their lips appeared the faintest of faint smiles. It was as though those lips were saying: 'Yes, but we are not quite animals!'

Hilary got up and sat down on his bed. Bianca stayed in the chair, looking straight before her, utterly inert, her head thrown back, her white throat gleaming, on her lips and in her eyes that flickering smile. Not a word more, nor a look, passed between them.

Then rising, without noise, she passed behind him and went out.

Hilary had a feeling in his mouth as though he had been chewing ashes. And a phrase—as phrases sometimes fill the spirit of a man without rhyme or reason—kept forming on his lips: 'The house of harmony!'

Presently he went to her door, and stood there listening. He could hear no sound whatever. If she had been crying—if she had been laughing—it would have been better than this silence. He put his hands up to his ears and ran downstairs.

Chapter 13

SOUND IN THE NIGHT

PASSING his study door, he halted at Mr Stone's; the thought of the old man, so steady and absorbed in the face of all external things, refreshed him.

Still in his brown woollen gown, Mr Stone was sitting with his eyes fixed on something in the corner, whence a little perfumed steam was rising.

'Shut the door,' he said; 'I am making cocoa; will you have a cup?'

'Am I disturbing you?' asked Hilary.

Mr Stone looked at him steadily before answering.

'If I work after cocoa, I find it clogs the liver.'

'Then, if you'll let me, sir, I'll stay a little.'

'It is boiling,' said Mr Stone. He took the saucepan off the flame, and, distending his frail cheeks, blew. Then, while the steam mingled with his frosty beard, he brought two cups from a cupboard, filled one of them, and looked at Hilary.

'I should like you,' he said, 'to hear three or four pages I have just completed; you may perhaps be able to suggest a word or two.'

He placed the saucepan back on the stove, and grasped the cup he had filled.

'I will drink my cocoa, and read them to you.'

Going to the desk, he stood, blowing at the cup.

Hilary turned up the collar of his coat against the night wind which was visiting the room, and glanced at the empty cup, for he was rather hungry. He heard a curious sound: Mr Stone was blowing his own tongue. In his haste to read, he had drunk too soon and deeply of the cocoa.

'I have burnt my mouth,' he said.

Hilary moved hastily towards him: 'Badly? Try cold milk, sir.'

Mr Stone lifted the cup.

'There is none,' he said, and drank again.

'What would I not give,' thought Hilary, 'to have his singleness of heart!'

There was the sharp sound of a cup set down. Then, out of a rustling of papers, a sort of droning rose:

' "The Proletariat—with a cynicism natural to those who really are in want, and even amongst their leaders only veiled when these attained a certain position in the public eye—desired indeed the wealth and leisure of their richer neighbours, but in their long night of struggle with existence they had only found the energy to formulate their pressing needs from day to day. They were a heaving, surging sea of creatures, slowly, without consciousness or real guidance, rising in long tidal movements to set the limits of the shore a little farther back, and cast afresh the form of social life; and on its pea-green bosom——" ' Mr Stone paused. 'She has copied it wrong,' he said; 'the word is "sea-green". "And on its sea-green bosom sailed a fleet of silver cockle-shells, wafted by the breath of those not in themselves driven by the wind of need. The voyage of these silver cockle-shells, all heading across each other's bows, was, in fact, the advanced movement of that time. In the stern of each of these little craft, blowing at the sails, was seated a by-product of the accepted system. These by-products we should now examine." '

Mr Stone paused, and looked into his cup. There were some grounds in it. He drank them, and went on:

' "The fratricidal principal of the survival of the fittest, which in those days was England's moral teaching, had made the country one huge butcher's shop. Amongst the carcasses of countless victims there had fattened and grown purple many butchers, physically strengthened by the smell of blood and sawdust. These had begotten many children. Following out the laws of Nature providing against surfeit, a proportion of these children were born with a feeling of distaste for blood and sawdust; many of them, compelled for the purpose of making money to follow in their father's practices, did so unwillingly; some, thanks to their fathers' butchery, were in a position to abstain from practising; but whether in practice or at leisure, distaste for the scent of blood and sawdust was the common feature that distinguished them. Qualities hitherto but little known, and generally despised—not, as we shall see, without some reason—were developed in them. Self-consciousness, aestheticism, a dislike for waste, a hatred of injustice; these—or some one of these, when coupled with that desire natural to men throughout all ages to accomplish something—constituted the motive forces which enabled them to work their bellows. In practical affairs those who were under the necessity of labouring were driven, under the then machinery of social life, to the humaner and less exacting kinds of butchery, such as the Arts, Education, the practice of Religions and Medicine, and the paid representation of their fellow-creatures. Those not so driven occupied themselves in observing and complaining of the existing state of things. Each year saw more of their silver cockle-shells putting out from port, and the cheeks of those who blew the sails more violently distended. Looking back on that pretty voyage, we see the reason why those ships were doomed never to move, but, seated on the sea-green bosom of that sea, to heave up and down, heading across each other's bows in the self-same place for ever. That reason, in a few words, was this : 'The man who blew should have been in the sea, not on the ship.' " '

The droning ceased. Hilary saw that Mr Stone was staring fixedly at his sheet of paper, as though the merits of this last sentence were surprising him. The droning instantly began again : ' "In social effort, as in the physical processes of Nature, there had ever been a single fertilising agent—the mysterious and wonderful attraction known as Love. To this—that merging of one being in another—had been due all the progressive variance of form, known by man under the name of Life. It was this merger, this mysterious, unconscious Love, which was lacking to the windy efforts of those who tried to sail that fleet. They were full of reason, conscience, horror, full of impatience, contempt, revolt; but they did not *love* the masses of their fellow-men : They could not fling themselves into the sea. Their hearts were glowing; but the wind that made them glow was not the salt and universal zephyr : it was the desert wind of scorn. As with the flowering of the aloe-tree—so long awaited, so strange and swift when once it comes—man had yet to wait for his delirious impulse to Universal Brotherhood, and the forgetfulness of Self." '

Mr Stone had finished, and stood gazing at his visitor with eyes that clearly saw beyond him. Hilary could not meet those eyes; he kept his own fixed on the empty cocoa cup. It was not, in fact, usual for those who heard Mr Stone read his manuscript to look him in the face. He stood thus absorbed so long that Hilary rose at last, and glanced into the saucepan. There was no cocoa in it. Mr Stone had only made enough for one. He had meant it for his visitor, but self-forgetfulness had supervened.

'You know what happens to the aloe, sir, when it has flowered?' asked Hilary, with malice.

Mr Stone moved, but did not answer.

'It dies,' said Hilary.

'No,' said Mr Stone; 'it is at peace.'

'When is self at peace, sir? The individual is surely as immortal as the universal. That is the eternal comedy of life.'

'What is?' said Mr Stone.

'The fight between the two.'

Mr Stone stood a moment looking wistfully at his son-in-law. He laid down the sheets of manuscript. 'It is time for me to do my exercises.' So saying, he undid the tasselled cord tied round the middle of his gown.

Hilary hastened to the door. From that point of vantage he looked back.

Divested of his gown and turned towards the window, Mr Stone was already rising on his toes, his arms were extended, his palms pressed hard together in the attitude of prayer, his trousers slowly slipping down.

'One, two, three, four, five!' There was a sudden sound of breath escaping. . . .

In the corridor upstairs, flooded with moonlight from a window at the end, Hilary stood listening again. The only sound that came to him was the light snoring of Miranda, who slept in the bathroom, not caring to lie too near to anyone. He went to his room, and for a long time sat buried in thought; then, opening the side window, he leaned out. On the trees of the next garden, and the sloping roofs of stables and out-houses, the moonlight had come down like a flight of milk-white pigeons; with outspread wings, vibrating faintly as though yet in motion, they covered everything. Nothing stirred. A clock was striking two. Past that flight of milk-white pigeons were black walls as yet unvisited. Then, in the stillness, Hilary seemed to hear, deep and very faint, the sound as of some monster breathing, or the far beating of muffled drums. From every side of the pale sleeping town it seemed to come, under the moon's cold glamour. It rose, and fell, and rose, with a weird, creepy rhythm, like a groaning of the hopeless and hungry. A hansom cab rattled down the High Street; Hilary strained his ears after the failing clatter of hoofs and bell. They died; there was silence. Creeping nearer, drumming, throbbing, he heard again the beating of that vast heart. It grew and grew. His own heart began thumping. Then, emerging from that sinister dumb groan, he distinguished a crunching sound, and knew that it was no muttering echo of men's struggles, but only the waggons coming into Covent Garden Market.

Chapter 14

A WALK ABROAD

THYME DALLISON, in the midst of her busy life, found leisure to record her recollections and ideas in the pages of old school notebooks. She had no definite purpose in so doing, nor did she desire the solace of luxuriating in her private feelings—this she would have scorned as out of date and silly. It was done from the fulness of youthful energy, and from the desire to express oneself what was 'in the air'. It was everywhere, that desire : among her fellow-students, among her young men friends, in her mother's drawing-room, and her aunt's studio. Like sentiment and marriage to the Victorian miss, so was this duty to express herself to Thyme; and, going hand-in-hand with it, the duty to have a good and jolly youth. She never read again the thoughts which she recorded, she took no care to lock them up, knowing that her liberty, development, and pleasure were sacred things which no one would dream of touching—she kept them stuffed down in a drawer among her handkerchiefs and ties and blouses, together with the indelible fragment of a pencil.

This journal, naïve and slipshod, recorded without order the current impression of things on her mind.

In the early morning of the 4th of May she sat, nightgowned, on the foot of her white bed, with chestnut hair all fluffy about her neck, eyes bright and cheeks still rosy with sleep, scribbling away and rubbing one bare foot against the other in the ecstasy of self-expression. Now and then, in the middle of a sentence, she would stop and look out of the window, or stretch herself deliciously, as though life were too full of joy for her to finish anything.

'I went into grandfather's room yesterday, and stayed while he was dictating to the little model. I do think grandfather's so splendid. Martin says an enthusiast is worse than useless; people, he says, can't afford to dabble in ideas or dreams. He calls grandfather's idea palaeolithic. I hate him to be laughed at. Martin's so cocksure. I don't think he'd find many men of eighty who'd bathe in the Serpentine all the year round, and do his own room, cook his own food, and live on about ninety pounds a year out of his pension of three hundred, and give all the rest away. Martin says that's unsound, and the "Book of Universal Brotherhood" rot. I don't care if it is; it's fine to go on writing it as he does all day. Martin admits that. That's the worst of him : he's so cool, you can't score him off; he seems to be always criticising you; it makes me wild. . . . That little model is a hopeless duffer. I could have taken it all down in half the time. She kept stopping and looking up with that mouth of hers half open, as if she had all day before her. Grandfather's so absorbed he doesn't notice; he likes to read the thing over and over, to hear how the words sound. That girl would be no good at any sort of work, except "sitting", I suppose. Aunt B. used to say she sat well. There's something queer about her face; it reminds me a little of that Botticelli Madonna in the National Gallery, the full-face one; not so much in the shape as in the expression—almost stupid, and yet as if things were going to happen to her. Her hands and arms are pretty, and her feet are smaller than mine. She's two years older than me. I asked her why she went in for being a model, which is beastly work. She said she was glad to get anything! I asked her why she didn't go into a shop or into service. She didn't answer at once, and then said she hadn't had any recommendations—didn't know where to try; then, all of a sudden, she grew quite sulky, and said she didn't want to. . . .'

Thyme paused to pencil in a sketch of the little model's profile. . . .

'She had on a really pretty frock, quite simple and well made—it must have cost three or four pounds. She can't be so very badly off, or somebody gave it her. . . .'

And again Thyme paused.

'She looked ever so much prettier in it than she used to in her old brown skirt, I thought. . . . Uncle Hilary came to dinner last night. We talked of social questions; we always discuss things when he comes. I can't help liking Uncle Hilary; he has such kind eyes, and he's so gentle that you never lose your temper with him. Martin calls him weak and unsatisfactory because he's not in touch with life. I should say it was more as if he couldn't bear to force anyone to do anything; he seems to see both sides of every question, and he's not good at making up his mind, of course. He's rather like Hamlet might have been, only nobody seems to know now what Hamlet was really like. I told him what I thought about the lower classes. One can talk to him. I hate father's way of making feeble little jokes, as if nothing were serious. I said I didn't think it was any use to dabble; we ought to go to the root of everything. I said that money and class distinctions are two bogeys we have got to lay. Martin says, when it comes to real dealing with social questions and the poor, all the people we know are amateurs. He says that we have got to shake ourselves free of all the old sentimental notions, and just work at putting everything to the test of Health. Father calls Martin a "Sanitist"; and Uncle Hilary says that if you wash people by *law* they'll all be as dirty again to-morrow. . . .'

Thyme paused again. A blackbird in the garden of the Square was uttering a long, low, chuckling trill. She ran to the window and peeped out. The bird was on a plane-tree, and, with throat uplifted, was letting through his yellow beak that delicious piece of self-expression. All things he seemed to praise—the sky, the sun, the trees, the dewy grass, himself!

'You darling!' thought Thyme. With a shudder of delight she dropped her notebook back into the drawer, flung off her night-gown, and flew into her bath.

That same morning she slipped quietly out at ten o'clock. Her Saturdays were free of classes, but she had to run the gauntlet of her mother's liking for her company and her father's wish for her to go with him to Richmond and play golf. For on Saturdays Stephen almost always left the precincts of the Courts before three o'clock. Then, if he could induce his wife or daughter to accompany him, he liked to get a round or two in preparation for Sunday, when he always started off at half-past ten and played all day. If Cecilia and Thyme failed him, he would go to his club, and keep himself in touch with every kind of social movement by reading the reviews.

Thyme walked along with her head up and a wrinkle in her brow, as though she were absorbed in serious reflection; if admiring glances were flung at her, she did not seem aware of them. Passing not far from Hilary's, she entered the Broad Walk, and crossed it to the farther end.

On a railing, stretching out his long legs and observing the passers-by, sat her cousin, Martin Stone. He got down as she came up.

'Late again,' he said. 'Come on!'

'Where are we going first?' Thyme asked.

'The Notting Hill district's all we can do to-day if we're to go again to Mrs Hughs'. I must be down at the hospital this afternoon.'

Thyme frowned. 'I do envy you living by yourself, Martin. It's silly having to live at home.'

Martin did not answer, but one nostril of his long nose was seen to curve, and Thyme acquiesced in this without remark. They walked for some minutes between tall houses, looking about them calmly. Then Martin said: 'All Purceys round here.'

Thyme nodded. Again there was silence; but in these pauses there was no embarrassment, no consciousness apparently that it was

silence, and their eyes—those young, impatient, interested eyes—
were for ever busy observing.

'Boundary line. We shall be in a patch directly.'

'Black?' asked Thyme.

'Dark blue—black farther on.'

They were passing down a long, grey, curving road, whose narrow houses, hopelessly unpainted, showed marks of grinding
poverty. The Spring wind was ruffling straw and little bits of paper
in the gutters; under the bright sunlight a bleak and bitter struggle
seemed raging. Thyme said:

'This street gives me a hollow feeling.'

Martin nodded. 'Worse than the real article. There's half a mile
of this. Here it's all grim fighting. Farther on they've given it up.'

And still they went on up the curving street, with its few pinched
shops and its unending narrow grimness.

At the corner of a by-street Martin said: 'We'll go down here.'

Thyme stood still, wrinkling her nose. Martin eyed her.

'Don't funk!'

'I'm not funking, Martin, only I can't stand the smells.'

'You'll have to get used to them.'

'Yes, I know; but—but I·forgot my eucalyptus.'

The young man took out a handkerchief which had not yet been
unfolded.

'Here, take mine.'

'They do make me feel so—it's a shame to take yours,' and she
took the handkerchief.

'That's all right,' said Martin. 'Come on!'

The houses of this narrow street, inside and out, seemed full of
women. Many of them had babies in their arms; they were working or looking out of windows or gossiping on doorsteps. And all
stopped to stare as the young couple passed. Thyme stole a look at
her companion. His long stride had not varied; there was the usual
pale, observant, sarcastic expression on his face. Clenching the
handkerchief in readiness, and trying to imitate his callous air, she
looked at a group of five women on the nearest doorstep. Three were
seated and two were standing. One of these, a young woman with
a round, open face, was clearly very soon to have a child; the other,
with a short, dark face and iron-grey, straggling hair, was smoking
a clay pipe. Of the three seated, one, quite young, had a face as
grey-white as a dirty sheet, and a blackened eye; the second, with
her ragged dress disarranged, was nursing a baby; the third, in the
centre, on the top step, with red arms akimbo, her face scored with

drink, was shouting friendly obscenities to a neighbour in the window opposite. In Thyme's heart rose the passionate feeling, 'How disgusting! how *disgusting!*' and since she did not dare to give expression to it, she bit her lips and turned her head from them, resenting, with all a young girl's horror, that her sex had given her away. The women stared at her, and in those faces, according to their different temperaments, could be seen first the same vague, hard interest that had been Thyme's when she first looked at them, then the same secret hostility and criticism, as though they too felt that by this young girl's untouched modesty, by her flushed cheeks and unsoiled clothes, their sex had given *them* away. With contemptuous movements of their lips and bodies, on that doorstep they proclaimed their emphatic belief in the virtue and reality of their own existences and in the vice and unreality of her intruding presence.

'Give the doll to Bill; 'e'd make 'er work for once, the ——' In a burst of laughter the epithet was lost.

Martin's lips curled.

'Purple just here,' he said.

Thyme's cheeks were crimson.

At the end of the little street he stopped before a shop.

'Come on,' he said, 'you'll see the sort of place where they buy their grub.'

In the doorway were standing a thin brown spaniel, a small fair woman with a high, bald forehead, from which the hair was gleaned into curl-papers, and a little girl with some affection of the skin.

Nodding coolly, Martin motioned them aside. The shop was ten feet square; its counters, running parallel to two of the walls, were covered with plates of cake, sausages, old ham-bones, peppermint sweets, and household soap; there was also bread, margarine, suet in bowls, sugar, bloaters—many bloaters—Captain's biscuits, and other things besides. Two or three dead rabbits hung against the wall. All was uncovered, so that what flies there were sat feeding socialistically. Behind the counter a girl of seventeen was serving a thin-faced woman with portions of a cheese which she was holding down with her strong, dirty hand, while she sawed it with a knife. On the counter, next the cheese, sat a quiet-looking cat.

They all glanced round at the two young people, who stood and waited.

'Finish what you're at,' said Martin, 'then give me three pennyworth of bull's-eyes.'

The girl, with a violent effort, finished severing the cheese. The thin-faced woman took it, and, coughing above it, went away. The girl, who could not take her eyes off Thyme, now served them with three pennyworth of bull's-eyes, which she took out with her fingers, for they had stuck. Putting them in a screw of newspaper, she handed them to Martin. The young man, who had been observing negligently, touched Thyme's elbow. She, who had stood with eyes cast down, now turned. They went out, Martin handing the bull's-eyes to the little girl with an affection of the skin.

The street now ended in a wide road formed of little low houses.

'Black,' said Martin, 'here; all down this road—casual labour, criminals, loafers, drunkards, consumps. Look at the faces!'

Thyme raised her eyes obediently. In this main thoroughfare it was not as in the by-street, and only dull or sullen glances, or none at all, were bent on her. Some of the houses had ragged plants on the window-sills; in one window a canary was singing. Then, at a bend, they came into a blacker reach of human river. Here were outbuildings, houses with broken windows, houses with windows boarded up, fried-fish shops, low public-houses, houses without doors. There were more men here than women, and those men were wheeling barrows full of rags and bottles, or not even full of rags and bottles; or they were standing by the public-houses gossiping or quarrelling in groups of three or four; or very slowly walking in the gutters, or on the pavements, as though trying to remember if they were alive. Then suddenly some young man with gaunt violence in his face would pass, pushing his barrow desperately, striding fiercely by. And every now and then, from a fried-fish or hardware shop, would come out a man in a dirty apron to take the sun and contemplate the scene, not finding in it, seemingly, anything that in any way depressed his spirit. Amongst the constant, crawling, shifting stream of passengers were seen women carrying food wrapped up in newspaper, or with bundles beneath their shawls. The faces of these women were generally either very red and coarse or of a sort of bluish-white; they wore the expression of such as know themselves to be existing in the way that Providence has arranged they should exist. No surprise, revolt, dismay, or shame was ever to be seen on those faces; in place of these emotions a drab and brutish acquiescence or mechanical coarse jocularity. To pass like this about their business was their occupation each morning of the year; it was needful to accept it. Not having any hope of ever being different, not being able to imagine any other life, they were not so wasteful of their strength as to attempt either to hope or to imagine. Here and there, too, very slowly passed old men and women, crawling along, like winter bees who, in some strange and evil moment, had forgotten to die in the sunlight of their toil, and, too old to be of use, had been chivied forth from their hive to perish slowly in the cold twilight of their days.

Down the centre of the street Thyme saw a brewer's dray creeping its way due south under the sun. Three horses drew it, with braided tails and beribboned manes, the brass glittering on their harness. High up, like a god, sat the drayman, his little slits of eyes above huge red cheeks fixed immovably on his horses' crests. Behind him, with slow, unceasing crunch, the dray rolled, piled up with hogsheads, whereon the drayman's mate lay sleeping. Like the slumbrous image of some mighty unrelenting Power, it passed, proud that its monstrous bulk contained all the joy and blessing those shadows on the pavement had ever known.

The two young people emerged on to the high road running east and west.

'Cross here,' said Martin, 'and cut down into Kensington. Nothing more of interest now till we get to Hound Street. Purceys and Purceys all round about this part.'

Thyme shook herself.

'O Martin, let's go down a road where there's some air. I feel so dirty.' She put her hand up to her chest.

'There's one here,' said Martin.

They turned to the left into a road that had many trees. Now that she could breathe and look about her, Thyme once more held her head erect and began to swing her arms.

'Martin, something must be done!'

The young doctor did not reply; his face still wore its pale, sarcastic, observant look. He gave her arm a squeeze with a half-contemptuous smile.

Chapter 15

SECOND PILGRIMAGE TO HOUND STREET

ARRIVING in Hound Street, Martin Stone and his companion went straight up to Mrs Hughs' front room. They found her doing the week's washing, and hanging out before a scanty fire part of the little that the week had been suffered to soil. Her arms were bare, her face and eyes red; the steam of soapsuds had congealed on them.

Attached to the bolster by a towel, under his father's bayonet and the oleograph depicting the Nativity, sat the baby. In the air

there was the scent of him, or walls, and washing, and red herrings. The two young people took their seat on the window-sill.

'May we open the window, Mrs Hughs?' said Thyme. 'Or will it hurt the baby?'

'No, miss.'

'What's the matter with your wrists?' asked Martin.

The seamstress, muffling her arms with the garment she was dipping in soapy water, did not answer.

'Don't do that. Let me have a look.'

Mrs Hughs held out her arms; the wrists were swollen and discoloured.

'The brute!' cried Thyme.

The young doctor muttered: 'Done last night. Got any arnica?'

'No, sir.'

'Of course not.' He laid a sixpence on the sill. 'Get some and rub it in. Mind you don't break the skin.'

Thyme suddenly burst out: 'Why don't you leave him, Mrs Hughs? Why do you live with a brute like that?'

Martin frowned.

'Any particular row,' he said, 'or only just the ordinary?'

Mrs Hughs turned her face to the scanty fire. Her shoulders heaved spasmodically.

Thus passed three minutes, then she again began rubbing the soapy garment.

'If you don't mind, I'll smoke,' said Martin. 'What's your baby's name? Bill? Here, Bill!' He placed his little finger in the baby's hand. 'Feeding him yourself?'

'Yes, sir.'

'What's his number?'

'I've lost three, sir; there's only his brother Stanley now.'

'One a year?'

'No, sir. I missed two years in the war, of course.'

'Hughs wounded out there?'

'Yes, sir—in the head.'

'Ah! And fever?'

'Yes, sir.'

Martin tapped his pipe against his forehead. 'Least drop of liquor goes to it, I suppose?'

Mrs Hughs paused in the dipping of a cloth; her tear-stained face expressed resentment, as though she had detected an attempt to find excuses for her husband.

'He didn't ought to treat me as he does,' she said.

All three now stood round the bed, over which the baby presided with solemn gaze.

Thyme said: 'I wouldn't care what he did, Mrs Hughs; I wouldn't stay another day if I were you. It's your duty as a woman.'

To hear her duty as a woman Mrs Hughs turned; slow vindictiveness gathered on her thin face.

'Yes, miss?' she said. 'I don't know what to do.'

'Take the children and go. What's the good of waiting? We'll give you money if you haven't got enough.'

But Mrs Hughs did not answer.

'Well?' said Martin, blowing out a cloud of smoke.

Thyme burst out again; 'Just go, the very minute your little boy comes back from school. Hughs'll never find you. It'll serve him right. No woman ought to put up with what you have; it's simply weakness, Mrs Hughs.'

As though that word had forced its way into her very heart and set the blood free suddenly, Mrs Hughs' face turned the colour of tomatoes. She poured forth words:

'And leave him to that young girl—and leave him to his wickedness! After I've been his wife eight years and borne him five! After I've done what I have for him! I never want no better husband than what he used to be, till *she* came with her pale face and her prinky manners, and—and her mouth that you can tell she's bad by. Let her keep to her profession—sitting naked's what she's fit for—coming here to decent folk——' And holding out her wrists to Thyme, who had shrunk back, she cried: 'He's never struck me before. I got these all because of her new clothes!'

Hearing his mother speak with such strange passion, the baby howled. Mrs Hughs stopped, and took him up. Pressing him close to her thin bosom, she looked above his little dingy head at the two young people.

'I got my wrists like this last night, wrestling with him. He swore he'd go and leave me, but I held him, I did. And don't you ever think that I'll let him go to that young girl—not if he kills me first!'

With those words the passion in her face died down. She was again a meek, mute woman.

During this outbreak, Thyme, shrinking, stood by the doorway with lowered eyes. She now looked up at Martin, clearly asking him to come away. The latter had kept his gaze fixed on Mrs Hughs, smoking silently. He took his pipe out of his mouth, and pointed with it at the baby.

'This gentleman,' he said, 'can't stand too much of that.'

272

In silence all three bent their eyes on the baby. His little fists, and nose, and forehead, even his little naked, crinkled feet, were thrust with all his feeble strength against his mother's bosom, as though he were striving to creep into some hole away from life. There was a sort of dumb despair in that tiny pushing of his way back to the place whence he had come. His head, covered with dingy down, quivered with his effort to escape. He had been alive so little; that little had sufficed. Martin put his pipe back into his mouth.

'This won't do, you know,' he said. 'He can't stand it. And look here! If you stop feeding him, I wouldn't give that for him to-morrow!' He held up the circle of his thumb and finger. 'You're the best judge of what sort of chance you've got of going on in your present state of mind!' Then, motioning to Thyme, he went down the stairs.

Chapter 16

BENEATH THE ELMS

SPRING was in the hearts of men, and their tall companions, trees. Their troubles, the stiflings of each other's growth, and all such things, seemed of little moment. Spring had them by the throat. It turned old men round, and made them stare at women younger than themselves. It made young men and women walking side by side touch each other, and every bird on the branches tune his pipe. Flying sunlight speckled the fluttered leaves, and flushed the cheeks of crippled boys who limped into the Gardens, till their pale Cockney faces shone with a strange glow.

In the Broad Walk, beneath those dangerous trees, the elms, people sat and took the sun—cheek by jowl, generals and nurse-maids, parsons and the unemployed. Above, in that Spring wind, the elm-tree boughs were swaying, rustling, creaking ever so gently, carrying on the innumerable talk of trees—their sapient, wordless conversation over the affairs of men. It was pleasant, too, to see and hear the myriad movement of the million little separate leaves, each shaped differently, flighting never twice alike, yet all obedient to the single spirit of their tree.

Thyme and Martin were sitting on a seat beneath the largest of all the elms. Their manner lacked the unconcern and dignity of the moment, when, two hours before, they had started forth on their discovery from the other end of the Broad Walk. Martin spoke:

273

'It's given you the hump! First sight of blood, and you're like all the rest of them!'

'I'm not, Martin. How perfectly beastly of you!'

'Oh yes, you are. There's plenty of aestheticism about you and your people—plenty of good intentions—but not an ounce of real business!'

'Don't abuse my people; they're just as kind as you!'

'Oh, they're kind enough, and they can see what's wrong. It's not that which stops them. But your dad's a regular official. He's got so much sense of what he ought not to do that he never does anything; just as Hilary's got so much consciousness of what he *ought* to do that *he* never does anything. You went to that woman's this morning with your ideas of helping her all cut and dried, and now that you find the facts aren't what you thought, you're stumped!'

'One can't believe anything they say. That's what I hate. I thought Hughs simply knocked her about. I didn't know it was her jealousy——'

'Of course you didn't. Do you imagine those people give anything away to our sort unless they're forced? They know better.'

'Well, I hate the whole thing—it's all so sordid!'

'O Lord!'

'Well, it is! I don't feel that I want to help a woman who can say and feel such horrid things, or the girl, or any of them.'

'Who cares what they say or feel? That's not the point. It's simply a case of common sense. Your people put that girl there, and they must get her to clear out again sharp. It's just a question of what's healthy.'

'Well, I know it's not healthy for me to have anything to do with, and I won't! I don't believe you can help people unless they want to be helped.'

Martin whistled.

'You're rather a brute, I think,' said Thyme.

'*A* brute, not rather a brute. That's all the difference.'

'For the worse!'

'I don't think so. Thyme!'

There was no answer.

'Look at me.'

Very slowly Thyme turned her eyes.

'Well?'

'Are you one of us, or are you not?'

'Of course I am.'

'You're not!'

274

'I am.'

'Well, don't let's fight about it. Give me your hand.'

He dropped his hand on hers. Her face had flushed rose colour. Suddenly she freed herself. 'Here's Uncle Hilary!'

It was indeed Hilary, with Miranda trotting in advance. His hands were crossed behind him, his face bent towards the ground. The two young people on the bench sat looking at him.

'Buried in self-contemplation,' murmured Martin; 'that's the way he always walks. I shall tell him about this!'

The colour of Thyme's face deepened from rose to crimson.

'No!'

'Why not?'

'Well—those new——' She could not bring out that word 'clothes'. It would have given her thoughts away.

Hilary seemed making for their seat, but Miranda, aware of Martin, stopped 'A man of action!' she appeared to say. 'The one who pulls my ears.' And turning, as though unconscious, she endeavoured to lead Hilary away. Her master, however, had already seen his niece. He came and sat down on the bench beside her.

'We wanted *you!*' said Martin, eyeing him slowly, as a young dog will eye another of a different age and breed. 'Thyme and I have been to see the Hughs in Hound Street. Things are blowing up for a mess. You, or whoever put the girl there, ought to get her away again as quick as possible.'

Hilary seemed at once to withdraw into himself.

'Well,' he said, 'let us hear all about it.'

'The woman's jealous of her: that's all the trouble!'

'Oh!' said Hilary; 'that's all the trouble?'

Thyme murmured: 'I don't see a bit why Uncle Hilary should bother. If they will be so horrid—I didn't think the poor were like that. I didn't think they had it in them. I'm sure the girl isn't worth it, or the woman either!'

'I didn't say they were,' growled Martin. 'It's a question of what's healthy.'

Hilary looked from one of his young companions to the other.

'I see,' he said. 'I thought perhaps the matter was more delicate.' Martin's lip curled.

'Ah, your precious delicacy! What's the good of that? What did it ever do? It's the curse that you're all suffering from. Why don't you act? You could think about it afterwards.'

A flush came into Hilary's sallow cheeks.

'Do you never think before you act, Martin?'

275

Martin got up and stood looking down on Hilary.

'Look here!' he said; 'I don't go in for your subtleties. I use my eyes and nose. I can see that the woman will never be able to go on feeding the baby in the neurotic state she's in. It's a matter of health for both of them.'

'Is everything a matter of health with you?'

'It is. Take any subject that you like. Take the poor themselves—what's wanted? Health. Nothing on earth but health! The discoveries and inventions of the last century have knocked the floor out of the old order; we've got to put a new one in, and we're going to put it in, too—the floor of health. The crowd doesn't yet see what it wants, but *they're looking for it*, and when we show them they'll catch on fast enough.'

'But who are "you"?' murmured Hilary.

'Who are we? I'll tell you one thing. While all the reformers are pecking at each other we shall quietly come along and swallow up the lot. We've simply grasped this elementary fact, that theories are no basis for reform. We go on the evidence of our eyes and noses; what we see and smell is wrong we correct by practical and scientific means.'

'Will you apply that to human nature?'

'It's human nature to want health.'

'I wonder! It doesn't look much like it at present.'

'Take the case of this woman.'

'Yes,' said Hilary, 'take her case. You can't make this too clear to me, Martin.'

'She's no use—poor sort altogether. The man's no use. A man who's been wounded in the head, and isn't a teetotaller, is done for. The girl's no use—regular pleasure-loving type!'

Thyme flushed crimson, and, seeing that flood of colour in his niece's face, Hilary bit his lips.

'The only things worth considering are the children. There's this baby—well, as I said, the important thing is that the mother should be able to look after it properly. Get hold of that, and let the other facts go hang.'

'Forgive me, but my difficulty is to isolate this question of the baby's health from all the other circumstances of the case.'

Martin grinned.

'And you'll make that an excuse, I'm certain, for doing nothing.'

Thyme slipped her hand into Hilary's.

'You *are* a brute, Martin,' she murmured.

The young man turned on her a look that said: 'It's no use calling

276

me a brute; I'm proud of being one. Besides, you know you don't dislike it.'

'It's better to be a brute than an amateur,' he said.

Thyme, pressing close to Hilary, as though she needed her protection, cried out :

'Martin, you really are a Goth!'

Hilary was still smiling, but his face quivered.

'Not at all,' he said. 'Martin's powers of diagnosis do him credit.' And, raising his hat, he walked away.

The two young people, both on their feet now, looked after him. Martin's face was a queer study of contemptuous compunction; Thyme's was startled, softened, almost tearful.

'It won't do him any harm,' muttered the young man. 'It'll shake him up.'

Thyme flashed a vicious look at him.

'I hate you sometimes,' she said. 'You're so coarse-grained—your skin's just like leather.'

Martin's hand descended on her wrist.

'And yours,' he said, 'is tissue-paper. You're all the same, you amateurs.'

'I'd rather be an amateur than a—than a bounder!'

Martin made a queer movement of his jaw, then smiled. That smile seemed to madden Thyme. She wrenched her wrist away and darted after Hilary.

Martin impassively looked after her. Taking out his pipe, he filled it with tobacco, slowly pressing the golden threads down into the bowl with his little finger.

Chapter 17

TWO BROTHERS

IT has been said that Stephen Dallison, when unable to get his golf on Saturdays, went to his club and read reviews. The two forms of exercise, in fact, were very similar : in playing golf you went round and round; in reading reviews you did the same, for in course of time you were assured of coming to articles that nullified articles already read. In both forms of sport the balance was preserved which keeps a man both sound and young.

And to be both sound and young was to Stephen an everyday necessity. He was essentially a Cambridge man, springy and undemonstrative, with just that air of taking a continual pinch of peculiarly perfect snuff. Underneath this manner he was a good worker, a good husband, a good father, and nothing could be urged against him except his regularity and the fact that he was never in the wrong. Where he worked, and indeed in other places, many men were like him. In one respect he resembled them, perhaps, too much—he disliked leaving the ground unless he knew precisely where he was coming down again.

He and Cecilia had 'got on' from the first. They had both desired to have one child—no more; they had both desired to keep up with the times—no more; they now both considered Hilary's position awkward—no more; and when Cecilia, in the special Jacobean bed, and taking care to let him have his sleep out first, had told him of this matter of the Hughs, they had both turned it over carefully, lying on their backs, and speaking in grave tones. Stephen was of opinion that poor old Hilary must look out what he was doing. Beyond this he did not go, keeping even from his wife the more unpleasant of what seemed to him the possibilities.

Then, in the words she had used to Hilary, Cecilia spoke:

'It's so sordid, Stephen.'

He looked at her, and almost with one accord they both said:

'But it's all nonsense!'

These speeches, so simultaneous, stimulated them to a robuster view. What was this affair, if real, but the sort of episode that they read of in their papers? What was it, if true, but a duplicate of some bit of fiction or drama which they daily saw described by that word 'sordid'? Cecilia, indeed, had used this word instinctively. It had come into her mind at once. The whole affair disturbed her ideals of virtue and good taste—that particular mental atmosphere mysteriously, inevitably woven round the soul by the conditions of special breeding and special life. If, then, this affair were real it was sordid, and if it were sordid it was repellent to suppose that her family could be mixed up in it; but her people *were* mixed up in it, therefore it must be—nonsense!

So the matter rested until Thyme came back from her visit to her grandfather, and told them of the little model's new pretty clothes. When she detailed this news they were all sitting at dinner, over the ordering of which Cecilia's loyalty had been taxed till her little headache came, so that there might be nothing too conventional to overnourish Stephen or so essentially aesthetic as not to nourish him at all. The manservant being in the room, they neither of them raised their eyes. But when he was gone to fetch the bird, each found the other looking furtively across the table. By some queer

278

misfortune the word 'sordid' had leaped into their minds again. Who had given her those clothes? But feeling that it was sordid to pursue this thought, they looked away, and, eating hastily, began pursuing it. Being man and woman, they naturally took a different line of chase, Cecilia hunting in one grove and Stephen in another.

Thus ran Stephen's pack of meditations:

'If old Hilary has been giving her money and clothes and that sort of thing, he's either a greater duffer than I took him for, or there's something in it. B.'s got herself to thank, but that won't help to keep Hughs quiet. He wants money, I expect. Oh, damn!'

Cecilia's pack ran other ways:

'I know the girl can't have bought those things out of her proper earnings. I believe she's a really bad lot. I don't like to think it, but it must be so. Hilary can't have been so stupid after what I said to him. If she really *is* bad, it simplifies things very much; but Hilary is just the sort of man who will never believe it. Oh dear!'

It was, to be quite fair, immensely difficult for Stephen and his wife—or any of their class and circle—in spite of genuinely good intentions, to really feel the existence of their 'shadows', except in so far as they saw them on the pavements. They knew that these people lived, because they saw them, but they did not *feel* it—with such extraordinary care had the web of social life been spun. They were, and were bound to be, as utterly divorced from understanding of, or faith in, all that shadowy life, as those 'shadows' in their by-streets were from knowledge or belief that gentlefolk really existed except in so far as they had money from them.

Stephen and Cecilia, and their thousands, knew these 'shadows' as 'the people', knew them as slums, as districts, as sweated industries, or different sorts of workers, knew them in the capacity of persons performing odd jobs for them; but as human beings possessing the same faculties and passions with themselves, they did not, could not, know them. The reason, the long reason, extending back through generations, was so plain, so very simple, that it was never mentioned—in their heart of hearts, where there was no room for cant, they knew it to be just a little matter of the senses. They knew that whatever money they might give, or time devote, their hearts could never open, unless—unless they closed their ears, and eyes, and noses. This little fact, more potent than all the teaching of philosophers, than every Act of Parliament, and all the sermons ever preached, reigned paramount, supreme. It divided class from class, man from his shadow—as the Great Underlying Law had set dark apart from light.

279

On this little fact, too gross to mention, they and their kind had in secret built and built, till it was not too much to say that laws, worship, trade, and every art were based on it, if not in theory, then in fact. For it must not be thought that those eyes were dull or that nose plain—no, no, those eyes could put two and two together; that nose, of myriad fancy, could imagine countless things unsmelled which must lie behind a state of life not quite its own. It could create, as from the scent of an old slipper dogs create their masters.

So Stephen and Cecilia sat, and their butler brought in the bird. It was a nice one, nourished down in Surrey, and as he cut it into portions the butler's soul turned sick within him—not because he wanted some himself, or was a vegetarian, or for any sort of principle, but because he was by natural gifts an engineer, and deadly tired of cutting up and handing birds to other people and watching while they ate them. Without a glimmer of expression on his face he put the portions down before the persons who, having paid him to do so, could not tell his thoughts.

That same night, after working at a Report on the present Laws of Bankruptcy, which he was then drawing up, Stephen entered the joint apartment with excessive caution, having first made all his dispositions, and, stealing to the bed, slipped into it. He lay there, offering himself congratulations that he had not awakened Cecilia, and Cecilia, who was wide awake, knew by his unwonted carefulness that he had come to some conclusion which he did not wish to impart to her. Devoured, therefore, by disquiet, she lay sleepless till the clock struck two.

The conclusion to which Stephen had come was this: Having twice gone through the facts—Hilary's corporeal separation from Bianca (communicated to him by Cecilia), cause unknowable; Hilary's interest in the little model, cause unknown; her known poverty; her employment by Mr Stone; her tenancy of Mrs Hughs' room; the latter's outburst to Cecilia; Hughs' threat; and, finally, the girl's pretty clothes—he had summed it up as just a common 'plant', to which his brother's possibly innocent, but in any case imprudent, conduct had laid him open. It was a man's affair. He resolutely tried to look on the whole thing as unworthy of attention, to feel that nothing would occur. He failed dismally, for three reasons. First, his inherent love of regularity, of having everything in proper order; secondly, his ingrained mistrust of and aversion from Bianca; thirdly, his unavowed conviction, for all his wish to be sympathetic to them, that the lower classes always wanted

something out of you. It was a question of how much they would
want, and whether it were wise to give them anything. He decided
that it would not be wise at all. What then? Impossible to say. It
worried him. He had a natural horror of any sort of scandal, and
he was very fond of Hilary. If only he knew the attitude Bianca
would take up! He could not even guess it.

Thus, on that Saturday afternoon, the 4th of May, he felt for
once such a positive aversion from the reading of reviews, as men
will feel from their usual occupations when their nerves have been
disturbed. He stayed late at Chambers, and came straight home
outside an omnibus.

The tide of life was flowing in the town. The streets were awash
with wave on wave of humanity, sucked into a thousand crossing
currents. Here men and women were streaming out from the
meeting of a religious congress, there streaming in at the gates of
some social function; like bright water confined within long
shelves of rock and dyed with myriad scales of shifting colour,
they thronged Rotten Row, and along the closed shop-fronts
were woven into an inextricable network of little human runlets.
And everywhere amongst this sea of men and women could be
seen their shadows, meandering like streaks of grey slime stirred
up from the lower depths by some huge, never-ceasing finger. The
innumerable roar of that human sea climbed out above the roofs
and trees, and somewhere in illimitable space blended, and slowly
reached the meeting-point of sound and silence—that Heart where
Life, leaving its little forms and barriers, clasps Death, and from
that clasp springs forth new-formed, within new barriers.

Above this crowd of his fellow-creatures Stephen drove, and
the same Spring wind that had made the elm-trees talk, whispered
to him, and tried to tell him of the million flowers it had fertilised,
the million leaves uncurled, the million ripples it had awakened
on the sea, of the million flying shadows flung by it across the
Downs, and how into men's hearts its scent had driven a million
longings and sweet pains.

It was but moderately successful, for Stephen, like all men of
culture and neat habits, took Nature only at those moments when
he had gone out to take her, and of her wild heart he had a secret
fear.

On his own doorstep he encountered Hilary coming out.

'I ran across Thyme and Martin in the Gardens,' the latter
said. 'Thyme brought me back to lunch, and here I've been ever
since.'

281

'Did she bring our young Sanitist in too?' asked Stephen dubiously.

'No,' said Hilary.

'Good! That young man gets on my nerves.'

Taking his elder brother by the arm, he added: 'Will you come in again, old boy, or shall we go for a stroll?'

'A stroll,' said Hilary.

Though different enough, perhaps because they were so different, these two brothers had the real affection for each other which depends on something deeper and more elementary than a similarity of sentiments, and is permanent because unconnected with the reasoning powers. It depended on the countless times they had kissed and wrestled as tiny boys, slept in small beds alongside, refused to 'tell' about each other, and even now and then taken up the burden of each other's peccadilloes. They might get irritated or tired of being in each other's company, but it would have been impossible for either to have been disloyal to the other in any circumstances, because of that traditional loyalty which went back to their cribs.

Preceded by Miranda, they walked along the flower walk towards the Park, talking of indifferent things, though in his heart each knew well enough what was in the other's.

Stephen broke through the hedge.

'Cis has been telling me,' he said, 'that this man Hughs is making trouble of some sort.'

Hilary nodded.

Stephen glanced a little anxiously at his brother's face; it struck him as looking different, neither so gentle nor so impersonal as usual.

'He's a ruffian, isn't he?'

'I can't tell you,' Hilary answered. 'Probably not.'

'He must be, old chap,' murmured Stephen. Then, with a friendly pressure of his brother's arm, he added: 'Look here old boy, can I be of any use?'

'In what?' asked Hilary.

Stephen took a hasty mental view of his position; he had been in danger of letting Hilary see that he suspected him. Frowning slightly, and with some colour in his clean-shaven face, he said:

'Of course, there's nothing in it.'

'In what?' said Hilary again.

'In what this ruffian says.'

'No,' said Hilary, 'there's nothing in it, though what there may be if people give me credit for what there isn't, is another thing.'

Stephen digested this remark, which hurt him. He saw that his suspicions had been fathomed, and this injured his opinion of his own diplomacy.

'You mustn't lose your head, old man,' he said at last.

They were crossing the bridge over the Serpentine. On the bright waters below, young clerks were sculling their inamoratas up and down; the ripples set free by their oars gleamed beneath the sun, and ducks swam lazily along the banks. Hilary leaned over.

'Look here, Stephen, I take an interest in this child—she's a helpless sort of little creature, and she seems to have put herself under my protection. I can't help that. But that's all. Do you understand?'

This speech produced a queer turmoil in Stephen, as though his brother had accused him of a petty view of things. Feeling that he must justify himself somehow, he began:

'Oh, of course I understand, old boy! But don't think, anyway, that I should care a damn—I mean as far as I'm concerned—even if you had gone as far as ever you liked, considering what you have to put up with. What I'm thinking of is the general situation.'

By this clear statement of his point of view Stephen felt he had put things back on a broad basis, and recovered his position as a man of liberal thought. He too leaned over, looking at the ducks. There was a silence. Then Hilary said:

'If Bianca won't get that child into some fresh place, I shall.'

Stephen looked at his brother in surprise, amounting almost to dismay; he had spoken with such unwonted resolution.

'My dear old chap,' he said. 'I wouldn't go to B. Women are so funny.'

Hilary smiled. Stephen took this for a sign of restored impersonality.

'I'll tell you exactly how the thing appeals to me. It'll be much better for you to chuck it altogether. Let Cis see to it.'

Hilary's eyes became bright with angry humour.

'Many thanks,' he said, 'but this is entirely our affair.'

Stephen answered hastily:

'That's exactly what makes it difficult for you to look at it all round. That fellow Hughs could make himself quite nasty. I wouldn't give him any sort of chance. I mean to say—giving the girl clothes and that kind of thing——'

'I see,' said Hilary.

'You know, old man,' Stephen went on hastily, 'I don't think you'll get Bianca to look at things in your light. If you were on—terms, of course it would be different. I mean the girl, you know, is rather attractive in her way.'

Hilary roused himself from contemplation of the ducks, and they moved on towards the Powder Magazine. Stephen carefully abstained from looking at his brother; the respect he had for Hilary—result, perhaps, of the latter's seniority, perhaps of the feeling that Hilary knew more of him than he of Hilary—was beginning to assert itself in a way he did not like. With every word, too, of this talk, the ground, instead of growing firmer, felt less and less secure. Hilary spoke:

'You mistrust my powers of action?'

'No, no,' said Stephen. 'I don't want you to act at all.'

Hilary laughed. Hearing that rather bitter laugh, Stephen felt a little ache about his heart.

'Come, old boy,' he said, 'we can trust each other, anyway.' Hilary gave his brother's arm a squeeze.

Moved by that pressure, Stephen spoke:

'I hate you to be worried over such a rotten business.'

The whizz of a motor-car rapidly approaching them became a sort of roar, and out of it a voice shouted: 'How are you?' A hand was seen to rise in salute. It was Mr Purcey driving his A.1. Damyer back to Wimbledon. Before him in the sunlight a little shadow fled; behind him the reek of petrol seemed to darken the road.

'There's a symbol for you,' muttered Hilary.

'How do you mean?' said Stephen dryly. The word 'symbol' was distasteful to him.

'The machine in the middle moving on its business; shadows like you and me skipping in front; oil and used-up stuff dropping behind. Society—body, beak, and bones.'

Stephen took time to answer. 'That's rather far-fetched,' he said. 'You mean these Hughs and people are the droppings?'

'Quite so,' was Hilary's sardonic answer. 'There's the body of that fellow and his car between our sort and them—and no getting over it, Stevie.'

'Well, who wants to? If you're thinking of our old friend's Fraternity, I'm not taking any.' And Stephen suddenly added: 'Look here, I believe this affair is all "a plant".'

'You see that Powder Magazine?' said Hilary. 'Well, this business that you call a "plant" is more like that. I don't want to

284

alarm you, but I think you, as well as our young friend Martin, are inclined to under-rate the emotional capacity of human nature.'

Disquietude broke up the customary mask on Stephen's face. 'I don't understand,' he stammered.

'Well, we're none of us machines, not even amateurs like me —not even under-dogs like Hughs. I fancy you may find a certain warmth, not to say violence, about this business. I tell you frankly that I don't live in married celibacy quite with impunity. I can't answer for anything, in fact. You had better stand clear, Stephen—that's all.'

Stephen marked his thin hands quivering, and this alarmed him as nothing else had done.

They walked on beside the water. Stephen spoke quietly, looking at the ground. 'How can I stand clear, old man, if you are going to get into a mess? That's impossible.'

He saw at once that this shot, which indeed was from his heart, had gone right home to Hilary's. He sought within him how to deepen the impression.

'You mean a lot to us,' he said. 'Cis and Thyme would feel it awfully if you and B.——' He stopped.

Hilary was looking at him; that faintly smiling glance, searching him through and through, suddenly made Stephen feel inferior. He had been detected trying to extract capital from the effect of his little piece of brotherly love. He was irritated at his brother's insight.

'I have no right to give advice, I suppose,' he said; 'but in my opinion you should drop it—drop it dead. The girl is not worth your looking after. Turn her over to that Society—Mrs Tallents Smallpeace's thing—whatever it's called.'

At a sound as of mirth Stephen, who was not accustomed to hear his brother laugh, looked round.

'Martin,' said Hilary, 'also wants the case to be treated on strictly hygienic grounds.'

Nettled by this, Stephen answered:

'Don't confound me with our young Sanitist, please; I simply think there are probably a hundred things you don't know about the girl which ought to be cleared up.'

'And then?'

'Then,' said Stephen, 'they could—er—deal with her accordingly.'

Hilary shrank so palpably at this remark that he added rather hastily:

'You call that cold-blooded, I suppose; but I think, you know, old chap, that you're too sensitive.'

Hilary stopped rather abruptly.

'If you don't mind, Stevie,' he said, 'we'll part here. I want to think it over.' So saying, he turned back, and sat down on a seat that faced the sun.

Chapter 18

THE PERFECT DOG

HILARY sat long in the sun, watching the pale bright waters and many well-bred ducks circling about the shrubs, searching with their round, bright eyes for worms. Between the bench where he was sitting and the spiked iron railings people passed continually—men, women, children of all kinds. Every now and then a duck would stop and cast her knowing glance at these creatures, as though comparing the condition of their forms and plumage with her own. 'If I had had the breeding of you,' she seemed to say, 'I could have made a better fist of it than that. A worse-looking lot of ducks, take you all round, I never wish to see!' And with a quick but heavy movement of her shoulders, she would turn away and join her fellows.

Hilary, however, got small distraction from the ducks. The situation gradually developing was something of a dilemma to a man better acquainted with ideas than facts, with the trimming of words than with the shaping of events. He turned a queer, perplexed, almost quizzical eye on it. Stephen had irritated him profoundly. He had such a way of pettifying things! Yet, in truth, the affair would seem ridiculous enough to an ordinary observer. What would a man of sound common sense, like Mr Purcey, think of it? Why not, as Stephen had suggested, drop it? Here, however, Hilary approached the marshy ground of feeling.

To give up befriending a helpless girl the moment he found himself personally menaced was exceedingly distasteful. But would she be friendless? Were there not, in Stephen's words, a hundred things he did not know about her? Had she not other resources? Had she not a story? But here, too, he was hampered by his delicacy: one did not pry into the private lives of others!

The matter, too, was hopelessly complicated by the domestic troubles of the Hughs family. No conscientious man—and what-

ever Hilary lacked, no one ever accused him of a lack of conscience
—could put aside that aspect of the case.

Wandering among these reflections were his thoughts about
Bianca. She was his wife. However he might feel towards her now,
whatever their relations, he must not put her in a false position.
Far from wishing to hurt her, he desired to preserve her, and
everyone, from trouble and annoyance. He had told Stephen that
his interest in the girl was purely protective. But since the night
when, leaning out into the moonlight, he heard the waggons
coming in to Covent Garden Market, a strange feeling had possessed him—the sensation of a man who lies, with a touch of fever
on him, listening to the thrum of distant music—sensuous, not
unpleasurable.

Those who saw him sitting there so quietly, with his face resting
on his hand, imagined, no doubt, that he was wrestling with some
deep, abstract proposition, some great thought to be given to mankind; for there was that about Hilary which forced everyone to
connect him instantly with the humaner arts.

The sun began to leave the long pale waters.

A nursemaid and two children came and sat down beside him.
Then it was that, underneath his seat, Miranda found what she had
been looking for all her life. It had no smell, made no movement,
was pale-grey in colour, like herself. It had no hair that she could
find; its tail was like her own; it took no liberties, was silent, had
no passions, committed her to nothing. Standing a few inches
from its head, closer than she had ever been of her free will to
any dog, she smelt its smell-lessness with a long, delicious snuffling,
wrinkling up the skin on her forehead, and through her upturned
eyes her little moonlight soul looked forth. 'How unlike you are,'
she seemed to say, 'to all the other dogs I know! I would love to
live with you. Shall I ever find a dog like you again? ''The latest—
sterilised cloth—see white label underneath: 4s. 3d.!'' ' Suddenly
she slithered out her slender grey-pink tongue and licked its nose.
The creature moved a little way and stopped. Miranda saw that it
had wheels. She lay down close to it, for she knew it was the
perfect dog.

Hilary watched the little moonlight lady lying vigilant, affectionate, beside this perfect dog, who could not hurt her. She panted
slightly, and her tongue showed between her lips.

Presently behind his seat he saw another idyll. A thin white
spaniel had come running up. She lay down in the grass quite close,
and three other dogs who followed, sat and looked at her. A poor,

dirty little thing she was, who seemed as if she had not seen a home for days. Her tongue lolled out, she panted piteously, and had no collar. Every now and then she turned her eyes, but though they were so tired and desperate, there was a gleam in them. 'For all its thirst and hunger and exhaustion, this is life!' they seemed to say. The three dogs, panting too, and watching till it should be her pleasure to begin to run again, seemed with their moist, loving eyes to echo: 'This is life!'

Because of this idyll, people near were moving on.

And suddenly the thin white spaniel rose, and, like a little harried ghost, slipped on amongst the trees, and the three dogs followed her.

Chapter 19

BIANCA

IN her studio that afternoon Bianca stood before her picture of the little model—the figure with parted pale-red lips and haunting, pale-blue eyes, gazing out of shadow into lamplight.

She was frowning, as though resentful of a piece of work which had the power to kill her other pictures. What force had moved her to paint like that? What had she felt while the girl was standing before her, still as some pale flower placed in a cup of water? Not love—there was no love in the presentment of that twilight figure; not hate—there was no hate in the painting of her dim appeal. Yet in the picture of this shadow girl, between the gloom and glimmer, was visible a spirit, driving the artist on to create that which had the power to haunt the mind.

Bianca turned away and went up to a portrait of her husband, painted ten years before. She looked from one picture to the other, with eyes as hard and stabbing as the points of daggers.

In the more poignant relationships of human life there is a point beyond which men and women do not quite truthfully analyse their feelings—they *feel* too much. It was Bianca's fortune, too, to be endowed to excess with that quality which, of all others, most obscures the real significance of human issues. Her pride had kept her back from Hilary, till she had felt herself a failure. Her pride had so revolted at that failure that she had led the way to utter estrangement. Her pride had forced her to the attitude of one who says: 'Live your own life; I should be ashamed to let you see that I care what happens between us.' Her pride had concealed

288

from her the fact that beneath her veil of mocking liberality there was an essential woman tenacious of her dues, avid of affection and esteem. Her pride prevented the world from guessing that there was anything amiss. Her pride even prevented Hilary from really knowing what had spoiled his married life—this ungovernable itch to be appreciated, governed by ungovernable pride. Hundreds of times he had been baffled by the hedge round that disharmonic nature. With each failure something had shrivelled in him, till the very roots of his affection had dried up. She had worn out a man who, to judge from his actions and appearance, was naturally long-suffering to a fault. Beneath all manner of kindness and considera-tion for each other—for their good taste, at all events, had never given way—this tragedy of a woman, who wanted to be loved, slowly killing the power of loving her in the man, had gone on year after year. It had ceased to be tragedy, as far as Hilary was con-cerned; the nerve of his love for her was quite dead, slowly frozen out of him. It was still active tragedy with Bianca, the nerve of whose jealous desire for his appreciation was not dead. Her in-stinct, too, ironically informed her that, had he been a man with some brutality, a man who had set himself to ride and master her, instead of one too delicate, he might have trampled down the hedge. This gave her a secret grudge against him, a feeling that it was not she who was to blame.

Pride was Bianca's fate, her flavour, and her charm. Like a shadowy hill-side behind glamorous bars of waning sunlight, she was enveloped in smiling pride—mysterious, one thinks, even to herself. This pride of hers took part even in her many generous impulses, kind actions which she did rather secretly and scoffed at herself for doing. She scoffed at herself continually, even for putting on dresses of colours which Hilary was fond of. She would not admit her longing to attract him.

Standing between those two pictures, pressing her mahl-stick against her bosom, she suggested somewhat the image of an Italian saint forcing the dagger of martyrdom into her heart.

That other person, who had once brought the thought of Italy into Cecilia's mind—the man Hughs—had been for the last eight hours or so walking the streets, placing in a cart the refuses of Life; nor had he at all suggested the aspect of one tortured by the passions of love and hate. For the first two hours he had led the horse without expression of any sort on his dark face, his neat soldier's figure garbed in the costume which had made 'West-minister' describe him as a 'dreadful foreign-lookin' man'. Now and then he had spoken to the horse; save for those speeches, of no great importance, he had been silent. For the next two hours, following the cart, he had used a shovel, and still his square, short face, with little black moustache and still blacker eyes, had given no sign of conflict in his breast. So he had passed the day. Apart from the fact, indeed, that men of any kind are not too given to expose private passions to public gaze, the circumstances of a life devoted from the age of twenty onwards to the service of his country, first as a soldier, now in the more defensive part of Vestry scavenger, had given him a kind of gravity. Life had cloaked him with passivity—the normal look of men whose bread and cheese depends on their not caring much for anything. Had Hughs allowed his inclinations play, or sought to express himself, he could hardly have been a private soldier; still less, on his retirement from that office with an honourable wound, would he have been selected out of many others as a Vestry scavenger. For such an occupation as the lifting from the streets of the refuses of Life—a calling greatly sought after, and, indeed, one of the few open to a man who had served his country—charm of manner, individuality, or the engaging quality of self-expression, were perhaps out of place.

He had never been trained in the voicing of his thoughts, and, ever since he had been wounded, felt at times a kind of desperate looseness in his head. It was not, therefore, remarkable that he should be liable to misconstruction, more especially by those who had nothing in common with him, except that somewhat negligible factor, common humanity. The Dallisons had misconstructed him as much as, but no more than, he had misconstructed them when, as 'Wesminister' had informed Hilary, he 'went on against the gentry'. He was, in fact, a ragged screen, a broken vessel, that let light through its holes. A glass or two of beer, the fumes of which his wounded head no longer dominated, and he at once became 'dreadful foreign'. Unfortunately, it was his custom, on finishing his work, to call at the 'Green Glory'. On this particular afternoon the glass had become three, and in sallying forth he had felt a confused sense of duty urging him to visit the house where this girl for whom he had conceived his strange infatuation 'carried on her games'. The 'no-tale-bearing' tradition of a soldier fought hard with this sense of duty; his feelings were mixed as he rang the bell and asked for Mrs Dallison. Habit, however, masked his face, and he stood before her at 'attention', his black eyes lowered, clutching his peaked cap.

Bianca noted curiously the scar on the left side of his cropped black head.

Whatever Hughs had to say was not said easily.

'I've come,' he began at last in a dogged voice, 'to let you know. I never wanted to come into this house. I never wanted to see no one.'

Bianca could see his lips and eyelids quivering in a way strangely out of keeping with his general stolidity.

'My wife has told you tales of me, I suppose. She's told you I knock her about, I daresay. I don't care what she tells you or any o' the people that she works for. But this I'll say: I never touched her but she touched me first. Look here! that's marks of hers!' and, drawing up his sleeve, he showed a scratch on his sinewy tattooed forearm. 'I've not come here about her; that's no business of anyone's.'

Bianca turned towards her pictures. 'Well?' she said, 'but what *have* you come about, please? You see I'm busy.'

Hughs' face changed. Its stolidity vanished, the eyes became as quick, passionate, and leaping as a dark torrent. He was more violently alive than she had ever seen a man. Had it been a woman she would have felt—as Cecilia had felt with Mrs Hughs—the indecency, the impudence of this exhibition; but from that male violence the feminine in her derived a certain satisfaction. So in Spring, when all seems lowering and grey, the hedges and trees suddenly flare out against the purple clouds, their twigs all in flame. The next moment that white glare is gone, the clouds are no longer purple, fiery light no longer quivers and leaps along the hedgerows. The passion in Hughs' face was gone as soon. Bianca felt a sense of disappointment, as though she could have wished her life held a little more of that. He stole a glance at her out of his dark eyes, which, when narrowed, had a velvety look, like the body of a wild bee, then jerked his thumb at the picture of the little model.

'It's about *her* I come to speak.'

Bianca faced him frigidly.

'I have not the slightest wish to hear.'

Hughs looked round, as though to find something that would help him to proceed; his eyes lighted on Hilary's portrait.

'Ah! I'd put the two together if I was you,' he said.

Bianca walked past him to the door.

'Either you or I must leave the room.'

The man's face was neither sullen now nor passionate, but simply miserable.

'Look here, lady,' he said, 'don't take it hard o' me coming here. I'm not out to do you any harm. I've got a wife of my own, and Gawd knows I've enough to put up with from her about this girl. I'll be going in the water one of these days. It's him giving her them clothes that set me coming here.'

Bianca opened the door. 'Please go,' she said.

'I'll go quiet enough,' he muttered, and, hanging his head, walked out.

Having seen him through the side door out into the street, Bianca went back to where she had been standing before he came. She found some difficulty in swallowing; for once there was no armour on her face. She stood there a long time without moving, then put the pictures back into their places and went down the little passage to the house. Listening outside her father's door, she turned the handle quietly and went in.

Mr Stone, holding some sheets of paper out before him, was dictating to the little model, who was writing laboriously with her face close above her arm. She stopped at Bianca's entrance. Mr Stone did not stop, but, holding up his other hand, said:

'I will take you through the last three pages again. Follow!'

Bianca sat down at the window.

Her father's voice, so thin and slow, with each syllable disjointed from the other, rose like monotony itself.

' "There was tra-cea-able indeed, in those days, certain rudi-mentary at-tempts to f-u-s-e the classes . . ." '

It went on unwavering, neither rising high nor falling low, as though the reader knew he had yet far to go, like a runner that brings great news across mountains, plains and rivers.

To Bianca that thin voice might have been the customary sighing of the wind, her attention was so fast fixed on the girl, who sat following the words down the pages with her pen's point.

Mr Stone paused.

'Have you got the word "insane"?' he asked.

The little model raised her face. 'Yes, Mr Stone.'

'Strike it out.'

With his eyes fixed on the trees he stood breathing audibly. The little model moved her fingers, freeing them from cramp. Bianca's curious, smiling scrutiny never left her, as though trying to fix an indelible image on her mind. There was something terrifying in that stare, cruel to herself, cruel to the girl.

'The precise word,' said Mr Stone, 'eludes me. Leave a blank. Follow! . . . "Neither that sweet fraternal interest of man in man, nor

a curiosity in phenomena merely as phenomena . . ." ' His voice
pursued its tenuous path through spaces, frozen by the calm eternal
presence of his beloved idea, which, like a golden moon, far and
cold, presided glamorously above the thin track of words. And still
the girl's pen-point traced his utterance across the pages. Mr Stone
paused again, and looking at his daughter as though surprised to see
her sitting there, asked:

'Do you wish to speak to me, my dear?'

Bianca shook her head.

'Follow!' said Mr Stone.

But the little model's glance had stolen round to meet the scrutiny
fixed on her.

A look passed across her face which seemed to say: 'What have
I done to you, that you should stare at me like this?'

Furtive and fascinated, her eyes remained fixed on Bianca, while
her hand moved, mechanically ticking the paragraphs. That silent
duel of eyes went on—the woman's fixed, cruel, smiling; the girl's
uncertain, resentful. Neither of them heard a word that Mr Stone
was reading. They treated it as, from the beginning, Life has treated
Philosophy—and to the end will treat it.

Mr Stone paused again, seeming to weigh his last sentences.

'That, I think,' he murmured to himself, 'is true.' And suddenly
he addressed his daughter. 'Do you agree with me, my dear?'

He was evidently waiting with anxiety for her answer, and the
little silver hairs that straggled on his lean throat beneath his beard
were clearly visible.

'Yes, father, I agree.'

'Ah!' said Mr Stone, 'I am glad that you confirm me. I was
anxious. Follow!'

Bianca rose. Burning spots of colour had settled in her cheeks.
She went towards the door, and the little model pursued her figure
with a long look, cringing, mutinous, and wistful.

Chapter 20

THE HUSBAND AND THE WIFE

IT was past six o'clock when Hilary at length reached home, preceded a little by Miranda, who almost felt within her the desire to
eat. The lilac bushes, not yet in flower, were giving forth spicy
fragrance. The sun still netted their top boughs, as with golden silk,
and a blackbird, seated on a low branch of the acacia-tree, was

summoning the evening. Mr Stone, accompanied by the little model, dressed in her new clothes, was coming down the path. They were evidently going for a walk, for Mr Stone wore his hat, old and soft and black, with a strong green tinge, and carried a paper parcel, which leaked crumbs of bread at every step.

The girl grew very red. She held her head down, as though afraid of Hilary's inspection of her new clothes. At the gate she suddenly looked up. His face said: 'Yes, you look very nice!' And into her eyes a look leaped such as one may see in dogs' eyes lifted in adoration to their masters' faces. Manifestly disconcerted, Hilary turned to Mr Stone. The old man was standing very still; a thought had evidently struck him.

'I have not, I think,' he said, 'given enough consideration to the question whether force is absolutely, or only relatively, evil. If I saw a man ill-treat a cat, should I be justified in striking him?'

Accustomed to such divagations, Hilary answered: 'I don't know whether you would be justified, but I believe that you would strike him.'

'I am not sure,' said Mr Stone. 'We are going to feed the birds.'

The little model took the paper bag. 'It's all dropping out,' she said. From across the road she turned her head. 'Won't you come, too?' she seemed to say.

But Hilary passed rather hastily into the garden and shut the gate behind him. He sat in his study, with Miranda near him, for fully an hour, without doing anything whatever, sunk in a strange half-pleasurable torpor. At this hour he should have been working at his book; and the fact that his idleness did not trouble him might well have given him uneasiness. Many thoughts passed through his mind, imaginings of things he had thought left behind for ever— sensations and longings which to the normal eye of middle age are but dried forms hung in the museum of memory. They started up at the whip of the still-living youth, and lost wildness at the heart of every man. Like the reviving flame of half-spent fires, longing for discovery leaped and flickered in Hilary—to find out once again what things were like before he went down the hill of age.

No trivial ghost was beckoning him; it was the ghost, with unseen face and rosy finger, that comes to men whose youth has gone.

Miranda, hearing him so silent, rose. At this hour it was her master's habit to scratch paper. She, who seldom scratched anything, because it was not delicate, felt dimly that this was what he should be doing. She held up a slim foot and touched his knee.

Receiving no discouragement, she delicately sprang into his lap, and, forgetting for once her modesty, placed her arms on his chest, and licked his face all over.

It was while receiving this embrace that Hilary saw Mr Stone and the little model returning across the garden. The old man was walking very rapidly, holding out the fragment of a broken stick. He was extremely pink.

Hilary went to meet them.

'What's the matter, sir?' he said.

'I cut him over the legs,' said Mr Stone. 'I do not regret it;' and he walked on to his room.

Hilary turned to the little model.

'It was a little dog. The man kicked it, and Mr Stone hit him. He broke his stick. There were several men; they threatened us.' She looked up at Hilary. 'I—I was frightened. Oh! Mr Dallison, isn't he—funny?'

'All heroes are funny,' murmured Hilary.

'He wanted to hit them again, after his stick was broken. Then a policeman came, and they all ran away.'

'That was quite as it should be,' said Hilary. 'And what did *you* do?'

Perceiving that she had not as yet made much effect, the little model cast down her eyes.

'I shouldn't have been frightened if *you* had been there!'

'Heavens!' muttered Hilary. 'Mr Stone is far more valiant than I.'

'I don't think he is,' she replied stubbornly, and again looked up at him.

'Well, good-night!' said Hilary hastily. 'You must run off. . . .'

That same evening, driving with his wife back from a long, dull dinner, Hilary began:

'I've something to say to you.'

An ironic 'Yes?' came from the other corner of the cab.

'There is some trouble with the little model.'

'Really!'

'This man Hughs has become infatuated with her. He has even said, I believe, that he was coming to see you.'

'What about?'

'Me.'

'And what is he going to say about you?'

'I don't know; some vulgar gossip—nothing true.'

There was a silence, and in the darkness Hilary moistened his dry lips.

Bianca spoke: 'May I ask how you knew of this?'

'Cecilia told me.'

A curious noise, like a little strangled laugh, fell on Hilary's ears.

'I am very sorry,' he muttered.

Presently Bianca said:

'It was good of you to tell me, considering that we go our own ways. What made you?'

'I thought it right.'

'And—of course, the man might have come to me!'

'*That* you need not have said.'

'One does not always say what one ought.'

'I have made the child a present of some clothes which she badly needed. As far as I know, that's all I've done!'

'Of course!'

This wonderful 'of course' acted on Hilary like a tonic. He said dryly:

'What do you wish me to do?'

'I?' No gust of the east wind, making the young leaves curl and shiver, the gas jets flare and die down in their lamps, could so have nipped the flower of amity. Through Hilary's mind flashed Stephen's almost imploring words: 'Oh, I wouldn't go to her! Women are so funny!'

He looked round. A blue gauze scarf was wrapped over his wife's dark head. There, in her corner, as far away from him as she could get, she was smiling. For a moment Hilary had the sensation of being stifled by fold on fold of that blue gauze scarf, as if he were doomed to drive for ever, suffocated, by the side of this woman who had killed his love for her.

'You will do what you like, of course,' she said suddenly.

A desire to laugh seized Hilary. 'What do you wish me to do?' 'You will do what you like, of course!' Could civilised restraint and tolerance go further?

'B.,' he said, with an effort, 'the wife is jealous. We put the girl into that house—we ought to get her out.'

Bianca's reply came slowly.

'From the first,' she said, 'the girl has been your property; do what you like with her. I shall not meddle!'

'I am not in the habit of regarding people as my property.'

'No need to tell me that—I have known you twenty years.'

Doors sometimes slam in the minds of the mildest and most restrained of men.

'Oh, very well! I have told you; you can see Hughs when he comes—or not, as you like.'

'I *have* seen him.'

Hilary smiled.

'Well, was his story very terrible?'

'He told me no story.'

'How was that?'

Bianca suddenly sat forward, and threw back the blue scarf, as though she, too, were stifling. In her flushed face her eyes were bright as stars; her lips quivered.

'Is it likely,' she said, 'that I should listen? That's enough, please, of these people.'

Hilary bowed. The cab, bearing them fast home turned into the last short cut. This narrow street was full of men and women circling round barrows and lighted booths. The sound of coarse talk and laughter floated out into air thick with the reek of paraffin and the scent of frying fish. In every couple of those men and women Hilary seemed to see the Hughs, that other married couple, going home to wedded happiness above the little model's head. The cab turned out of the gay alley.

'Enough, please, of these people!'

That same night, past one o'clock, he was roused from sleep by hearing bolts drawn back. He got up, hastened to the window, and looked out. At first he could distinguish nothing. The moonless night, like a dark bird, had nested in the garden; the sighing of the lilac bushes was the only sound. Then, dimly, just below him, on the steps of the front door, he saw a figure standing.

'Who is that?' he called.

The figure did not move.

'Who are you?' said Hilary again.

The figure raised its face, and by the gleam of his white beard Hilary knew that it was Mr Stone.

'What is it, sir?' he said. 'Can I do anything?'

'No,' answered Mr Stone. 'I am listening to the wind. It has visited everyone to-night.' And lifting his hand, he pointed out into the darkness.

Chapter 21

A DAY OF REST

CECILIA'S house in the Old Square was steeped from roof to basement in the peculiar atmosphere brought by Sunday to houses whose inmates have no need of religion or of rest.

Neither she nor Stephen had been to church since Thyme was christened; they did not expect to go again 'till she was married, and they felt that even to go on these occasions was against their principles; but for the sake of other people's feelings they had made the sacrifice, and they meant to make it once more, when the time came. Each Sunday, therefore, everything tried to happen exactly as it happened on every other day, with indifferent success. This was because, for all Cecilia's resolutions, a joint of beef and Yorkshire pudding would appear on the luncheon-table, notwithstanding the fact that Mr Stone—who came when he remembered that it was Sunday—did not devour the higher mammals. Every week, when it appeared, Cecilia, who for some reason carved on Sundays, regarded it with a frown. Next week she would really discontinue it; but when next week came, there it was, with its complexion that reminded her so uncomfortably of cabmen. And she would partake of it with unexpected heartiness. Something very old and deep, some horrible whole-hearted appetite, derived, no doubt, from Mr Justice Carfax, rose at that hour precisely every week to master her. Having given Thyme the second helping which she invariably took, Cecilia, who detested carving, would look over the fearful joint at a piece of glass procured by her in Venice, and at the daffodils standing upright in it, apparently without support. Had it not been for this piece of beef, which had made itself smelt all the morning, and would make itself felt all the afternoon, it need never have come into her mind at all that it was Sunday—and she would cut herself another slice.

To have told Cecilia that there was still a strain of the Puritan in her would have been to occasion her some uneasiness, and provoked a strenuous denial; yet her way of observing Sunday furnished indubitable evidence of this peculiar fact. She did more that day than any other. For, in the morning she invariably 'cleared off' her correspondence; at lunch she carved the beef; after lunch she cleared off the novel or book on social questions she was reading; went to a concert, clearing off a call on the way back; and on first

Sundays—a great bore—stayed at home to clear off the friends
who came to visit her. In the evening she went to some play or
other, produced by Societies for the benefit of persons compelled,
like her, to keep a Sunday with which they felt no sympathy.

On this particular 'first Sunday', having made the circuit of her
drawing-room, which extended the whole breadth of her house, and
through long, low windows cut into leaded panes, looked out both
back and front, she took up Mr Balladyce's latest book. She sat, with
her paper-knife pressed against the tiny hollow in her flushed cheek,
and pretty little bits of lace and real old jewellery nestling close to
her. And while she turned the pages of Mr Balladyce's book, Thyme
sat opposite in a bright blue frock, and turned the pages of Dar-
win's work on earth-worms.

Regarding her 'little daughter', who was so much more solid than
herself, Cecilia's face wore a very sweet, faintly surprised expression.

'My kitten is a bonny thing,' it seemed to say. 'It is queer that I
should have a thing so large.'

Outside in the Square Gardens a shower, the sunlight, and blossoms, were entangled. It was the time of year when all the world
had kittens; young things were everywhere—soft, sweet, uncouth.
Cecilia felt this in her heart. It brought depth into her bright, quick
eyes. What a secret satisfaction it was that she had once so far
committed herself as to have borne a child! What a queer vague
feeling she sometimes experienced in the Spring—almost amounting to a desire to bear another! So one may mark the warm eye of
a staid mare, following with her gaze the first strayings of her foal.
'I must get used to it,' she seems to say. 'I certainly do miss the little
creature, though I used to threaten her with my hoofs, to show I
couldn't be bullied by anything of that age. And there she goes!
Ah, well!'

Remembering suddenly, however, that she was sitting there to
clear off Mr Balladyce, because it was so necessary to keep up with
what he wrote, Cecilia dropped her gaze to the page before her; and
instantly, by uncomfortable chance, not the choice pastures of Mr
Balladyce appeared, where women might browse at leisure, but a
vision of the little model. She had not thought of her for quite an
hour; she had tired herself out with thinking—not, indeed, of her,
but of all that hinged on her, ever since Stephen had spoken of his
talk with Hilary. Things Hilary had said seemed to Cecilia's delicate
and rather timid soul so ominous, so unlike himself. Was there
really going to be complete disruption between him and Bianca—

worse, an ugly scandal? She, who knew her sister better, perhaps, than anyone, remembered from schoolroom days Bianca's moody violence when anything had occurred to wound her—remembered, too, the long fits of brooding that followed. This affair, which she had tried to persuade herself was exaggerated, loomed up larger than ever. It was not an isolated squib; it was a lighted match held to a train of gunpowder. This girl of the people, coming from who knew where, destined for who knew what—this young, not very beautiful, not even clever child, with nothing but a sort of queer haunting naïveté to give her charm—might even be a finger used by Fate! Cecilia sat very still before that sudden vision of the girl. There was no staid mare to guard *that* foal with the dark devotion of her eye. There was no wise whinnying to answer back those tiny whinnies; no long look round to watch the little creature nodding to sleep on its thin trembling legs in the hot sunlight; no ears to prick up and hoofs to stamp at the approach of other living things. These thoughts passed through Cecilia's mind and were gone, being too far and pale to stay. Turning the page which she had not been reading, she heaved a sigh. Thyme sighed also.

'These worms are fearfully interesting,' she said. 'Is anybody coming in this afternoon?'

'Mrs Tallents Smallpeace was going to bring a young man in, a Signor Pozzi—Egregio Pozzi, or some such name. She says he is the coming pianist.' Cecilia's face was spiced with faint amusement. Some strain of her breeding (the Carfax strain, no doubt) still heard such names and greeted such proclivities with an inclination to derision.

Thyme snatched up her book. 'Well,' she said, 'I shall be in the attic. If anyone interesting comes you might send up to me.'

She stood, luxuriously stretching, and turning slowly round in a streak of sunlight so as to bathe her body in it. Then, with a long soft yawn, she flung up her chin till the sun streamed on her face. Her eyelashes rested on cheeks already faintly browned; her lips were parted; little shivers of delight ran down her; her chestnut hair glowed, burnished by the kisses of the sun.

'Ah!' Cecilia thought, 'if that other girl were like this, now, I could understand well enough!'

'Oh, Lord!' said Thyme, 'there they are!' She flew towards the door.

'My dear,' murmured Cecilia, 'if you *must* go, do please tell Father.'

A minute later Mrs Tallents Smallpeace came in, followed by a young man with an interesting, pale face and a crop of dusky hair.

Let us consider for a minute the not infrequent case of a youth cursed with an Italian mother and a father of the name of Potts, who had baptised him William. He had emanated from the lower classes, he might with impunity have ground an organ under the name of Bill; but springing from the bourgeoisie, and playing Chopin at the age of four, his friends had been confronted with a problem of no mean difficulty. Heaven, on the threshold of his career, had intervened to solve it. Hovering, as it were, with one leg raised before the gladiatorial arena of musical London, where all were waiting to turn their thumbs down on the figure of the native Potts, he had received a letter from his mother's birthplace. It was inscribed: 'Egregio Signor·Pozzi'. He was saved. By the simple inversion of the first two words, the substitution of z's for t's without so fortunately making any difference in the sound, and the retention of that i, all London knew him now to be the rising pianist.

He was a quiet, well-mannered youth, invaluable just then to Mrs Tallents Smallpeace, a woman never happy unless slightly leading a genius in strings.

Cecilia, while engaging them to right and left in her half-sympathetic, faintly mocking way—as if doubting whether they really wanted to see her or she them—heard a word of fear.

'Mr Purcey.'

'Oh, Heaven!' she thought.

Mr Purcey, whose A.1. Damyer could be heard outside, advanced in his direct and simple way.

'I thought I'd give my car a run,' he said. 'How's your sister?' And seeing Mrs Tallents Smallpeace, he added: 'How do you do? We met the other day.'

'We did,' said Mrs Tallents Smallpeace, whose little eyes were sparkling. 'We talked about the poor, do you remember?'

Mr Purcey, a sensitive man if you could get through his skin, gave her a shrewd look. 'I don't quite cotton to this woman,' he seemed saying; 'there's a laugh about her I don't like.'

'Ah! yes—you were tellin' me about them.'

'Oh, Mr Purcey, but you had heard of them, you remember!'

Mr Purcey made a movement of his face which caused it to seem all jaw. It was a sort of unconscious declaration of a somewhat formidable character. So one may see bulldogs, those amiable animals, suddenly disclose their tenacity.

'It's rather a blue subject,' he said bluntly.

Something in Cecilia fluttered at those words. It was like the

301

saying of a healthy man looking at a box of pills which he did not mean to open. Why could not she and Stephen keep that lid on, too? And at this moment, to her deep astonishment, Stephen entered. She had sent for him, it is true, but had never expected he would come.

His entrance, indeed, requires explanation.

Feeling, as he said, a little 'off colour', Stephen had not gone to Richmond to play golf. He had spent the day instead in the company of his pipe and those ancient coins, of which he had the best collection of any man he had ever met. His thoughts had wandered from them, more than he thought proper, to Hilary and that girl. He had felt from the beginning that he was so much more the man to deal with an affair like this than poor old Hilary. When, therefore, Thyme put her head into his study and said, 'Father, Mrs Tallents Smallpeace!' he had first thought, 'That busybody!' and then, 'I wonder—perhaps I'd better go and see if I can get anything out of her.'

In considering Stephen's attitude towards a woman so firmly embedded in the various social movements of the day, it must be remembered that he represented that large class of men who, unhappily too cultivated to put aside, like Mr Purcey, all blue subjects, or deny the need for movements to make them less blue, still could not move, for fear of being out of order. He was also temperamentally distrustful of anything too feminine; and Mrs Tallents Smallpeace was undoubtedly extremely feminine. Her merit, in his eyes, consisted of her attachment to Societies. So long as mankind worked through Societies, Stephen, who knew the power of rules and minute books, did not despair of too little progress being made. He sat down beside her, and turned the conversation on her chief work—'the Maids in Peril'.

Searching his face with those eyes so like little black bees sipping honey from all the flowers that grew, Mrs Tallents Smallpeace said:

'Why don't you get your wife to take an interest in our work?'

To Stephen this question was naturally both unexpected and annoying, one's wife being the last person he wished to interest in other people's movements. He kept his head.

'Ah, well!' he said, 'we haven't all got a talent for that sort of thing.'

The voice of Mr Purcey travelled suddenly across the room.

'Do tell me! How do you go to work to worm things out of them?'

Mrs Tallents Smallpeace, prone to laughter, bubbled.

'Oh, that is such a delicious expression, Mr Purcey! I almost think we ought to use it in our Report. Thank you!'

Mr Purcey bowed. 'Not at all!' he said.

Mrs Tallents Smallpeace turned again to Stephen.

'We have our trained inquirers. That is the advantage of Societies such as ours; so that we don't personally have the unpleasantness. Some cases do baffle everybody. It's such very delicate work.'

'You sometimes find you let in a rotter?' said Mr Purcey—'or, I should say, a rotter lets you in! Ha, ha!'

Mrs Tallents Smallpeace's eyes flew deliciously down his figure.

'Not often,' she said; and turning rather markedly once more to Stephen: 'Have you any special case that you are interested in, Mr Dallison?'

Stephen consulted Cecilia with one of those masculine half-glances so discreet that Mrs Tallents Smallpeace intercepted it without looking up. She found it rather harder to catch Cecilia's reply, but she caught it before Stephen did. It was, 'You'd better wait, perhaps,' conveyed by a tiny raising of the left eyebrow and a slight movement to the right of the lower lip. Putting two and two together, she felt within her bones that they were thinking of the little model. And she remembered the interesting moment in the omnibus when that attractive-looking man had got out so hastily.

There was no danger whatever from Mrs Tallents Smallpeace feeling anything. The circle in which she moved did not now talk scandal, or, indeed, allude to matters of that sort without deep sympathy; and in the second place she was really far too good a fellow, with far too dear a love of life, to interfere with anybody else's love of it. At the same time it was interesting.

'That little model, now,' she said, 'what about her?'

'Is that the girl I saw?' broke in Mr Purcey, with his accustomed shrewdness.

Stephen gave him the look with which he was accustomed to curdle the blood of persons who gave evidence before Commissions.

'This fellow is impossible,' he thought.

The little black bees flying below Mrs Tallents Smallpeace's dark hair, done in the Early Italian fashion, tranquilly sucked honey from Stephen's face.

'She seemed to me,' she answered, 'such a very likely type.'

303

'Ah!' murmured Stephen, 'there would be, I suppose, a danger——' And he looked angrily at Cecilia.

Without ceasing to converse with Mr Purcey and Signor Egregio Pozzi, she moved her left eye upwards. Mrs Tallents Smallpeace understood this to mean: 'Be frank, and guarded!' Stephen, however, interpreted it otherwise. To him it signified: 'What the deuce do you look at me for?' And he felt justly hurt. He therefore said abruptly:

'What would you do in a case like that?'

Mrs Tallents Smallpeace, sliding her face sideways, with a really charming little smile, asked softly:

'In a case like what?'

And her little eyes fled to Thyme, who had slipped into the room, and was whispering to her mother.

Cecilia rose.

'You know my daughter,' she said. 'Will you excuse me just a minute? I'm so very sorry.' She glided towards the door, and threw a flying look back. It was one of those social moments precious to those who are escaping them.

Mrs Tallents Smallpeace was smiling, Stephen frowning at his boots; Mr Purcey stared admiringly at Thyme, and Thyme, sitting very upright, was calmly regarding the unfortunate Egregio Pozzi, who apparently could not bring himself to speak.

When Cecilia found herself outside, she stood still a moment to compose her nerves. Thyme had told her that Hilary was in the dining-room, and wanted specially to see her.

As in most women of her class and bringing-up, Cecilia's qualities of reticence and subtlety, the delicate treading of her spirit, were seen to advantage in a situation such as this. Unlike Stephen, who had shown at once that he had something on his mind, she received Hilary with that exact shade of friendly, intimate, yet cool affection long established by her as the proper manner towards her husband's brother. It was not quite sisterly, but it was very nearly so. It seemed to say: 'We understand each other as far as it is right and fitting that we should; we even sympathise with the difficulties we have each of us experienced in marrying the other's sister or brother, as the case may be. We know the worst. And we like to see each other, too, because there are bars between us, which make it almost piquant.'

Giving him her soft little hand, she began at once to talk of things farthest from her heart. She saw that she was deceiving Hilary, and this feather in the cap of her subtlety gave her pleasure.

But her nerves fluttered at once when he said: 'I want to speak to you, Cis. You know that Stephen and I had a talk yesterday, I suppose?'

Cecilia nodded.

'I have spoken to B.!'

'Oh!' Cecilia murmured. She longed to ask what Bianca had said, but did not dare, for Hilary had his armour on, the retired, ironical look which he always wore when any subject was broached for which he was too sensitive.

She waited.

'The whole thing is distasteful to me,' he said; 'but I must do something for this child. I can't leave her completely in the lurch.'

Cecilia had an inspiration.

'Hilary,' she said softly, 'Mrs Tallents Smallpeace is in the drawing-room. She was just speaking of the girl to Stephen. Won't you come in, and arrange with her quietly?'

Hilary looked at his sister-in-law for a moment without speaking, then said:

'I draw the line there. No, thank you. I'll see this through myself.'

Cecilia fluttered out:

'Oh, but, Hilary, what do you mean?'

'I am going to put an end to it.'

It needed all Cecilia's subtlety to hide her consternation. End to what? Did he mean that he and B. were going to separate?

'I won't have all this vulgar gossip about the poor girl. I shall go and find another room for her.'

Cecilia sighed with relief.

'Would you—would you like me to come too, Hilary?'

'It's very good of you,' said Hilary dryly. 'My actions appear to rouse suspicion.'

Cecilia blushed.

'Oh, that's absurd! Still, no one could think *anything* if I come with you. Hilary, have you thought that if she continues coming to father——'

'I shall tell her that she mustn't!'

Cecilia's heart gave two thumps, the first with pleasure, the second with sympathy.

'It will be horrid for you,' she said. 'You hate doing anything of that sort.'

Hilary nodded.

'But I'm afraid it's the only way,' went on Cecilia, rather hastily.

305

'And, of course, it will be no good saying anything to Father; one must simply let him suppose that she has got tired of it.'

Again Hilary nodded.

'He will think it very funny,' murmured Cecilia pensively. 'Oh, and have you thought that taking her away from where she is will only make those people talk the more?'

Hilary shrugged his shoulders.

'It may make that man furious,' Cecilia added.

'It will.'

'Oh, but then, of course, if you don't see her afterwards, they will have no—no excuse at all.'

'I shall not see her afterwards,' s id Hilary, 'if I can avoid it.'

Cecilia looked at him.

'It's very sweet of you, Hilary.'

'What is sweet?' asked Hilary stonily.

'Why, to take all this trouble. Is it really necessary for you to do anything?' But looking in his face, she went on hastily: 'Yes, yes, it's best. Let's go at once. Oh, those people in the drawing-room! Do wait ten minutes.'

A little later, running up to put her hat on, she wondered why it was that Hilary always made her want to comfort him. Stephen never affected her like this.

Having little or no notion where to go, they walked in the direction of Bayswater. To place the Park between Hound Street and the little model was the first essential. On arriving at the other side of the Broad Walk, they made instinctively away from every sight of green. In a long, grey street of dismally respectable appearance they found what they were looking for, a bed-sitting room furnished, advertised on a card in the window. The door was opened by the landlady, a tall woman of narrow build, with a West-Country accent, and a rather hungry sweetness running through her hardness. They stood talking with her in a passage, whose oilcloth of variegated pattern emitted a faint odour. The staircase could be seen climbing steeply up past walls covered with a shining paper cut by narrow red lines into small yellow squares. An almanack, of so floral a design that nobody would surely want to steal it, hung on the wall; below it was an umbrella stand without umbrellas. The dim little passage led past two grimly closed doors painted rusty red to two half-open doors with dull glass in their panels. Outside, in the street from which they had mounted by stone steps, a shower of sleet had begun to fall.

Hilary shut the door, but the cold spirit of that shower had already slipped into the bleak, narrow house.

'This is the apartment, m'm,' said the landlady, opening the first of the rusty-coloured doors. The room, which had a paper of blue roses on a yellow ground, was separated from another room by double doors.

'I let the rooms together sometimes, but just now that room's taken—a young gentleman in the City; that's why I'm able to let this cheap.'

Cecilia looked at Hilary. 'I hardly think——'

The landlady quickly turned the handles of the doors, showing that they would not open.

'I keep the key,' she said. 'There's a bolt on both sides.'

Reassured, Cecilia walked round the room as far as this was possible, for it was practically all furniture. There was the same little wrinkle across her nose as across Thyme's nose when she spoke of Hound Street. Suddenly she caught sight of Hilary. He was standing with his back against the door. On his face was a strange and bitter look, such as a man might have on seeing the face of Ugliness herself, feeling that she was not only without him, but within—a universal spirit; the look of a man who had thought that he was chivalrous, and found that he was not; of a leader about to give an order that he would not himself have executed.

Seeing that look, Cecilia said with some haste:

'It's all very nice and clean; it will do very well, I think. Seven shillings a week, I believe you said. We will take it for a fortnight, at all events.'

The first glimmer of a smile appeared on the landlady's grim face, with its hungry eyes, sweetened by patience.

'When would she be coming in?' she asked.

'When do you think, Hilary?'

'I don't know,' muttered Hilary. 'The sooner the better—if it must be. To-morrow, or the day after.'

And with one look at the bed, covered with a piece of cheap red-and-yellow tasselled tapestry, he went out into the street. The shower was over, but the house faced north, and no sun was shining on it.

Chapter 22

HILARY PUTS AN END TO IT

LIKE flies caught among the impalpable and smoky threads of cob-webs, so men struggle in the webs of their own natures, giving here a start, there a pitiful small jerking, long sustained, and failing into stillness. Enmeshed they were born, enmeshed they die, fight-ing according to their strength to the end; to fight in the hope of freedom, their joy; to die, not knowing they are beaten, their reward. Nothing, too, is more to be remarked than the manner in which Life devises for each man the particular dilemmas most suited to his nature; that which to the man of gross, decided, or fanatic turn of mind appears a simple sum, to the man of delicate and speculative temper seems to have no answer.

So it was with Hilary in that special web wherein his spirit strug-gled, sunrise unto sunset, and by moonlight afterward. Inclina-tion, and the circumstances of a life which had never forced him to grips with either men or women, had detached him from the necessity for giving or taking orders. He had almost lost the faculty. Life had been a picture with blurred outlines melting into a softly shaded whole. Not for years had anything seemed to him quite a case for 'Yes' or 'No'. It had been his creed, his delight, his business, too, to try and put himself in everybody's place, so that now there were but few places where he did not, speculatively speaking, feel at home.

Putting himself into the little model's place gave him but small delight. Making due allowance for the sentiment men naturally import into their appreciation of the lives of women, his concep-tion of her place was doubtless not so very wrong.

Here was a child, barely twenty years of age, country bred, neither a lady nor quite a working-girl, without a home or rela-tives, according to her own account—at all events, without those who were disposed to help her—without apparently any sort of friend; helpless by nature, and whose profession required a more than common wariness—this girl he was proposing to set quite adrift again by cutting through the single slender rope which tethered her. It was like digging up a little rose-tree planted with one's own hands in some poor shelter, just when it had taken root, and setting it where the full winds would beat against it. To do so brusque and, as it seemed to Hilary, so in-humane a thing was foreign to his nature. There was also the little matter of that touch of fever—the distant music he had been hear-ing since the waggons came in to Covent Garden.

With a feeling that was almost misery, therefore, he waited for her on Monday afternoon, walking to and fro in his study, where all the walls were white, and all the woodwork coloured like the leaf of a cigar; where the books were that colour too, in Hilary's special deerskin binding; where there were no flowers nor any sunlight coming through the windows, but plenty of sheets of paper—a room that youth seemed to have left for ever, the room of middle age!

He called her in with the intention of at once saying what he had to say, and getting it over in the fewest words. But he had not reckoned fully either with his own nature or with woman's instinct. Nor had he allowed—being, for all his learning, perhaps because of it, singularly unable to gauge the effects of simple actions—for the proprietary relations he had established in the girl's mind by giving her those clothes.

As a dog whose master has it in his mind to go away from him, stands gazing up with tragic inquiry in his eyes, scenting to his soul that coming cruelty—as a dog thus soon to be bereaved, so stood the little model.

By the pose of every limb, and a fixed gaze bright as if tears were behind it, and by a sort of trembling, she seemed to say: 'I know why you have sent for me.'

When Hilary saw her stand like that he felt as a man might when told to flog his fellow-creature. To gain time he asked her what she did with herself all day. The little model evidently tried to tell herself that her foreboding had been needless.

Now that the mornings were nice—she said with some anima-tion—she got up much earlier, and did her needlework first thing; she then 'did out' the room. There were mouse-holes in her room, and she had bought a trap. She had caught a mouse last night. She hadn't liked to kill it; she had put it in a tin box, and let it go when she went out. Quick to see that Hilary was interested in this, as well he might be, she told him that she could not bear to see cats hungry or lost dogs, especially lost dogs, and she des-cribed to him one that she had seen. She had not liked to tell a policeman; they stared so hard. Those words were of strange omen, and Hilary turned his head away. The little model, perceiving that she had made an effect of some sort, tried to deepen it. She had heard they did all sorts of things to people—but, seeing at once from Hilary's face that she was not improving her effect, she broke off suddenly, and hastily began to tell him of her breakfast, of how comfortable she was now she had got her clothes; how she liked her room; how old Mr Creed was very funny, never taking any notice of her when he met her in the morning. Then followed a minute account of where she had been trying to get work; of an engagement promised; Mr Lennard, too, still wanted her to pose to him. At this she flashed a look at Hilary, then cast down her eyes. She could get plenty of work if she began that way. But she hadn't, because he had told her not, and, of course, she didn't want to; she liked coming to Mr Stone so much. And she got on very well, and she liked London, and she liked the shops. She mentioned neither Hughs nor Mrs Hughs. In all this rigmarole, told with such obvious purpose, stolidity was strangely mingled with almost cunning quickness to see the effect made; but the dog-like devotion was never quite out of her eyes when they were fixed on Hilary.

This look got through the weakest places in what little armour Nature had bestowed on him. It touched one of the least conceited and most amiable of men profoundly. He felt it an honour that anything so young as this should regard him in that way. He had always tried to keep out of his mind that which might have given him the key to her special feeling for himself—those words of the painter of still life: 'She's got a story of some sort.' But it flashed across him suddenly like an inspiration: If her story were the simplest of all stories—the direct, rather brutal, love affair of a village boy and girl—would not she, naturally given to surrender, be forced this time to the very antithesis of that young animal amour which had brought on her such sharp consequences?

But, wherever her devotion came from, it seemed to Hilary the grossest violation of the feelings of a gentleman to treat it ungratefully. Yet it was as if for the purpose of saying, 'You are a nuisance to me, or worse!' that he had asked her to his study. Her presence had hitherto chiefly roused in him the half-amused, half-tender feelings of one who strokes a foal or calf, watching its soft uncouthness; now, about to say good-bye to her, there was the question of whether that was the only feeling.

Miranda, stealing out between her master and his visitor, growled.

The little model, who was stroking a china ash-tray with her ungloved, inky fingers, muttered, with a smile, half pathetic, half

310

cynical: 'She doesn't like me! She knows I don't belong here. She hates me to come. She's jealous!'

Hilary said abruptly:

'Tell me! Have you made any friends since you've been in London?'

The girl flashed a look at him that said:

'Could I make *you* jealous?'

Then, as though guilty of a far too daring·thought, drooped her head, and answered:

'No.'

'Not one?'

The little model repeated almost passionately: 'No. I don't want any friends; I only want to be let alone.'

Hilary began speaking rapidly.

'But these Hughs have not left you alone. I told you, I thought you ought to move; I've taken another room for you quite away from them. Leave your furniture with a week's rent, and take your trunk quietly away tomorrow in a cab without saying a word to anyone. This is the new address, and here's the money for your expenses. They're dangerous for you, those people.'

The little model muttered desperately: 'But I don't care what they do!'

Hilary went on: 'Listen! You mustn't come here again, or the man will trace you. We will take care you have what's necessary till you can get other work.'

The little model looked up at him without a word. Now that the thin link which bound her to some sort of household gods had snapped, all the patience and submission bred in her by village life, by the hard facts of her story, and by these last months in London, served her well enough. She made no fuss. Hilary saw a tear roll down her cheek.

He turned his head away, and said: 'Don't cry, my child!'

Quite obediently the little model swallowed the tear. A thought seemed to strike her:

'But I could see you, Mr Dallison, couldn't I, sometimes?'

Seeing from his face that this was not in the programme, she stood silent again, looking up at him.

It was a little difficult for Hilary to say: 'I can't see you because my wife is jealous!' It was cruel to tell her: 'I don't want to see you!'—besides, it was not true.

'You'll soon be making friends,' he said at last, 'and you can always write to me;' and with a queer smile he added: 'You're only just beginning life; you mustn't take these things to heart; you'll find plenty of people better able to advise and help you than ever I shall be!'

The little model answered this by seizing his hand with both of hers. She dropped it again at once, as if guilty of presumption, and stood with her head bent. Hilary, looking down on the little hat which, by his special wish, contained no feathers, felt a lump rise in his throat.

'It's funny,' he said; 'I don't know your Christian name.'

'Ivy,' muttered the little model.

'Ivy! Well, I'll write to you. But you must promise me to do exactly as I said.'

The girl looked up; her face was almost ugly—like a child's in whom a storm of feeling is repressed.

'Promise!' repeated Hilary.

With a bitter droop of her lower lip, she nodded, and suddenly put her hand to her heart. The action, of which she was clearly unconscious, so naïvely, so almost automatically was it done, nearly put an end to Hilary's determination.

'Now you must go,' he said.

The little model choked, grew very red, and then quite white.

'Aren't I even to say good-bye to Mr Stone?'

Hilary shook his head.

'He'll miss me,' she said desperately. 'He will. I know he will!'

'So shall I,' said Hilary. 'We can't help that.'

The little model drew herself up to her full height; her breast heaved beneath the clothes which had made her Hilary's. She was very like 'The Shadow' at that moment, as though whatever Hilary might do there she would be—a little ghost, the spirit of the helpless submerged world, for ever haunting with its dumb appeal the minds of men.

'Give me your hand,' said Hilary.

The little model put out her not too white, small hand. It was soft, clinging, and as hot as fire.

'Good-bye, my dear, and bless you!'

The little model gave him a look with who-knows-what of reproach in it, and, faithful to her training, went submissively away.

Hilary did not look after her, but, standing by the lofty mantelpiece above the ashes of the fire, rested his forehead on his arm. Not even a fly's buzzing broke the stillness. There was sound

312

for all that—not of distant music, but of blood beating in his ears
and temples.

Chapter 23

THE 'BOOK OF UNIVERSAL BROTHERHOOD'

IT is fitting that a few words should be said about the writer of
the 'Book of Universal Brotherhood'.

Sylvanus Stone, having graduated very highly at the London
University, had been appointed at an early age lecturer to more
than one Public Institution. He had soon received the professional
robes due to a man of his profound learning in the natural sciences,
and from that time till he was seventy his life had flowed on in one
continual round of lectures, addresses, disquisitions, and arguments on the subjects in which he was a specialist. At the age
of seventy, long after his wife's death and the marriages of his
three children, he had for some time been living by himself, when
a very serious illness—the result of liberties taken with an iron
constitution by a single mind—prostrated him.

During the long convalescence following this illness the power
of contemplation, which the Professor had up to then given to
natural science, began to fix itself on life at large. But the mind
which had made of natural science an idea, a passion, was not
content with vague reflections on life. Slowly, subtly, with irresis-
tible centrifugal force—with a force which perhaps it would not
have acquired but for that illness—the idea, the passion of Universal Brotherhood had sucked into itself all his errant wonderings
on the riddle of existence. The single mind of this old man, divorced
by illness from his previous existence, pensioned and permanently
shelved, began to worship a new star, that with every week and
month and year grew brighter, till all other stars had lost their
glimmer and died out.

At the age of seventy-four he had begun his book. Under the
spell of his subject and of advancing age, his extreme inattention
to passing matters became rapidly accentuated. His figure had become almost too publicly conspicuous before Bianca, finding
him one day seated on the roof of his lonely little top-storey flat,
the better to contemplate his darling Universe, had inveigled him
home with her, and installed him in a room in her own house.
After the first day or two he had not noticed any change to speak
of.

His habits in his new home were soon formed, and once formed, they varied not at all; for he admitted into his life nothing that took him from the writing of his book.

On the afternoon following Hilary's dismissal of the little model, being disappointed of his amanuensis, Mr Stone had waited for an hour, reading his pages over and over to himself. He had then done his exercises. At the usual time for tea he had sat down, and, with his cup and brown bread-and-butter alternately at his lips, had looked long and fixedly at the place where the girl was wont to sit. Having finished, he left the room and went about the house. He found no one but Miranda, who, seated in the passage leading to the studio, was trying to keep one eye on the absence of her master and the other on the absence of her mistress. She joined Mr Stone maintaining a respect-compelling interval behind him when he went before, and before him when he went behind. When they had finished hunting, Mr Stone went down to the garden gate. Here Bianca found him presently, motionless, without a hat, in the full sun, craning his white head in the direction from which he knew the little model habitually came.

The mistress of the house was herself returning from her annual visit to the Royal Academy, where she still went, as dogs, from some perverted sense, will go and sniff round other dogs to whom they have long taken a dislike. A loose-hanging veil depended from her mushroom-shaped and coloured hat. Her eyes were brightened by her visit.

Mr Stone soon seemed to take in who she was, and stood regarding her a minute without speaking. His attitude towards his daughters was rather like that of an old drake towards two swans whom he has inadvertently begotten—there was inquiry in it, disapproval, admiration, and faint surprise.

'Why has she not come?' he said.

Bianca winced behind her veil. 'Have you asked Hilary?'

'I cannot find him,' answered Mr Stone. Something about his patient stooping figure and white head, on which the sunlight was falling, made Bianca slip her hand through his arm.

'Come in, Dad. I'll do your copying.'

Mr Stone looked at her intently, and shook his head.

'It would be against my principles; I cannot take an unpaid service. But if you would come, my dear, I should like to read to you. It is stimulating.'

At that request Bianca's eyes grew dim. Pressing Mr Stone's shaggy arm against her breast, she moved with him towards the house.

'I think I may have written something that will interest you,' Mr Stone said, as they went along.

'I am sure you have,' Bianca murmured.

'It is universal,' said Mr Stone; 'it concerns birth. Sit at the table. I will begin, as usual, where I left off yesterday.'

Bianca took the little model's seat, resting her chin on her hand, as motionless as any of the statues she had just been viewing.

It almost seemed as if Mr Stone were feeling nervous. He twice arranged his papers; cleared his throat; then, lifting a sheet suddenly, took three steps, turned his back on her, and began to read.

'"In that slow, incessant change of form to form, called Life, men, made spasmodic by perpetual action, had seized on a certain moment, no more intrinsically notable than any other moment, and had called it Birth. This habit of honouring one single instant of the universal process to the disadvantage of all the other instants had done more, perhaps, than anything to obfuscate the crystal clearness of the fundamental flux. As well might such as watch the process of the green, unfolding earth, emerging from the brumous arms of winter, isolate a single day and call it Spring. In the tides of rhythm by which the change of form to form was governed"'—Mr Stone's voice, which had till then been but a thin, husky murmur, gradually grew louder and louder, as though he were addressing a great concourse—'"the golden universal haze in which men should have flown like bright wingbeats round the sun gave place to the parasitic halo which every man derived from the glorifying of his own nativity. To this primary mistake could be traced his intensely personal philosophy. Slowly but surely there had dried up in his heart the wish to be his brother."'

He stopped reading suddenly.

'I see him coming in,' he said.

The next minute the door opened, and Hilary entered.

'She has not come,' said Mr Stone; and Bianca murmured:

'We miss her!'

'Her eyes,' said Mr Stone, 'have a peculiar look; they help me to see into the future. I have noticed the same look in the eyes of female dogs.'

With a little laugh, Bianca murmured again:

'That is good!'

'There is one virtue in dogs,' said Hilary, 'which human beings lack—they are incapable of mockery.'

But Bianca's lips, parted, indrawn, seemed saying: 'You ask too

315

much! I no longer attract you. Am I to sympathise in the attraction this common little girl has for you?'

Mr Stone's gaze was fixed intently on the wall.

'The dog,' he said, 'has lost much of its primordial character.'

And, moving to his desk, he took up his quill pen.

Hilary and Bianca made no sound, nor did they look at one another; and in this silence, so much more full of meaning than any talk, the scratching of the quill went on. Mr Stone put it down at last, and, seeing two persons in the room, said:

'Looking back at those days when the doctrine of evolution had reached its pinnacle, one sees how the human mind, by its habit of continual crystallisations, had destroyed all the meaning of the process. Witness, for example, that sterile phenomenon, the pagoda of "caste"! Like this Chinese building, so was Society then formed. Men were living there in layers, as divided from each other, class from class——' He took up the quill, and again began to write.

'You understand, I suppose,' said Hilary in a low voice, 'that she has been told not to come?'

Bianca moved her shoulders.

With a most unwonted look of anger, he added:

'Is it within the scope of your generosity to credit me with the desire to meet your wishes?'

Bianca's answer was a laugh so strangely hard, so cruelly bitter, that Hilary involuntarily turned, as though to retrieve the sound before it reached the old man's ears.

Mr Stone had laid down his pen. 'I shall write no more to-day,' he said; 'I have lost my feeling—I am not myself.' He spoke in a voice unlike his own.

Very tired and worn his old figure looked; as some lean horse, whose sun has set, stands with drooped head, the hollows in his neck showing under his straggling mane. And suddenly, evidently quite oblivious that he had any audience, he spoke:

'O great Universe, I am an old man of a faint spirit, with no singleness of purpose. Help me to write on—help me to write a book such as the world has never seen!'

A dead silence followed that strange prayer; then Bianca, with tears rolling down her face, got up and rushed out of the room.

Mr Stone came to himself. His mute, white face had suddenly grown scared and pink. He looked at Hilary.

'I fear that I forgot myself. Have I said anything peculiar?'

316

Not feeling certain of his voice, Hilary shook his head, and he, too, moved towards the door.

Chapter 24

SHADOWLAND

'EACH of us has a shadow in those places—in those streets.'

That saying of Mr Stone's, which—like so many of his sayings—had travelled forth to beat the air, might have seemed, even 'in those days', not altogether without meaning to anyone who looked into the room of Mr Joshua Creed in Hound Street.

This aged butler lay in bed waiting for the inevitable striking of a small alarum clock placed in the very centre of his mantelpiece. Flanking that round and ruthless arbiter, which drove him day by day to stand up on feet whose time had come to rest, were the effigies of his past triumphs. On the one hand, in a papier-mâché frame, slightly tinged with smuts, stood a portrait of the 'Honorable Bateson', in the uniform of his peculiar Yeomanry. Creed's former master's face wore that dare-devil look with which he had been wont to say : 'D——n it, Creed! lend me a pound. I've got no money!' On the other hand, in a green frame that had once been plush, and covered by a glass with a crack in the left-hand corner, was a portrait of the Dowager Countess of Glengower, as this former mistress of his appeared, conceived by the local photographer, laying the foundation-stone of the local almshouse. During the wreck of Creed's career, which, following on a lengthy illness, had preceded his salvation by the *Westminster Gazette*, these two household gods had lain at the bottom of an old tin trunk, in the possession of the keeper of a lodging-house, waiting to be bailed out. The 'Honorable Bateson' was now dead, nor had he paid as yet the pounds he had borrowed. Lady Glengower, too, was in heaven, remembering that she had forgotten all her servants in her will. He who had served them was still alive, and his first thought, when he had secured his post on the *Westminster*, was to save enough to rescue them from a dishonourable confinement. It had taken him six months. He had found them keeping company with three pairs of woollen drawers; an old but respectable black tail-coat; a plaid cravat; a Bible; four socks, two of which had toes and two of which had heels; some darning-cotton and a needle; a pair of elastic-sided boots; a comb and a sprig of white heather, wrapped up with a little piece of shaving-soap and two pipe-cleaners in a bit of the *Globe*

317

newspaper; also two collars, whose lofty points, separated by gaps of quite two inches, had been wont to reach their master's gills; the small alarum clock aforesaid; and a tie-pin formed in the likeness of Queen Victoria at the date of her first Jubilee. How many times had he not gone in thought over those stores of treasure while he was parted from them! How many times since they had come back to him had he not pondered with a slow but deathless anger on the absence of a certain shirt, which he could have sworn had been amongst them!

But now he lay in bed waiting to hear the clock go off, with his old bristly chin beneath the bedclothes, and his old discoloured nose above. He was thinking the thoughts which usually came into his mind about this hour—that Mrs Hughs ought not to scrape the butter off his bread for breakfast in the way she did; that she ought to take that sixpence off his rent; that the man who brought his late editions in the cart ought to be earlier, letting 'that man' get his *Pell Mells* off before him, when he himself would be having the one chance of his day; that, sooner than pay the ninepence which the bootmaker had proposed to charge for resoling him, he would wait until the summer came—'low-class o' feller' as he was, he'd be glad enough to sole him then for sixpence!

And the high-souled critic, finding these reflections sordid, would have thought otherwise, perhaps, had it been standing on those feet (now twitching all by themselves beneath the bedclothes) up to eleven o'clock the night before, because there were still twelve numbers of the late edition that nobody would buy. No one knew more surely than Joshua Creed himself that, if he suffered himself to entertain any large and lofty views of life, he would infallibly find himself in that building to keep out of which he was in the habit of addressing to God his only prayer to speak of. Fortunately, from a boy up, together with a lengthy, oblong, square-jawed face, he had been given by Nature a single-minded view of life. In fact, the mysterious, stout tenacity of a soul born in the neighbourhood of Newmarket could not have been done justice to had he constitutionally seen—any more than Mr Stone himself—two things at a time. The one thing he had seen, for the five years that he had now stood outside Messrs Rose and Thorn's, was the workhouse; and, as he was not going there so long as he was living, he attended carefully to all little matters of expense in this somewhat sordid way.

While attending thus, he heard a scream. Having by temperament considerable caution, but little fear, he waited till he heard an-

other, and then got out of bed. Taking the poker in his hand, and
putting on his spectacles, he hurried to the door. Many a time and
oft in old days had he risen in this fashion to defend the plate of
the 'Honorable Bateson' and the Dowager Countess of Glengower
from the periodical attacks of his imagination. He stood with his
ancient nightgown flapping round his still more ancient legs,
slightly shivering; then, pulling the door open, he looked forth. On
the stairs just above him Mrs Hughs, clasping her baby with one
arm, was holding the other out at full length between herself and
Hughs. He heard the latter say: 'You've drove me to it; I'll do a
swing for you!' Mrs Hughs' thin body brushed past into his room;
blood was dripping from her wrist. Creed saw that Hughs had his
bayonet in his hand. With all his might he called out: 'Ye ought
to be ashamed of yourself!' raising the poker to a position of de-
fence. At this moment—more really dangerous than any he had
ever known—it was remarkable that he instinctively opposed to
it his most ordinary turns of speech. It was as though the extravagance of this un-English violence had roused in him the full
measure of a native moderation. The sight of the naked steel deeply
disgusted him; he uttered a long sentence. What did Hughs call this
—'disgracin' of the house at this time in the mornin'? Where was
he brought up? Call 'imself a soldier, attackin' of old men and
women in this way? He ought to be ashamed!

While these words were issuing between the yellow stumps of
teeth in that withered mouth, Hughs stood silent, the back of his
arm covering his eyes. Voices and a heavy tread were heard. Dis-
tinguishing in that tread the advancing footsteps of the Law,
Creed said: 'You attack me if you dare!'

Hughs dropped his arm. His short, dark face had a desperate look,
as of a caged rat; his eyes were everywhere at once.

'All right, daddy,' he said; 'I won't hurt *you*. She's drove my
head all wrong again. Catch hold o' this; I can't trust myself.' He
held out the bayonet.

'Westminister' took it gingerly in his shaking hand.

'To use a thing like that!' he said. 'An' call yourself an Englishman! I'll ketch me death standin' here, I will.'

Hughs made no answer, leaning against the wall. The old butler
regarded him severely. He did not take a wide or philosophic view
of him, as a tortured human being, driven by the whips of passion
in his dark blood; a creature whose moral nature was the warped,
stunted tree his life had made it; a poor devil half destroyed by
drink and by his wound. The old butler took a more single-minded

319

and old-fashioned line. 'Ketch 'old of 'im!' he thought. 'With these low fellers there's nothin' else to be done. Ketch 'old of 'im until he squeals.'

Nodding his ancient head, he said:

'Here's an orficer. I shan't speak for yer; you deserves all you'll get, and more.'

Later, dressed in an old Newmarket coat, given him by some client, and walking towards the police-station alongside Mrs Hughs, he was particularly silent, presenting a front of some austerity, as became a man mixed up in a low class of incident like this. And the seamstress, very thin and scared, with her wounded wrist slung in a muffler of her husband's, and carrying the baby on her other arm, because the morning's incident had upset the little thing, slipped along beside him, glancing now and then into his face.

Only once did he speak, and to himself:

'I don't know what they'll say to me down at the orfice, when I go again—missin' my day like this! Oh dear, what a misfortune! What put it into him to go on like that?'

At this, which was far from being intended as encouragement, the waters of speech broke up and flowed from Mrs Hughs. She had only told Hughs how that young girl had gone, and left a week's rent, with a bit of writing to say she wasn't coming back; it wasn't *her* fault that she was gone—that ought never to have come there at all, a creature that knew no better than to come between husband and wife. She couldn't tell no more than he could where that young girl had gone!

The tears, stealing forth, chased each other down the seamstress's thin cheeks. Her face had now but little likeness to the face with which she had stood confronting Hughs when she informed him of the little model's flight. None of the triumph which had leaped out of her bruised heart, none of the strident malice with which her voice, whether she would or no, strove to avenge her wounded sense of property; none of that unconscious abnegation, so very near to heroism, with which she had rushed and caught up her baby from beneath the bayonet, when, goaded by her malice and triumph, Hughs had rushed to seize that weapon. None of all that, but, instead, a pitiable terror of the ordeal before her—a pitiful, mute, quivering distress, that this man, against whom, two hours before, she had felt such a store of bitter rancour, whose almost murderous assault she had so narrowly escaped, should now be in this plight.

The sight of her emotion penetrated through his spectacles to something lying deep in the old butler.

'Don't you take on,' he said; 'I'll stand by yer. He shan't treat yer with impuniness.'

To his uncomplicated nature the affair was still one of tit for tat. Mrs Hughs became mute again. Her torn heart yearned to cancel the penalty that would fall on all of them, to deliver Hughs from the common enemy—the Law; but a queer feeling of pride and bewilderment, and a knowledge, that, to demand an eye for an eye was expected of all self-respecting persons, kept her silent.

Thus, then, they reached the great consoler, the grey resolver of all human tangles, haven of men and angels, the police court. It was situated in a back street. Like trails of ooze, when the tide, neither ebb nor flow, is leaving and making for some estuary, trails of human beings were moving to and from it. The faces of these shuffling 'shadows' wore a look as though masked with some hard but threadbare stuff—the look of those whom Life has squeezed into a last resort. Within the porches lay a stagnant marsh of suppliants, through whose centre trickled to and fro that stream of ooze. An old policeman, too, like some grey lighthouse, marked the entrance to the port of refuge. Close to that lighthouse the old butler edged his way. The love of regularity, and of an established order of affairs, born in him and fostered by a life passed in the service of the 'Honorable Bateson' and the other gentry, made him cling instinctively to the only person in this crowd whom he could tell for certain to be on the side of law and order. Something in his oblong face and lank, scanty hair parted precisely in the middle, something in that high collar supporting his lean gills, not subservient exactly, but as it were suggesting that he was in league against all this low-class of fellow, made the policeman say to him :

'What's your business, daddy?'

'Oh!' the old butler answered. 'This poor woman. I'm a witness to her battery.'

The policeman cast his not unkindly look over the figure of the seamstress. 'You stand here,' he said; 'I'll pass you in directly.'

And soon by his offices the two were passed into the port of refuge.

They sat down side by side on the edge of a long, hard, wooden bench; Creed fixing his eyes, whose colour had run into a brownish rim round their centres, on the magistrate, as in old days sun-worshippers would sit blinking devoutly at the sun; and Mrs Hughs fixing her eyes on her lap, while tears of agony trickled down her face. On her unwounded arm the baby slept. In front of them, and unregarded, filed one by one those shadows who had drunk the day

321

before too deeply of the waters of forgetfulness. To-day, instead, they were to drink the water of remembrance, poured out for them with no uncertain hand. And somewhere very far away, it may have been that Justice sat with her ironic smile watching men judge their shadows. She had watched them so long about that business. With her elementary idea that hares and tortoises should not be made to start from the same mark, she had a little given up expecting to be asked to come and lend a hand; they had gone so far beyond her. Perhaps she knew, too, that men no longer punished, but now only reformed, their erring brothers, and this made her heart as light as the hearts of those who had been in the prisons where they were no longer punished.

The old butler, however, was not thinking of her; he had thoughts of a simpler order in his mind. He was reflecting that he had once valeted the nephew of the late Lord Justice Hawthorn, and in the midst of this low-class business the reminiscence brought him refreshment. Over and over to himself he conned these words: 'I interpylated in between them, and I says, "Ye ought to be ashamed of yourself; call yourself an Englishman, I says, attackin' of old men and women with cold steel, I says!"' And suddenly he saw that Hughs was in the dock.

The dark man stood with his hands pressed to his sides, as though at attention on parade. A pale profile, broken by a line of black moustache, was all 'Westminister' could see of that impassive face, whose eyes, fixed on the magistrate, alone betrayed the fires within. The violent trembling of the seamstress roused in Joshua Creed a certain irritation, and seeing the baby open his black eyes, he nudged her, whispering: 'Ye've woke the baby!'

Responding to words, which alone perhaps could have moved her at such a moment, Mrs Hughs rocked this dumb spectator of the drama. Again the old butler nudged her.

'They want yer in the box,' he said.

Mrs Hughs rose, and took her place.

He who wished to read the hearts of this husband and wife who stood at right angles, to have their wounds healed by Law, would have needed to have watched the hundred thousand hours of their wedded life, known and heard the million thoughts and words which had passed in the dim spaces of their world, to have been cognisant of the million reasons why they neither of them felt that they could have done other than they had done. Reading their hearts by the light of knowledge such as this, he would not have been surprised that, brought into this place of remedy, they seemed to enter into a sudden league. A look passed between them. It was not friendly, it had no appeal; but it sufficed. There seemed to be expressed in it the knowledge bred by immemorial experience and immemorial time: This Law before which we stand was not made by us! As dogs, when they hear the crack of a far whip, will shrink, and in their whole bearing show wary quietude, so Hughs and Mrs Hughs, confronted by the questionings of Law, made only such answers as could be dragged from them. In a voice hardly above a whisper Mrs Hughs told her tale. They had fallen out. What about? She did not know. Had he attacked her? He had had it in his hand. What then? She had slipped, and hurt her wrist against the point. At this statement Hughs turned his eyes on her, and seemed to say: 'You drove me to it; I've got to suffer, for all your trying to get me out of what I've done. I gave you one, and I don't want your help. But I'm glad you stick to me against this —— Law!' Then, lowering his eyes, he stood motionless during her breathless little outburst. He was her husband; she had borne him five; he had been wounded in the war. She had never wanted him brought here.

No mention of the little model. . . .

The old butler dwelt on this reticence of Mrs Hughs' when, two hours afterwards, in pursuance of his instinctive reliance on the gentry, he called on Hilary.

The latter, surrounded by books and papers—for, since his dismissal of the girl, he had worked with great activity—was partaking of lunch, served to him in his study on a tray.

'There's an old gentleman to see you, sir; he says you know him; his name is Creed.'

'Show him in,' said Hilary.

Appearing suddenly from behind the servant in the doorway, the old butler came in at a stealthy amble; he looked round, and, seeing a chair, placed his hat beneath it, then advanced, with nose and spectacles upturned, to Hilary. Catching sight of the tray, he stopped, checked in an evident desire to communicate his soul.

'Oh dear,' he said, 'I'm intrudin' on your luncheon. I can wait; I'll go and sit in the passage.'

Hilary, however, shook his hand, faded now to skin and bone, and motioned him to a chair.

He sat down on the edge of it, and again said:

'I'm intrudin' on yer.'

'Not at all. Is there anything I can do?'

Creed took off his spectacles, wiped them to help himself to see more clearly what he had to say, and put them on again.

'It's a-concerning of these domestic matters,' he said. 'I come up to tell yer, knowing as you're interested in this family.'

'Well,' said Hilary. 'What has happened?'

'It's along of the young girl's having left them, as you may know.'

'Ah!'

'It's brought things to a crisax,' explained Creed.

'Indeed, how's that?'

The old butler related the facts of the assault. 'I took 'is bayonet away from him,' he ended; 'he didn't frighten *me*.'

'Is he out of his mind?' asked Hilary.

'I've no conscience of it,' replied Creed. 'His wife, she's gone the wrong way to work with him, in my opinion, but that's particular to women. She's a-goaded of him respecting a certain party. I don't say but what that young girl's no better than what she ought to be; look at her profession, and her a country girl, too! She must be what she oughtn't to. But he ain't the sort o' man you can treat like that. You can't get thorns from figs; you can't expect it from the lower orders. They only give him a month, considerin' of him bein' wounded in the war. It'd been more if they'd a-known he was a-hankerin' after that young girl—a married man like him; don't ye think so, sir?'

Hilary's face had assumed its retired expression. 'I cannot go into that with you,' it seemed to say.

Quick to see the change, Creed rose. 'But I'm intrudin' on your dinner,' he said—'your luncheon, I should say. The woman goes on irritatin' of him, but he must expect of that, she bein' his wife. But what a misfortune! He'll be back again in no time, and what'll happen then? It won't improve him, shut up in one of them low prisons!' Then, raising his old face to Hilary: 'Oh dear! It's like a-walkin' on a black night, when ye can't see your 'and before yer.'

Hilary was unable to find a suitable answer to this simile.

The impression made on him by the old butler's recital was queerly twofold; his more fastidious side felt distinct relief that he had severed connection with an episode capable of developments so sordid and conspicuous. But all the side of him—and Hilary was a complicated product—which felt compassion for the helpless, his suppressed chivalry, in fact, had also received its fillip. The old butler's references to the girl showed clearly how the hands of all men and women were against her. She was that pariah, a young girl without property or friends, spiritually soft, physically alluring.

To recompense 'Westminister' for the loss of his day's work, to make a dubious statement that nights were never so black as they appeared to be, was all that he could venture to do. Creed hesitated in the doorway.

'Oh dear,' he said, 'there's a-one thing that the woman was a-saying that I've forgot to tell you. It's a-concernin' of what this 'ere man was boastin' in his rage. "Let them," he says, "as is responsive for the movin' of her look out," he says; "I ain't done with them!" That's conspiracy, I should think!'

Smiling away this diagnosis of Hughs' words, Hilary shook the old man's withered hand, and closed the door. Sitting down again at his writing-table, he buried himself almost angrily in his work. But the queer, half-pleasurable, fevered feeling, which had been his, since the night he walked down Piccadilly, and met the image of the little model, was unfavourable to the austere process of his thoughts.

Chapter 25

MR STONE IN WAITING

THAT same afternoon, while Mr Stone was writing, he heard a voice saying:

'Dad, stop writing just a minute, and talk to me.'

Recognition came into his eyes. It was his younger daughter.

'My dear,' he said, 'are you unwell?'

Keeping his hand, fragile and veined and chill, under her own warm grasp, Bianca answered: 'Lonely.'

Mr Stone looked straight before him.

'Loneliness,' he said, 'is man's chief fault;' and seeing his pen lying on the desk, he tried to lift his hand. Bianca held it down. At that hot clasp something seemed to stir in Mr Stone. His cheeks grew pink.

'Kiss me, Dad.'

Mr Stone hesitated. Then his lips resolutely touched her eye. 'It is wet,' he said. He seemed for a moment struggling to grasp the meaning of moisture in connection with the human eye. Soon his face again became serene. 'The heart,' he said, 'is a dark well; its depth unknown. I have lived eighty years. I am still drawing water.'

'Draw a little for me, Dad.'

This time Mr Stone looked at his daughter anxiously, and suddenly spoke, as if afraid that if he waited he might forget.

'You are unhappy!'

Bianca put her face down to his tweed sleeve. 'How nice your coat smells!' she murmured.

'You are unhappy,' repeated Mr Stone.

Bianca dropped his hand, and moved away.

Mr Stone followed her. 'Why?' he said. Then, grasping his brow, he added: 'If it would do you any good, my dear, to hear a page or two, I could read to you.'

Bianca shook her head.

'No; talk to me!'

Mr Stone answered simply: 'I have forgotten.'

'You talk to that little girl,' murmured Bianca.

Mr Stone seemed to lose himself in reverie.

'If that is true,' he said, following out his thoughts, 'it must be due to the sex instinct not yet quite extinct. It is stated that the blackcock will dance before his females to a great age, though I have never seen it.'

'If you dance before *her*,' said Bianca, with her face averted, 'can't you even talk to me?'

'I do not dance, my dear,' said Mr Stone; 'I will do my best to talk to you.'

There was a silence, and he began to pace the room. Bianca, by the empty fireplace, watched a shower of rain driving past the open window.

'This is the time of year,' said Mr Stone suddenly, 'when lambs leap off the ground with all four legs at a time.' He paused as though for an answer; then, out of the silence, his voice rose again—it sounded different: 'There is nothing in Nature more symptomatic of that principle which should underlie all life. Live in the future; regret nothing; leap! A lamb that has left earth with all four legs at once is the symbol of true life. That she must come down again is but an inevitable accident. "In those days men were living on their pasts. They leaped with one, or, at the most, two legs at a time; they never left the ground, or in leaving, they wished to know the reason why. It was this paralysis" '—Mr Stone did not pause, but, finding himself close beside his desk, took up his pen—' "it was this paralysis of the leaping nerve which undermined their progress. Instead of millions of leaping lambs, ignorant of why they leaped, they were a flock of sheep lifting up one leg and asking whether it was or was not worth their while to lift another." '

The words were followed by a silence, broken only by the scratching of the quill with which Mr Stone was writing.

Having finished, he again began to pace the room, and coming suddenly on his daughter, stopped short. Touching her shoulder timidly, he said: 'I was talking to you, I think, my dear; where were we?'

Bianca rubbed her cheek against his hand.

'In the air, I think.'

'Yes, yes,' said Mr Stone, 'I remember. You must not let me wander from the point again.'

'No, dear.'

'Lambs,' said Mr Stone, 'remind me at times of that young girl who comes to copy for me. I make her skip to promote her circulation before tea. I myself do this exercise.' Leaning against the wall, with his feet twelve inches from it, he rose slowly on his toes. 'Do you know that exercise? It is excellent for the calves of the legs, and for the lumbar regions.' So saying, Mr Stone left the wall, and began again to pace the room; the whitewash had also left the wall, and clung in a large square patch on his shaggy coat.

'I have seen sheep in Spring,' he said, 'actually imitate their lambs in rising from the ground with all four legs at once.' He stood still. A thought had evidently struck him.

'If Life is not all Spring, it is of no value whatsoever; better to die, and to begin again. Life is a tree putting on a new green gown; it is a young moon rising—no, that is not so, we do not see the young moon rising—it is a young moon setting, never younger than when we are about to die——'

Bianca cried out sharply: 'Don't, Father! Don't talk like that; it's so untrue! Life is all autumn, it seems to me!'

Mr Stone's eyes grew very blue.

'That is a foul heresy,' he stammered; 'I cannot listen to it. Life is the cuckoo's song; it is a hill-side bursting into leaf; it is the wind; I feel it in me every day!'

He was trembling like a leaf in the wind he spoke of, and Bianca moved hastily towards him, holding out her arms. Suddenly his lips began to move; she heard him mutter: 'I have lost force; I will boil some milk. I must be ready when she comes.' And at those words her heart felt like a lump of ice.

Always that girl! And without again attracting his attention she went away. As she passed out through the garden she saw him at the window holding a cup of milk, from which the steam was rising.

Chapter 26

THIRD PILGRIMAGE TO HOUND STREET

LIKE water, human character will find its level; and Nature, with her way of fitting men to their environment, had made young Martin Stone what Stephen called a 'Sanitist'. There had been nothing else for her to do with him.

This young man had come into the social scheme at a moment when the conception of existence as a present life corrected by a life to come, was tottering; and the conception of the world as an upper-class preserve somewhat seriously disturbed.

Losing his father and mother at an early age, and brought up till he was fourteen by Mr Stone, he had formed the habit of thinking for himself. This had rendered him unpopular, and added force to the essential single-heartedness transmitted to him through his grandfather. A particular aversion to the sights and scents of suffering, which had caused him as a child to object to killing flies, and to watching rabbits caught in traps, had been regulated by his training as a doctor. His fleshly horror of pain and ugliness was now disciplined, his spiritual dislike of them forced into a philosophy. The peculiar chaos surrounding all young men who live in large towns and think at all, had made him gradually reject all abstract speculation; but a certain fire of aspiration coming, we may suppose, through Mr Stone, had nevertheless impelled him to embrace something with all his might. He had therefore embraced health. And living, as he did, in the Euston Road, to be in touch with things, he had every need of the health which he embraced.

Late in the afternoon of the day when Hughs had committed his assault, having three hours of respite from his hospital, Martin dipped his face and head into cold water, rubbed them with a corrugated towel, put on a hard bowler hat, took a thick stick in his hand, and went by Underground to Kensington.

With his usual cool, high-handed air he entered his aunt's house, and asked for Thyme. Faithful to his definite, if somewhat crude theory, that Stephen and Cecilia and all their sort were amateurs, he never inquired for them, though not unfrequently he would, while waiting, stroll into Cecilia's drawing-room, and let his sarcastic glance sweep over the pretty things she had collected, or, lounging in some luxurious chair, cross his long legs, and fix his eyes on the ceiling.

Thyme soon came down. She wore a blouse of some blue stuff bought by Cecilia for the relief of people in the Balkan States, a skirt of purplish tweed woven by Irish gentlewomen in distress, and held in her hand an open envelope addressed in Cecilia's writing to Mrs Tallents Smallpeace.

'Hallo!' she said.

Martin answered by a look that took her in from head to foot.

'Get on a hat! I haven't got much time. That blue thing's new.'

'It's pure flax. Mother bought it.'

'It's rather decent. Hurry up!'

Thyme raised her chin; that lazy movement showed her round, creamy neck in all its beauty.

'I feel rather slack,' she said; 'besides, I must get back to dinner, Martin.'

'Dinner!'

Thyme turned quickly to the door. 'Oh, well, I'll come,' and ran upstairs.

When they had purchased a postal order for ten shillings, placed it in the envelope addressed to Mrs Tallents Smallpeace, and passed the hundred doors of Messrs Rose and Thorn, Martin said: 'I'm going to see what that precious amateur has done about the baby. If he hasn't moved the girl, I expect to find things in a pretty mess.'

Thyme's face changed at once.

'Just remember,' she said, 'that I don't want to go there. I don't see the good, when there's such a tremendous lot waiting to be done.'

'Every other case, except the one in hand!'

'It's not *my* case. You're so disgustingly unfair, Martin. I don't like those people.'

'Oh, you amateur!'

Thyme flushed crimson. 'Look here!' she said, speaking with dignity, 'I don't care what you call *me*, but I won't have you call Uncle Hilary an amateur.'

'What is he, then?'

'I like him.'

'That's conclusive.'

'Yes, it is.'

Martin did not reply, looking sideways at Thyme with his queer, protective smile. They were passing through a street superior to Hound Street in its pretensions to be called a slum.

'Look here!' he said suddenly; 'a man like Hilary's interest in all this sort of thing is simply sentimental. It's on his nerves. He takes philanthropy just as he'd take sulphonal for sleeplessness.'

Thyme looked shrewdly up at him.

'Well,' she said, 'it's just as much on your nerves. You see it from the point of view of health; he sees it from the point of view of sentiment, that's all.'

'Oh! you think so?'

'You just treat all these people as if they were in hospital.'

The young man's nostrils quivered. 'Well, and how should they be treated?'

'How would you like to be looked at as a "case"?' muttered Thyme.

Martin moved his hand in a slow half-circle.

'These houses and these people,' he said, 'are in the way—in the way of you and me, and everyone.'

Thyme's eyes followed that slow, sweeping movement of her cousin's hand. It seemed to fascinate her.

'Yes, of course; I know,' she murmured. 'Something must be done!'

And she reared her head up, looking from side to side, as if to show him that she, too, could sweep away things. Very straight, and solid, fair, and fresh, she looked just then.

Thus, in the hypnotic silence of high thought the two young 'Sanitists' arrived in Hound Street.

In the doorway of No. 1 the son of the lame woman, Mrs Budgen —the thin, white youth as tall as Martin, but not so broad—stood, smoking a dubious-looking cigarette. He turned his lack-lustre, jeering gaze on the visitors.

'Who d'you want?' he said. 'If it's the girl, she's gone away, and left no address.'

'I want Mrs Hughs,' said Martin.

The young man coughed. 'Right-o! You'll find *her*; but for *him*, apply Wormwood Scrubs.'

'Prison! What for?'

'Stickin' her though the wrist with his bayonet;' and the young man let a long, luxurious fume of smoke trickle through his nose.

'How horrible!' said Thyme.

Martin regarded the young man, unmoved. 'That stuff you're smoking's rank,' he said. 'Have some of mine; I'll show you how to make them. It'll save you one and three per pound of baccy, and won't rot your lungs.'

Taking out his pouch, he rolled a cigarette. The white young man bent his dull wink on Thyme, who, wrinkling her nose, was pretending to be far away.

Mounting the narrow stairs that smelt of walls and washing and red herrings, Thyme spoke: 'Now, you see, it wasn't so simple as you thought. I don't want to go up; I don't want to see her. I shall wait for you here.' She took her stand in the open doorway of the little model's empty room. Martin ascended to the second floor.

There, in the front room, Mrs Hughs was seen standing with the baby in her arms beside the bed. She had a frightened and uncertain air. After examining her wrist, and pronouncing it a scratch, Martin looked long at the baby. The little creature's toes were stiffened against its mother's waist, its eyes closed, its tiny fingers crisped against her breast. While Mrs Hughs poured forth her tale, Martin stood with his eyes still fixed on the baby. It could not be gathered from his face what he was thinking, but now and then he moved his jaw, as though he were suffering from toothache. In truth, by the look of Mrs Hughs and her baby, his recipe did not seem to have achieved conspicuous success. He turned away at last from the trembling, nerveless figure of the seamstress, and went to the window. Two pale hyacinth plants stood on the inner edge; their perfume penetrated through the other savours of the room—and very strange they looked, those twin, starved children of the light and air.

'These are new,' he said.

'Yes, sir,' murmured Mrs Hughs. 'I brought them upstairs. I didn't like to see the poor things left to die.'

From the bitter accent of these words Martin understood that they had been the little model's.

'Put them outside,' he said; 'they'll never live in here. They want watering, too. Where are your saucers?'

Mrs Hughs laid the baby down, and, going to the cupboard where all the household gods were kept, brought out two old, dirty saucers. Martin raised the plants, and as he held them, from one close, yellow petal there rose up a tiny caterpillar. It reared a green, transparent body, feeling its way to a new resting-place. The little writhing shape seemed, like the wonder and mystery of life, to mock the young doctor, who watched it with eyebrows raised, having no hand at liberty to remove it from the plant.

'*She* came from the country. There's plenty of men there for her!'

Martin put the plants down, and turned round to the seamstress.

'Look here!' he said, 'it's no good crying over spilt milk. What you've got to do is to set to and get some work.'

'Yes, sir.'

'Don't say it in that sort of way,' said Martin, 'you must rise to the occasion.'

'Yes, sir.'

'You want a tonic. Take this half-crown, and get in a dozen pints of stout, and drink one every day.'

And again Mrs Hughs said, 'Yes, sir.'

'And about that baby.'

Motionless, where it had been placed against the foot-rail of the bed, the baby sat with its black eyes closed. The small grey face was curled down on the bundle of its garments.

'It's a silent gentleman,' Martin muttered.

'It never was a one to cry,' said Mrs Hughs.

'That's lucky, anyway. When did you feed it last?'

Mrs Hughs did not reply at first. 'About half-past six last evening, sir.'

'What?'

'It slept all night; but to-day, of course, I've been all torn to pieces; my milk's gone. I've tried it with the bottle, but it wouldn't take it.'

Martin bent down to the baby's face, and put his finger on its chin; bending lower yet, he raised the eyelid of the tiny eye.

'It's dead,' he said.

At the word 'dead' Mrs Hughs, stooping behind him, snatched the baby to her throat. With its drooping head close to her face, she clutched and rocked it without sound. Full five minutes this desperate mute struggle with eternal silence lasted—the feeling, and warming, and breathing on the little limbs. Then, sitting down, bent almost double over her baby, she moaned. That single sound was followed by utter silence. The tread of footsteps on the creaking stairs broke it. Martin, rising from his crouching posture by the bed, went towards the door.

His grandfather was standing there, with Thyme behind him.

'She has left her room,' said Mr Stone. 'Where has she gone?'

Martin, understanding that he meant the little model, put his finger to his lips, and, pointing to Mrs Hughs, whispered:

'This woman's baby has just died.'

Mr Stone's face underwent the queer discoloration that marked the sudden summoning of his far thoughts. He stepped past Martin, and went up to Mrs Hughs.

He stood there a long time gazing at the baby, and at the dark head bending over it with such despair. At last he spoke:

'Poor woman! He is at peace.'

Mrs Hughs looked up, and, seeing that old face, with its hollows and thin silver hair, she spoke:

'He's dead, sir.'

Mr Stone put out his veined and fragile hand, and touched the baby's toes. 'He is flying; he is everywhere; he is close to the sun—Little brother!' And turning on his heel, he went out.

Thyme followed him as he walked on tiptoe down stairs that seemed to creak the louder for his caution. Tears were rolling down her cheeks.

Martin sat on, with the mother and her baby, in the close, still room, where, like strange visiting spirits, came stealing whiffs of the perfume of hyacinths.

Chapter 27

STEPHEN'S PRIVATE LIFE

MR STONE and Thyme, in coming out, again passed the tall, white young man. He had thrown away the hand-made cigarette, finding that it had not enough saltpetre to make it draw, and was smoking one more suited to the action of his lungs. He directed towards them the same lack-lustre, jeering stare.

Unconscious, seemingly, of where he went, Mr Stone walked with his eyes fixed on space. His head jerked now and then, as a dried flower will shiver in a draught.

Scared at these movements, Thyme took his arm. The touch of that soft young arm squeezing his own brought speech back to Mr Stone.

'In those places . . .' he said, 'in those streets! . . . I shall not see the flowering of the aloe—I shall not see the living peace! "As with dogs, each couched over his proper bone, so men were living then!"' He sank back into silence.

Thyme, watching him askance, pressed still closer to his side, as though to try and warm him back to every day.

'Oh!' went her fluttered thoughts. 'I do wish grandfather would say something one could understand. I wish he would lose that dreadful stare.'

Mr Stone spoke in answer to his grand-daughter's thoughts.

'I have seen a vision of fraternity. A barren hillside in the sun, and on it a man of stone talking to the wind. I have heard an owl hooting in the daytime; a cuckoo singing in the night.'

'Grandfather, grandfather!'

333

To that appeal Mr Stone responded: 'Yes, what is it?'

But Thyme, thus challenged, knew not what to say, having spoken out of terror.

'If the poor baby had lived,' she stammered out, 'it would have grown up. . . . It's all for the best, isn't it?'

'Everything is for the best,' said Mr Stone. '"In those days men, possessed by thoughts of individual life, made moan at death, careless of the great truth that the world was one unending song."'

Thyme thought: 'I have never seen him as bad as this!' She drew him on more quickly. With deep relief she saw her father, latchkey in hand, turning into the Old Square.

Stephen, who was still walking with his springy step, though he had come on foot the whole way from the Temple, hailed them with his hat. It was tall and black, and very shiny, neither quite oval nor positively round, and had a little curly brim. In this and his black coat, cut so as to show the front of him and cover the behind, he looked his best. The costume suited his long, rather narrow face, corrugated by two short parallel lines slanting downwards from his eyes and nostrils on either cheek; suited his neat, thin figure and the close-lipped corners of his mouth. His permanent appointment in the world of Law had ousted from his life (together with all uncertainty of income) the need for putting on a wig and taking his moustache off; but he still preferred to go clean-shaved.

'Where have you two sprung from?' he inquired, admitting them into the hall.

Mr Stone gave him no answer, but passed into the drawing-room, and sat down on the verge of the first chair he came across, leaning forward with his hands between his knees.

Stephen, after one dry glance at him, turned to his daughter.

'My child,' he said softly, 'what have you brought the old boy here for? If there happens to be anything of the high mammalian order for dinner, your mother will have a fit.'

Thyme answered: 'Don't chaff, father!'

Stephen, who was very fond of her, saw that for some reason she was not herself. He examined her with unwonted gravity. Thyme turned away from him. He heard, to his alarm, a little gulping sound.

'My dear!' he said.

Conscious of her sentimental weakness, Thyme made a violent effort.

'I've seen a baby dead,' she cried in a quick, hard voice; and, without another word, she ran upstairs.

In Stephen there was a horror of emotion that amounted almost to disease. It would have been difficult to say when he had last shown emotion; perhaps not since Thyme was born, and even then not to anyone except himself, having first locked the door, and then walked up and down, with his teeth almost meeting in the mouthpiece of his favourite pipe. He was unaccustomed, too, to witness this weakness on the part of other people. His looks and speech unconsciously discouraged it, so that if Cecilia had been at all that way inclined, she must long ago have been healed. Fortunately, she never had been, having too much distrust of her own feelings to give way to them completely. And Thyme, that healthy product of them both, at once younger for her age, and older, than they had ever been, with her incapacity for nonsense, her love for open air and facts—that fresh, rising plant, so elastic and so sane— she had never given them a single moment of uneasiness.

Stephen, close to his hat-rack, felt soreness in his heart. Such blows as Fortune had dealt, and meant to deal him, he had borne, and he could bear, so long as there was nothing in his own manner, or in that of others, to show him they *were* blows.

Hurriedly depositing his hat, he ran to Cecilia. He still preserved the habit of knocking on her door before he entered, though she had never, so far, answered, 'Don't come in!' because she knew his knock. The custom gave, in fact, the measure of his idealism. What he feared, or what he thought he feared, after nineteen years of un-checked entrance, could never have been ascertained; but there it was, that flower of something formal and precise, of something reticent, within his soul.

This time, for once, he did not knock, and found Cecilia hooking up her tea-gown and looking very sweet. She glanced at him with mild surprise.

'What's this, Cis,' he said, 'about a baby dead? Thyme's quite upset about it; and your dad's in the drawing-room!'

With the quick instinct that was woven into all her gentle tread-ing, Cecilia's thoughts flew—she could not have told why—first to the little model, then to Mrs Hughs.

'Dead?' she said. 'Oh, poor woman!'

'What woman?' Stephen asked.

'It must be Mrs Hughs.'

The thought passed darkly through Stephen's mind: 'Those people again! What now?' He did not express it, being neither brutal nor lacking in good taste.

A short silence followed, then Cecilia said suddenly: 'Did you say that father was in the drawing-room? There's fillet of beef, Stephen!'

Stephen turned away. 'Go and see Thyme!' he said.

Outside Thyme's door Cecilia paused, and, hearing no sound, tapped gently. Her knock not being answered, she slipped in. On the bed of that white room, with her face pressed into the pillow, her little daughter lay. Cecilia stood aghast. Thyme's whole body was quivering with suppressed sobs.

'My *darling*!' said Cecilia, 'what is it?'

Thymes answer was inarticulate.

Cecilia sat down on the bed and waited, drawing her fingers through the girl's hair, which had fallen loose; and while she sat there she experienced all that sore, strange feeling—as of being skinned—which comes to one who watches the emotion of someone near and dear without knowing the exact cause.

'This is dreadful,' she thought. 'What am I to do?'

To see one's child cry was bad enough, but to see her cry when that child's whole creed of honour and conduct for years past had precluded this relief as unfeminine, was worse than disconcerting.

Thyme raised herself on her elbow, turning her face carefully away.

'I don't know what's the matter with me,' she said, choking. 'It's —it's purely physical.'

'Yes, darling,' murmured Cecilia; 'I know.'

'Oh, Mother!' said Thyme suddenly, 'it looked so tiny.'

'Yes, yes, my sweet.'

Thyme faced round; there was a sort of passion in her darkened eyes, rimmed pink with grief, and in all her flushed, wet face.

'Why should it have been choked out like that? It's—it's so brutal!'

Cecilia slid an arm round her.

'I'm so distressed you saw it, dear,' she said.

'And grandfather *was* so——' A long sobbing quiver choked her utterance.

'Yes, yes,' said Cecilia; 'I'm sure he was.'

Clasping her hands together in her lap, Thyme muttered: 'He called him "Little Brother".'

A tear trickled down Cecilia's cheek, and dropped on her daughter's wrist. Feeling that it was not her own tear, Thyme started up.

'It's weak and ridiculous,' she said. 'I won't! Oh, go away,

Mother, please. I'm only making you feel bad, too. You'd better go and see to grandfather.'

Cecilia saw that she would cry no more, and since it was the sight of tears which had so disturbed her, she gave the girl a little hesitating stroke, and went away. Outside she thought: 'How dreadfully unlucky and pathetic; and there's father in the drawing-room!' Then she hurried down to Mr Stone.

He was sitting where he had first placed himself, motionless. It struck her suddenly how frail and white he looked. In the shadowy light of her drawing-room, he was almost like a spirit sitting there in his grey tweed—silvery from head to foot. Her conscience smote her. It is written of the very old that they shall pass, by virtue of their long travel, out of the country of the understanding of the young, till the natural affections are blurred by creeping mists such as steal across the moors when the sun is going down. Cecilia's heart ached with a little ache for all the times she had thought: 'If father were only not quite so——'; for all the times she had shunned asking him to come to them, because he was so——; for all the silences she and Stephen had maintained after he had spoken; for all the little smiles she had smiled. She longed to go and kiss his brow, and make him feel that she was aching. But she did not dare; he seemed so far away; it would be ridiculous.

Coming down the room, and putting her slim foot on the fender with a noise, so that if possible he might both see and hear her, she turned her anxious face towards him, and said: 'Father!'

Mr Stone looked up, and seeing somebody who seemed to be his elder daughter, answered: 'Yes, my dear?'

'Are you sure you're feeling quite the thing? Thyme said she thought seeing that poor baby had upset you.'

Mr Stone felt his body with his hand.

'I am not conscious of any pain,' he said.

'Then you'll stay to dinner, dear, won't you?'

Mr Stone's brow contracted as though he were trying to recall his past.

'I have had no tea,' he said. Then, with a sudden, anxious look at his daughter: 'The little girl has not come to me. I miss her. Where is she?'

The ache within Cecilia became more poignant.

'It is now two days,' said Mr Stone, 'and she has left her room in that house—in that street.'

Cecilia, at her wits' end, answered: 'Do you really miss her, Father?'

'Yes,' said Mr Stone. 'She is like——' His eyes wandered round the room as though seeking something that would help him to express himself. They fixed themselves on the far wall. Cecilia, following their gaze, saw a little solitary patch of sunlight dancing and trembling there. It had escaped the screen of trees and houses, and, creeping through some chink, had quivered in. 'She is like that,' said Mr Stone, pointing with his finger. 'It is gone!' His finger dropped; he uttered a deep sigh.

'How dreadful this is!' Cecilia thought. 'I never expected him to feel it, and yet I can do nothing!' Hastily she asked: 'Would it do if you had Thyme to copy for you? I'm sure she'd love to come.'

'She is my grand-daughter,' Mr Stone said simply. 'It would not be the same.'

Cecilia could think of nothing now to say but: 'Would you like to wash your hands, dear?'

'Yes,' said Mr Stone.

'Then will you go up to Stephen's dressing-room for hot water, or will you wash them in the lavatory?'

'In the lavatory,' said Mr Stone. 'I shall be freer there.'

When he had gone Cecilia thought: 'Oh dear, how shall I get through the evening? Poor darling, he is so single-minded!'

At the sounding of the dinner-gong they all assembled—Thyme from her bedroom with cheeks and eyes still pink, Stephen with veiled inquiry in his glance, Mr Stone from freedom in the lavatory —and sat down, screened, but so very little, from each other by sprays of white lilac. Looking round her table, Cecilia felt rather like one watching a dew-belled cobweb, most delicate of all things in the world, menaced by the tongue of a browsing cow.

Both soup and fish had been achieved, however, before a word was spoken. It was Stephen who, after taking a mouthful of dry sherry, broke the silence.

'How are you getting on with your book, sir?' he said.

Cecilia heard that question with something like dismay. It was so bald; for, however inconvenient Mr Stone's absorption in his manuscript might be, her delicacy told her how precious beyond life itself that book was to him. To her relief, however, her father was eating spinach.

'You must be getting near the end, I should think,' proceeded Stephen.

Cecilia spoke hastily: 'Isn't this white lilac lovely, Dad?'

338

Mr Stone looked up.

'It is not white; it is really pink. The test is simple.' He paused with his eyes fixed on the lilac.

'Ah!' thought Cecilia, 'now, if I can only keep him on natural science—he used to be so interesting.'

'All flowers are one!' said Mr Stone. His voice had changed.

'Oh!' thought Cecilia, 'he is gone!'

'They have but a single soul. In those days men divided, and sub-divided them, oblivious of the one pale spirit that underlay those seemingly separate forms.'

Cecilia's glance passed swiftly from the man-servant to Stephen. She saw one of her husband's eyes rise visibly. Stephen did so hate one thing to be confounded with another.

'Oh, come sir,' she heard him say; 'you don't surely tell us that dandelions and roses have the same pale spirit!'

Mr Stone looked at him wistfully.

'Did I say that?' he said. 'I had no wish to be dogmatic.'

'Not at all, sir, not at all,' murmured Stephen.

Thyme, leaning over to her mother, whispered: 'Oh, Mother, don't let grandfather be queer; I can't bear it to-night!'

Cecilia, at her wits' end, said hurriedly:

'Dad, will you tell us what sort of character you think that little girl who comes to you has?'

Mr Stone paused in the act of drinking water; his attention had evidently been riveted; he did not, however, speak. And Cecilia, see-ing that the butler, out of the perversity which she found so con-spicuous in her servants, was about to hand him beef, made a desperate movement with her lips. 'No, Charles, not there, not there!'

The butler, tightening his lips, passed on. Mr Stone spoke:

'I had not considered that. She is rather of a Celtic than an Anglo-Saxon type; the cheek-bones are prominent; the jaw is not massive; the head is broad—if I can remember I will measure it; the eyes are of a peculiar blue, resembling chicory flowers; the mouth——' Mr Stone paused.

Cecilia thought: 'What a lucky find! Now perhaps he will go on all right!'

'I do not know,' Mr Stone resumed, speaking in a far-off voice, 'whether she would be virtuous.'

Cecilia heard Stephen drinking sherry; Thyme, too, was drinking something; she herself drank nothing, but; pink and quiet, for she was a well-bred woman, said:

339

'You have no new potatoes, dear. Charles, give Mr Stone some new potatoes.'

By the almost vindictive expression on Stephen's face she saw, however, that her failure had decided him to resume command of the situation. 'Talking of brotherhood, sir,' he said dryly, 'would you go so far as to say that a new potato is the brother of a bean?'

Mr Stone, on whose plate these two vegetables reposed, looked almost painfully confused.

'I do not perceive,' he stammered, 'any difference between them.'

'It's true,' said Stephen; 'the same pale spirit can be extracted from them both.'

Mr Stone looked up at him.

'You laugh at me,' he said. 'I cannot help it; but you must not laugh at life—that is blasphemy.'

Before the piercing wistfulness of that sudden gaze Stephen was abashed. Cecilia saw him bite his lower lip.

'We're talking too much,' he said; 'we really must let your father eat!' And the rest of the dinner was achieved in silence.

When Mr Stone, refusing to be accompanied, had taken his departure, and Thyme had gone to bed, Stephen withdrew to his study. This room, which had a different air from any other portion of the house, was sacred to his private life. Here, in specially designed compartments, he kept his golf clubs, pipes, and papers. Nothing was touched by anyone except himself, and twice a week by one peculiar housemaid. Here was no bust of Socrates, no books in deerskin bindings, but a bookcase filled with treatises on law, Blue Books, reviews, and the novels of Sir Walter Scott; two black oak cabinets stood side by side against the wall filled with small drawers. When these cabinets were opened and the drawers drawn forward there emerged a scent of metal polish. If the green-baize covers of the drawers were lifted, there were seen coins, carefully arranged with labels—as one may see plants growing in rows, each with its little name tied on. To these tidy rows of shining metal discs Stephen turned in moments when his spirit was fatigued. To add to them, touch them, read their names, gave him the sweet, secret feeling which comes to a man who rubs one hand against the other. Like a dram-drinker, Stephen drank—in little doses—of the feeling these coins gave him. They were his creative work, his history of the world. To them he gave that side of him which refused to find its full expression in summarising law, playing golf, or reading the reviews; that side of a man which aches, he knows not wherefore, to construct something ere he die. From Rameses to

George IV the coins lay within those drawers—links of the long unbroken chain of authority.

Putting on an old black velvet jacket laid out for him across a chair, and lighting the pipe that he could never bring himself to smoke in his formal dinner clothes, he went to the right-hand cabinet, and opened it. He stood with a smile, taking up coins one by one. In this particular drawer they were of the best Byzantine dynasty, very rare. He did not see that Cecilia had stolen in, and was silently regarding him. Her eyes seemed doubting at that moment whether or no she loved him who stood there touching that other mistress of his thoughts—that other mistress with whom he spent so many evening hours. The little green-baize cover fell. Cecilia said suddenly:

'Stephen, I feel as if I must tell father where that girl is!'

Stephen turned.

'My dear child,' he answered in his special voice, which, like champagne, seemed to have been dried by artifice, 'you don't want to reopen the whole thing?'

'But I can see he really is upset about it; he's looking so awfully white and thin.'

'He ought to give up that bathing in the Serpentine. At his age it's monstrous. And surely any other girl will do just as well?'

'He seems to set store by reading to her specially.'

Stephen shrugged his shoulders. It had happened to him on one occasion to be present when Mr Stone was declaiming some pages of his manuscript. He had never forgotten the discomfort of the experience. 'That crazy stuff,' as he had called it to Cecilia afterwards, had remained on his mind, heavy and damp, like a cold linseed poultice. His wife's father was a crank, and perhaps even a little more than a crank, a wee bit 'touched'—that *she* couldn't help, poor girl; but any allusion to his cranky produce gave Stephen pain. Nor had he forgotten his experience at dinner.

'He seems to have grown fond of her,' murmured Cecilia.

'But it's absurd at his time of life!'

'Perhaps that makes him feel it more; people do miss things when they are old!'

Stephen slid the drawer back into its socket. There was dry decision in that gesture.

'Look here! Let's exercise a little common sense; it's been sacrificed to sentiment all through this wretched business. One wants to be kind, of course; but one's got to draw the line.'

'Ah!' said Cecilia; 'where?'

'The thing,' went on Stephen, 'has been a mistake from first to last. It's all very well up to a certain point, but after that it becomes destructive of all comfort. It doesn't do to let these people come into personal contact with you. There are the proper channels for that sort of thing.'

Cecilia's eyes were lowered, as though she did not dare to let him see her thoughts.

'It seems so horrid,' she said; 'and father is not like other people.'

'He is not,' said Stephen dryly; 'we had a pretty good instance of that this evening. But Hilary and your sister are. There's something most distasteful to me, too, about Thyme's going about slumming. You see what she's been let in for this afternoon. The notion of that baby being killed through the man's treatment of his wife, and that, no doubt, arising from the girl's leaving them, is most repulsive!'

To these words Cecilia answered with a sound almost like a gasp. 'I hadn't thought of that. Then we're responsible; it was we who advised Hilary to make her change her lodging.'

Stephen stared; he regretted sincerely that his legal habit of mind had made him put the case so clearly.

'I can't imagine,' he said, almost violently, 'what possesses everybody! We—responsible! Good gracious! Because we gave Hilary some sound advice! What next?'

Cecilia turned to the empty hearth.

'Thyme has been telling me about that poor little thing. It seems so dreadful, and I can't get rid of the feeling that we're—we're all mixed up with it!'

'Mixed up with what?'

'I don't know; it's just a feeling like—like being haunted.'

Stephen took her quietly by the arm.

'My dear old girl,' he said, 'I'd no idea that you were run down like this. To-morrow's Thursday, and I can get away at three. We'll motor down to Richmond, and have a round or two!'

Cecilia quivered; for a moment it seemed that she was about to burst out crying. Stephen stroked her shoulder steadily. Cecilia must have felt his dread; she struggled loyally with her emotion.

'That will be very jolly,' she said at last.

Stephen drew a deep breath.

'And don't you worry, dear,' he said, 'about your dad; he'll have forgotten the whole thing in a day or two; he's far too wrapped up in his book. Now trot along to bed; I'll be up directly.'

Before going out Cecilia looked back at him. How wonderful was that look, which Stephen did not—perhaps intentionally—

see. Mocking, almost hating, and yet thanking him for having refused to let her be emotional and yield herself up for once to what she felt, showing him too how clearly she saw through his own masculine refusal to be made to feel, and how she half-admired it—all this was in that look, and more. Then she went out.

Stephen glanced quickly at the door, and, pursing up his lips, frowned. He threw the window open, and inhaled the night air.

'If I don't look out,' he thought, 'I shall be having her mixed up with this. I was an ass ever to have spoken to old Hilary. I ought to have ignored the matter altogether. It's a lesson not to meddle with people in those places. I hope to God she'll be herself tomorrow!'

Outside, under the soft black foliage of the Square, beneath the slim sickle of the moon, two cats were hunting after happiness; their savage cries of passion rang in the blossom-scented air like a cry of dark humanity in the jungle of dim streets. Stephen, with a shiver of disgust, for his nerves were on edge, shut the window with a slam.

Chapter 28

HILARY HEARS THE CUCKOO SING

IT was not left to Cecilia alone to remark how very white Mr Stone looked in these days.

The wild force which every year visits the world, driving with its soft violence snowy clouds and their dark shadows, breaking through all crusts and sheaths, covering the earth in a fierce embrace; the wild force which turns form to form, and with its million leapings, swift as the flight of swallows and the arrow-darts of the rain, hurries everything on to sweet mingling—this great, wild force of universal life, so-called the Spring, had come to Mr Stone, like new wine to some old bottle. And Hilary, to whom it had come, too, watching him every morning setting forth with a rough towel across his arm, wondered whether the old man would not this time leave his spirit swimming in the chill waters of the Serpentine—so near that spirit seemed to breaking through its fragile shell.

Four days had gone by since the interview at which he had sent away the little model, and life in his household—that quiet backwater choked with lilies—seemed to have resumed the tranquillity enjoyed before this intrusion of rude life. The paper whiteness

343

of Mr Stone was the only patent evidence that anything disturbing had occurred—that and certain feelings about which the strictest silence was preserved.

On the morning of the fifth day, seeing the old man stumble on the level flagstones of the garden, Hilary finished dressing hastily, and followed. He overtook him walking forward feebly beneath the candelabra of flowering chestnut-trees, with a hail-shower striking white on his high shoulders; and, placing himself alongside, without greeting—for forms were all one to Mr Stone—he said:

'Surely you don't mean to bathe during a hail-storm, sir! Make an exception this once. You're not looking quite yourself.'

Mr Stone shook his head; then, evidently following out a thought which Hilary had interrupted, he remarked:

'The sentiment that men call honour is of doubtful value. I have not as yet succeeded in relating it to universal brotherhood.'

'How is that, sir?'

'In so far,' said Mr Stone, 'as it consists in fidelity to principle, one might assume it worthy of conjunction. The difficulty arises when we consider the nature of the principle. . . . There is a family of young thrushes in the garden. If one of them finds a worm, I notice that his devotion to that principle of self-preservation which prevails in all low forms of life forbids his sharing it with any of the other little thrushes.'

Mr Stone had fixed his eyes on distance.

'So it is, I fear,' he said, 'with "honour". In those days men looked on women as thrushes look on worms——'

He paused, evidently searching for a word; and Hilary, with a faint smile, said:

'And how did women look on men, sir?'

Mr Stone observed him with surprise. 'I did not perceive that it was you,' he said. 'I have to avoid brain action before bathing.'

They had crossed the road dividing the Gardens from the Park, and, seeing that Mr Stone had already seen the water where he was about to bathe, and would now see nothing else, Hilary stopped beside a little lonely birch-tree. This wild, small, graceful visitor, who had long bathed in winter, was already draping her bare limbs in a scarf of green. Hilary leaned against her cool, pearly body. Below were the chilly waters, now grey, now starch-blue, and the pale forms of fifteen or twenty bathers. While he stood shivering in the frozen wind, the sun, bursting through the hail-cloud, burned his cheeks and hands. And suddenly he heard, clear,

344

but far off, the sound which, of all others, stirs the hearts of men :
'Cuckoo, cuckoo!'

Four times over came the unexpected call. Whence had that
ill-advised, indelicate grey bird flown into this great haunt of men
and shadows? Why had it come with its arrowy flight and mocking
cry to pierce the heart and set it aching? There were trees enough
outside the town, cloud-swept hollows, tangled brakes of furze just
coming into bloom, where it could preside over the process of
Spring. What solemn freak was this which made it come and sing
to one who had no longer any business with the Spring?

With a real spasm in his heart Hilary turned away from that
distant bird, and went down to the water's edge. Mr Stone was
swimming, slower than man had ever swum before. His silver
head and lean arms alone were visible, parting the water feebly;
suddenly he disappeared. He was but a dozen yards from the shore;
and Hilary, alarmed at not seeing him reappear, ran in. The water
was not deep. Mr Stone, seated at the bottom, was doing all he
could to rise. Hilary took him by his bathing-dress, raised him
to the surface, and supported him towards the land. By the time
they reached the shore he could just stand on his legs. With the
assistance of a policeman, Hilary enveloped him in garments and
got him to a cab: He had regained some of his vitality, but did not
seem aware of what had happened.

'I was not in as long as usual,' he mused, as they passed out into
the high road.

'Oh, I think so, sir.'

Mr Stone looked troubled.

'It is odd,' he said. 'I do not recollect leaving the water.'

He did not speak again till he was being assisted from the cab.

'I wish to recompense the man. I have half a crown indoors.'

'I will get it, sir,' said Hilary.

Mr Stone, who shivered violently now that he was on his feet,
turned his face up to the cabman.

'Nothing is nobler than the horse,' he said; 'take care of him.'

The cabman removed his hat. 'I will, sir,' he answered.

Walking by himself, but closely watched by Hilary, Mr Stone
reached his room. He groped about him as though not distinguish-
ing objects too well through the crystal clearness of the fundamental flux.

'If I might advise you,' said Hilary, 'I would get back into bed
for a few minutes. You seem a little chilly.'

Mr Stone, who was indeed shaking so that he could hardly

stand, allowed Hilary to assist him into bed and tuck the blankets round him.

'I must be at work by ten o'clock,' he said.

Hilary, who was also shivering, hastened to Bianca's room. She was just coming down, and exclaimed at seeing him all wet. When he had told her of the episode she touched his shoulder.

'What about you?'

'A hot bath and drink will set me right. You'd better go to *him*.'

He turned towards the bathroom, where Miranda stood, lifting a white foot. Compressing her lips, Bianca ran downstairs. Startled by his tale, she would have taken his wet body in her arms, if the ghosts of innumerable moments had not stood between. So this moment passed too, and itself became a ghost.

Mr Stone, greatly to his disgust, had not succeeded in resuming work at ten o'clock. Failing simply because he could not stand on his legs, he had announced his intention of waiting until half-past three, when he should get up, in preparation for the coming of the little girl. Having refused to see a doctor, or have his temperature taken, it was impossible to tell precisely what degree of fever he was in. In his cheeks, just visible over the blankets, there was more colour than there should have been; and his eyes, fixed on the ceiling, shone with suspicious brilliancy. To the dismay of Bianca—who sat as far out of sight as possible, lest he should see her, and fancy that she was doing him a service—he pursued his thoughts aloud:

'Words—words—they have taken away brotherhood!' Bianca shuddered, listening to that uncanny sound. '"In those days of words they called it death—*mors pallida*. They saw that word like a gigantic granite block suspended over them, and slowly coming down. Some, turning up their faces at the sight, trembled painfully, awaiting their obliteration. Others, unable, while they still lived, to face the thought of nothingness, inflated by some spiritual wind, and thinking always of their individual forms, called out unceasingly that those selves of theirs would and must survive this word—that in some fashion, which no man could understand, each self-conscious entity reaccumulated after distribution. Drunk with this thought, these, too, passed away. Some waited for it with grim, dry eyes, remarking that the process was molecular, and thus they also met their so-called death."'

His voice ceased, and in place of it rose the sound of his tongue moistening his palate. Bianca, from behind, placed a glass of barley-water to his lips. He drank it with a slow, clucking noise; then, see-

346

ing that a hand held the glass, said: 'Is that you? Are you ready for me? Follow. "In those days no one leaped up to meet pale riding Death; no one saw in her face that she was brotherhood incarnate; no one with a heart as light as gossamer kissed her feet, and, smiling, passed into the Universe." ' His voice died away, and when next he spoke it was in a quick, husky whisper: 'I must —I must—I must——' There was silence; then he added: 'Give me my trousers.'

Bianca placed them by his bed. The sight seemed to reassure him. He was once more silent.

For more than an hour after this he was so absolutely still that Bianca rose continually to look at him. Each time, his eyes, wide open, were fixed on a little dark mark across the ceiling; his face had a look of the most singular determination, as though his spirit were slowly, relentlessly, regaining mastery over his fevered body. He spoke suddenly:

'Who is there?'

'Bianca.'

'Help me out of bed!'

The flush had left his face, the brilliance had faded from his eyes; he looked just like a ghost. With a sort of terror Bianca helped him out of bed. This weird display of mute white will-power was unearthly.

When he was dressed in his woollen gown and seated before the fire, she gave him a cup of strong beef-tea, with brandy. He swallowed it with great avidity.

'I should like some more of that,' he said, and fell asleep.

While he was asleep Cecilia came, and the two sisters watched his slumber, and, watching it, felt nearer to each other than they had for many years. Before she went away Cecilia whispered:

'B., if he seems to want that little girl while he's like this, don't you think she ought to come?'

Bianca answered: 'I don't know where she is.'

'I do.'

'Ah!' said Bianca; 'of course!' And she turned her head away.

Disconcerted by that sarcastic little speech, Cecilia was silent; then, summoning all her courage, she said:

'Here's the address, B. I've written it down for you;' and, with puckers of anxiety in her face, she left the room.

Bianca sat on in the old golden chair, watching the deep hollows beneath the sleeper's temples, the puffs of breath stirring

the silver round his mouth. Her ears burned crimson. Carried
out of herself by the sight of that old form, dearer to her than she
had thought, fighting its great battle for the sake of its idea, her
spirit grew all tremulous and soft within her. With eagerness she
embraced the thought of self-effacement. It did not seem to matter
whether she were first with Hilary. Her spirit should so manifest
its capacity for sacrifice that she would be first with him through
sheer nobility. At this moment she could almost have taken that
common little girl into her arms and kissed her. So would all
disquiet end! Some harmonious messenger had fluttered to her for
a second—the gold-winged bird of peace. In this sensuous exaltation her nerves vibrated like the strings of a violin.

When Mr Stone woke it was past three o'clock, and Bianca at
once handed him another cup of strong beef-tea.

He swallowed it, and said: 'What is this?'

'Beef-tea.'

Mr Stone looked at the empty cup.

'I must not drink it. The cow and the sheep are on the same
plane as man.'

'But how do you feel, dear?'

'I feel,' said Mr Stone, 'able to dictate what I have already
written—not more. Has she come?'

'Not yet; but I will go and find her if you like.'

Mr Stone looked at his daughter wistfully.

'That will be taking up your time,' he said.

Bianca answered: 'My time is of no consequence.'

Mr Stone stretched his hands out to the fire.

'I will not consent,' he said, evidently to himself, 'to be a drag
on anyone. If that has come, then I must go!'

Bianca, placing herself beside him on her knees, pressed her
hot cheek against his temple.

'But it has not come, Dad.'

'I hope not,' said Mr Stone. 'I wish to end my book first.'

The sudden grim coherence of his last two sayings terrified
Bianca more than all his feverish utterances.

'I rely on your sitting quite still,' she said, 'while I go and find
her.' And with a feeling in her heart as though two hands had
seized and were pulling it asunder, she went out.

Some half-hour later Hilary slipped quietly in, and stood
watching at the door. Mr Stone, seated on the very verge of his
armchair, with his hands on its arms, was slowly rising to his feet,
and slowly falling back again, not once, but many times, practising

a standing posture. As Hilary came into his line of sight, he said:
'I have succeeded twice.'

'I am very glad,' said Hilary. 'Won't you rest now, sir?'

'It is my knees,' said Mr Stone. 'She has gone to find her.'

Hilary heard those words with bewilderment, and, sitting down
on the other chair, waited.

'I have fancied,' said Mr Stone, looking at him wistfully, 'that
when we pass away from life we may become the wind. Is that
your opinion?'

'It is a new thought to me,' said Hilary.

'It is not tenable,' said Mr Stone. 'But it is restful. The wind is
everywhere and nowhere, and nothing can be hidden from it. When
I have missed that little girl, I have tried, in a sense, to become
the wind; but I have found it difficult.'

His eyes left Hilary's face, whose mournful smile he had not
noticed, and fixed themselves on the bright fire. ' "In those days," '
he said ' "men's relation to the eternal airs was the relation of a
billion little separate draughts blowing against the south-west
wind. They did not wish to merge themselves in that soft, moon-
uttered sigh, but blew in its face through crevices, and cracks, and
keyholes, and were borne away on the pellucid journey, whistling out their protests." '

He again tried to stand, evidently wishing to get to his desk to
record this thought, but, failing, looked painfully at Hilary. He
seemed about to ask for something, but checked himself.

'If I practise hard,' he murmured, 'I shall master it.'

Hilary rose and brought him paper and a pencil. In bending, he
saw that Mr Stone's eyes were dim with moisture. This sight
affected him so that he was glad to turn away and fetch a book
to form a writing-pad.

When Mr Stone had finished, he sat back in his chair with closed
eyes. A supreme silence reigned in the bare room above those two
men of different generations and of such strange dissimilarity
of character. Hilary broke that silence.

'I heard the cuckoo sing to-day,' he said, almost in a whisper,
lest Mr Stone should be asleep.

'The cuckoo,' replied Mr Stone, 'has no sense of brotherhood.'

'I forgive him—for his song,' murmured Hilary.

'His song,' said Mr Stone, 'is alluring; it excites the sexual
instinct.'

Then to himself he added:

'She has not come, as yet!'

349

Even as he spoke there was heard by Hilary a faint tapping on the door. He rose and opened it. The little model stood outside.

Chapter 29

RETURN OF THE LITTLE MODEL

THAT same afternoon in High Street, Kensington, 'Westminister', with his coat-collar raised against the inclement wind, his old hat spotted with rain, was drawing at a clay pipe and fixing his iron-rimmed gaze on those who passed him by. It had been a day when singularly few as yet had bought from him his faintly green-tinged journal, and the low class of fellow who sold the other evening prints had peculiarly exasperated him. His single mind, always torn to some extent between an ingrained loyalty to his employers and those politics of his which differed from his paper's, had vented itself twice since coming on his stand; once in these words to the seller of 'Pell Mells': 'I stupulated with you not to come beyond the lamp-post. Don't you never speak to me again— a-crowdin' of me off my stand'; and once to the younger vendors of the less expensive journals, thus: 'Oh, you boys! I'll make you regret of it—a-snappin' up my customers under my very nose! Wait until ye're old!' To which the boys had answered: 'All right, daddy; don't you have a fit. You'll be a deader soon enough without that, y'know!'

It was now his time for tea, but 'Pell Mell' having gone to partake of this refreshment, he waited on, hoping against hope to get a customer or two of that low fellow's. And while in blank insulation he stood there a timid voice said at his elbow:

'Mr Creed!'

The aged butler turned, and saw the little model.

'Oh,' he said dryly, 'it's you, is it?' His mind, with its incessant love of rank, knowing that she earned her living as a handmaid to that disorderly establishment, the House of Art, had from the first classed her as lower than a lady's-maid. Recent events had made him think of her unkindly. Her new clothes, which he had not been privileged to see before, while giving him a sense of Sunday, deepened his moral doubts.

'And where are you living now?' he said in tones incorporating these feelings.

'I'm not to tell you.'

'Oh, very well. Keep yourself to yourself.'

The little model's lower lip drooped more than ever. There were dark marks beneath her eyes; her face was altogether rather pinched and pitiful.

'Won't you tell me any news?' she said in her matter-of-fact voice.

The old butler gave a strange grunt.

'Ho!' he said. 'The baby's dead, and buried to-morrer.'

'Dead!' repeated the little model.

'I'm a-goin' to the funeral—Brompton Cemetery. Half-past nine I leave the door. And that's a-beginnin' at the end. The man's in prison, and the woman's gone a shadder of herself.'

The little model rubbed her hands against her skirt.

'What did he go to prison for?'

'For assaultin' of her; I was witness to his battery.'

'Why did he assault her?'

Creed looked at her, and, wagging his head, answered:

'That's best known to them as caused of it.'

The little model's face went the colour of carnations.

'I can't help what he does,' she said. 'What should *I* want him for—a man like that? It wouldn't be *him* I'd want!' The genuine contempt in that sharp burst of anger impressed the aged butler.

'I'm not a-sayin' anything,' he said; 'it's all a-one to me. I never mixes up with no other people's business. But it's very ill-convenient. I don't get my proper breakfast. That poor woman—she's half off her head. When the baby's buried I'll have to go and look out for another room before he gets a-comin' out.'

'I hope they'll keep him there,' muttered the little model suddenly.

'They give him a month,' said Creed.

'Only a month!'

The old butler looked at her. 'There's more stuff in you,' he seemed to say, 'than ever I had thought.'

'Because of his servin' of his country,' he remarked aloud.

'I'm sorry about the poor little baby,' said the little model in her stolid voice.

'Westminister' shook his head. 'I never suspected *him* of goin' to live,' he said.

The girl, biting the finger-tip of her white cotton glove, was staring out at the traffic. Like a pale ray of light entering the now dim cavern of the old man's mind, the thought came to Creed that he did not quite understand her. He had in his time had occasion to class many young persons, and the feeling that he did not

351

quite know her class of person was like the sensation a bat might have, surprised by daylight.

Suddenly, without saying good-bye to him, she walked away.

'Well,' he thought, looking after her, 'your manners ain't improved by where you're living, nor your apperiance neither, for all your new clothes.' And for some time he stood thinking of the stare in her eyes and that abrupt departure.

Through the crystal clearness of the fundamental flux the mind could see at the same moment Bianca leaving her front gate.

Her sensuous exaltation, her tremulous longing after harmony, had passed away; in her heart, strangely mingled, were these two thoughts: 'If only she were a lady!' and, 'I am glad she is not a lady!'

Of all the dark and tortuous places of this life the human heart is the most dark and tortuous; and of all human hearts none are less clear, more intricate, than the hearts of all that class of people among whom Bianca had her being. Pride was a simple quality when joined with a simple view of life, based on the plain philosophy of property; pride was no simple quality when the hundred paralysing doubts and aspirations of a social conscience also hedged it round. In thus going forth with the full intention of restoring the little model to her position in the household, her pride fought against her pride, and her woman's sense of ownership in the man whom she had married wrestled with the acquired sentiments of freedom, liberality, equality, good taste. With her spirit thus confused, and her mind so at variance with itself, she was really acting on the simple instinct of compassion.

She had run upstairs from Mr Stone's room, and now walked fast, lest that instinct, the most physical, perhaps, of all—awakened by sights and sounds, and requiring constant nourishment—should lose its force.

Rapidly, then, she made her way to the grey street in Bayswater where Cecilia had told her that the girl now lived.

The tall, gaunt landlady admitted her.

'Have you a Miss Barton lodging here?' Bianca asked.

'Yes,' said the landlady, 'but I think she's out.'

She looked into the little model's room.

'Yes,' she said, 'she's out; but if you'd like to leave a note you could write in here. If you're looking for a model, she wants work, I believe.'

That modern faculty of pressing on an aching nerve was

assuredly not lacking to Bianca. To enter the girl's room was jabbing at the nerve indeed.

She looked round her. The mental vacuity of that little room! There was not one single thing—with the exception of a torn copy of *Tit-Bits*—which suggested that a mind of any sort lived there. For all that, perhaps because of that, it was neat enough.

'Yes,' said the landlady, 'she keeps her room tidy. Of course, she's a country girl—comes from down my way.' She said this with a dry twist of her grim, but not unkindly, features. 'If it weren't for that,' she went on, 'I don't think I should care to let to one of her profession.'

Her hungry eyes, gazing at Bianca, had in them the aspirations of all Nonconformity.

Bianca pencilled on her card:

'If you can come to my father to-day or to-morrow, please do.'
'Will you give her this, please? It will be quite enough.'

'I'll give it her,' the landlady said; 'she'll be glad of it, I daresay. I see her sitting here. Girls like that, if they've got nothing to do—see, she's been moping on her bed. . . .'

The impress of a form was, indeed, clearly visible on the red and yellow tasselled tapestry of the bed.

Bianca cast a look at it.

'Thank you,' she said; 'good day.'

With the jabbed nerve aching badly she came slowly homewards.

Before the garden gate the little model herself was gazing at the house, as if she had been there some time. Approaching from across the road, Bianca had an admirable view of that young figure, now very trim and neat, yet with something in its lines—more graceful, perhaps, but less refined—which proclaimed her not a lady; a something fundamentally undisciplined or disciplined by the material facts of life alone, rather than by a secret creed of voluntary rules. It showed here and there in ways women alone could understand; above all, in the way her eyes looked out on that house which she was clearly longing to enter. Not 'Shall I go in?' was in that look, but 'Dare I go in?'

Suddenly she saw Bianca. The meeting of these two was very like the ordinary meeting of a mistress and her maid. Bianca's face had no expression, except the faint, distant curiosity which seems to say: 'You are a sealed book to me; I have always found you so. What you really think and do I shall never know.'

The little model's face wore a half-caught-out, half-stolid look.

353

'Please go in,' Bianca said; 'my father will be glad to see you.'

She held the garden gate open for the girl to pass through. Her feeling at that moment was one of slight amusement at the futility of her journey. Not even this small piece of generosity was permitted her, it seemed.

'How are you getting on?'

The little model made an impulsive movement at such an unexpected question. Checking it at once, she answered:

'Very well, thank you; that is, not very——'

'You will find my father tired to-day; he has caught a chill. Don't let him read too much, please.'

The little model seemed to try and nerve herself to make some statement, but failing, passed into the house.

Bianca did not follow, but stole back into the garden, where the sun was still falling on a bed of wallflowers at the far end. She bent down over these flowers till her veil touched them. Two wild bees were busy there, buzzing with smoky wings, clutching with their black, tiny legs at the orange petals, plunging their black, tiny tongues far down into the honeyed centres. The flowers quivered beneath the weight of their small dark bodies. Bianca's face quivered too, bending close to them, nor making the slightest difference to their hunt.

Hilary, who, as it has been seen, lived in thoughts about events rather than in events themselves, and to whom crude acts and words had little meaning save in relation to what philosophy could make of them, greeted the girl's appearance in the corridor outside Mr Stone's apartment with a startled face. But the little model, who mentally lived very much from hand to mouth, and had only the philosophy of wants, acted differently. She knew that for the last five days, like a spaniel dog shut away from where it feels it ought to be, she had wanted to be where she was now standing; she knew that, in her new room with its rust-red doors, she had bitten her lips and fingers till blood came, and, as newly caged birds will flutter, had beaten her wings against those walls with blue roses on a yellow ground. She remembered how she had lain, brooding, on that piece of red and yellow tapestry, twisting its tassels, staring through half-closed eyes at nothing.

There was something different in her look at Hilary. It had lost some of its childish devotion; it was bolder, as if she had lived and felt, and brushed a good deal more down off her wings during those few days.

'Mrs Dallison told me to come,' she said. 'I thought I might.
Mr Creed told me about *him* being in prison.'

Hilary made way for her, and, following her into Mr Stone's
presence, shut the door.

'The truant has returned,' he said.

Hearing herself called so unjustly by that name, the little
model flushed deeply, and tried to speak. She stopped at the
smile on Hilary's face, and gazed from him to Mr Stone and back
again, the victim of mingled feelings.

Mr Stone was seen to have risen to his feet, and to be very
slowly moving towards his desk. He leaned both arms on his
papers for support, and, seeming to gather strength, began sorting
out his manuscript.

Through the open window the distant music of a barrel-organ
came drifting in. Faint, and much too slow, was the sound of
the waltz it played, but there was invitation, allurement, in that
tune. The little model turned towards it, and Hilary looked hard
at her. The girl and that sound together—there, quite plain,
was the music he had heard for many days, like a man lying with
the touch of fever on him.

'Are you ready?' said Mr Stone.

The little model dipped her pen in ink. Her eyes crept towards
the door, where Hilary was still standing with the same expression
on his face. He avoided her eyes, and went up to Mr Stone.

'Must you read to-day, sir?'

Mr Stone looked at him with anger.

'Why not?' he said.

'You are hardly strong enough.'

Mr Stone raised his manuscript.

'We are three days behind;' and very slowly he began dictating: '"Bar-ba-rous ha-bits in those days, such as the custom
known as War——"' His voice died away; it was apparent that
his elbows, leaning on the desk, alone prevented his collapse.

Hilary moved the chair, and, taking him beneath the arms,
lowered him gently into it.

Noticing that he was seated, Mr Stone raised his manuscript
and read on: '"—were pursued regardless of fraternity. It was
as though a herd of horn-èd cattle driven through green pastures
to that Gate, where they must meet with certain dissolution,
had set about to prematurely gore and disembowel each
other, out of a passionate devotion to those individual shapes
which they were so soon to lose. So men—tribe against tribe, and

country against country—glared across the valleys with their ensanguined eyes; they could not see the moonlit wings, or feel the embalming airs of brotherhood." '

Slower and slower came his sentences, and as the last word died away he was heard to be asleep, breathing through a tiny hole left beneath the eave of his moustache. Hilary, who had waited for that moment, gently put the manuscript on the desk, and beckoned to the girl. He did not ask her to his study, but spoke to her in the hall.

'While Mr Stone is like this he misses you. You will come, then, at present, please, so long as Hughs is in prison. How do you like your room?'

The little model answered simply: 'Not very much.'

'Why not?'

'It's lonely there. I shan't mind, now I'm coming here again.'

'Only for the present,' was all Hilary could find to say.

The little model's eyes were lowered.

'Mrs Hughs' baby's to be buried to-morrow,' she said suddenly.

'Where?'

'In Brompton Cemetery. Mr Creed's going.

'What time is the funeral?'

The girl looked up stealthily.

'Mr Creed's going to start at half-past nine.'

'I should like to go myself,' said Hilary.

A gleam of pleasure passing across her face was instantly obscured behind the cloud of her stolidity. Then, as she saw Hilary move nearer to the door, her lip began to droop.

'Well, good-bye,' he said.

The little model flushed and quivered. 'You don't even look at me,' she seemed to say: 'you haven't spoken kindly to me once.' And suddenly she said in a hard voice:

'Now I shan't go to Mr Lennard's any more.'

'Oh, then you have been to him!'

Triumph at attracting his attention, fear of what she had admitted, supplication, and a half-defiant shame—all this was in her face.

'Yes,' she said.

Hilary did not speak.

'I didn't care any more when you told me I wasn't to come here.'

Still Hilary did not speak.

'I haven't done anything wrong,' she said, with tears in her voice.

356

'No no,' said Hilary; 'of course not!'

The little model choked.

'It's my profession.'

'Yes, yes,' said Hilary; 'it's all right.'

'I don't care what he thinks; I won't go again so long as I can come here.'

Hilary touched her shoulder.

'Well, well,' he said, and opened the front door.

The little model, tremulous, like a flower kissed by the sun after rain, went out with a light in her eyes.

The master of the house returned to Mr Stone. Long he sat looking at. the old man's slumber. 'A thinker meditating upon action!' So might Hilary's figure, with its thin face resting on its hand, a furrow between the brows, and that painful smile, have been entitled in any catalogue of statues.

Chapter 30

FUNERAL OF A BABY

FOLLOWING out the instinct planted so deeply in human nature for treating with the utmost care and at great expense when dead those, who, when alive, have been served with careless parsimony, there started from the door of No. I in Hound Street a funeral procession of three four-wheeled cabs.

The first bore the little coffin, on which lay a great white wreath (gift of Cecilia and Thyme). The second bore Mrs Hughs, her son Stanley, and Joshua Creed. The third bore Martin Stone.

In the first cab Silence was presiding with the scent of lilies over him who in his short life had made so little noise, the small grey shadow that had crept so quietly into being, and, taking his chance when he was not noticed, had crept so quietly out again. Never had he felt so restful, so much at home, as in that little common coffin, washed as he was to an unnatural whiteness, and wrapped in his mother's only spare sheet. Away from all the strife of men he was journeying to a greater peace. His little aloe-plant had flowered; and, between the open windows of the only carriage he had ever been inside, the wind—which, who knows? he had perhaps become—stirred the fronds of fern and the flowers of his funeral wreath. Thus he was going from that world where all men were his brothers.

From the second cab the same wind was rigidly excluded, and

357

there was silence, broken by the aged butler's breathing. Dressed
in his Newmarket coat, he was recalling with a certain sense of
luxury past journeys in four-wheeled cabs—occasions when, seated
beside a box corded and secured with sealing-wax, he had taken his
master's plate for safety to the bank; occasions when, under a roof
piled up with guns and boxes, he had sat holding the 'Honorable
Bateson's' dog; occasions when, with some young person by his
side, he had driven at the tail of a baptismal, nuptial or funeral
cortège. These memories of past grandeur came back to him with
curious poignancy, and for some reason the words kept rising in
his mind: 'For richer for poorer, for better for worser, in health
and in sick places, till death do us part.' But in the midst of the
exaltation of these recollections the old heart beneath his old red
flannel chest-protector—that companion of his exile—twittering
faintly at short intervals, made him look at the woman by his side.
He longed to convey to her some little of the satisfaction he felt
in the fact that this was by no means the low class of funeral it
might have been. He doubted whether, with her woman's mind, she
was getting all the comfort she could out of three four-wheeled
cabs and a wreath of lilies. The seamstress's thin face, with its
pinched, passive look, was indeed thinner, quieter, than ever. What
she was thinking of he could not tell. There were so many things she
might be thinking of. She, too, no doubt, had seen her grandeur, if
but in the solitary drive away from the church where, eight years
ago, she and Hughs had listened to the words now haunting Creed.
Was she thinking of that; of her lost youth and comeliness, and her
man's dead love; of the long descent to shadowland; of the other
children she had buried; of Hughs in prison; of the girl that had 'put
a spell on him'; or only of the last precious tugs the tiny lips at
rest in the first four-wheeled cab had given at her breast? Or was
she, with a nicer feeling for proportion, reflecting that, had not
people been so kind, she might have had to walk behind a funeral
provided by the parish?

The old butler could not tell, but he—whose one desire now,
coupled with the wish to die outside a workhouse, was to save
enough to bury his own body without the interference of other
people—was inclined to think she must be dwelling on the brighter
side of things; and, designing to encourage her, he said: 'Wonderful
improvement in these 'ere four-wheel cabs! Oh dear, yes! I remember of them when they were the shadders of what they are at the
present time of speakin'.'

The seamstress answered in her quiet voice: 'Very comfortable this is. Sit still, Stanley!' Her little son, whose feet did not reach the floor, was drumming his heels against the seat. He stopped and looked at her, and the old butler addressed him.

'You'll a-remember of this occasion,' he said, 'when you gets older.'

The little boy turned his black eyes from his mother to him who had spoken last.

'It's a beautiful wreath,' continued Creed. 'I could smell of it all the way up the stairs. There's been no expense spared; there's white laylock in it—that's a class of flower that's very extravagant.'

A train of thought having been roused too strong for his discretion, he added: 'I saw that young girl yesterday. She came interrogatin' of me in the street.'

On Mrs Hughs' face, where till now expression had been buried, came such a look as one may see on the face of an owl—hard, watchful, cruel; harder, more cruel, for the softness of the big dark eyes.

'She'd show a better feeling,' she said, 'to keep a quiet tongue. Sit still, Stanley!'

Once more the little boy stopped drumming his heels, and shifted his stare from the old butler back to her who spoke. The cab, which had seemed to hesitate and start, as though jibbing at something in the road, resumed its ambling pace. Creed looked through the well-closed window. There before him, so long that it seemed to have no end, like a building in a nightmare, stretched that place where he did not mean to end his days. He faced towards the horse again. The colour had deepened in his nose. He spoke:

'If they'd a-give me my last edition earlier, 'stead of sending of it down after that low-class feller's taken all my customers, that'd make a difference to me o' two shillin's at the utmost in the week, and all clear savin's.' To these words, dark with hidden meaning, he received no answer save the drumming of the small boy's heels; and, reverting to the subject he had been distracted from, he murmured: 'She was a-wearin' of new clothes.'

He was startled by the fierce tone of a voice he hardly knew. 'I don't want to hear about her; she's not for decent folk to talk of.'

The old butler looked round askance. The seamstress was trembling violently. Her fierceness at such a moment shocked him. 'Dust to dust,' he thought.

'Don't you be considerate of it,' he said at last, summoning all his knowledge of the world; 'she'll come to her own place.' And at the sight of a slow tear trickling over her burning cheek, he added hurriedly: 'Think of your baby—I'll see yer through. Sit still, little boy—sit still! Ye're disturbin' of your mother.'

Once more the little boy stayed the drumming of his heels to look at him who spoke; and the closed cab rolled on with its slow, jingling sound.

In the third four-wheeled cab, where the windows again were wide open, Martin Stone, with his hands thrust deep into the pockets of his coat, and his long legs crossed, sat staring at the roof, with a sort of twisted scorn on his pale face.

Just inside the gate, through which had passed in their time so many dead and living shadows, Hilary stood waiting. He could probably not have explained why he had come to see this tiny shade committed to the earth—in memory, perhaps, of those two minutes when the baby's eyes had held parley with his own, or in the wish to pay a mute respect to her on whom life had weighed so hard of late. For whatever reason he had come, he was keeping quietly to one side. And unobserved, he, too, had his watcher—the little model, sheltering behind a tall grave.

Two men in rusty black bore the little coffin; then came the white-robed chaplain; then Mrs Hughs and her little son; close behind, his head thrust forward with trembling movements from side to side, old Creed; and, last of all, young Martin Stone. Hilary joined the young doctor. So the five mourners walked.

Before a small dark hole in a corner of the cemetery they stopped. On this forest of unflowered graves the sun was falling; the east wind, with its faint reek, touched the old butler's plastered hair, and brought moisture to the corners of his eyes, fixed with absorption on the chaplain. Words and thoughts hunted in his mind.

'He's gettin' Christian burial. Who gives this woman away? I do. Ashes to ashes. I never suspected him of livin'.' The conning of the burial service, shortened to fit the passing of that tiny shade, gave him pleasurable sensation; films came down on his eyes; he listened like some old parrot on its perch, his head a little to one side.

'Them as dies young,' he thought, 'goes straight to heaven. We trusts in God—all mortial men; his godfathers and his godmothers in his baptism. Well, so it is! *I'm* not afeared o' death!'

Seeing the little coffin tremble above the hole, he craned his head still further forward. It sank; a smothered sobbing rose. The old butler touched the arm in front of him with shaking fingers.

'Don't 'e,' he whispered; 'he's a-gone to glory.'

But, hearing the dry rattle of the earth, he took out his own handkerchief and put it to his nose.

'Yes, he's a-gone,' he thought; 'another little baby. Old men an' maidens, young men an' little children; it's a-goin' on all the time. Where 'e is now there'll be no marryin', no, nor givin' out in marriage; till death do us part.'

The wind, sweeping across the filled-in hole, carried the rustle of his husky breathing, the dry, smothered sobbing of the seamstress, out across the shadows' graves, to those places, to those streets. . . .

From the baby's funeral Hilary and Martin walked away together, and far behind them, across the road, the little model followed. For some time neither spoke; then Hilary, stretching out his hand towards a squalid alley, said:

'They haunt us and drag us down. A long, dark passage. Is there a light at the far end, Martin?'

'Yes,' said Martin gruffly.

'I don't see it.'

Martin looked at him.

'Hamlet!'

Hilary did not reply.

The young man watched him sideways. 'It's a disease to smile like that!'

Hilary ceased to smile. 'Cure me, then,' he said, with sudden anger, 'you man of health!'

The young 'Sanitist's' sallow cheeks flushed. 'Atrophy of the nerve of action,' he muttered; 'there's no cure for that!'

'Ah!' said Hilary: 'All kinds of us want social progress in our different ways. You, your grandfather, my brother, myself; there are four types for you. Will you tell me any one of us is the right man for the job? For instance, action's not natural to me.'

'Any act,' answered Martin, 'is better than no act.'

'And myopia is natural to you, Martin. Your prescription in this case has not been too successful, has it?'

'I can't help it if people will be d—d fools.'

'There you hit it. But answer me this question: Isn't a social conscience, broadly speaking, the result of comfort and security?'

Martin shrugged his shoulders.

'And doesn't comfort also destroy the power of action?'

Again Martin shrugged.

'Then, if those who have the social conscience and can see what is

361

wrong have lost their power of action, how can you say there is any light at the end of this dark passage?'

Martin took his pipe out, filled it, and pressed the filling with his thumb.

'There *is* light,' he said at last, 'in spite of all invertebrates. Good-bye! I've wasted enough time,' and he abruptly strode away.

'And in spite of myopia?' muttered Hilary.

A few minutes later, coming out from Messrs Rose and Thorn's, where he had gone to buy tobacco, he came suddenly on the little model, evidently waiting.

'I was at the funeral,' she said; and her face added plainly : 'I've followed you.' Uninvited, she walked on at his side.

'This is not the same girl,' he thought, 'that I sent away five days ago. She has lost something, gained something. I don't know her.'

There seemed such a stubborn purpose in her face and manner. It was like the look in a dog's eyes that says : 'Master, you thought to shut me away from you; I know now what that is like. Do what you will, I mean in future to be near you.'

This look, by its simplicity, frightened one to whom the primi-tive was strange. Desiring to free himself of his companion, yet not knowing how, Hilary sat down in Kensington Gardens on the first bench they came to. The little model sat down beside him. The quiet siege laid to him by this girl was quite uncanny. It was as though someone were binding him with toy threads, swelling slowly into rope before his eyes. In this fear of Hilary's there was at first much irritation. His fastidiousness and sense of the ridiculous were roused. What did this little creature with whom he had no thoughts and no ideas in common, whose spirit and his could never hope to meet, think that she could get from him? Was she trying to weave a spell over him too, with her mute, stubborn adoration? Was she trying to change his protective weakness for her to another sort of weakness? He turned and looked; she dropped her eyes at once, and sat still as a stone figure.

As in her spirit, so in her body, she was different; her limbs looked freer, rounder; her breath seemed stirring her more deeply; like a flower of early June she was opening before his very eyes. This, though it gave him pleasure, also added to his fear. The strange silence, in its utter naturalness—for what could he talk about with her?—brought home to him more vividly than anything before, the barriers of class. All he thought of was how not to be ridiculous! She was inviting him in some strange, unconscious, subtle way to treat her as a woman, as though in spirit she had linked her round young arms about his neck, and through her half-closed lips were whispering the eternal call of sex to sex. And he, a middle-aged and cultivated man, conscious of everything, could not even speak for fear of breaking through his shell of delicacy. He hardly breathed, disturbed to his very depths by the young figure sitting by his side, and by the dread of showing that disturbance.

Beside the cultivated plant the self-sown poppy rears itself; round the stem of a smooth tree the honeysuckle twines; to a trim wall the ivy clings.

In her new-found form and purpose this girl had gained a strange, still power; she no longer felt it mattered whether he spoke or looked at her; her instinct, piercing through his shell, was certain of the throbbing of his pulses, the sweet poison in his blood.

The perception of this still power, more than all else, brought fear to Hilary. He need not speak; she would not care! He need not even look at her; she had but to sit there silent, motionless, with the breath of youth coming through her parted lips, and the light of youth stealing through her half-closed eyes.

And abruptly he got up and walked away.

Chapter 31

SWAN SONG

THE new wine, if it does not break the old bottle, after fierce effervescence seethes and bubbles quietly.

It was so in Mr Stone's old bottle, hour by hour and day by day, throughout the month. A pinker, robuster look came back to his cheeks; his blue eyes, fixed on distance, had in them more light; his knees regained their powers; he bathed, and, all unknown to him, for he only saw the waters he cleaved with his ineffably slow stroke, Hilary and Martin, on alternate weeks, and keeping at a proper distance, for fear he should see them doing him a service, attended at that function in case Mr Stone should again remain too long seated at the bottom of the Serpentine. Each morning after his cocoa and porridge he could be heard sweeping out his room with extraordinary vigour, and as ten o'clock came near anyone who listened would remark a sound of air escaping, as he moved up and down on his toes in preparation for the labours of the day. No letters, of course, nor any newspapers disturbed the supreme and perfect self-containment of this life devoted to Fraternity— no letters, partly because he lacked a known address, partly because for years he had not answered them; and with regard to newspapers, once a month he went to a Public Library, and could be seen with the last four numbers of two weekly reviews before him, making himself acquainted with the habits of those days, and moving his lips as though in prayer. At ten each morning anyone in the corridor outside his room was startled by the whirr of an alarum clock; perfect silence followed; then rose a sound of shuffling, whistling, rustling, broken by sharply muttered words; soon from this turbid lake of sound the articulate, thin fluting of an old man's voice streamed forth. This, alternating with the squeak of a quill pen, went on till the alarum clock once more went off. Then he who stood outside could smell that Mr Stone would shortly eat; if, stimulated by that scent, he entered, he might see the author of the 'Book of Universal Brotherhood' with a baked potato in one hand and a cup of hot milk in the other; on the table, too, the ruined forms of eggs, tomatoes, oranges, bananas, figs, prunes, cheese, and honeycomb, which had passed into other forms already, together with a loaf of wholemeal bread. Mr Stone would presently emerge in his cottage-woven tweeds, and old hat of green-black felt; or, if wet, in a long coat of yellow gaberdine, and sou'-wester cap of the same material; but always with a little osier fruit-bag in his hand. Thus equipped, he walked down to Rose and Thorn's, entered, and to the first man he saw handed the osier fruit-bag, some coins, and a little book containing seven leaves, headed 'Food: Monday, Tuesday, Wednesday', and so forth. He then stood looking through the pickles in some jar or other at things beyond, with one hand held out, fingers upwards, awaiting the return of his little osier fruit-bag. Feeling presently that it had been restored to him, he would turn and walk out of the shop. Behind his back, on the face of the department, the same protecting smile always rose. Long habit had perfected it. All now felt that, though so very different from themselves, this aged customer was dependent on them. By not one single farthing or one pale slip of cheese would they have defrauded him for all the treasures of the moon, and any new salesman who laughed at that old client was promptly told to 'shut his head'.

Mr Stone's frail form, bent somewhat to one side by the increased gravamen of the osier bag, was now seen moving homewards. He arrived perhaps ten minutes before the three o'clock alarum, and soon passing through preliminary chaos, the articulate, thin fluting of his voice streamed forth again, broken by the squeaking and spluttering of his quill.

But towards four o'clock signs of cerebral excitement became visible; his lips would cease to utter sounds, his pen to squeak. His face, with a flushed forehead, would appear at the open window. As soon as the little model came in sight—her eyes fixed, not on his window, but on Hilary's—he turned his back, evidently waiting for her to enter by the door. His first words were uttered in a tranquil voice: 'I have several pages. I have placed your chair. Are you ready? Follow!'

Except for that strange tranquillity of voice and the disappearance of the flush on his brow, there was no sign of the rejuvenescence that she brought, of such refreshment as steals on the traveller who sits down beneath a lime-tree towards the end of a long day's journey; no sign of the mysterious comfort distilled into his veins by the sight of her moody young face, her young, soft limbs. So from some stimulant men very near their end will draw energy, watching, as it were, a shape beckoning them forward, till suddenly it disappears in darkness.

In the quarter of an hour sacred to their tea and conversation he never noticed that she was always listening for sounds beyond; it was enough that in her presence he felt singleness of purpose strong within him.

When she had gone, moving languidly, moodily away, her eyes darting about for signs of Hilary, Mr Stone would sit down rather suddenly and fall asleep, to dream, perhaps, of Youth—Youth with its scent of sap, its close beckonings; Youth with its hopes and fears; Youth that hovers round us so long after it is dead! His spirit would smile behind its covering—that thin china of his face; and, as dogs hunting in their sleep work their feet, so he worked the fingers resting on his woollen knees.

The seven o'clock alarum woke him to the preparation of the evening meal. This eaten, he began once more to pace up and down, to pour words out into the silence, and to drive his squeaking quill.

So was being written a book such as the world had never seen!

But the girl who came so moodily to bring him refreshment, and went so moodily away, never in these days caught a glimpse of that which she was seeking.

Since the morning when he had left her abruptly, Hilary had made a point of being out in the afternoons and not returning till past six o'clock. By this device he put off facing her and himself, for he could no longer refuse to see that he had himself to face. In the few minutes of utter silence when the girl sat beside him, magnetic, quivering with awakening force, he had found that the male in him was far from dead. It was no longer vague, sensuous feeling; it was warm, definite desire. The more she was in his thoughts, the less spiritual his feeling for this girl of the people had become.

In those days he seemed much changed to such as knew him well. Instead of the delicate, detached, slightly humorous suavity which he had accustomed people to expect from him, the dry kindliness which seemed at once to check confidence and yet to say, 'If you choose to tell me anything, I should never think of passing judgment on you, whatever you have done'—instead of that rather abstracted, faintly quizzical air, his manner had become absorbed and gloomy. He seemed to jib away from his friends. His manner at the 'Pen and Ink' was wholly unsatisfying to men who liked to talk. He was known to be writing a new book; they suspected him of having 'got into a hat'—this Victorian expression, found by Mr Balladyce in some chronicle of post-Thackerayan manners, and revived by him in his incomparable way, as who should say, 'What delicious expressions those good bourgeois had!' now flourished in second childhood.

In truth, Hilary's difficulty with his new book was merely the one of not being able to work at it at all. Even the housemaid who 'did' his study noticed that day after day she was confronted by Chapter XXIV, in spite of her master's staying in, as usual, every morning.

The change in his manner and face, which had grown strained and harassed, had been noticed by Bianca, though she would have died sooner than admit she had noticed anything about him. It was one of those periods in the lives of households like an hour of a late summer's day—brooding, electric, as yet quiescent, but charged with the currents of coming storms.

Twice only in those weeks while Hughs was in prison did Hilary see the girl. Once he met her when he was driving home; she blushed crimson and her eyes lighted up. And one morning, too, he passed her on the bench where they had sat together. She was staring straight before her, the corners of her mouth drooping discontentedly. She did not see him.

To a man like Hilary—for whom running after women had been about the last occupation in the world, who had, in fact, always fought shy of them and imagined that they would always fight shy of him—there was an unusual enticement and dismay in the feeling that a young girl really was pursuing him. It was at once too good, too unlikely, and too embarrassing to be true. His sudden feeling for her was the painful sensation of one who sees a ripe nectarine

hanging within reach. He dreamed continually of stretching out his hand, and so he did not dare, or thought he did not dare, to pass that way. All this did not favour the tenor of a studious, introspective life; it also brought a sense of unreality that made him avoid his best friends.

This, partly, was why Stephen came to see him one Sunday, his other reason for the visit being the calculation that Hughs would be released on the following Wednesday.

'This girl,' he thought, 'is going to the house still, and Hilary will let things drift till he can't stop them, and there'll be a real mess.'

The fact of the man's having been in prison gave a sinister turn to an affair regarded hitherto as merely sordid by Stephen's orderly and careful mind.

Crossing the garden, he heard Mr Stone's voice issuing through the open window.

'Can't the old crank stop even on Sundays?' he thought.

He found Hilary in his study, reading a book on the civilisation of the Maccabees, in preparation for a review. He gave Stephen but a dubious welcome.

Stephen broke ground gently.

'We haven't seen you for an age. I hear our old friend at it. Is he working double tides to finish his *magnum opus*? I thought he observed the day of rest.'

'He does as a rule,' said Hilary.

'Well, he's got the girl there now dictating.'

Hilary winced. Stephen continued with greater circumspection.

'You couldn't get the old boy to finish by Wednesday, I suppose? He must be quite near the end by now.'

The notion of Mr Stone's finishing his book by Wednesday procured a pale smile from Hilary.

'Could you get your Law Courts,' he said, 'to settle up the affairs of mankind for good and all by Wednesday?'

'By Jove! Is it as bad as that? I thought, at any rate, he must be meaning to finish some day.'

'When men are brothers,' said Hilary, 'he will finish.'

Stephen whistled.

'Look here, dear boy!' he said, 'that ruffian comes out on Wednesday. The whole thing will begin over again.'

Hilary rose and paced the room. 'I refuse,' he said, 'to consider Hughs a ruffian. What do we know about him, or any of them?'

'Precisely! What do we know of this girl?'

'I am not going to discuss that,' Hilary said shortly.

For a moment the faces of the two brothers wore a hard, hostile look, as though the deep difference between their characters had at last got the better of their loyalty. They both seemed to recognise this, for they turned their heads away.

'I just wanted to remind you,' Stephen said, 'though you know your own business best, of course.' And at Hilary's nod he thought: 'That's just exactly what he doesn't!'

He soon left, conscious of an unwonted awkwardness in his brother's presence. Hilary watched him out through the wicket gate, then sat down on the solitary garden bench.

Stephen's visit had merely awakened perverse desires in him.

Strong sunlight was falling on that little London garden, disclosing its native shadowiness; streaks, and smudges such as Life smears over the faces of those who live too consciously. Hilary, beneath the acacia-tree not yet in bloom, marked an early butterfly flitting over the geraniums blossoming round an old sundial. Blackbirds were holding evensong; the late perfume of the lilac came stealing forth into air faintly smeethed with chimney smoke. There was brightness, but no glory, in that little garden; scent, but no strong air blown across golden lakes of buttercups, from seas of springing clover, or the wind-silver of young wheat; music, but no full choir of sound, no hum. Like the face and figure of its master, so was this little garden, whose sundial the sun seldom reached—refined, self-conscious, introspective, obviously a creature of the town. At that moment, however, Hilary was not looking quite himself; his face was flushed, his eyes angry, almost as if he had been a man of action.

The voice of Mr Stone was still audible, fitfully quavering out into the air, and the old man himself could now and then be seen holding up his manuscript, his profile clear-cut against the darkness of the room. A sentence travelled out across the garden:

' "Amidst the tur-bu-lent dis-cov-eries of those days, which, like cross-currented and multi-billowed seas, lapped and hollowed every rock——" '

A motor-car dashing past drowned the rest, and when the voice rose again it was evidently dictating another paragraph.

' "In those places, in those streets, the shadows swarmed, whispering and droning like a hive of dying bees, who, their honey eaten, wander through the winter day seeking flowers that are frozen and dead." '

A great bee that had been busy with the lilac began to circle,

booming, round his hair. Suddenly Hilary saw him raise both his
arms.

'"In huge congeries, crowded, devoid of light and air, they were
assembled, these bloodless imprints from forms of higher caste.
They lay, like the reflection of leaves which, fluttering free in the
sweet winds, let fall to the earth wan resemblances. Imponderous,
dark ghosts, wandering ones chained to the ground, they had no hope
of any Lovely City, nor knew whence they had come. Men cast them
on the pavements and marched on. They did not in Universal
Brotherhood clasp their shadows to sleep within their hearts—for
the sun was not then at noon, when no man has a shadow."'

As those words of swan song died away he swayed and trembled,
and suddenly disappeared below the sight-line, as if he had sat
down. The little model took his place in the open window. She
started at seeing Hilary; then, motionless, stood gazing at him. Out
of the gloom of the opening her eyes were all pupil, two spots of
the surrounding darkness imprisoned in a face as pale as any flower.
As rigid as the girl herself, Hilary looked up at her.

A voice behind him said: 'How are you? I thought I'd give my
car a run.' Mr Purcey was coming from the gate, his eyes fixed on
the window where the girl stood. 'How is your wife?' he added.

The bathos of this visit roused an acid fury in Hilary. He sur-
veyed Mr Purcey's figure from his cloth-topped boots to his tall hat,
and said: 'Shall we go in and find her?'

As they went along Mr Purcey said: 'That's the young—the—er
—model I met in your wife's studio, isn't it? Pretty girl!'

Hilary compressed his lips.

'Now, what sort of living do those girls make?' pursued Mr Purcey. 'I suppose they've most of them other resources. Eh, what?'

'They make the living God will let them, I suppose, as other
people do.'

Mr Purcey gave him a sharp look. It was almost as if Dallison
had meant to snub him.

'Oh, exactly! I should think this girl would have no difficulty.'
And suddenly he saw a curious change come over 'that writing fellow', as he always afterwards described Hilary. Instead of a mild,
pleasant-looking chap enough, he had become a regular cold devil.

'My wife appears to be out,' Hilary said. 'I also have an engagement.'

In his surprise and anger Mr Purcey said with great simplicity,
'Sorry I'm *de trop*!' and soon his car could be heard bearing him
away with some unnecessary noise.

Chapter 32

BEHIND BIANCA'S VEIL

BUT Bianca was not out. She had been a witness of Hilary's long look at the little model. Coming from her studio through the glass passage to the house, she could not, of course, see what he was gazing at, but she knew as well as if the girl had stood before her in the dark opening of the window. Hating herself for having seen, she went to her room and lay on her bed with her hands pressed to her eyes. She was used to loneliness—that necessary lot of natures such as hers; but the bitter isolation of this hour was such as to drive even her lonely nature to despair.

She rose at last, and repaired the ravages made in her face and dress, lest anyone should see that she was suffering. Then, first making sure that Hilary had left the garden, she stole out.

She wandered towards Hyde Park. It was Whitsuntide, a time of fear to the cultivated Londoner. The town seemed all arid jollity and paper bags whirled on a dusty wind. People swarmed everywhere in clothes which did not suit them; desultory, dead-tired creatures who, in these few green hours of leisure out of the sandy eternity of their toil, were not suffered to rest, but were whipped on by starved instincts to hunt pleasures which they longed for too dreadfully to overtake.

Bianca passed an old tramp asleep beneath a tree. His clothes had clung to him so long and lovingly that they were falling off, but his face was calm as though masked with the finest wax. Forgotten were his sores and sorrows; he was in the blessed fields of sleep.

Bianca hastened away from the sight of such utter peace. She wandered into a grove of trees that had almost eluded the notice of the crowd. They were limes, guarding still within them their honey bloom. Their branches of light, broad leaves, near heart-shaped, were spread out like wide skirts. The tallest of these trees, a beautiful, gay creature, stood tremulous, like a mistress waiting for her tardy lover. What joy she seemed to promise, what delicate enticement, with every veined quivering leaf! And suddenly the sun caught hold of her, raised her up to him, kissed her all over; she gave forth a sigh of happiness, as though her very spirit had travelled through her lips up to her lover's heart.

A woman in a lilac frock came stealing through the trees towards

Bianca, and sitting down not far off, kept looking quickly round under her sunshade.

Presently Bianca saw what she was looking for. A young man in black coat and shining hat came swiftly up and touched her shoulder. Half hidden by the foliage they sat, leaning forward, prodding gently at the ground with stick and parasol; the stealthy murmur of their talk, so soft and intimate that no word was audible, stole across the grass; and secretly he touched her hand and arm. They were not of the holiday crowd, and had evidently chosen out this vulgar afternoon for a stolen meeting.

Bianca rose and hurried on amongst the trees. She left the Park. In the streets many couples, not so careful to conceal their intimacy, were parading arm-in-arm. The sight of them did not sting her like the sight of those lovers in the Park; they were not of her own order. But presently she saw a little boy and girl asleep on the door-step of a mansion, with their cheeks pressed close together and their arms round each other, and again she hurried on. In the course of that long wandering she passed the building which 'Westminister' was so anxious to avoid. In its gateway an old couple were just about to separate, one to the men's, the other to the women's quarters. Their toothless mouths were close together. 'Well, good-night, mother!' 'Good-night, father, good-night—take care o' yourself!'

Once more Bianca hurried on.

It was past nine when she turned into the Old Square, and rang the bell of her sister's house with the sheer physical desire to rest—somewhere that was not her home.

At one end of the long, low drawing-room Stephen, in evening dress, was reading aloud from a review. Cecilia was looking dubiously at his sock, where she seemed to see a tiny speck of white that might be Stephen. In the window at the far end Thyme and Martin were exchanging speeches at short intervals; they made no move at Bianca's entrance; and their faces said: 'We have no use for that handshaking nonsense!'

Receiving Cecilia's little, warm, doubting kiss and Stephen's polite, dry handshake, Bianca motioned to him not to stop reading. He resumed. Cecilia, too, resumed her scrutiny of Stephen's sock.

'Oh dear!' she thought. 'I know B.'s come here because she's unhappy. Poor thing! Poor Hilary! It's that wretched business again, I suppose.'

Skilled in every tone of Stephen's voice, she knew that Bianca's entry had provoked the same train of thought in him; to her he seemed reading out these words: 'I disapprove—I disapprove. She's Cis's sister. But if it wasn't for old Hilary I wouldn't have the subject in the house!'

Bianca, whose subtlety recorded every shade of feeling, could see that she was not welcome. Leaning back with veil raised, she seemed listening to Stephen's reading, but in fact she was quivering at the sight of those two couples.

Couples, couples—for all but her! What crime had she committed? Why was the china of her cup flawed so that no one could drink from it? Why had she been made so that nobody could love her? This, the most bitter of all thoughts, the most tragic of all questionings, haunted her.

The article which Stephen read—explaining exactly how to deal with people so that from one sort of human being they might become another, and going on to prove that if, after this conversion, they showed signs of a reversion, it would then be necessary to know the reason why—fell dryly on ears listening to that eternal question: Why is it with me as it is? It is not fair!—listening to the constant murmuring of her pride: I am not wanted here or anywhere. Better to efface myself!

From their end of the room Thyme and Martin scarcely looked at her. To them she was Aunt B., an amateur, the mockery of whose eyes sometimes penetrated their youthful armour; they were besides too interested in their conversation to perceive that she was suffering. The skirmish of that conversation had lasted now for many days—ever since the death of the Hughs' baby.

'Well,' Martin was saying, 'what are you going to do? It's no good to base it on the baby; you must know your own mind all round. You can't go rushing into real work on mere sentiment.'

'You went to the funeral, Martin. It's bosh to say you didn't feel it too!'

Martin deigned no answer to this insinuation.

'We've gone past the need for sentiment,' he said: 'it's exploded; so is Justice, administered by an upper class with a patch over one eye and a squint in the other. When you see a dying donkey in a field, you don't want to refer the case to a society, as your dad would; you don't want an essay of Hilary's, full of sympathy with everybody, on "Walking in a field: with reflections on the end of donkeys"—you want to put a bullet in the donkey.'

'You're always down on Uncle Hilary,' said Thyme.

'I don't mind Hilary himself; I object to his type.'

'Well, he objects to yours,' said Thyme.

372

'I'm not so sure of that,' said Martin slowly; 'he hasn't got character enough.'

Thyme raised her chin, and, looking at him through half-closed eyes, said : 'Well, I do think, of all the conceited persons I ever met you're the worst.'

Martin's nostril curled.

'Are you prepared,' he said, 'to put a bullet in the donkey, or are you not?'

'I only see one donkey, and not a dying one!'

Martin stretched out his hand and gripped her arm below the elbow. Retaining it luxuriously, he said : 'Don't wander!'

Thyme tried to free her arm. 'Let go!'

Martin was looking straight into her eyes. A flush had risen in his cheeks.

Thyme, too, went the colour of the old-rose curtain behind which she sat.

'Let go!'

'I won't! I'll *make* you know your mind. What do you mean to do? Are you coming in a fit of sentiment, or do you mean business?'

Suddenly, half-hypnotised, the young girl ceased to struggle. Her face had the strangest expression of submission and defiance— a sort of pain, a sort of delight. So they sat full half a minute staring at each other's eyes. Hearing a rustling sound, they looked, and saw Bianca moving to the door. Cecilia, too, had risen.

'What is it, B.?'

Bianca, opening the door, went out. Cecilia followed swiftly, too late to catch even a glimpse of her sister's face behind the veil. . . .

In Mr Stone's room the green lamp burned dimly, and he who worked by it was sitting on the edge of his camp-bed, attired in his old brown woollen gown and slippers.

And suddenly it seemed to him that he was not alone.

'I have finished for to-night,' he said. 'I am waiting for the moon to rise. She is nearly full; I shall see her face from here.'

A form sat down by him on the bed, and a voice said softly : 'Like a woman's.'

Mr Stone saw his younger daughter. 'You have your hat on. Are you going out, my dear?'

'I saw your light as I came in.'

'The moon,' said Mr Stone, 'is an arid desert. Love is unknown there.'

'How can your bear to look at her, then?' Bianca whispered.

Mr Stone raised his finger. 'She has risen.'

The wan moon had slipped out into the darkness. Her light stole across the garden and through the open window to the bed where they were sitting.

'Where there is no love, Dad,' Bianca said, 'there can be no life, can there?'

Mr Stone's eyes seemed to drink the moonlight.

'That,' he said, 'is the great truth. The bed is shaking!'

With her arms pressed tight across her breast, Bianca was struggling with violent, noiseless sobbing. That desperate struggle seemed to be tearing her to death before his eyes, and Mr Stone sat silent, trembling. He knew not what to do. From his frosted heart years of Universal Brotherhood had taken all knowledge of how to help his daughter. He could only sit touching her tremulously with thin fingers.

The form beside him, whose warmth he felt against his arm, grew stiller, as though, in spite of its own loneliness, his helplessness had made it feel that he, too, was lonely. It pressed a little closer to him. The moonlight, gaining pale mastery over the flickering lamp, filled the whole room.

Mr Stone said: 'I want her mother!'

The form beside him ceased to struggle.

Finding out an old, forgotten way, Mr Stone's arm slid round that quivering body.

'I do not know what to say to her,' he muttered, and slowly he began to rock himself.

'Motion,' he said, 'is soothing.'

The moon passed on. The form beside him sat so still that Mr Stone ceased moving. His daughter was no longer sobbing. Suddenly her lips seared his forehead.

Trembling from that desperate caress, he raised his fingers to the spot and looked round.

She was gone.

Chapter 33

HILARY DEALS WITH THE SITUATION

TO understand the conduct of Hilary and Bianca at what 'West-minister' would have called this 'crisax', not only their feelings as sentient human beings, but their matrimonial philosophy, must be taken into account. By education and environment they belonged to a section of society which had 'in those days' abandoned the more old-fashioned views of marriage. Such as composed this section, finding themselves in opposition, not only to the orthodox proprietary creed, but even to their own legal rights, had been driven to an attitude of almost blatant freedom. Like all folk in opposition, they were bound, as a simple matter of principle, to disagree with those in power, to view with a contemptuous resentment that majority which said, 'I believe the thing is mine, and mine it shall remain'—a majority which by force of numbers made this creed the law. Unable legally to be other than the proprietors of wife or husband, as the case might be, they were obliged, even in the most happy unions, to be very careful not to become disgusted with their own position. Their legal status was, as it were, a goad, spurring them on to show their horror of it. They were like children sent to school with trousers that barely reached their knees, aware that they could neither reduce their stature to the proportions of their breeches nor make their breeches grow. They were furnishing an instance of that immemorial 'change of form to form' to which Mr Stone had given the name of Life. In a past age thinkers and dreamers and 'artistic pigs', rejecting the forms they found, had given unconscious shape to this marriage law, which, after they had become the wind, had formed itself out of their exiled pictures and thoughts and dreams. And now this particular law in turn was the dried rind, devoid of pips or speculation; and the thinkers and dreamers and 'artistic pigs' were again rejecting it, and again themselves in exile.

This exiled faith, this honour amongst thieves, animated a little conversation between Hilary and Bianca on the Tuesday following the night when Mr Stone sat on his bed to watch the rising moon.

Quietly Bianca said: 'I think I shall be going away for a time.'

'Wouldn't you rather that I went instead?'

'You are wanted; I am not.'

That ice-cold, ice-clear remark contained the pith of the whole matter; and Hilary said:

'You are not going at once?'

'At the end of the week, I think.'

Noting his eyes fixed on her, she added:

'Yes; we're neither of us looking quite our best.'

'I am sorry.'

'I know you are.'

This had been all. It had been sufficient to bring Hilary once more face to face with the situation.

Its constituent elements remained the same; relative values had much changed. The temptations of St Anthony were becoming more poignant every hour. He had no 'principles' to pit against them : he had merely the inveterate distaste for hurting anybody, and a feeling that if he yielded to his inclination he would be faced ultimately with a worse situation than ever. It was not possible for him to look at the position as Mr Purcey might have done, if *his* wife had withdrawn from him and a girl had put herself in his way. Neither hesitation because of the defenceless position of the girl, nor hesitation because of his own future with her, would have troubled Mr Purcey. He—good man—in his straightforward way, would have only thought about the present—not, indeed, intending to have a future with a young person of that class. Consideration for a wife who had withdrawn from the society of Mr Purcey would also naturally have been absent from the equation. That Hilary worried over all these questions was the mark of his 'fin de sièclism'. And in the meantime the facts demanded a decision.

He had not spoken to this girl since the day of the baby's funeral, but in that long look from the garden he had in effect said : 'You are drawing me to the only sort of union possible to us!' And she in effect had answered : 'Do what you like with me!'

There were other facts, too, to be reckoned with. Hughs would be released to-morrow; the little model would not stop her visits unless forced to; Mr Stone could not well do without her; Bianca had in effect declared that she was being driven out of her own house. It was this situation which Hilary, seated beneath the bust of Socrates, turned over and over in his mind. Long and painful reflection brought him back continually to the thought that he himself, and not Bianca, had better go away. He was extremely bitter and contemptuous towards himself that he had not done so long ago. He made use of the names Martin had given him. 'Hamlet', 'Amateur', 'Invertebrate'. They gave him, unfortunately, little comfort.

In the afternoon he received a visit. Mr Stone came in with his osier fruit-bag in his hand. He remained standing, and spoke at once.

'Is my daughter happy?'

At this unexpected question Hilary walked over to the fire-place.

'No,' he said at last; 'I am afraid she is not.'

'Why?'

Hilary was silent; then, facing the old man, he said:

'I think she will be glad, for certain reasons, if I go away for a time.'

'When are you going?' asked Mr Stone.

'As soon as I can.'

Mr Stone's eyes, wistfully bright, seemed trying to see through heavy fog.

'She came to me, I think,' he said; 'I seem to recollect her crying. You are good to her?'

'I have tried to be,' said Hilary.

Mr Stone's face was discoloured by a flush. 'You have no children,' he said painfully; 'do you live together?'

Hilary shook his head.

'You are estranged?' said Mr Stone.

Hilary bowed. There was a long silence. Mr Stone's eyes had travelled to the window.

'Without love there cannot be life,' he said at last; and fixing his wistful gaze on Hilary, asked: 'Does she love another?'

Again Hilary shook his head.

When Mr Stone next spoke it was clearly to himself.

'I do not know why I am glad. Do you love another?'

At this question Hilary's eyebrows settled in a frown. 'What do you mean by love?' he said.

Mr Stone did not reply; it was evident that he was reflecting deeply. His lips began to move: 'By love I mean the forgetfulness of self. Unions are frequent in which only the sexual instincts, or the remembrance of self, are roused——'

'That is true,' muttered Hilary.

Mr Stone looked up; painful traces of confusion showed in his face. 'We were discussing something.'

'I was telling you,' said Hilary, 'that it would be better for your daughter if I go away for a time.'

'Yes,' said Mr Stone; 'you are estranged.'

Hilary went back to his stand before the empty fireplace.

'There is one thing, sir,' he said, 'on my conscience to say before I go, and I must leave it to you to decide. The little girl who comes to you no longer lives where she used to live.'

'In that street . . .' said Mr Stone.

Hilary went on quickly. 'She was obliged to leave because the husband of the woman with whom she used to lodge became infatuated with her. He has been in prison, and comes out to-morrow. If she continues to come here he will, of course, be able to find

377

her. I'm afraid he will pursue her again. Have I made it clear to you?'

'No,' said Mr Stone.

'The man,' resumed Hilary patiently, 'is a poor, violent creature, who has been wounded in the head; he is not quite responsible. He may do the girl an injury.'

'What injury?'

'He has stabbed his wife already.'

'I will speak to him,' said Mr Stone.

Hilary smiled. 'I am afraid that words will hardly meet the case. She ought to disappear.'

There was silence.

'My book!' said Mr Stone.

It smote Hilary to see how white his face had become. 'It's better,' he thought, 'to bring his will-power into play; she will never come here, anyway, after I'm gone.'

But, unable to bear the tragedy in the old man's eyes, he touched him on the arm.

'Perhaps she will take the risk, sir, if you ask her.'

Mr Stone did not answer, and, not knowing what more to say, Hilary went back to the window. Miranda was slumbering lightly out there in the speckled shade, where it was not too warm and not too cold, her cheek resting on her paw and white teeth showing.

Mr Stone's voice rose again. 'You are right; I cannot ask her to run a risk like that!'

'She is just coming up the garden,' Hilary said huskily. 'Shall I tell her to come in?'

'Yes,' said Mr Stone.

Hilary beckoned.

The girl came in, carrying a tiny bunch of lilies of the valley; her face fell at sight of Mr Stone; she stood still, raising the lilies to her breast. Nothing could have been more striking than the change from her look of fluttered expectancy to a sort of hard dismay. A spot of red came into both her cheeks. She gazed from Mr Stone to Hilary and back again. Both were staring at her. No one spoke. The little model's bosom began heaving as though she had been running; she said faintly, 'Look; I brought you this, Mr Stone!' and held out to him the bunch of lilies. But Mr Stone made no sign. 'Don't you like them?'

Mr Stone's eyes remained fastened on her face.

To Hilary this suspense was, evidently, most distressing. 'Come, will you tell her, sir,' he said, 'or shall I?'

Mr Stone spoke.

'I shall try and write my book without you. You must not run this risk. I cannot allow it.'

The little model turned her eyes from side to side. 'But I *like* to copy out your book,' she said.

'The man will injure you,' said Mr Stone.

The little model looked at Hilary.

'I don't care if he does; I'm not afraid of him. I can look after myself; I'm used to it.'

'*I* am going away,' said Hilary quietly.

After a desperate look, that seemed to ask, 'Am I going, too?' the little model stood as though frozen.

Wishing to end the painful scene, Hilary went up to Mr Stone. 'Do you want to dictate to her this afternoon, sir?'

'No,' said Mr Stone.

'Nor to-morrow?'

'No.'

'Will you come a little walk with me?'

Mr Stone bowed.

Hilary turned to the little model. 'It is good-bye, then,' he said.

She did not take his hand. Her eyes, turned sideways, glinted; her teeth were fastened on her lower lip. She dropped the lilies, suddenly looked up at him, gulped, and slunk away. In passing she had smeared the lilies with her foot.

Hilary picked up the fragments of the flowers, and dropped them into the grate. The fragrance of the bruised blossoms remained clinging to the air.

'Shall we get ready for our walk?' he said.

Mr Stone moved feebly to the door, and very soon they were walking silently towards the Gardens.

Chapter 34

THYME'S ADVENTURE

THIS same afternoon Thyme, wheeling a bicycle and carrying a light valise, was slipping into a back street out of the Old Square. Putting her burden down at the pavement's edge, she blew a whistle. A hansom-cab appeared, and a man in ragged clothes, who seemed to spring out of the pavement, took hold of her valise. His lean, unshaven face was full of wolfish misery.

'Get off with you!' the cabman said.

'Let him do it!' murmured Thyme.

The cab-runner hoisted up the trunk, then waited motionless beside the cab.

Thyme handed him two coppers. He looked at them in silence, and went away.

'Poor man,' she thought; 'that's one of the things we've got to do away with!'

The cab now proceeded in the direction of the Park, Thyme following on her bicycle, and trying to stare about her calmly.

'This,' she thought, 'is the end of the old life. I won't be romantic, and imagine I'm doing anything special; I must take it all as a matter of course.' She thought of Mr Purcey's face—'that person!' —if he could have seen her at this moment turning her back on comfort. 'The moment I get there,' she mused, 'I shall let mother know; she can come out to-morrow, and see for herself. I can't have hysterics about my disappearance, and all that. They must get used to the idea that I mean to be in touch with things. I can't be stopped by what anybody thinks!'

An approaching motor-car brought a startled frown across her brow. Was it 'that person'? But though it was not Mr Purcey and his A.1. Damyer, it was somebody so like him as made no difference. Thyme uttered a little laugh.

In the Park a cool light danced and glittered on the trees and water, and the same cool, dancing glitter seemed lighting the girl's eyes.

The cabman, unseen, took an admiring look at her. 'Nice little bit, this!' it said.

'Grandfather bathes here,' thought Thyme. 'Poor darling! I pity everyone that's old.'

The cab passed on under the shade of trees out into the road.

'I wonder if we have only one self in us,' thought Thyme. 'I sometimes feel that I have two—Uncle Hilary would understand what I mean. The pavements are beginning to smell horrid already, and it's only June to-morrow. Will mother feel my going very much? How glorious if one didn't feel!'

The cab turned into a narrow street of little shops.

'It must be dreadful to have to serve in a small shop. What millions of people there are in the world! Can anything be of any use? Martin says what matters is to do one's job; but what *is* one's job?'

The cab emerged into a broad, quiet square.

'But I'm not going to think of anything,' thought Thyme; 'that's fatal. Suppose father stops my allowance; I should have to earn my living as a typist, or something of that sort; but he won't, when he sees I mean it. Besides, mother wouldn't let him.'

The cab entered the Euston Road, and again the cabman's broad face was turned towards Thyme with an inquiring stare.

'What a hateful road!' Thyme thought. 'What dull, ugly, common-looking faces all the people seem to have in London! as if they didn't care for anything but just to get through their day somehow. I've only seen two really pretty faces!'

The cab stopped before a small tobacconist's on the south side of the road.

'Have I got to live here?' thought Thyme.

Through the open door a narrow passage led to a narrow staircase covered with oilcloth. She raised her bicycle and wheeled it in. A Jewish-looking youth emerging from the shop accosted her.

'Your gentleman friend says you are to stay in your rooms, please, until he comes.'

His warm red-brown eyes dwelt on her lovingly. 'Shall I take your luggage up, miss?'

'Thank you; I can manage.'

'It's the first floor,' said the young man.

The little rooms which Thyme entered were stuffy, clean, and neat. Putting her trunk down in her bedroom, which looked out on a bare yard, she went into the sitting-room and threw the window up. Down below the cabman and tobacconist were engaged in conversation. Thyme caught the expression on their faces—a sort of leering curiosity.

'How disgusting and horrible men are!' she thought, moodily staring at the traffic. All seemed so grim, so inextricable, and vast, out there in the grey heat and hurry, as though some monstrous devil were sporting with a monstrous ant-heap. The reek of petrol and of dung rose to her nostrils. It was so terribly big and hopeless; it was so ugly! 'I shall never do anything,' thought Thyme—'never —never! Why doesn't Martin come?'

She went into her bedroom and opened her valise. With the scent of lavender that came from it, there sprang up a vision of her white bedroom at home, and the trees of the green garden and the blackbirds on the grass.

The sound of footsteps on the stairs brought her back into the sitting-room. Martin was standing in the doorway.

Thyme ran towards him, but stopped abruptly. 'I've come, you see. What made you choose this place?'

'I'm next door but two; and there's a girl here—one of us. She'll show you the ropes.'

'Is she a lady?'

Martin raised his shoulders. 'She *is* what is called a lady,' he said; 'but she's the right sort, all the same. Nothing will stop her.'

At this proclamation of supreme virtue, the look on Thyme's face was very queer. 'You don't trust me,' it seemed to say, 'and you trust that girl. You put me here for her to watch over me! . . .'

'I want to send this telegram,' she said aloud.

Martin read the telegram. 'You oughtn't to have funked telling your mother what you meant to do.'

Thyme crimsoned. 'I'm not cold-blooded, like you.'

'This is a big matter,' said Martin. 'I told you that you had no business to come at all if you couldn't look it squarely in the face.'

'If you want me to stay you had better be more decent to me, Martin.'

'It must be your own affair,' said Martin.

Thyme stood at the window, biting her lips to keep the tears back from her eyes. A very pleasant voice behind her said: 'I do think it's so splendid of you to come!'

A girl in grey was standing there—thin, delicate, rather plain, with a nose ever so little to one side, lips faintly smiling, and large, shining, greenish eyes.

'I am Mary Daunt. I live above you. Have you had some tea?'

In the gentle question of this girl with the faintly smiling lips and shining eyes Thyme fancied that she detected mockery.

'Yes, thanks. I want to be shown what my work's to be, at once, please.'

The grey girl looked at Martin.

'Oh! Won't to-morrow do for all that sort of thing? I'm sure you must be tired. Mr Stone, do make her rest!'

Martin's glance seemed to say: 'Please leave your femininities!'

'If you mean business, your work will be the same as hers,' he said; 'you're not qualified. All you can do will be visiting, noting the state of the houses and the condition of the children.'

The girl in grey said gently: 'You see, we only deal with sanitation and the children. It seems hard on the grown people and the old to leave them out; but there's sure to be so much less money than we want, so that it *must* all go towards the future.'

382

There was a silence. The girl with the shining eyes added softly:
'1950!'

'1950!' repeated Martin. It seemed to be some formula of faith.

'I must send this telegram!' muttered Thyme.

Martin took it from her and went out.

Left alone in the little room, the two girls did not at first speak.
The girl in grey was watching Thyme half timidly, as if she could
not tell what to make of this young creature who looked so charming, and kept shooting such distrustful glances.

'I think it's so awfully sweet of you to come,' she said at last. 'I
know what a good time you have at home; your cousin's often
told me. Don't you think he's splendid?'

To that question Thyme made no answer.

'Isn't this work horrid,' she said—'prying into people's houses?'

The grey girl smiled. 'It *is* rather awful sometimes. I've been at it
six months now. You get used to it. I've had all the worst things
said to me by now, I should think.'

Thyme shuddered.

'You see,' said the grey girl's faintly smiling lips, 'you soon get
the feeling of having to go through with it. We all realise it's got
to be done, of course. Your cousin's one of the best of us: nothing
seems to put him out. He has such a nice sort of scornful kindness.
I'd rather work with him than anyone.'

She looked past her new associate into that world outside, where
the sky seemed all wires and yellow heat-dust. She did not notice
Thyme appraising her from head to foot, with a stare hostile and
jealous, but pathetic, too, as though confessing that this girl was
her superior.

'I'm sure I can't do that work!' she said suddenly.

The grey girl smiled. 'Oh, *I* thought that at first.' Then, with
an admiring look: 'But I do think it's rather a shame for you,
you're so pretty. Perhaps they'd put you on to tabulation work,
though that's awfully dull. We'll ask your cousin.'

'No; I'll do the whole or nothing.'

'Well,' said the grey girl, 'I've got one house left to-day. Would
you like to come and see the sort of thing?'

She took a small notebook from a side pocket in her skirt.

'I can't get on without a pocket. You must have something that
you can't leave behind. I left four little bags and two dozen handkerchiefs in five weeks before I came back to pockets. It's rather
a horrid house, I'm afraid!'

'*I* shall be all right,' said Thyme shortly.

In the shop doorway the young tobacconist was taking the evening air. He greeted them with his polite but constitutionally leering smile.

'Good-evening, mith,' he said; 'nithe evening!'

'He's rather an awful little man,' the grey girl said when they had achieved the crossing of the street; 'but he's got quite a nice sense of humour.'

'Ah!' said Thyme.

They had turned into a by-street, and stopped before a house which had obviously seen better days. Its windows were cracked, its doors unpainted, and down in the basement could be seen a pile of rags, an evil-looking man seated by it, and a blazing fire. Thyme felt a little gulping sensation. There was a putrid scent as of burning refuse. She looked at her companion. The grey girl was consulting her notebook, with a faint smile on her lips. And in Thyme's heart rose a feeling that was almost hatred for this girl, who was so business-like in the presence of such sights and scents.

The door was opened by a young red-faced woman, who looked as if she had been asleep.

The grey girl screwed up her shining eyes. 'Oh, do you mind if we come in a minute?' she said. 'It would be so good of you. We're making a report.'

'There's nothing to report here,' the young woman answered. But the grey girl had slipped as gently past as though she had been the very spirit of adventure.

'Of course, I see that, but just as a matter of form, you know.'

'I've parted with most of my things,' the young woman said defensively, 'since my husband died. It's a hard life.'

'Yes, yes, but not worse than mine—always poking my nose into other people's houses.'

The young woman was silent, evidently surprised.

'The landlord ought to keep you in better repair,' said the grey girl. 'He owns next door, too, doesn't he?'

The young woman nodded. 'He's a bad landlord. All down the street 'ere it's the same. Can't get nothing done.'

The grey girl had gone over to a dirty bassinette where a half-naked child sprawled. An ugly little girl with fat red cheeks was sitting on a stool beside it, close to an open locker wherein could be seen a number of old meat bones.

'Your chickabiddies?' said the grey girl. 'Aren't they sweet?'

The young woman's face became illumined by a smile.

384

'They're healthy,' she said.

'That's more than can be said for all the children in the house, I expect,' murmured the grey girl.

The young woman replied emphatically, as though voicing an old grievance: 'The three on the first floor's not so bad, but I don't let 'em 'ave anything to do with that lot at the top.'

Thyme saw her new friend's hand hover over the child's head like some pale dove. In answer to that gesture, the mother nodded. 'Just that; you've got to clean 'em every time they go near them children at the top.'

The grey girl looked at Thyme. 'That's where we've got to go, evidently,' she seemed to say.

'A dirty lot!' muttered the young woman.

'It's very hard on you.'

'It is. I'm workin' at the laundry all day when I can get it. I can't look after the children—they get everywhere.'

'Very hard,' murmured the grey girl. 'I'll make a note of that.'

Together with the little book, in which she was writing furiously, she had pulled out her handkerchief, and the sight of this handkerchief reposing on the floor gave Thyme a queer satisfaction, such as comes when one remarks in superior people the absence of a virtue existing in oneself.

'Well, we mustn't keep you, Mrs—Mrs——?'

'Cleary.'

'Cleary. How old's this little one? Four? And the other? Two? They *are* ducks. Good-bye!'

In the corridor outside the grey girl whispered: 'I do like the way we all pride ourselves on being better than someone else. I think it's so hopeful and jolly. Shall we go up and see the abyss at the top?'

Chapter 35

A YOUNG GIRL'S MIND

A YOUNG girl's mind is like a wood in Spring—now a rising mist of bluebells and flakes of dappled sunlight; now a world of still, wan, tender saplings, weeping they know not why. Through the curling twigs of boughs just green, its wings fly towards the stars; but the next moment they have drooped to mope beneath the damp bushes. It is ever yearning for and trembling at the future; in its secret places all the countless shapes of things that are to be are taking stealthy counsel of how to grow up without

385

letting their gown of mystery fall. They rustle, whisper, shriek suddenly, and as suddenly fall into a delicious silence. From the first hazel-bush to the last may-tree it is an unending meeting-place of young solemn things eager to find out what they are, eager to rush forth to greet the kisses of the wind and sun, and for ever trembling back and hiding their faces. The spirit of that wood seems to lie with her ear close to the ground, a pale petal of a hand curved like a shell behind it, listening for the whisper of her own life. There she lies, white and supple, with dewy, wistful eyes, sighing: 'What is my meaning? Ah, I am everything! Is there in all the world a thing so wonderful as I? . . . Oh, I am nothing —my wings are heavy; I faint, I die!'

When Thyme, attended by the grey girl, emerged from the abyss at the top, her cheeks were flushed and her hands clenched. She said nothing. The grey girl, too, was silent, with a look such as a spirit divested of its body by long bathing in the river of reality might bend on one who has just come to dip her head. Thyme's quick eyes saw that look, and her colour deepened. She saw, too, the glance of the Jewish youth when Martin joined them in the doorway.

'Two girls now,' he seemed to say. 'He goes it, this young man!'

Supper was laid in her new friend's room—pressed beef, potato salad, stewed prunes, and ginger ale. Martin and the grey girl talked. Thyme ate in silence, but though her eyes seemed fastened on her plate, she saw every glance that passed between them, heard every word they said. Those glances were not remarkable, nor were those words particularly important, but they were spoken in tones that seemed important to Thyme. 'He never talks to me like that,' she thought.

When supper was over they went out into the streets to walk, but at the door the grey girl gave Thyme's arm a squeeze, her cheek a swift kiss, and turned back up the stairs.

'Aren't you coming?' shouted Martin.

Her voice was heard answering from above: 'No, not to-night.'

With the back of her hand Thyme rubbed off the kiss. The two cousins walked out amongst the traffic.

The evening was very warm and close; no breeze fanned the reeking town. Speaking little, they wandered among endless darkening streets, whence to return to the light and traffic of the Euston Road seemed like coming back to Heaven. At last, close again to her new home, Thyme said: 'Why should one bother? It's all a horrible great machine, trying to blot us out; people are like insects when you put your thumb on them and smear them on a book. I hate—I loathe it!'

'They might as well be healthy insects while they last,' answered Martin.

Thyme faced round at him. 'I shan't sleep to-night, Martin; get out my bicycle for me.'

Martin scrutinised her by the light of the street lamp. 'All right,' he said; 'I'll come too.'

There are, say moralists, roads that lead to Hell, but it was on a road that leads to Hampstead that the two young cyclists set forth towards eleven o'clock. The difference between the character of the two destinations was soon apparent, for whereas man taken in bulk had perhaps made Hell, Hampstead had obviously been made by the upper classes. There were trees and gardens, and instead of dark canals of sky banked by the roofs of houses and hazed with the yellow scum of London lights, the heavens spread out in a wide trembling pool. From that rampart of the town, the Spaniard's Road, two plains lay exposed to left and right; the scent of may-tree blossom had stolen up the hill; the rising moon clung to a fir-tree bough. Over the country the far stars presided, and sleep's dark wings were spread above the fields—silent, scarce breathing, lay the body of the land. But to the south, where the town, that restless head, was lying, the stars seemed to have fallen and were sown in the thousand furrows of its great grey marsh, and from the dark miasma of those streets there travelled up a rustle, a whisper, the far allurement of some deathless dancer, dragging men to watch the swirl of her black, spangled drapery, the gleam of her writhing limbs. Like the song of the sea in a shell was the murmur of that witch of motion, clasping to her the souls of men, drawing them down into a soul whom none had ever seen at rest.

Above the two young cousins, scudding along that ridge between the country and the town, three thin white clouds trailed slowly towards the west—like tired sea-birds drifting exhausted far out from land on a sea blue to blackness with unfathomable depth.

For an hour those two rode silently into the country.

'Have we come far enough?' Martin said at last.

Thyme shook her head. A long, steep hill beyond a little sleeping village had brought them to a standstill. Across the shadowy fields a pale sheet of water gleamed out in moonlight. Thyme turned down towards it.

'I'm hot,' she said; 'I want to bathe my face. Stay here. Don't come with me.'

She left her bicycle, and, passing through a gate, vanished among the trees.

Martin stayed leaning against the gate. The village clock struck one. The distant call of a hunting owl, 'Qu-wheek, qu-wheek!' sounded through the grave stillness of this last night of May. The moon at her curve's summit floated at peace on the blue surface of the sky, a great closed water-lily. And Martin saw through the trees scimitar-shaped reeds clustering black along the pool's shore. All about him the may-flowers were alight. It was such a night as makes dreams real and turns reality to dreams.

'All moonlit nonsense!' thought the young man, for the night had disturbed his heart.

But Thyme did not come back. He called to her, and in the death-like silence following his shouts he could hear his own heart beat. He passed in through the gate. She was nowhere to be seen. Why was she playing him this trick?

He turned up from the water among the trees, where the incense of the may-flowers hung heavy in the air.

'Never look for a thing!' he thought, and stopped to listen. It was so breathless that the leaves of a low bough against his cheek did not stir while he stood there. Presently he heard faint sounds, and stole towards them. Under a beech-tree he almost stumbled over Thyme, lying with her face pressed to the ground. The young doctor's heart gave a sickening leap; he quickly knelt down beside her. The girl's body, pressed close to the dry beech-mat, was being shaken by long sobs. From head to foot it quivered; her hat had been torn off, and the fragrance of her hair mingled with the fragrance of the night. In Martin's heart something seemed to turn over and over, as when a boy he had watched a rabbit caught in a snare. He touched her. She sat up, and, dashing her hand across her eyes, cried: 'Go away! Oh, go away!'

He put his arm round her and waited. Five minutes passed. The air was trembling with a sort of pale vibration, for the moonlight had found a hole in the dark foliage and flooded on to the ground beside them, whitening the black beech-husks. Some tiny bird, disturbed by these unwonted visitors, began chirruping and fluttering, but was soon still again. To Martin, so strangely close to this young creature in the night, there came a sense of utter disturbance.

'Poor little thing!' he thought; 'be careful of her, comfort her!'

Hardness seemed so broken out of her, and the night so wonderful! And there came into the young man's heart a throb of the knowledge—very rare with him, for he was not, like Hilary, a philosophising person—that she was as real as himself—suffering, hoping, feeling, not his hopes and feelings, but her own. His fingers kept pressing her shoulder through her thin blouse. And the touch of those fingers was worth more than any words, as this night, all moonlit dreams, was worth more than a thousand nights of sane reality.

Thyme twisted herself away from him at last.

'I can't,' she sobbed. 'I'm not what you thought me—I'm not made for it!'

A scornful little smile curled Martin's lip. So that was it! But the smile soon died away. One did not hit what was already down!

Thyme's voice wailed through the silence. 'I thought I could— but I want beautiful things. I can't bear it all so grey and horrible. I'm not like *that girl*. I'm—an—amateur!'

'If I kissed her——' Martin thought.

She sank down again, burying her face in the dark beech-mat. The moonlight had passed on. Her voice came faint and stifled, as out of the tomb of faith. 'I'm no good. I never shall be. I'm as bad as mother!'

But to Martin there was only the scent of her hair.

'No,' murmured Thyme's voice, 'I'm only fit for miserable Art. . . . I'm only fit for—nothing!'

They were so close together on the dark beech-mat that their bodies touched, and a longing to clasp her in his arms came over him.

'I'm a selfish beast!' moaned the smothered voice. 'I don't really care for all these people—I only care because they're ugly for me to see!'

Martin reached his hand out to her hair. If she had shrunk away he would have seized her, but as though by instinct she let it rest there. And at her sudden stillness, strange and touching, Martin's quick passion left him. He slipped his arm round her and raised her up, as if she had been a child, and for a long time sat listening with a queer twisted smile to the moanings of her lost illusions.

The dawn found them still sitting there against the bole of the beech-tree. Her lips were parted; the tears had dried on her sleeping face, pillowed against his shoulder, while he still watched her sideways with the ghost of that twisted smile.

And beyond the grey water, like some tired wanton, the moon in an orange hood was stealing down to her rest between the trees.

Chapter 36

STEPHEN SIGNS CHEQUES

WHEN Cecilia received the mystic document containing these words: 'Am quite all right. Address, 598, Euston Road, three doors off Martin. Letter follows explaining.—Thyme,' she had not even realised her little daughter's departure. She went up to Thyme's room at once, and opening all the drawers and cupboards, stared into them one by one. The many things she saw there allayed the first pangs of her disquiet.

'She has only taken one little trunk,' she thought, 'and left all her evening frocks.'

This act of independence alarmed rather than surprised her, such had been her sense of the unrest in the domestic atmosphere during the last month. Since the evening when she had found Thyme in floods of tears because of the Hughs' baby, her maternal eyes had not failed to notice something new in the child's demeanour—a moodiness, an air almost of conspiracy, together with an emphatic increase of youthful sarcasm. Fearful of probing deep, she had sought no confidence, nor had she divulged her doubts to Stephen.

Amongst the blouses a sheet of blue ruled paper, which had evidently escaped from a notebook, caught her eye. Cecilia read: 'That poor little dead thing was so grey and pinched, and I seemed to realise all of a sudden how awful it is for them. I must—I must—I *will* do something!'

Cecilia dropped the sheet of paper; her hand was trembling. There was no mystery in that departure now, and Stephen's words came into her mind: 'It's all very well up to a certain point, and nobody sympathises with them more than I do; but after that it becomes destructive of all comfort, and that does no good to anyone.'

The sound sense of those words had made her feel queer when they were spoken; they were even more sensible than she had thought. Did her little daughter, so young and pretty, seriously mean to plunge into the rescue work of dismal slums, to cut herself adrift from sweet sounds and scents and colours, from music and art, from dancing, flowers, and all that made life beautiful? The secret forces of fastidiousness, an inborn dread of the fanatical, and all her real ignorance of what such a life was like, rose in Cecilia with a force that made her feel quite sick. Better that she herself should do this thing than that her own child should be deprived of air and light and all the just environment of her youth and beauty. 'She must come back—she must listen to me!' she thought. 'We will begin together; we will start a nice little *crèche* of our own, or perhaps Mrs Tallents Smallpeace could find us some regular work on one of her committees.'

Then suddenly she conceived a thought which made her blood run positively cold. What if it were a matter of heredity? What if Thyme had inherited her grandfather's single-mindedness? Martin was giving proof of it. Things, she knew, often skipped a generation and then set in again. Surely, surely, it could not have done that! With longing, yet with dread, she waited for the sound of Stephen's latchkey. It came at its appointed time.

Even in her agitation Cecilia did not forget to spare him, all she could. She began by giving him a kiss, and then said casually: 'Thyme has got a whim into her head.'

'What whim?'

'It's rather what you might expect,' faltered Cecilia, 'from her going about so much with Martin:'

Stephen's face assumed at once an air of dry derision; there was no love lost between him and his young nephew-in-law.

'The Sanitist?' he said; 'ah! Well?'

'She has gone off to do work to some place in the Euston Road. I've had a telegram. Oh, and I found this, Stephen.'

She held out to him half-heartedly the two bits of paper, one pinkish-brown, the other blue. Stephen saw that she was trembling. He took them from her, read them, and looked at her again. He had a real affection for his wife, and the tradition of consideration for other people's feelings was bred in him, so that at this moment, so vitally disturbing, the first thing he did was to put his hand on her shoulder and give it a reassuring squeeze. But there was also in Stephen a certain primitive virility, pickled, it is true, at Cambridge, and in the Law Courts dried, but still preserving something of its possessive and assertive quality, and the second thing he did was to say, 'No, I'm damned!'

In that little sentence lay the whole psychology of his attitude towards this situation and all the difference between two classes of the population. Mr Purcey would undoubtedly have said: '*Well*, I'm damned!' Stephen, by saying '*No*, I'm damned!' betrayed that before he could be damned he had been obliged to wrestle and contend with something, and Cecilia, who was always wrestling too, knew this something to be that queer new thing, a Social Conscience, the dim bogey stalking pale about the houses of those who, through the accidents of leisure or of culture, had once left the door open to the suspicion: Is it possible that there is a class of people besides my own, or am I dreaming? Happy the millions, poor or rich, not yet condemned to watch the wistful visiting or hear the husky mutter of that ghost, happy in their homes, blessed by a less disquieting god. Such were Cecilia's inner feelings.

Even now she did not quite plumb the depths of Stephen's; she felt his struggle with the ghost, she felt and admired his victory. What she did not, could not, perhaps, realise, was the precise nature of the outrage inflicted on him by Thyme's action. With her —being a woman—the matter was more practical; she did not grasp, had never grasped, the architectural nature of Stephen's mind —how really hurt he was by what did not seem to him in due and proper order.

He spoke: 'Why on earth, if she felt like that, couldn't she have gone to work in the ordinary way? She could have put herself in connection with some proper charitable society—I should never have objected to that. It's all that young Sanitary idiot!'

'I believe,' Cecilia faltered, 'that Martin's *is* a society. It's a kind of medical Socialism, or something of that sort. He has tremendous faith in it.'

Stephen's lip curled.

'He may have as much faith as he likes,' he said, with the restraint that was one of his best qualities, 'so long as he doesn't infect my daughter with it.'

Cecilia said suddenly: 'Oh! what are we to do, Stephen? Shall I go over there to-night?'

As one may see a shadow pass down on a cornfield, so came the cloud on Stephen's face. It was as though he had not realised till then the full extent of what this meant. For a minute he was silent.

'Better wait for her letter,' he said at last. 'He's her cousin, after all, and Mrs Grundy's dead—in the Euston Road, at all events.'

So, trying to spare each other all they could of anxiety, and careful to abstain from any hint of trouble before the servants, they dined and went to bed.

At that hour between the night and morning, when man's vitality is lowest, and the tremors of his spirit, like birds of ill omen, fly round and round him, beating their long plumes against his cheeks, Stephen awoke.

It was very still. A bar of pearly-grey dawn showed between the filmy curtains, which stirred with a regular, faint movement, like the puffing of a sleeper's lips. The tide of the wind, woven in Mr Stone's fancy of the souls of men, was at low ebb. Feebly it fanned the houses and hovels where the myriad forms of men lay sleeping, unconscious of its breath; so faint life's pulse, that men and shadows seemed for that brief moment mingled in the town's sleep. Over the million varied roofs, over the hundred-million little different shapes of men and things, the wind's quiet, visiting wand had stilled all into the wonder state of nothingness, when life is passing into death, death into new life, and self is at its feeblest.

And Stephen's self, feeling the magnetic currents of that ebb-tide drawing it down into murmurous slumber, out beyond the sandbars of individuality and class, threw up its little hands and began to cry for help. The purple sea of self-forgetfulness, under the dim, impersonal sky, seemed to him so cold and terrible. It had no limit that he coud see, no rules but such as hung too far away, written in the hieroglyphics of paling stars. He could feel no order in the lift and lap of the wan waters round his limbs. Where would those waters carry him? To what depth of still green silence? Was his own little daughter to go down into this sea that knew no creed but that of self-forgetfulness, that respected neither class nor person— this sea where a few wandering streaks seemed all the evidence of the precious differences between mankind? God forbid it!

And, turning on his elbow, he looked at her who had given him this daughter. In the mystery of his wife's sleeping face—the face of her most near and dear to him—he tried hard not to see a likeness to Mr Stone. He fell back somewhat comforted with the thought: 'That old chap has his one idea—his Universal Brotherhood. He's absolutely absorbed in it. I don't see it in Cis's face a bit. Quite the contrary.'

But suddenly a flash of clear, hard cynicism amounting to inspiration utterly disturbed him: The old chap, indeed, was so wrapped up in himself and his precious book as to be quite unconscious that anyone else was alive. Could one be everybody's brother if one were blind to their existence? But this freak of Thyme's was an actual try to be everybody's sister. For that, he supposed, one *must* forget oneself. Why, it was really even a worse case than that of Mr Stone! And to Stephen there was something awful in this thought.

The first small bird of morning, close to the open window, uttered a feeble chirrup. Into Stephen's mind there leaped without reason recollection of the morning after his first term at school, when, awakened by the birds, he had started up and fished out from under his pillow his catapult and the box of shot he had brought home and taken to sleep with him. He seemed to see again those leaden shot with their bluish sheen, and to feel them, round, and soft, and heavy, rolling about his palm. He seemed to hear Hilary's surprised voice saying: 'Hallo, Stevie! you awake?'

No one had ever had a better brother than old Hilary. His only fault was that he had always been too kind. It was his kindness that had done for him, and made his married life a failure. He had never asserted himself enough with that woman, his wife. Stephen turned over on his other side. 'All this confounded business,' he thought, 'comes from over-sympathising. That's what's the matter with Thyme, too.' Long he lay thus, while the light grew stronger, listening to Cecilia's gentle breathing, disturbed to his very marrow by these thoughts.

The first post brought no letter from Thyme, and the announcement soon after, that Mr Hilary had come to breakfast, was received by both Stephen and Cecilia with a welcome such as the anxious give to anything which shows promise of distracting them.

Stephen made haste down. Hilary, with a very grave and harassed face, was in the dining-room. It was he, however, who, after one look at Stephen, said:

'What's the matter, Stevie?'

Stephen took up the *Standard*. In spite of his self-control, his hand shook a little.

'It's a ridiculous business,' he said. 'That precious young Sanitist has so worked his confounded theories into Thyme that she has gone off to the Euston Road to put them into practice, of all things!'

At the half-concerned amusement on Hilary's face his quick and rather narrow eyes glinted.

'It's not exactly for you to laugh, Hilary,' he said. 'It's all of a piece with your cursed sentimentality about those Hughs, and that girl. I knew it would end in a mess.'

Hilary answered this unjust and unexpected outburst by a look, and Stephen, with the strange feeling of inferiority which would come to him in Hilary's presence against his better judgment, lowered his own glance.

'My dear boy,' said Hilary, 'if any bit of my character has crept into Thyme, I'm truly sorry.'

Stephen took his brother's hand and gave it a good grip; and, Cecilia coming in, they all sat down.

Cecilia at once noted what Stephen in his preoccupation had not —that Hilary had come to tell them something. But she did not like to ask him what it was, though she knew that in the presence of their trouble Hilary was too delicate to obtrude his own. She did not like, either, to talk of her trouble in the presence of his. They all talked, therefore, of indifferent things—what music they had heard, what plays they had seen—eating but little, and drinking tea. In the middle of a remark about the opera, Stephen, looking up, saw Martin himself standing in the doorway. The young Sanitist looked pale, dusty, and dishevelled. He advanced towards Cecilia, and said with his usual cool determination:

'I've brought her back, Aunt Cis.'

At that moment, fraught with such relief, such pure joy, such desire to say a thousand things, Cecilia could only murmur: 'Oh, Martin!'

Stephen, who had jumped up, asked: 'Where is she?'

'Gone to her room.'

'Then perhaps,' said Stephen, regaining at once his dry composure, 'you will give us some explanation of this folly.'

'She's no use to us at present.'

'Indeed!'

'None.'

'Then,' said Stephen, 'kindly understand that we have no use for *you* in future, or any of your sort.'

Martin looked round the table, resting his eyes on each in turn.

'You're right,' he said. 'Good-bye!'

Hilary and Cecilia had risen, too. There was silence. Stephen crossed to the door.

'You seem to me,' he said suddenly, in his driest voice, 'with your new manners and ideas, quite a pernicious youth.'

Cecilia stretched her hands out towards Martin, and there was a faint tinkling, as of chains.

'You must know, dear,' she said, 'how anxious we've all been. Of course, your uncle doesn't mean that.'

The same scornful tenderness with which he was wont to look at Thyme passed into Martin's face.

'All right, Aunt Cis,' he said; 'if Stephen doesn't mean it, he ought to. To mean things is what matters.' He stooped and kissed her forehead. 'Give that to Thyme for me,' he said. 'I shan't see her for a bit.'

'You'll never see her, sir,' said Stephen dryly, 'if I can help it! The liquor of your Sanitism is too bright and effervescent.'

395

Martin's smile broadened. 'For old bottles,' he said, and with another slow look round went out.

Stephen's mouth assumed its driest twist. 'Bumptious young devil!' he said. 'If that is the new young man, defend us!'

Over the cool dining-room, with its faint scent of pinks, of melon, and of ham, came silence. Suddenly Cecilia glided from the room. Her light footsteps were heard hurrying, now that she was not visible, up to Thyme.

Hilary, too, had moved towards the door. In spite of his pre-occupation, Stephen could not help noticing how very worn his brother looked.

'You look quite seedy, old boy,' he said. 'Will you have some brandy?'

Hilary shook his head.

'Now that you've got Thyme back,' he said, 'I'd better let you know my news. I'm going abroad to-morrow. I don't know whether I shall come back again to live with B.'

Stephen gave a low whistle; then, pressing Hilary's arm, he said: 'Anything you decide, old man, I'll always back you in, but——'

'I'm going alone.'

In his relief Stephen violated the laws of reticence.

'Thank Heaven for that! I was afraid you were beginning to lose your head about that girl.'

'I'm not quite fool enough,' said Hilary, 'to imagine that such a liaison would be anything but misery in the long-run. If I took the child I should have to stick to her; but I'm not proud of leaving her in the lurch, Stevie.'

The tone of his voice was so bitter that Stephen seized his hand.

'My dear old man, you're too kind. Why, she's no hold on you —not the smallest in the world!'

'Except the hold of this devotion I've roused in her, God knows how, and her destitution.'

'You let these people haunt you,' said Stephen. 'It's quite a mistake—it really is.'

'I had forgotten to mention that I am not an iceberg,' muttered Hilary.

Stephen looked into his face without speaking, then with the utmost earnestness he said:

'However much you may be attracted, it's simply unthinkable for a man like you to go outside his class.'

'Class! Yes!' muttered Hilary: 'Good-bye!' And with a long grip of his brother's hand he went away.

Stephen turned to the window. For all the care and contrivance bestowed on the view, far away to the left the back courts of an alley could be seen; and as though some gadfly had planted in him its small poisonous sting, he moved back from the sight at once.

'Confusion!' he thought. 'Are we never to get rid of these infernal people?'

His eyes lighted on the melon. A single slice lay by itself on a blue-green dish. Leaning over a plate, with a desperation quite unlike himself, he took an enormous bite. Again and again he bit the slice, then almost threw it from him, and dipped his fingers in a bowl.

'Thank God!' he thought, 'that's over! What an escape!'

Whether he meant Hilary's escape or Thyme's was doubtful, but there came on him a longing to rush up to his little daughter's room and hug her. He suppressed it, and sat down at the bureau; he was suddenly experiencing a sensation such as he had sometimes felt on a perfect day, or after physical danger, of too much benefit, of something that he would like to return thanks for, yet knew not how. His hand stole to the inner pocket of his black coat. It stole out again; there was a cheque-book in it. Before his mind's eye, starting up one after the other, he saw the names of the societies he supported, or meant sometime, if he could afford it, to support. He reached his hand out for a pen. The still, small noise of the nib travelling across the cheques mingled with the buzzing of a single fly.

These sounds Cecilia heard, when, from the open door, she saw the thin back of her husband's neck, with its softly graduated hair, bent forward above the bureau. She stole over to him, and pressed herself against his arm.

Stephen, staying the progress of his pen, looked up at her. Their eyes met, and, bending down, Cecilia put her cheek to his.

Chapter 37

THE FLOWERING OF THE ALOE

THIS same day, returning through Kensington Gardens, from his preparations for departure, Hilary came suddenly on Bianca standing by the shores of the Round Pond.

To the eyes of the frequenters of these Elysian fields, where so many men and shadows daily steal recreation, to the eyes of all drinking in those green gardens their honeyed draught of peace, this husband and wife appeared merely a distinguished-looking couple, animated by a leisured harmony. For the time was not yet when men were one, and could tell by instinct what was passing in each other's hearts.

In truth, there were not too many people in London who, in their situation, would have behaved with such seemliness—not too many so civilised as they!

Estranged, and soon to part, they retained the manner of accord up to the last. Not for them the matrimonial brawl, the solemn accusation and recrimination, the pathetic protestations of proprietary rights. For them no sacred view that at all costs they must make each other miserable—not ever the belief that they had the right to do so. No, there was no reli f for their sore hearts. They walked side by side, treating each otl er's feelings with respect, as if there had been no terrible heart-burnings throughout the eighteen years in which they had first loved, then, through mysterious disharmony, drifted apart; as if there were now between them no question of this girl.

Presently Hilary said:

· 'I've been into town and made my preparations; I'm starting tomorrow for the mountains. There will be no necessity for you to leave your father.'

'Are you taking her?'

It was beautifully uttered, without a trace of bias or curiosity, with an unforced accent, neither indifferent nor too interested— no one could have told whether it was meant for generosity or malice. Hilary took it for the former.

'Thank you,' he said; 'that comedy is finished.'

Close to the edge of the Round Pond a swan-like cutter was putting out to sea; in the wake of this fair creature a tiny scooped-out bit of wood, with three feathers for masts, bobbed and trembled; and the two small ragged boys who owned that little galley were stretching bits of branch out towards her over the bright waters.

Bianca looked, without seeing, at this proof of man's pride in his own property. A thin gold chain hung round her neck; suddenly she thrust it into the bosom of her dress. It had broken into two, between her fingers.

They reached home without another word.

At the door of Hilary's study sat Miranda. The little person answered his caress by a shiver of her sleek skin, then curled herself down again on the spot she had already warmed.

'Aren't you coming in with me?' he said.

Miranda did not move.

The reason for her refusal was apparent when Hilary had entered. Close to the long bookcase, behind the bust of Socrates, stood the little model. Very still, as if fearing to betray itself by sound or movement, was her figure in its blue-green frock, and a brimless toque of brown straw, with two purplish roses squashed together into a band of darker velvet. Beside those roses a tiny peacock's feather had been slipped in—unholy little visitor, slanting backward, trying, as it were, to draw all eyes, yet to escape notice. And, wedged between the grim white bust and the dark bookcase, the girl herself was like some unlawful spirit which had slid in there, and stood trembling and vibrating, ready to be shuttered out.

Before this apparition Hilary recoiled towards the door, hesitated, and returned.

'You should not have come here,' he muttered, 'after what we said to you yesterday.'

The little model answered quickly: 'But I've seen Hughs, Mr Dallison. He's found out where I live. Oh, he does look dreadful; he frightens me. I can't ever stay there now.'

She had come a little out of her hiding-place, and stood fidgeting her hands and looking down.

'She's not speaking the truth,' thought Hilary.

The little model gave him a furtive glance. 'I *did* see him,' she said. 'I must go right away now; it wouldn't be safe, would it?' Again she gave him that swift look.

Hilary thought suddenly: 'She is using my own weapon against me. If she *has* seen the man, he didn't frighten her. It serves me right!' With a dry laugh, he turned his back.

There was a rustling sound. The little model had moved out of her retreat, and stood between him and the door. At this stealthy action, Hilary felt once more the tremor which had come over him when he sat beside her in the Broad Walk after the baby's funeral. Outside in the garden a pigeon was pouring forth a continuous love-song; Hilary heard nothing of it, conscious only of the figure of the girl behind him—that young figure which had twined itself about his senses.

'Well, what is it you want?' he said at last.

The little model answered by another question. 'Are you really going away, Mr Dallison?'

'I am.'

She raised her hands to the level of her breast, as though she meant to clasp them together; without doing so, however, she dropped them to her sides. They were cased in very worn suède gloves, and in this dire moment of embarrassment Hilary's eyes fastened themselves on those slim hands moving against her skirt.

The little model tried at once to slip them away behind her. Suddenly she said in her matter-of-fact voice: 'I only wanted to ask—Can't I come too?'

At this question, whose simplicity might have made an angel smile, Hilary experienced a sensation as if his bones had been turned to water. It was strange—delicious—as though he had been suddenly offered all that he wanted of her, without all those things that he did not want. He stood regarding her silently. Her cheeks and neck were red; there was a red tinge, too, in her eyelids, deepening the 'chicory-flower' colour of her eyes. She began to speak, repeating a lesson evidently learned by heart.

'I wouldn't be in your way. I wouldn't cost much. I could do everything you wanted. I could learn typewriting. I needn't live too near, or that, if you didn't want me, because of people talking; I'm used to being alone. Oh, Mr Dallison, I could do everything for you. I wouldn't mind *anything*, and I'm not like some girls; I do know what I'm talking about.'

'Do you?'

The little model put her hands up, and, covering her face, said: 'If you'd try and see!'

Hilary's sensuous feeling almost vanished; a lump rose in his throat instead.

'My child,' he said, 'you are too generous!'

The little model seemed to know instinctively that by touching his spirit she had lost ground. Uncovering her face, she spoke breathlessly, growing very pale:

'Oh no, I'm not. I *want* to be let come; I don't want to stay here. I know I'll get into mischief if you don't take me—oh, I know I will!'

'If I were to let you come with me,' said Hilary, 'what then? What sort of companion should I be to you, or you to me? You know very well. Only one sort. It's no use pretending, child, that we've any interests in common.'

The little model came closer.

'I know what I am,' she said, 'and I don't want to be anything else. I can do what you tell me to, and I shan't ever complain. I'm not worth any more!'

'You're worth more,' muttered Hilary, 'than I can ever give you, and I'm worth more than you can ever give me.'

The little model tried to answer, but her words would not pass her throat; she threw her head back trying to free them, and stood, swaying. Seeing her like this before him, white as a sheet, with her eyes closed and her lips parted, as though about to faint, Hilary seized her by the shoulders. At the touch of those soft shoulders, his face became suffused with blood, his lips trembled. Suddenly her eyes opened ever so little between their lids, and looked at him. And the perception that she was not really going to faint, that it was a little desperate wile of this child Dalilah, made him wrench away his hands. The moment she felt that grasp relax she sank down and clasped his knees, pressing them to her bosom so that he could not stir. Closer and closer she pressed them to her, till it seemed as though she must be bruising her flesh. Her breath came in sobs; her eyes were closed; her lips quivered upwards. In the clutch of her clinging body there seemed suddenly the whole of woman's power of self-abandonment. It was just that, which, at this moment, so horribly painful to him, prevented Hilary from seizing her in his arms—just that queer seeming self-effacement, as though she were lost to knowledge of what she did. It seemed too brutal, too like taking advantage of a child.

From calm is born the wind, the ripple from the still pool, self out of nothingness—so all passes imperceptibly, no man knows how. The little model's moment of self-oblivion passed, and into her wet eyes her plain, twisting spirit suddenly writhed up again, for all the world as if she had said: 'I won't let you go; I'll keep you—I'll keep you.'

Hilary broke away from her, and she fell forward on her face.

'Get up, child,' he said—'get up; for God's sake, don't lie there!'

She rose obediently, choking down her sobs, mopping her face with a small, dirty handkerchief. Suddenly, taking a step towards him, she clenched both her hands and struck them downwards.

'I'll go to the bad,' she said—'I *will*—if you don't take me!' And, her breast heaving, her hair all loose, she stared straight into his face with her red-rimmed eyes. Hilary turned suddenly, took a book up from the writing-table, and opened it. His face was again suffused with blood; his hands and lips trembled; his eyes had a queer fixed stare.

'Not now, not now,' he muttered; 'go away now. I'll come to you to-morrow.'

The little model gave him the look a dog gives you when it asks

if you are deceiving him. She made a sign on her breast, as a
Catholic might make the sign of his religion, drawing her fingers
together, and clutching at herself with them, then passed her little
dirty handkerchief once more over her eyes, and, turning round,
went out.

Hilary remained standing where he was, reading the open book
without apprehending what it was.

There was a wistful sound, as of breath escaping hurriedly. Mr
Stone was standing in the open doorway.

'She has been here,' he said. 'I saw her go away.'

Hilary dropped the book; his nerves were utterly unstrung. Then,
pointing to a chair, he said: 'Won't you sit down, sir?'

Mr Stone came close up to his son-in-law.

'Is she in trouble?'

'Yes,' murmured Hilary.

'She is too young to be in trouble. Did you tell her that?'

Hilary shook his head.

'Has the man hurt her?'

Again Hilary shook his head.

'What is her trouble, then?' said Mr Stone.

The closeness of this catechism, the intent stare of the old man's
eyes, were more than Hilary could bear. He turned away.

'You ask me something that I cannot answer.'

'Why?'

'It is a private matter.'

With the blood still beating in his temples, his lips still quivering,
and the feeling of the girl's clasp round his knees, he almost hated
this old man who stood there putting such blind questions.

Then suddenly in Mr Stone's eyes he saw a startling change; as in
the face of a man who regains consciousness after days of vacancy.
His whole countenance had become alive with a sort of jealous
understanding. The warmth which the little model brought to his
old spirit had licked up the fog of his Idea, and made him see what
was going on before his eyes.

At that look Hilary braced himself against the wall.

A flush spread slowly over Mr Stone's face. He spoke with
rare hesitation. In this sudden coming back to the world of men
and things he seemed astray.

'I am not going,' he stammered, 'to ask you any more. I could
not pry into a private matter. That would not be——' His voice
failed; he looked down.

Hilary bowed, touched to the quick by the return to life of this old man, so long lost to facts, and by the delicacy in that old face.

'I will not intrude further on your trouble,' said Mr Stone, 'whatever it may be. I am sorry that you are unhappy, too.'

Very slowly, and without again looking up at his son-in-law, he went out.

Hilary remained standing where he had been left against the wall.

Chapter 38

THE HOME-COMING OF HUGHS

HILARY had evidently been right in thinking the little model was not speaking the truth when she said she had seen Hughs, for it was not until early on the following morning that three persons traversed the long winding road leading from Wormwood Scrubs to Kensington. They preserved silence, not because there was nothing in their hearts to be expressed, but because there was too much; and they walked in the giraffe-like formation peculiar to the lower classes—Hughs in front; Mrs Hughs to the left, a foot or two behind; and a yard behind her, to the left again, her son Stanley. They made no sign of noticing anyone in the road besides themselves, and no one in the road gave sign of noticing that they were there; but in their three minds, so differently fashioned, a verb was dumbly, and with varying emotion, being conjugated:

> 'I've been in prison.'
> 'You've been in prison.'
> 'He's been in prison.'

Beneath the seeming acquiescence of a man subject to domination from his birth up, those four words covered in Hughs such a whirlpool of surging sensation, such a ferocity of bitterness, and madness, and defiance, that no outpouring could have appreciably relieved its course. The same four words summed up in Mrs Hughs so strange a mingling of fear, commiseration, loyalty, shame, and trembling curiosity at the new factor which had come into the life of all this little family walking giraffe-like back to Kensington that to have gone beyond them would have been like plunging into a wintry river. To their son the four words were as a legend of romance, conjuring up no definite image, lighting merely the glow of wonder.

'Don't lag, Stanley. Keep up with your father.'

The little boy took three steps at an increased pace, then fell behind again. His black eyes seemed to answer: 'You say that because you don't know what else to say.' And without alteration in their giraffe-like formation, but again in silence, the three proceeded.

In the heart of the seamstress doubt and fear were being slowly knit into dread of the first sound to pass her husband's lips. What would he ask? How should she answer? Would he talk wild, or would he talk sensible? Would he have forgotten that young girl, or had he nursed and nourished his wicked fancy in the house of grief and silence? Would he ask where the baby was? Would he speak a kind word to her? But alongside her dread there was fluttering within her the undying resolution not to 'let him go from her, if it were ever so, to that young girl.'

'Don't lag, Stanley!'

At the reiteration of those words Hughs spoke.

'Let the boy alone; You'll be nagging at the baby next!'

Hoarse and grating, like sounds issuing from a damp vault, was this first speech.

The seamstress's eyes brimmed over.

'I won't get the chance,' she stammered out. 'He's gone!'

Hughs' teeth gleamed like those of a dog at bay.

'Who's taken him? You let me know the name.'

Tears rolled down the seamstress's cheeks; she could not answer. Her little son's thin voice rose instead:

'Baby's dead. We buried him in the ground. I saw it. Mr Creed came in the cab with me.'

White flecks appeared suddenly at the corners of Hughs' lips. He wiped the back of his hand across his mouth, and once more, giraffe-like, the little family marched on. . . .

'Westminister', in his threadbare summer jacket—for the day was warm—had been standing for some little time in Mrs Budgen's doorway on the ground floor at Hound Street. Knowing that Hughs was to be released that morning early, he had, with the circumspection and foresight of his character, reasoned thus: 'I shan't lie easy in my bed, I shan't hev no peace until I know that low feller's not a-goin' to misdemean himself with me. It's no good to go a-puttin' of it off. I don't want him comin' to my room attackin' of old men. I'll be previous with him in the passage. The lame woman 'll let me. I shan't trouble her. She'll be palliable between me and him, in case he goes for to attack me. *I* ain't afraid of him.'

But, as the minutes of waiting went by, his old tongue, like that of a dog expecting chastisement, appeared ever more frequently to moisten his twisted, discoloured lips. 'This comes of mixin' up with soldiers,' he thought, 'and a low-class o' man like that. I ought to ha' changed my lodgin's. He'll be askin' me where that young girl is, I shouldn't wonder, an' him lost his character and his job, and everything, and all because o' women!'

He watched the broad-faced woman, Mrs Budgen, in whose grey eyes the fighting light so fortunately never died, painfully doing out her rooms, and propping herself against the chest of drawers whereon clustered china cups and dogs as thick as toadstools on a bank.

'I've told my Charlie,' she said, 'to keep clear of Hughs a bit. They comes out as prickly as hedgehogs. Pick a quarrel as soon as look at you, they will.'

'Oh dear,' thought Creed, 'she's full o' cold comfort.' But, careful of his dignity, he answered: 'I'm a-waitin' here to engage the situation. You don't think he'll attack of me with definition at this time in the mornin'?'

The lame woman shrugged her shoulders. 'He'll have had a drop of something,' she said, 'before he comes home. They gets a cold feelin' in the stomach in them places, poor creatures!'

The old butler's heart quavered up into his mouth. He lifted his shaking hand, and put it to his lips, as though to readjust himself.

'Oh yes,' he said; 'I ought to ha' given notice, and took my things away; but there, poor woman, it seemed a-hittin' of her when she was down. And I don't *want* to make no move. I ain't got no one else that's interested in me. This woman's very good about mendin' of my clothes. Oh dear, yes; she don't grudge a little thing like that!'

The lame woman hobbled from her post of rest, and began to make the bed with the frown that always accompanied a task which strained the contracted muscles of her leg. 'If you don't help your neighbour, your neighbour don't help you,' she said sententiously.

Creed fixed his iron-rimmed gaze on her in silence. He was considering perhaps how he stood with regard to Hughs in the light of that remark.

'I attended of his baby's funeral,' he said. 'Oh dear, he's here a'ready!'

The family of Hughs, indeed, stood in the doorway. The spiritual process by which 'Westminister' had gone through life

was displayed completely in the next few seconds. 'It's so important for me to keep alive and well,' his eyes seemed saying. 'I know
the class of man you are, but now you're here it's not a bit o' use
me bein' frightened. I'm bound to get up-sides with you. Ho! yes;
keep yourself to yourself, and don't you let me hev any o'
your nonsense, 'cause I won't stand it. Oh dear, no!'

Beads of perspiration stood thick on his patchily coloured forehead; with lips stiffening, and intently staring eyes, he waited
for what the released prisoner would say.

Hughs, whose face had blanched in the prison to a sallow grey-
white hue, and whose black eyes seemed to have sunk back into his
head, slowly looked the old man up and down. At last he took his
cap off, showing his cropped hair.

'*You* got me that, daddy,' he said, 'but I don't bear you malice.
Come up and have a cup o' tea with us.'

And, turning on his heel, he began to mount the stairs, followed
by his wife and child. Breathing hard, the old butler mounted
too.

In the room on the second floor, where the baby no longer
lived, a haddock on the table was endeavouring to be fresh; round
it were slices of bread on plates, a piece of butter in a pie-dish, a
teapot, brown sugar in a basin, and, side by side, a little blue jug of
cold milk and a half-empty bottle of red vinegar. Close to one plate
a bunch of stocks and gillyflowers reposed on the dirty tablecloth,
as though dropped and forgotten by the God of Love. Their faint
perfume stole through the other odours. The old butler fixed his
eyes on it.

'The poor woman bought that,' he thought, 'hopin' for to remind
him of old days. She had them flowers on her weddin'-day, I
shouldn't wonder!' This poetical conception surprising him, he
turned towards the little boy, and said: 'This'll be a memorial.
to you, as you gets older.' And without another word all sat down.

They ate in silence, and the old butler thought: 'That 'addick
ain't what it was; but a beautiful cup o' tea. He don't eat nothing;
he's more ameniable to reason than I expected. There's no one
won't be too pleased to see him now!'

His eyes, travelling to the spot from which the bayonet had
been removed, rested on the print of the Nativity. ' "Suffer little
children to come unto *Me*," ' he thought, ' "and forbid them not".
He'll be glad to hear there was two carriages followed him home.'

And, taking his time, he cleared his throat in preparation for
speech. But before the singular muteness of this family sounds

would not come. Finishing his tea, he tremblingly arose. Things that he might have said jostled in his mind. 'Very pleased to 'a seen you. Hope you're in good health at the present time of speaking. Don't let me intrude on you. We've all a-got to die some time or other!' They remained unuttered. Making a vague movement of his skinny hand, he walked feebly but quickly to the door. When he stood but half-way within the room, he made his final effort.

'I'm not a-goin' to say nothing,' he said;—'*that'd* be superlative! I wish you a good-morning.'

Outside he waited a second, then grasped the banister.

'For all he sets so quiet, they've done him no good in that place,' he thought. 'Them eyes of his!' And slowly he descended, full of a sort of very deep surprise. 'I misjudged of him,' he was thinking; 'he never was nothing but a 'armless human being. We all has our predijuices—I misjudged of him. They've broke his 'eart between 'em—that they have.'

The silence in the room continued after his departure. But when the little boy had gone to school, Hughs rose and lay down on the bed. He rested there, unmoving, with his face towards the wall, his arms clasped round his head to comfort it. The seamstress, stealing about her avocations, paused now and then to look at him. If he had raged at her, if he had raged at everything, it would not have been so terrifying as this utter silence, which passed her comprehension—this silence as of a man flung by the sea against a rock, and pinned there with the life crushed out of him. All her inarticulate longing, now that her baby was gone, to be close to something in her grey life, to pass the unfranchisable barrier dividing her from the world, seemed to well up, to flow against this wall of silence and recoil.

Twice or three times she addressed him timidly by name, or made some trivial remark. He did not answer, as though in very truth he had been the shadow of a man lying there. And the injustice of this silence seemed to her so terrible. Was she not his wife? Had she not borne him five, and toiled to keep him from that girl? Was it her fault if she had made his life a hell with her jealousy, as he had cried out that morning before he went for her, and was 'put away'? He was her 'man'. It had been her right—nay, more, her duty!

And still he lay there silent. From the narrow street where no traffic passed, the cries of a coster and distant whistlings mounted through the unwholesome air. Some sparrows in the

407

eave were chirruping incessantly. The little sandy house-cat had stolen in, and, crouched against the door-post, was fastening her eyes on the plate which held the remnants of the fish. The seamstress bowed her forehead to the flowers on the table; unable any longer to bear the mystery of this silence, she wept. But the dark figure on the bed only pressed his arms closer round his head, as though there were within him a living death passing the speech of men.

The little sandy cat, creeping across the floor, fixed its claws in the backbone of the fish, and drew it beneath the bed.

Chapter 39

THE DUEL

BIANCA did not see her husband after their return together from the Round Pond. She dined out that evening, and in the morning avoided any interview. When Hilary's luggage was brought down and the cab summoned, she slipped up to take shelter in her room. Presently the sound of his footsteps coming along the passage stopped outside her door. He tapped. She did not answer.

Good-bye would be a mockery! Let him go with the words unsaid! And as though the thought had found its way through the closed door, she heard his footsteps recede again. She saw him presently go out to the cab with his head bent down, saw him stoop and pat Miranda. Hot tears sprang into her eyes. She heard the cab-wheels roll away.

The heart is like the face of an Eastern woman—warm and glowing, behind swathe on swathe of fabric. At each fresh touch from the fingers of Life, some new corner, some hidden curve or angle, comes into view, to be seen last of all—perhaps never to be seen—by the one who owns them.

When the cab had driven away there came into Bianca's heart a sense of the irreparable, and, mysteriously entwined with that arid ache, a sort of bitter pity. What would happen to this wretched girl now that he was gone? Would she go completely to the bad—till she became one of those poor creatures like the figure in 'The Shadow', who stood beneath lamp-posts in the streets? Out of this speculation, which was bitter as the taste of aloes, there came to her a craving for some palliative, some sweetness, some expression of that instinct of fellow-feeling deep in each human breast, however disharmonic. But even with that

408

craving was mingled the itch to justify herself, and prove that she could rise above jealousy.

She made her way to the little model's lodging.

A child admitted her into the bleak passage that served for hall. The strange medley of emotions passing through Bianca's breast while she stood outside the girl's door did not show in her face, which wore its customary restrained, half-mocking look.

The little model's voice faintly said: 'Come in.'

The room was in disorder, as though soon to be deserted. A closed and corded trunk stood in the centre of the floor; the bed, stripped of clothing, lay disclosed in all the barrenness of discoloured ticking. The china utensils of the washstand were turned head downwards. Beside that washstand the little model, with her hat on—the hat with the purplish-pink roses and the little peacock's feather—stood in the struck, shrinking attitude of one who, coming forward in the expectation of a kiss, has received a blow.

'You are leaving here, then?' Bianca said quietly.

'Yes,' the girl murmured.

'Don't you like this part? Is it too far from your work?'

Again the little model whispered: 'Yes.'

Bianca's eyes travelled slowly over the blue beflowered walls and rust-red doors; through the dusty closeness of this dismantled room a rank scent of musk and violets rose, as though a cheap essence had been scattered as libation. A small empty scent-bottle stood on the shabby looking-glass.

'Have you found new lodgings?'

The little model edged closer to the window. A stealthy watchfulness was creeping into her shrinking, dazed face.

She shook her head.

'I don't know where I'm going.'

Obeying a sudden impulse to see more clearly, Bianca lifted her veil. 'I came to tell you,' she said, 'that I shall always be ready to help you.'

The girl did not answer, but suddenly through her black lashes she stole a look upward at her visitor. 'Can *you*,' it seemed to say, '*you*—help me? Oh no; I think not!' And as though she had been stung by that glance, Bianca said with deadly slowness:

'It is my business, of course, entirely, now that Mr Dallison has gone abroad.'

The little model received this saying with a quivering jerk. It might have been an arrow transfixing her white throat. For a moment she seemed almost about to fall, but gripping the window-sill, held herself erect. Her eyes, like an animal's in pain darted here, there, everywhere, then rested on her visitor's breast, quite motionless. This stare, which seemed to see nothing, but to be doing, as it were, some mortal calculation, was uncanny. Colour came gradually back into her lips and eyes and cheeks; she seemed to have succeeded in her calculation, to be reviving from that stab.

And suddenly Bianca understood. This was the meaning of the packed trunk, the dismantled room. He was going to take her, after all!

In the turmoil of this discovery two words alone escaped her: 'I see!'

They were enough. The girl's face at once lost all trace of its look of mortal calculation, brightened, became guilty, and from guilty sullen.

The antagonism of all the long past months was now declared between these two—Bianca's pride could no longer conceal, the girl's submissiveness no longer obscure it. They stood like duellists, one on each side of the trunk—that common, brown-japanned, tin trunk, corded with rope. Bianca looked at it.

'You,' she said, 'and he? Ha, ha; ha, ha! Ha, ha, ha!'

Against that cruel laughter—more poignant than a hundred homilies on caste, a thousand scornful words—the little model literally could not stand; she sat down in the low chair where she had evidently been sitting to watch the street. But as a taste of blood will infuriate a hound, so her own laughter seemed to bereave Bianca of all restraint.

'What do you imagine he's taking you for, girl? Only out of pity! It's not exactly the emotion to live on in exile. In exile—but that you do not understand!'

The little model staggered to her feet again. Her face had grown painfully red.

'He wants me!' she said.

'Wants you? As he wants his dinner. And when he's eaten it—what then? No, of course he'll never abandon you; his conscience is too·tender. But you'll be round his neck—like this!' Bianca raised her arms, looped, and dragged them slowly down, as a mermaid's arms drag at a drowning sailor.

The little model stammered: 'I'll do what he tells me! I'll do what he tells me!'

Bianca stood silent, looking at the girl, whose heaving breast and little peacock's feather, whose small round hands twisting in front of her, and scent about her clothes, all seemed an offence.

'And do you suppose that he'll tell you what he wants? Do you imagine *he'll* have the necessary brutality to get rid of you? He'll think himself bound to keep you till you leave him, as I suppose you will some day!'

The girl dropped her hands. 'I'll never leave him—never!' she cried out passionately.

'Then Heaven help him!' said Bianca.

The little model's eyes seemed to lose all pupil, like two chicory flowers that have no dark centres. Through them, all that she was feeling struggled to find an outlet; but, too deep for words, those things would not pass her lips, utterly unused to express emotion. She could only stammer:

'I'm not—I'm not—I will——' and press her hands again to her breast.

Bianca's lip curled.

'I see; you imagine yourself capable of sacrifice. Well, you have your chance. Take it!' She pointed to the corded trunk. 'Now's your time; you have only to disappear!'

The little model shrank back against the window-sill. 'He wants me!' she muttered. 'I *know* he wants me.'

Bianca bit her lips till the blood came.

'Your idea of sacrifice,' she said, 'is perfect! If you went now, in a month's time he'd never think of you again.'

The girl gulped. There was something so pitiful in the movements of her hands that Bianca turned away. She stood for several seconds staring at the door, then, turning round again, said:

'Well?'

But the girl's whole face had changed. All tear-stained, indeed, she had already masked it with a sort of immovable stolidity.

Bianca went swiftly up to the trunk.

'You *shall*!' she said. 'Take that thing and go!'

The little model did not move.

'So you won't?'

The girl trembled violently all over. She moistened her lips, tried to speak, failed, again moistened them, and this time murmured: 'I'll only—I'll only—if *he* tells me!'

'So you still imagine he will tell you!'

The little model merely repeated: 'I won't—I won't do anything without *he* tells me!'

Bianca laughed. 'Why, it's like a dog!' she said.

But the girl had turned abruptly to the window. Her lips were parted. She was shrinking, fluttering, trembling at what she saw. She was indeed like a spaniel dog who sees her master coming. Bianca had no need of being told that Hilary was outside. She went into the passage and opened the front door.

He was coming up the steps, his face worn like that of a man in fever, and at the sight of his wife he stood quite still, looking into her face.

Without the quiver of an eyelid, without the faintest trace of emotion, or the slightest sign that she knew him to be there, Bianca passed and slowly walked away.

Chapter 40

FINISH OF THE COMEDY

THOSE who may have seen Hilary driving towards the little model's lodgings saw one who, by a fixed red spot in either cheek, and the over-compression of his quivering lips, betrayed the presence of that animality which underlies even the most cultivated men.

After eighteen hours of the purgatory of indecision, he had not so much decided to pay that promised visit on which hung the future of two lives, as allowed himself to be borne towards the girl.

There was no one in the passage to see him after he had passed Bianca in the doorway, but it was with a face darkened by the peculiar stabbing look of wounded egoism that he entered the little model's room.

The sight of it coming so closely on the struggle she had just been through was too much for the girl's self-control.

Instead of going up to him, she sat down on the corded trunk and began to sob. It was the sobbing of a child whose school-treat has been cancelled, of a girl whose ball-dress has not come home in time. It only irritated Hilary, whose nerves had already borne all they could bear. He stood literally trembling, as though each one of these common little sobs were a blow falling on the drumskin of his spirit, and through every fibre he took in the

412

features of the dusty, scent-besprinkled room—the brown tin trunk, the dismantled bed, the rust-red doors.

And he realised that she had burned her boats to make it impossible for a man of sensibility to disappoint her!

The little model raised her face and looked at him. What she saw must have been less reassuring even than the first sight had been, for it stopped her sobbing. She rose and turned to the window, evidently trying with handkerchief and powder-puff to repair the ravages caused by her tears; and when she had finished she still stood there with her back to him. Her deep breathing made her young form quiver from her waist up to the little peacock's feather in her hat; and with each supple movement it seemed offering itself to Hilary.

In the street a barrel-organ had begun to play the very waltz it had played the afternoon when Mr Stone had been so ill. Those two were neither of them conscious of that tune, too absorbed in their emotions; and yet, quietly, it was bringing something to the girl's figure—like the dowering of scent that the sun brings to a flower. It was bringing the compression back to Hilary's lips, the flush to his ears and cheeks, as a draught of wind will blow to redness a fire that has been choked. Without knowing it, without sound, inch by inch he moved nearer to her; and as though, for all there was no sign of his advance, she knew of it, she stayed utterly unmoving except for the deep breathing that so stirred the warm youth in her. In that stealthy progress was the history of life and the mystery of sex. Inch by inch he neared her; and she swayed, mesmerising his arms to fold round her thus poised, as if she must fall backward; mesmerising him to forget that there was anything there, anything in all the world, but just her young form waiting for him—nothing but that!

The barrel-organ stopped; the spell had broken! She turned round to him. As a wind obscures with grey wrinkles the still green waters of enchantment wherein some mortal has been gazing, so Hilary's reason suddenly swept across the situation, and showed it once more as it was. Quick to mark every shade that passed across his face, the girl made as though she would again burst into tears; then, since tears had been so useless, she pressed her hand over her eyes.

Hilary looked at that round, not too cleanly hand. He could see her watching him between her fingers. It was uncanny, almost horrible, like the sight of a cat watching a bird; and he stood appalled at the terrible reality of his position, at the sight of his own future with this girl, with her traditions, customs, life, the thousand and one things that he did not know about her, that he would have to live with if he once took her. A minute passed, which seemed eternity, for into it was condensed every force of her long pursuit, her instinctive clutching at something that she felt to be security, her reaching upwards, her twining round him.

Conscious of all this, held back by that vision of his future, yet whipped towards her by his senses, Hilary swayed like a drunken man. And suddenly she sprang at him, wreathed her arms round his neck, and fastened her mouth to his. The touch of her lips was moist and hot. The scent of stale violet powder came from her, warmed by her humanity. It penetrated to Hilary's heart. He started back in sheer physical revolt.

Thus repulsed, the girl stood rigid, her breast heaving, her eyes unnaturally dilated, her mouth still loosened by the kiss. Snatching from his pocket a roll of notes, Hilary flung them on the bed.

'I can't take you!' he almost groaned. 'It's madness! it's impossible!' And he went out into the passage. He ran down the steps and got into his cab. An immense time seemed to pass before it began to move. It started at last, and Hilary sat back in it, his hands clenched, as still as a dead man.

His mortified face was recognised by the landlady, returning from her morning's visit to the shops. The gentleman looked, she thought, as if he had received bad news! She not unnaturally connected his appearance with her lodger. Tapping on the girl's door, and receiving no answer, she went in.

The little model was lying on the dismantled bed, pressing her face into the blue and white ticking of the bolster. Her shoulders shook, and a sound of smothered sobbing came from her. The landlady stood staring silently.

Coming of Cornish chapel-going stock, she had never liked this girl, her instinct telling her that she was one for whom life had already been to much. Those for whom life had so early been too much, she knew, were always 'ones for pleasure'! Her experience of village life had enabled her to construct the little model's story—that very simple, very frequent little story. Sometimes, indeed, trouble of that sort was soon over and forgotten; but sometimes, if the young man didn't do the right thing by her, and the girl's folk took it hardly, well, then——! So had run the reasoning of this good woman. Being of the same class, she had looked at her lodger from the first without obliquity of vision.

But seeing her now apparently so overwhelmed, and having something soft and warm down beneath her granitic face and hungry eyes, she touched her on the back.

'Come, now!' she said; 'you mustn't take on! What is it?'

The little model shook off the hand as a passionate child shakes itself free of consolation. 'Let me alone!' she muttered.

The landlady drew back. 'Has anyone done you a harm?' she said.

The little model shook her head.

Baffled by this dumb grief, the landlady was silent; then, with the stolidity of those whose lives are one long wrestling with fortune, she muttered:

'I don't like to see *anyone* cry like that!'

And finding that the girl remained obstinately withdrawn from sight or sympathy, she moved towards the door.

'Well,' she said, with ironical compassion, 'if you want me, I'll be in the kitchen.'

The little model remained lying on her bed. Every now and then she gulped, like a child flung down on the grass apart from its comrades, trying to swallow down its rage, trying to bury in the earth its little black moment of despair. Slowly those gulps grew fewer, feebler, and at last died away. She sat up, sweeping Hilary's bundle of notes, on which she had been lying, to the floor.

At sight of that bundle she broke out afresh, flinging herself down sideways with her cheek on the wet bolster; and, for some time after her sobs had ceased again, still lay there. At last she rose and dragged herself over to the looking-glass, scrutinising her streaked, discoloured face, the stains in the cheeks, the swollen eyelids, the marks beneath her eyes; and listlessly she tidied herself. Then, sitting down on the brown tin trunk, she picked the bundle of notes off the floor. They gave forth a dry peculiar crackle. Fifteen ten-pound notes—all Hilary's travelling money. Her eyes opened wider and wider as she counted; and tears, quite suddenly, rolled down on to those thin slips of paper.

Then slowly she undid her dress, and forced them down till they rested, with nothing but her vest between them and the quivering warm flesh which hid her heart.

415

Chapter 41

THE HOUSE OF HARMONY

AT half-past ten that evening Stephen walked up the stone-flagged pathway of his brother's house.

'Can I see Mrs Hilary?'

'Mr Hilary went abroad this morning, sir, and Mrs Hilary has not yet come in.'

'Will you give her this letter? No, I'll wait, I suppose I can wait for her in the garden?'

'Oh yes, sir!'

'Very well.'

'I'll leave the door open, sir, in case you want to come in.'

Stephen walked across to the rustic bench and sat down. He stared gloomily through the dusk at his patent-leather boots, and every now and then he flicked his evening trousers with the letter Across the dark garden, where the boughs hung soft, unmoved by wind, the light from Mr Stone's open window flowed out in a pale river; moths, born of the sudden heat, were fluttering up this river to its source.

Stephen looked irritably at the figure of Mr Stone, which could be seen, bowed, and utterly still, beside his desk; so, by lifting the spy-hole thatch, one may see a convict in his cell stand gazing at his work, without movement, numb with solitude.

'He's getting awfully broken up,' thought Stephen. 'Poor old chap! His ideas are killing him. They're not human nature, never will be.' Again he flicked his trousers with the letter, as though that document emphasised the fact. 'I can't help being sorry for the sublime old idiot!'

He rose, the better to see his father-in-law's unconscious figure. It looked as lifeless and as cold as though Mr Stone had followed some thought below the ground, and left his body standing there to await his return. Its appearance oppressed Stephen.

'You might set the house on fire,' he thought; 'he'd never notice.'

Mr Stone's figure moved; the sound of a long sigh came out to Stephen in the windless garden. He turned his eyes away, with the sudden feeling that it was not the thing to watch the old chap like this; then, getting up, he went indoors. In his brother's study he stood turning over the knick-knacks on the writing-table.

'I warned Hilary that he was burning his fingers,' he thought.

At the sound of the latchkey he went back to the hall.

However much he had secretly disapproved of her from the beginning, because she had always seemed to him such an uncomfortable and tantalising person, Stephen was impressed that night by the haunting unhappiness of Bianca's face; as if it had been suddenly disclosed to him that she could not help herself. This was disconcerting, being, in a sense, a disorderly way of seeing things.

'You look tired, B.,' he said. 'I'm sorry, but I thought it better to bring this round to-night.'

Bianca glanced at the letter.

'It is to you,' she said. 'I don't wish to read it, thank you.'

Stephen compressed his lips.

'But I wish you to hear it, please,' he said. 'I'll read it out, if you'll allow me.

"CHARING CROSS STATION.

"DEAR STEVIE,

"I told you yesterday morning that I was going abroad alone. Afterwards I changed my mind—I meant to take her. I went to her lodgings for the purpose. I have lived too long amongst sentiments for such a piece of reality as that. Class has saved me; it has triumphed over my most primitive instincts.

"I am going alone—back to my sentiments. No slight has been placed on Bianca—but my married life having become a mockery, I shall not return to it. The following address will find me, and I shall ask you presently to send on my household gods.

"Please let Bianca know the substance of this letter.

"Ever your affectionate brother,

"HILARY DALLISON." '

With a frown Stephen folded up the letter, and restored it to his breast pocket.

'It's more bitter than I thought,' he reflected; 'and yet he's done the only possible thing!'

Bianca was leaning her elbow on the mantelpiece with her face turned to the wall. Her silence irritated Stephen, whose loyalty to his brother longed to find a vent.

'I'm very much relieved, of course,' he said at last. 'It would have been fatal.'

She did not move, and Stephen became increasingly aware that this was a most awkward matter to touch on.

'Of course,' he began again. 'But, B., I don't think you—rather—

I mean——' And again he stopped before her utter silence, her utter immobility. Then unable to go away without having in some sort expressed his loyalty to Hilary, he tried once more: 'Hilary is the kindest man I know. It's not his fault if he's out of touch with life—if he's not fit to deal with things. He's *negative*!'

And having thus in a single word, somewhat to his own astonishmen, described his brother, he held out his hand.

The hand which Bianca placed in it was feverishly hot. Stephen felt suddenly compunctious.

'I'm awfully sorry,' he stammered, 'about the whole thing. I'm awfully sorry for you——'

Bianca drew back her hand.

With a little shrug Stephen turned away.

'What are you to do with women like that?' was his thought, and saying dryly, 'Good-night, B.,' he went.

For some time Bianca sat in Hilary's chair. Then, by the faint glimmer coming through the half-open door, she began to wander round the room, touching the walls, the books, the prints, all the familar things among which he had lived so many years.

In that dim continual journey she was like a disharmonic spirit traversing the air above where its body lies.

The door creaked behind her. A voice said sharply:

'What are you doing in this house?'

Mr Stone was standing beside the bust of Socrates. Bianca went up to him.

'Father!'

Mr Stone stared. 'It is you! I thought it was a thief! Where is Hilary?'

'Gone away.'

'Alone?'

Bianca bowed her head. 'It is very late, Dad,' she whispered.

Mr Stone's hand moved as though he would have stroked her. 'The human heart,' he murmured, 'is the tomb of many feelings.'

Bianca put her arm round him.

'You must go to bed, Dad,' she said, trying to get him to the door, for in her heart something seemed giving way.

Mr Stone stumbled; the door swung to; the room was plunged in darkness. A hand, cold as ice, brushed her cheek. With all her force she stifled a scream.

'I am here,' Mr Stone said.

His hand, wandering downwards, touched her shoulder, and

she seized it with her own burning hand. Thus linked, they groped their way out into the passage towards his room.

'Good-night, dear,' Bianca murmured.

By the light of his now open door Mr Stone seemed to try and see her face, but she would not show it him. Closing the door gently, she stole upstairs.

Sitting down in her bedroom by the open window, it seemed to her that the room was full of people—her nerves were so unstrung. It was as if walls had not the power this night to exclude human presences. Moving, or motionless, now distinct, then covered suddenly by the thick veil of some material object, they circled round her quiet figure, lying back in the chair with shut eyes. These disharmonic shadows flitting in the room made a stir like the rubbing of dry straw or the hum of bees among clover stalks. When she sat up they vanished, and the sounds became the distant din of homing traffic; but the moment she closed her eyes, her visitors again began to steal round her with that dry, mysterious hum.

She fell asleep presently, and woke with a start. There, in a glimmer of pale light, stood the little model, as in the fatal picture Bianca had painted of her. Her face was powder white, with shadows beneath the eyes. Breath seemed coming through her parted lips, just touched with colour. In her hat lay the tiny peacock's feather beside the two purplish-pink roses. A scent came from her, too—but faint, as ever was the scent of chicory flower. How long had she been standing there? Bianca started to her feet, and as she rose the vision vanished.

She went towards the spot. There was nothing in that corner but moonlight; the scent she had perceived was merely that of the trees drifting in.

But so vivid had that vision been that she stood at the window, panting for air, passing her hand again and again across her eyes.

Outside, over the dark gardens, the moon hung full and almost golden. Its honey-pale light filtered down on every little shape of tree, and leaf, and sleeping flower. That soft, vibrating radiance seemed to have woven all into one mysterious whole, stilling disharmony, so that each little separate shape had no meaning to itself.

Bianca looked long at the rain of moonlight falling on the earth's carpet, like a covering shower of blossom which bees have sucked and spilled. Then, below her, out through candescent space, she saw a shadow dart forth along the grass, and to her fright a voice rose, tremulous and clear, seeming to seek enfranchisement beyond the barrier of the dark trees : 'My brain is clouded. Great Universe! I cannot write! I can no longer discover to my brothers that they are one. I am not worthy to stay here. Let me pass into You, and die!'

Bianca saw her father's fragile arms stretch out into the night through the sleeves of his white garment, as though expecting to be received at once into the Universal Brotherhood of the thin air.

There ensued a moment, when, by magic, every little dissonance in all the town seemed blended into a harmony of silence, as it might be the very death of self upon the earth.

Then, breaking that trance, Mr Stone's voice rose again, trembling out into the night, as though blown through a reed.

'Brothers!' he said.

Behind the screen of lilac bushes at the gate Bianca saw the dark helmet of a policeman. He stood there staring steadily in the direction of that voice. Raising his lantern, he flashed it into every corner of the garden, searching for those who had been addressed. Satisfied, apparently, that no one was there, he moved it to right and left, lowered it to the level of his breast, and walked slowly on.

This book,
designed by William B. Taylor,
is a production of
Heron Books, London

Printed in Great Britain by offset litho at
Taylor Garnett Evans & Co. Ltd.
Watford, Herts